Fancy Free in the Back Thirty!

by
Colin Manuel

**Illustrations by
Ben Crane**

Fancy Free in the Back Thirty!

E-Book ISBN: 978-0-9918604-5-6
Paperback ISBN: 978-0-9918604-4-9

Additional copies of this book may be ordered by visiting the
PPG Online Bookstore at:

🍁 **PolishedPublishingGroup**

shop.polishedpublishinggroup.com

or by contacting the author at phone 403-845-4914, by fax 403-844-8482
or e-mail at colinmanuel@hotmail.com

Due to the dynamic nature of the Internet,any website addresses mentioned within this book may have been changed or discontinued since publication.

This is for all those farmers who struggle daily,
for all those whose roots are still deep in the soil,
for all those country folk who told us their tales,
especially for Clayton Cole and the Cole family.
Their auction mart brought so many of us together,
to become the start of so many never-ending stories.
For Mark and Annie Bertagnolli, their friendship
is a constant beacon even on the darkest of days,
and of course,
for my long-suffering wife Felicity who, like Sabine,
went on a wild safari not knowing how it might end!

Contents

In the farming community, there are characters that are truly one of a kind. Irreverent, sometimes outrageous, these are the folk who enrich the landscape beyond any measure. So if some of these characters resemble people you know, make this a salute to them for being who they are. As much as the stories herein are gleaned from real life, they are intended as no more than that, stories. If they should offend anyone, that was never the intention: to be offended in our world is like a conscious decision to charge through a barb wire fence…it's such a waste of energy!

Chapter One
BEDEVILED BY NUMBERS
AND ... PIG LATIN!

*N*umbers.

Numbers insist on telling you the date and the time, measuring your measly acres or your bulging waistline, counting your scarce bushels or your manifold blessings, assessing your entire life in Arabesque hieroglyphics.

Put those same numbers into the hands and the mouths of others, and they will account for your poverty and your health. Some will even make declarations about your fiscal wellness or your age staying consistently at 29, declarations that will be used as evidence for or against you. To those in the know, numbers supposedly show that you are a brilliant or an incompetent manager, a thrifty or a careless housekeeper, a solid or a sloppy provider. Numbers can show you as being too old, too young, or too downright indeterminate to qualify for this or that. In the ledgers of yore or in the hard drives of today, your financial custodians—the bankers and the accountants and all of the other miscellaneous know-alls and wannabes—scan your worth and determine whether you should be encouraged to sail on to greater glory or be pushed aside into the debtors' scrap yard. Your inquisitor needs only to press a key or two and hey presto, "Mr. Hanlon, I have to tell you that your debt-equity ratio is sorely under stress, your credit-worthiness is highly suspect, and you are living in a manner to which you ought not become accustomed. In short, your income is not keeping pace with your chosen lifestyle."

When Aubrey and Sabine Hanlon bought the farm near Rocky Mountain House, Alberta, back in '76, neither of them had any intention of embracing the farm as a full-time occupation. It was not that they saw such an occupation as somehow beneath them, not at all. They were just smart enough at the time not to throw themselves headlong into a world about which they had to confess they knew little. After all, Aubrey was a retired policeman whose dream had always been to own a few quiet acres in the country. Sabine, often misread as a classic china doll type from the city, saw the farm primarily as an escape from the cramped confines of the little "shoebox" they had owned in South Edmonton. Besides, there was absolutely no way she was about to go digging around in the dirt and risk cracking those immaculately manicured fingernails. Yet it had not taken long before both of them had absorbed the farming bug into their bloodstream—as much by default as by design, it was true. Once they had tasted the true flavor of their own free-range meat chickens, how could they ever go back to those plasticized packages that passed as "roasters" in the local supermarket? Once they had rescued their first near-dead calf from a snow bank and nursed it back to life, they had become immediately emotionally entangled, hopelessly and permanently so. Then of course there was Nellie, the "Hanlon Sacred Cow" and founding mother of the herd, the little red cow with the one stubby horn and the white patch over one eye— the one animal they hated to love but love they did, ornery old bag that she was anyway. Then there had been Miss Piggy, the lovable old sow won in a draw at the trade show, a beast that had confirmed for them animals have their own personalities, as if they needed such confirmation after Nellie! Their experiences, the highs and lows of those early days on the farm chronicled in *Footloose in the Front Forty*, forever bonded them to the soil and to the fauna and flora, the animals and the plants that it nurtured.

And then came the real challenges: first the drought and then the B.S.E. or the dreaded "mad cow disease", both of which threatened to overwhelm them. That was when they were called upon to make a critical choice; quit while they were still ahead, or hunker down and go with the flow. "Farming will always be cursed by its cycles," said one old-timer to Aubrey. "You gotta learn to hang on tight and ride 'em out." So Aubrey and Sabine hunkered down, treading water in the back thirty, in a manner of speaking, naturally.

This is where the whole business of numbers came back into play. One day, Aubrey found himself in conversation with... who else but the new Loans Officer at the local Credit Union. He was a mustachioed type, an import from the city who saw his cowboy image as an act of pretended solidarity with his agricultural clientele. He was one of those well-worn gentlemen whose pomposity and book knowledge combined to confuse him enough to believe he had real-life experience. Not that his position of Loans Officer gave him much room for maneuver given the cast-iron bank policies and the computer-generated instant calculations that dictated his every move, almost down to tying his own shoelaces. Of course it had to be said, Alfred Burlap would never, ever be seen in shoes with laces;

they required too much of an effort to bend over a well-padded paunch, and besides, that would deflect too much attention from his genuine snakeskin boots from Idaho.

"Yessir, now let me tell *you,* in today's world, a small-time farmer-rancher type like we have around these here parts needs at least a couple a hundred critters to calve out if he wants to make it further than the gatepost. Course, a man like you, retired cop's pension and so forth, you get to live the good life courtesy of a public pension and the good ol' taxpayer. Not that you don't deserve it, mind you," he added hurriedly when he saw Aubrey's frown. "Now me, I wouldn't have done your job if they had paid me ten times what they pay me, chasing after all them lawbreakers with their seatbelt violations and parking infractions and stuff."

"And so ends another beautiful friendship with the banker," Aubrey was thinking, at this precise moment interested simply in signing up for the small consumer loan that would allow them to buy a small runabout vehicle for Sabine. The fellow's smug pseudo-western wisdom born of imagined life in the slow lane should be recycled into horse droppings as far as Aubrey was concerned.

Nonetheless… nonetheless he had got to thinking about what the man had said. The Hanlons could easily handle sixty or seventy head of cows, certainly in terms of workload. Okay, they would be a bit tight on the land base but they could always buy the additional hay and rent the extra pasture they needed. The problem as he saw it right now was that they had reached something of an impasse; they were neither one thing nor the other. Neither farmers nor ranchers, they were still classed as "hobbyists", as if what they did on their farm was a low-key version of the rich at play. Aubrey replayed that banker's line over and over in his mind, that a small farmer-rancher type "needed at least two hundred critters" to make a go of it. He mentally thanked the man for adding some legitimacy to the argument he would put forward to Sabine. The problem was, how was he to get his wife's attention without her first flipping her lid? If she were to do that before actually listening to what he had to say, there would be no hope, no hope at all. Yet, he would always happily admit, his wife had a capacity to surprise him.

It was she, after all, who had gone out on a limb and arranged the purchase of hay during the big drought, at a time when he was all of a dither and ready to cash in their chips because he thought that was what his wife would want. But he underestimated her capacity to fight. It was Sabine who had made the statement he would always remember: "For once in our lives, let us be the contrarians. Let all the others sell their cows at fire sale prices. We stay and fight." But staying and fighting was one thing, expanding was quite another. What if the beef industry took years to get back on its feet after B.S.E.? What if the Yankees never again opened their precious border to Canadian cattle? What if another disastrous drought was to show its face? What if Sabine decided that her husband had finally gone off his rocker?

One of the joys of country living and of being your own boss is that you can always take time out and chew the fat with the neighbor. Chewing the fat is not just an idling away of your time; it is an agricultural if not social imperative in the country, what the upwardly mobile city types like to call "networking" or "interfacing". It is the best way to keep up with what is happening on costs of hay, fertilizer, fuel, and all of those inputs that keep the wheels turning. Of course it is also the best way to stay connected to the latest in gossip, all further spiced with every telling of the story.

"Ah yes, they say Mrs. Wiseman's lodger gets free rent; she says it's because he does a lot of maintenance."

"By the way, did you hear that John Upham managed to set his woodshed on fire again? He did the same darn thing last year, burning the dead grass in his yard. Had to call the firemen out of Rocky before it got to his house. Crazy old firebug, that's what he is!"

Weddings, christenings and funerals, accidents and scandals of every hue, all are grist for the mill and make for a lively community.

This particular day, Aubrey and Sabine had stopped to check on their old bachelor neighbor, Stanley Himilton; they had seen no sign of him for over a week and had to assure themselves that he was okay. Normally by this time of the year, late spring, he would be out disking the field west of the house for the umpteenth time that season. When some people get bored, they watch a movie or read a book. Not Stanley, he would jump in his tractor and go disking. He was a firm believer in leaving no sod unbroken, in having a seedbed that was as fine as any talcum powder from the east.

Stanley answered the door of his beautifully maintained older mobile home. He was badly stooped and clearly in some pain and had to use a cane to keep his balance. "Darned arthritis, anyway," he said, his eyes lighting up at the prospect of some company. Sabine had become one of his favorites, what with her always razzing him gently about his ability to grow a better garden, flowers and vegetables, than any farm wife in the neighborhood. "I'll plug in the coffee."

It was when the three of them were seated at the kitchen table that Stanley dropped his bombshell, after the customary wailing about the weather, of course. "I've decided it's time to quit. Sell up."

"What did you say?" Aubrey could not quite believe what he was hearing.

"Sell up. I'm gonna sell up. Move into town. Are you folks interested?" He always directed the conversation at Sabine if she was around, as if Aubrey was something of a lesser planet—which he was, being as Sabine was a shining star as far as Stanley was concerned.

Her answer was automatic, unrehearsed. "Of course we are, aren't we, honey?" Her eyes dared Aubrey to say no.

"It all comes down to numbers," said Aubrey warily. "It depends on the cost."

"Well yes and no," said Stanley with certainty. "You see, I want my land to go to people who will care about it. I homesteaded this place, you know. Cleared the land with horses and mules. There's no way on earth I'm gonna turn it over to some fancy dude with millions of dollars so's he can first rape the place, 'scuze me Ma'am, then turn right around and sell it to make a second fortune when he probably never even worked for his first one."

"We'd never do that if we bought it, would we, honey?" said Sabine.

"No, but we still need to know what you want for it," Aubrey came back, still too cautious to believe his luck.

"Just what you people think it's worth to you," replied Stanley enigmatically, but staring at Sabine in a way that said he trusted her implicitly. "You see, I've got me a place in town so I want to move as soon as I can."

Aubrey might have been floundering but Sabine was right there with Stanley. "The fairest way is to have your farm appraised, and then neither side gets the short end of the stick, no?"

"I'd go along with that," Stanley agreed at once. "That at least gives us a figure to go on."

"Then it's settled then, right dear?" Sabine leaned back in her chair, suddenly realizing that not only had she done all the talking for the Hanlon side, but she had also pretty much clinched the deal.

"Fine by me," said Aubrey, somewhat bemused that what he had wanted was falling into place so quickly.

"I'll get on to it right away," said Stanley, convincing Sabine that this was what the crafty old devil had been planning all along.

"And so shall we, right honey?" echoed Sabine, her mind already visualizing a vast herd of Hanlon cattle grazing contentedly up on the hill that they could see from their sitting room-window; a hill that could soon be theirs.

Numbers. Money, lots of it, wheelbarrows full of dollars! But where would they borrow them from—a hundred thousand dollars, to be exact.

"Go talk to my buddy Peter at the AFSC offices in Red Deer," said Pete, Aubrey's farmer-mentor. "He'll set you up without all the hubble-bubble trouble you'll have if you go to the banks. Say, have you met that new Loans Officer at the Credit Union yet?"

When Aubrey said that he had, Pete launched into a diatribe about pretend cowboys that wouldn't know a rocking horse from a brood mare, not that Aubrey was any more knowledgeable than the banker when it came to brood mares. Naturally enough, Pete had to know how much they were paying for the land and so forth, but his statement that the Hanlons could not have got a better deal anywhere was very reassuring.

So it was that Aubrey and Sabine found themselves in the offices of the Agriculture Financial Services Corporation, the AFSC, in downtown Red Deer, armed with an appraisal and an accepted offer less than the appraisal's value, which showed just how much Stanley Himilton cared about who would own his land. "We have a ten o'clock appointment with a Mister, er, a Mister Peter er, with Peter," said Sabine to the receptionist, realizing that she had failed to memorize the man's last name. "I'm afraid we're a few minutes late," she added as the woman glanced up at a clock showing 10:20 AM.

"Please have a seat," said the woman graciously, well versed in "farmer time". "I'll go and tell him that you are here."

Aubrey knew it! How he hated these sorts of meetings, formalized interviews, call them what they would. Somehow, he always felt like a prisoner in the dock. Soon, no doubt, an officious little man in a pinstripe suit would appear out of the mahogany woodwork and offer them a limp handshake, before bombarding them with a dazzling array of useless knowledge and leaving them feeling like paupers begging for crumbs from the rich man's table. Why was it these people always seemed to act as if it was *their* money you wanted to borrow? Taken as a whole, his past experiences together with the short wait only made him want to grab his cap and run. God forbid, but if the man were to start in on the issue of law and order because he, Aubrey, was an ex-cop, he would have no hesitation in walking out. Damn it, even if the fellow was foolish enough to show any irritation with their being late, he would still walk out. It wasn't their fault that there had been road construction on the way in, for heaven's sake, and then they had encountered the usual rigmarole of finding a parking spot. In contrast, Sabine eased herself quietly into an old copy of *Cosmopolitan*, clearly at ease with herself and the situation. Aubrey could only find a copy of *Barley Growers* magazine, yet quickly found himself fascinated with another more savory connotation of the word "smut".

"Mr. and Mrs. Hanlon," the melodious voice penetrated their separate worlds. They both looked up.

Peter Walshe was as far from Aubrey's officious little man in a pinstripe suit as he could possibly get. First, he could never be described as a small man. Second, he was dressed as many farmers would dress on a visit to the town, which of course tended to put his clients at ease immediately. Officious? Far from it. Engaging? A resounding yes. As soon as they had made their introductions, Aubrey had forgotten all about his earlier misgivings, which in turn made the process of borrowing such a huge chunk of money a little easier to swallow. Mr. Walshe's office was notable neither for the amount of paperwork on show nor for the inevitable electronic gadgetry so essential to the modern day office, but for its lack of pretension. Indeed, it appeared that the man was a golf nut; all kinds of knick-knacks attested to it. For Aubrey, golf was a contagious disease that he and Sabine had not yet contracted, but he could see the day coming. The brochure for the category of loan for which they were applying indicated that the loan was for "beginning farmers". Aubrey was convinced that at some point in the next five minutes Mr. Walshe would have to inform them politely that they were not beginning farmers at all, and so would be ineligible. Their having farmed for seven or so years did not fit Aubrey's conception of a "beginning farmer". He had to ask.

"Let me put it this way, Mr. Hanlon, may I call you Aubrey? As far as this office is concerned, either you are beginning, expanding on the beginning, or beginning on the expanding. Which one is it?" The smile that came with this logic disarmed Aubrey immediately, allowing him to trust the loans specialist completely. They went on to talk about the things that farmers like to talk about: the freak snowstorm of ten days ago, the weather in general, the weather forecast for next week and the rest of summer, the indifferent calf prices of last fall, the projected moderate rise for the coming fall, and all things calculated to settle down a nervous farmer's heart rate. There was no mention of golf; farmers don't talk about golf.

"I will need to come out to the farm for a big look-see before we can get down to the nitty-gritty and the paperwork," Mr. Walshe announced suddenly, at the same time trying to gage just how much of a china doll type the woman sitting before him really was. Would she be little more than a fashion statement with a farm hat, a silent partner whose only support for her man would be a flickering of those eyelashes in times of stress? "You can both show me around and fill me in about what you are doing, and what you hope to do. That'll give me a handle as to how best to structure our plans. What do you think?"

Aubrey had not missed the phrase "our plans" and was very gratified. This had to be the first time ever a moneylender had intimated any sort of togetherness with what he and the bank intended to do. Then, actually being asked what they thought would be best, asked in a genuinely sincere tone, well, that had to be a bit of a first too. Once again though, Sabine was ahead of him. "Sounds perfect for us, don't you think Aub?"

"Uh, yes, perfect," Aubrey heard himself confirming.

"Good. Just let me take a look at my calendar. How about Tuesday of next week?" Peter Walshe smiled. "In the afternoon, around, say, two o'clock? That should give you the time to finish up your chores, yes?"

"Good enough for us," Sabine again responded. "Right, Aub?"

"Right", agreed Aubrey, wondering at the same time whether Mr. Walshe was beginning to get the impression that Aubrey was very much at the beck and call of his wife, the power not so much behind but on the throne; or as Pete would say, "the power behind the drone."

And so the scene was set. The following Tuesday was to be the day, and all would unfold as it would; hopefully as it should.

Murphy's Law number 302 or 303, the infamous Murphy Code, a spin-off hybrid of the Napoleonic Code and English common law, states that "on the one day when you need things to flow as smoothly and regularly as most other days, some form of malevolent interference should be expected: anything from a glitch to a catastrophe, with perhaps a couple of way stations in between." Any and every small farmer is familiar with the routine; there is always a critically-placed post about to fall down, an unattended hole for someone or some animal to tumble into, a length of barbed wire fencing crying out for a dozen staples, a board that should have been re-nailed last spring, or a machine that is in the road and should have been removed before somebody saw fit to rub noses with it. Always, Mister Farmer is distracted, diverted, waylaid, ambushed by events, and the minor chore never gets done. Aubrey knew that the post to one side of the cattle waterer in the big corral needed replacing, knew it to be urgent, and fully intended to get right to it. But then again, it was still standing was it not? Surely it would do the job for another day, another month, another year maybe? As Pete always insisted, a fence is more psychological than physical; certainly a useful principle to believe in when one's fence is decrepit. If the truth be known, even the wooden platform on which the cattle waterer was mounted could just as well be replaced too, being that it was experimenting with various forms of disintegration, rot, and such. Ah well, the slack time of early summer would give Aubrey the break he needed to attend to these minor problems.

"You know, dear, maybe we should put the cows in the big corral so that we have them confined in one place for Mr. Walshe to see them.

"Good thinking," Aubrey said, without doing any thinking himself. "I'll go get 'em in with a couple of buckets of chop. You go on baking those cookies. If we can't impress him with our fancy farming, at least we can work on his taste buds."

Since the man in question was due within the hour, Aubrey had already showered and changed into his "town duds" as he called them.

"Shouldn't you change back into some work clothes, honey? You'll get yourself all dirty, no?" Sabine always felt obliged to "manage" her husband when it came down to dress code and appearance.

"Sheesh! All I'm gonna do is take two buckets of chop into the corral," Aubrey replied irritably. "I'm not about to do an hour's farming. You know how the cows will always come for a mouthful of chop."

Aubrey was quite right. One rattle of the plastic chop pails brought the cows out of the trees and through the corral gate in an instant. Nellie, for one, would never miss out on chop, no chance, and she brought the twenty-nine other mamas with her. All Aubrey had to do was to shut the gate and head back to the house. "See what I mean," he bragged to his mate, "when it comes to handling cows, your man is the best."

"So it would seem," she responded somewhat enigmatically.

But Aubrey could not sit still. Minutes before Mr. Walshe was due, he decided to check on the cows, not that they could go anywhere. But he was nervous, his mind taking him back to his schooldays. For some reason, he felt as if he was showing what might be very indifferent homework to a teacher he really hoped to impress. When he got up to the corral, the cows were all crowded around the waterer, as they always were after they had had a bite of chop. It was unfortunate for Aubrey that cows know no decorum. Unlike humans, they have no conception of how to behave in a lineup. They were pushing and shoving at each other, one bovine face snatching a couple of laps at the water before another head barged in and took over. Aubrey could see what was about to happen, could clearly see the one rotten post debating whether it should continue its passive resistance or simply flop over. Powerless to do anything other than to use his famous *basso profundo* voice, Aubrey yelled at them to stop being so bloody silly. It was enough, more than enough.

Petunia, flighty young Petunia, took one startled look at her master and flattened the post, and a five-foot section of plank fence with it, simultaneously communicating her sense of extreme panic to the others.

She took off into the freshly germinated barley field, directly over the fence from the corral. There is no such concept as "one-at-a-time" in cow logic; all of them insisted on cramming themselves through the five-foot gap at the same time. It was inevitable really. The waterer was torn off its decayed moorings and toppled over sideways, the polythene feeder pipe breaking off and spewing water obscenely, defiantly into the air.

"You bloody stupid sons of…, sons of…, of bit…baboons," Aubrey shouted, his commitment to Sabine to cut down on agriculturally inspired swearing leaving him floundering for alternative vocabulary. "I hate you all, all of you, you, you progeny of, of… of…of a bloody ostrich farm." The absence of any logic was far from his mind this day as he charged after them, only to trip headlong into the sloppy mix of mud and manure that surrounds any waterer, particularly one in need of gravel. The broken pipe charitably doused him with ice-cold water, finishing off the rendering down of his city clothes. Slowly he got to his knees, rising up out of the mud like one of the smaller dinosaurs of the Pleistocene period surfacing from a bog. Dinosaurs, though, were reputedly clumsy and moved slowly. Aubrey was altogether different.

The instant he realized that his "girls" were now contentedly grazing on his newly sprung barley crop, he went ballistic. A second tumble back into the mud, followed by a second shower of frigid H2O stoked his ire further. A couple of the cows watched almost curiously as he got up once more, wiped mud and sh…, (well let's not go there, he willed himself to think), out of his eyes and his mouth, and suddenly galloped off to the gate that led from the barley field to the pasture in the trees. Nellie, undisputed matriarch of the herd and principal mood-reader of the only man in her life, unwisely decided that this would be a bad day to get into a confrontation. She promptly led her cohorts off to the opposite corner of the field, which in turn prompted her master to run, not just run, to gallop across the field cussing madly as he went. It was an abandonment of all dignity and all Sabine-inspired vocabulary. Quite the spectacle for Sabine and Mr. Walshe who were making their way up to the corral to see what Aubrey might be doing.

"Leave the good man be!" was Mr. Walshe's response to Sabine's utter consternation. "The poor fellow needs a moment or two to finish up his venting."

"But, but, please excuse the language, it's so foul and Aubrey really isn't like that."

"Pig Latin, nothing more," replied Mr. Walshe casually. "Let's go see those ducks you were talking about. That way, your husband can resolve his problems with some dignity and without interference from onlookers." They retreated gracefully.

On the other hand, "dignified" was the last adjective that could have been applied to Aubrey. Fighting mad, he was still racing across the barley field like a prematurely de-hibernated grizzly bear. Nellie got the message, maybe a little too quickly judging by the depth of the hoof prints she and the herd left behind them as they bolted for the open gate. Only then did Aubrey come to a stop and take stock, which was the moment he spotted the backs of the departing spectators. "Shoot me up my ass, 'er my buttocks, 'er my rump!" he yelled out loud. "They heard it all! Saw it all too, knowing my luck." He looked down. Splattered with an aromatic mix of mud and manure, his brown leather town shoes oozing slop, his body exuding a fetid shitty pungency from every pore, he near melted in embarrassment. Not that he could do anything about it; the damage had already been done. Sheepishly, the bedraggled Aubrey made his way back to the yard.

"Good day, good sir," Mr. Walshe greeted him as Aubrey rounded the corner of the shop. "Clearly you have been a very busy fellow." Aubrey regarded him closely to see if this might be a very clumsy attempt at humour.

"You could say that, Mister Walshe."

"Peter. Just call me Peter."

"Peter. Wouldn't you know it, the cows got out. Broke a post on one side of the waterer. Had to take the whole bloody waterer out too, didn't they?"

"Didn't I tell you to replace that post last summer?" Sabine interjected loftily. "Besides, your pig Latin was awful, absolutely awful."

"Pig Latin? What the hell is pig Latin?" Aubrey responded gruffly.

"That's what Peter called your cursing and swearing," Sabine responded. "Says you're a truly talented linguist. Now go and make yourself presentable before we take him back up to see the cows and all the other things. In the meantime, I'll show him my vegetable garden. He's got to get the message that I do things around here too," she added, as if to ensure that Mr. Walshe did not make the assumption that so many seemed to make—the assumption that she was the queen and Aubrey the knave.

Aubrey knew when he had lost momentum. He squelched off, first to turn off the water supply to the corral and then to reappear ten minutes later as the respectable country gentleman he saw himself to be, even if his reserve pair of "city shoes" was a little too scuffed to pass a close-up look.

"Well now, that looks better," said Mr. Walshe, Peter, when Aubrey came back out. "Now let's see how you really do things around here." The smile was genuine even if the word "really" might have suggested he was being judgmental, which he wasn't. Aubrey did not know him well enough yet. Sabine, however, had already laid the groundwork, had surprised Mr. Walshe with her garden and her array of vegetables, enough to sustain an army on the march. She was undoubtedly much more than the city maid she appeared to be. That conclusion was emphasized by the information that Aubrey was banished from the garden. He didn't know a carrot top from a spring onion, while hilling potatoes exacerbated a back injury he never knew he had—an injury he always remembered at the most propitious moment. No, Sabine was far from the china doll everyone took her for, Peter Walshe decided.

As they toured the buildings, the shop, the machines in their dedicated sheds, the two barns, Aubrey saw his own place through an entirely different pair of eyes. The lean on the two center poles of the main machine shed seemed drastically more pronounced than usual, so he dared not brag that it was he who had built it. The hole in the tin roof of the cow barn where Sabine had foolishly tried to scrape the snow off the roof with the front-end loader seemed to gape at him in mockery, but if Peter even saw it he made no mention. Every blemish on every machine (none of the machines were anywhere near new) clamoured to be noticed. "Look at me! Look at me!" they screamed. They positively vied for Peter Walshe's attention: the hole in the side cover of the haybine where Aubrey had run into an altercation with a fence; the partially removed top shaft of the round baler, a "repair in transition"; the unmistakable dent in the rear fender of the chore tractor where a round bale had "jumped off" the hay wagon to play "kissy-kissy" with the tractor.

Oh well, he and Sabine had made a silent, if not agreed-on, pact that neither one of them would parade the other's foolishness. And as if in contrition, or perhaps thinking their continued existence depended on it, the cows and their offspring came back out of the trees when they were called, and Mr. Walshe got a real good look. Maybe they would have acted less charitably had they known that their pampered status was about to be reduced by a doubling of their number if the proposed financing was to be accepted.

"I have to say," said Aubrey in an attempt to erase lingering negative images that Mr. Walshe may have retained, "normally, they are very well behaved."

"Oh yes," echoed Sabine. "They have really become pets."

Pets! Peter Walshe knew all about the connotation of "pets" when applied to cows. He had seen "pets" put their owners over the fence more than once. He had been chased once by a Red Angus bull who was "such a pet, you can do anything with him." He knew what was about to come. Either Aubrey or Sabine would attempt a long-winded history of every cow in the herd: how this one had undergone an abortion in '97, or wait a minute, was it '96; how that one had given birth to twins in '01; how the other full red one was surely a purebred Red Angus that had been abused in heiferhood, you could tell from the way she carried herself and sought to exterminate any humankind with whom she was not familiar. Or he would get a long-winded sermon on hybrid vigour and the benefits of out-crossing or line-breeding or…, but the good Mr. Walshe knew how to rescue himself.

"You know, we'd best take a quick boo at the land. That'll give me time to stop and have that quick coffee with you before I go back to the office. That'll give you, Aubrey, some time to deal with the waterer, and I can get back to Red Deer and get things in motion. If you don't mind coming into Red Deer next week to sign the papers, we'll have this thing all sewn up in no time." The speech was notable for what was not said: that seemingly the Hanlons had passed the test; that Mr. Walshe was a keen observer and so attuned to the rigours of farm life he knew that cows had to have water and that if he was to overstay his visit, Aubrey would be doing his repairs in the dark.

So it came to pass a week later that Aubrey and Sabine got themselves trussed up even more tightly in numbers, big numbers represented by a twenty-year mortgage taken out on Stanley Himilton's place. To make it productive right away, they would have to double the number of cows and purchase at least another thirty cow/calf pairs. Their roller-coaster with numbers was about to get faster and more death-defying!

Chapter Two
MRS. PAVAROTTI,
"IN FLAGRANTE INFLECTO"

For both Aubrey and Sabine, ex-city folks that they were, agricultural machinery came to be looked upon as a necessary evil, something that stood between them and their having to do everything by hand. But as they got themselves deeper into the farming experience, they realized that they could barely make it with their collection of "clunkers", Aubrey's description of their limited range of machinery comprising the single reliable working tractor, the old haybine, the relatively new baler, and a prehistoric plow that was one step up from the horse-drawn version.

They had already tried the route of custom machinery operators, but those people always seemed to show up when it suited them and not you, Aubrey lamented. The trouble was, he realized after those first few years in the front forty and the back thirty, there was usually only a small window between bouts of weather to get the essential jobs done when they were supposed to be done. You can only hay when the sun shines. If you possess your own machinery and can make it work the way it's supposed to, then you do not get caught out by the smooth promises of the custom man, the one who says he is on his way as you and he speak, but who takes a week or more to arrive. By then it is raining incessantly, the hay is turning black, and you are turning apoplectic red or dumpy blue because all the neighbors harvested their hay in perfect shape while yours is lying in sodden swaths in the field. If it's not your hay that is getting rained on, then it is your grain that is getting rinsed out or even snowed upon because the man with the combine says, "Oh, but you're next on the list". Or maybe it's your land that is getting to be severely rutted because the corral cleaners in all their excremental wisdom did not arrive with their heavy equipment when they said they would arrive.

Which is why Aubrey and Sabine were forced into buying their line of "clunkers": first the haybine and the balers (round and square), then a manure spreader and "Big Bertha", their second tractor. (Their third if you counted the old International antique that only started if she felt like it, and even then had barely enough power to pull the skin off a banana.) If there was such a thing as a student of Canadian agricultural machine history, he or she would have found on the Hanlon spread an array of machinery that truly reflected a century, the long march of progress from sodbusters and homesteaders through to today. Not that the Hanlons were too much different from many of the farmers around them and whose castoffs they bought.

Of course there had to be the obvious connection between farming practices and machinery, between what the wise men called "methodology and technology". Because Aubrey and Sabine embraced the notion of rotation, they got into growing grain and feeding it to the cows the following spring once the calves were born. This in turn called for a plow, a disc, a seed drill, a swather and a combine. It also necessitated a mixer mill to grind the grain into the more palatable "chop", and a square baler so that hay could be fed into the mix with the grain. There was also that fuzzy connection between wants and needs, with Clayton Cole, Aubrey's favorite auctioneer, exploiting that fuzziness to maximum effect … which was how Aubrey acquired the swather and the notoriety that went with the "defrocking" of a Hutterite matron as told in *Footloose in the Front Forty*. To add to their grief, farmers must also have what Aubrey called "the peripherals": the rake to turn over the hay, the bin for storing the grain, the auger for getting the grain into the bin, the sled for stacking the square bales, the post-pounder for work on the fences, and on and on it all went. All too often, these too had their story.

Take the grain bin, for instance. Aubrey bought it at a Cole's Auction, some thirty miles away from home. He probably would not have bid on it had he known he would have to hire a specialist bin-moving man whose fees were in line with those of a fast-talking lawyer. Worse yet, the fees increased when the man could not set it up on arrival at the Hanlon farm because Aubrey had not known enough to put down a gravel pad for the bin to sit on. "The floor will rot out within a year if you don't do it," said the man a little too dramatically. The man should also have advised Aubrey to place it away from the shade of a copse of poplar trees, but he didn't. Still, he enjoyed charging his naïve customer for time spent and mileage traveled; if he could have got away with it, he would have charged Aubrey a consulting fee like people do in the oilfield. Within fourteen months, Aubrey had a good fourteen hundred bushels of grain to put into the bin. That was when his mind circled back to one of the man's comments. "I dunno why you didn't get a ladder with this bin because you're gonna need one, that's for sure."

"Nah, we'll manage," said Aubrey in blissful ignorance, ignorance deliberately fortified by the man's offer to sell him a ladder for a further two hundred dollars.

Improvisation is one of the building bricks of farming; it is highly commendable, though often very dangerous. When Aubrey realized that he would have to find a way to shin up the bin to open the lid, then the ladder that the man had talked about was suddenly an imperative. Not a problem for Aubrey's creative mind. In an instant, it had recalled the emergency escape ladder, still wrapped in its box in the basement—the same ladder that they had bought for any possible urgent evacuation of their flat in Edmonton. Sabine, now very competent in the old loader tractor, hoisted Aubrey up in the bucket and he hooked the ladder onto the lip of the bin. His hubris was somewhat short-lived, however, as the ladder unrolled away beneath him. Basically all it amounted to was two lengths of light chain with metal rungs bolted between them. Tarzan of the apes is about to be reborn, Aubrey was thinking. He masked his concerns from Sabine as she lowered him to the ground; it was better that she remained blithely unaware of his misgivings. Climbing up the contraption called for all the skills and the fine-tuned balance of an orangutan, and he lacked that one prerequisite for balance—the tail. Quickly marooning him halfway up, the device seemed to take a notion to swing and twist and carry on in an effort to shake him off. No help to him was the wife down below, screeching useless directives, urging him to climb up or down, as if these were easily practicable options. As so often with devices mechanical, this one was also defiant of the laws of everything, from physics to gravity. Desperation forced Aubrey to think things out by himself. With his feet firmly on the rungs, the toes tucked into the steel corrugations of the bin, he managed to stabilize himself and then courageously climbed up to the roof. It has to be said here that in the country you can get away with things that would land you in a mental institution in the town. Standing now on the sloping roof, Tarzan struck the necessary pose for his wife and let out the equally necessary blood-curdling scream to announce his triumphant arrival to all the creatures of the jungle. Then he opened the lid.

Coming down from the bin was a wilder variation of the going-up story. This was the same orangutan that went up, but now the beast appeared to be descending the jungle vine in a state of intoxication, his wife urging him to be careful and so forth in a shrill tone that suggested she was about to witness the untimely demise of her mate. As Aubrey got closer to the bottom of the bin, the ladder again began its twisting and turning; only this time Aubrey fell off and hit the ground with a thud/ splat combination. Sabine's voice stopped in mid-sentence convinced her husband was surely dead. Seconds later, his gales of uncontrollable laughter had infected her too, and they howled together. Orangutans likely howl too, right?

Ah, but the bin got itself well-filled, even if the adventure had to be repeated once more, this time for the closing of the lid. Two weeks later, there was a freak ten-minute windstorm. A massive poplar that was too tired to stay rooted any longer toppled over onto the bin roof, wrecking it almost completely. Now Aubrey was to learn that even the peripherals would need repairing on occasion, and this was no "Kwik-Fix". This was a full eight-hour job, assuming that he could find replacement roof panels for a bin so old. For the time being, and for eight successive years, Aubrey had to cover the roof with a tarp hung at the edges with old car tires to keep it from blowing off.

Then again, another of the peripherals had to make its point; the auger, perhaps feeling somehow outdone by the bin, conspired to give Aubrey another job he had not counted on. It was cold, and he had been wearing his heavy winter work gloves as he transferred some grain into a tote in the back of his pickup to help out a neighbor who had run short. Somehow, a glove came off and fell into the tub from which the auger was drawing the grain. Warned too many times never to put limb close to auger, Aubrey chose to let the glove go, seeing it quickly sucked in by the exposed flighting of the auger. Five seconds later there was a "whump". The engine went into sudden labour, and then the auger gave birth to a mangled glove and a cascade of grain midway up the tubing where it was corroded and worn out. The "R & R" sequence—"Wreck & Repair"— that Aubrey applied to all machinery had triumphed again,.

"But 'wreck' starts with a 'w'," admonished Sabine.

"Poetic license, my dear", insisted her mate. "Farming is in need of more poetry."

"You're so wight," Sabine replied with a resigned smile.

Then there was the day when Aubrey first took issue with the squirrels. "They're so cute, are they not?" Sabine gushed, but such beauty simply blights the eye of those with no experience of squirrels. Sabine had even taken to dispensing charity to them in her very own version of the Squirrel Food Bank. She took to leaving little piles of cat food in strategic spots: down at the machine sheds, above the main workbench in the shop, and in the granary where they stored square bales. Aubrey's protests at this largesse fell on deaf ears, not that his protests were that spirited when he knew how much of a lost cause it was. After all, he had to admit that he too found the squirrels to be cute, and, truth be known, he was never averse to charity enterprises where nothing more than a few handfuls of cat food were involved. That is, until he began to notice how many tools and such had mysteriously fallen out of place in the shop—tins of screws and cotter pins scattered together on the floor, that sort of thing. Was Sabine that clumsy he got to thinking? And why couldn't she pick up after herself?

Then it was the plague of cats. Whiskered faces, easily startled, peered at him in their feral state. Skittish yes, but apparently ready to scratch his eyes out should he venture too close. Worse yet, they seemed happily intent on taking up residence close to this easy food supply. Something had to be done, but how was he to get Sabine on side?

It all came to a head the day he rolled his first batch of grain as the days slid inexorably into winter. Sabine was there to direct and supervise as he maneuvered the mixer mill into place alongside the grain bin and inserted the auger through the door. Like a pilot making pre-takeoff checks, Aubrey made sure he had pulled all the appropriate levers and made the right settings before he jumped into the tractor to engage the power takeoff. Sabine was at her usual post, slightly to one side, looking on. Her love affair with squirrels ended the moment he engaged the power takeoff, (the pto), and a traumatized squirrel burst out of the discharge auger, landing squarely on Sabine's head. She went down, happily for the squirrel, as it made a bound for the nearest tree and safety. Aubrey, caring husband that he had to be, shut down the operation, climbed out of the tractor and hauled his wife back onto her feet. She was bedraggled, yes, but none the worse for wear except for a sudden pathological hatred towards squirrels whose only folly had been for one of their number to mess with a city-turned-country girl's hair. Sabine resembled Medusa, the Gorgon sister of Greek mythology, the same who had snakes for hair and eyes that if looked into directly would turn the beholder into stone. Her hair was wild, disheveled, and full of dust and bits of twig; there was even a disconcerted beetle of some sort. Aubrey could not help it. He started to laugh. Since her attempt to turn her husband into stone did not seem to be working, Sabine abandoned the scene for the house and the shampoo. Aubrey thought it might be solicitous to follow her but had to surrender halfway, succumbing to the second bellyful of laughter that he had been suppressing so well. That was the same moment that he heard a loud crash and was just in time to see a second squirrel darting out of his shop. Aha, so it wasn't Sabine at all, it was those pesky squirrels that were making all the mess. It did not take much to convince Sabine that her Squirrel Food Bank should be no more—not if they were going to set up house in Aubrey's peripherals.

The main line of machinery was another story, and one naturally written with bigger numbers. First off, with their expansion, the old Massey tractor with the front-end loader would not be sufficient. Besides, thingamajigs kept falling off, breaking off, or plumb wearing out. The alternator stopped alternating, the starter stopped starting, the water pump quit pumping, and finally the steering took Aubrey for an unscheduled detour through the ditch.

"You need tie-rod ends," said the partsman. "Replace both left and right. Unfortunately, your tractor is that ancient we don't keep them in stock any more. But you're in luck. My computer tells me that there are some in Boise, Idaho. I hate to tell you this, but if you want them then you're liable for the freight."

"How much are these tie-rod end things?" asked Aubrey finding the partsman just a little too glib about spending his money.

"Oh, not bad as tie-rod ends go. A hundred and seventy each."

"One hundred and seventy?" The question came out as more of a screech. "One hundred and seventy each? Like two hundred and forty for both?" Aubrey was breathless.

"Three hundred and forty. Plus freight. Maybe forty or fifty bucks, I don't know. Do you still want them?" The man reached for his coffee, clearly too comfortable with the whining of his customers.

"Yes. Yes, I still want them," responded Aubrey, suddenly feeling very old.

The main line of machinery, as distinct from the peripherals, included all those machines that did the essential work, those jobs without which the farm could not be a farm at all. Needless to say, the cost of both running and maintaining them was exponentially higher in dollars and in time, especially in time for somebody as mechanically unschooled as Aubrey Hanlon. But at least he did try and better himself in this respect. He took a course in welding, offered by a teacher at the school in Caroline. He became quite good at welding two pieces of metal together when they were at waist height on a flat surface. Folks who went on about how difficult welding was just had not tried it, which was surely it, no? Aubrey was so convinced of his own new-found ability that he went home and decided to repair the hay deflector where it had broken under his haybine.

His confidence disintegrated as fast as the metal he was trying to weld. Lying under the machine, sparks flying indiscriminately into his coveralls, all twisted up like a contortionist, Aubrey struggled manfully. The results were not pretty but the job was done and the welding would hold, at least for a time—like minutes rather than hours—but he was not to know that. Aubrey was quite proud of himself in fact, until his good friend Pete chose that very moment to arrive in the yard and burst his bubble. Never one to stand on ceremony, Pete climbed under the machine next to Aubrey to see what his neighbor was doing. There was a short silence before Pete lay back and stared out at the clear blue sky above. Finally he said, "You know Aub, I never knew that crows could shit upside down."

Lying there, Aubrey was thinking to himself that this was a useless piece of information if ever he had heard one, but he would give Pete the benefit of the doubt and humour him nonetheless. "I didn't know that either," he said, his eyes scanning the sky so that he might see crows excreting upside down for himself. It was only when Pete started to laugh that it dawned on Aubrey. Pete was talking about his welding, mocking it. "You miserable, played-out, old fart," was the best he could come up with. But he could not just leave it there. "But then again, I'll bet even your welding upside down is more like a trail of elephant diarrhea."

"You got that right," Pete laughed. "Maybe it's time to do another course, you and I, 'Welding Upside Down' or 'Welding for Crow Crappers'" which started them into the world of courses, another story in itself.

Staying with the theme of stories, every machine came to have its own tale for Aubrey and Sabine, usually in the form of an adventurous learning curve involved in ascertaining how the monstrosity was supposed to operate. For a non-mechanical couple, that learning curve tended to be steeper and more dramatic than for those other more favored beings, the mechanically-gifted. Knowing not so much what was supposed to happen when you pulled on a certain lever, but what *might* happen if you were to pull on it out of sequence or at the wrong time, became something they learned by bitter experience. Aubrey was the first to protest that even the most gifted of farmers made the same kind of *faux pas* as he did, and they were nothing but damnable liars if they could not fess up to it. Naturally, booboos that you made were more bearable if nobody saw you make them, or if you could conveniently pass the blame on to another, not that this was easily done. Like when Aubrey took delivery of the fertilizer spreader the very first time he had ever used one. He had to get the man at the depot to demonstrate how to arrive at the right settings and what levers he needed to pull or push to activate the machine. The good man went one better, he actually set the machine for the one hundred and twenty pounds to the acre of fertilizer that Aubrey intended to use, actually engaged the ground drive lever so that Aubrey would know exactly what to do. This was all done in far too chatty a fashion for the foreman who was watching them and who was suddenly compelled to ask his underling if he had a piano tied to his butt or what.

"Oh, oh, you'd better drive around back and let old Sourpuss load you up," said the young and garrulous Mr. Congeniality, dropping Aubrey like a hot potato.

In the first mile on the way home, three cars passed Aubrey, all honking at him. Damn but I must be going too fast, he thought to himself, recalling the 40 km per hour sticker and the slow moving vehicle sign on the back of the machine. Being the good cop he had always tried to be, he obeyed his instincts and dropped his speed. Two more cars went by, but this time only one of them honked. Then a battered old Chevy pickup zipped in front of him, the driver signaling that he should stop at once.

"Say, young fellah," said the grizzled old cowboy, grinning widely as he approached Aubrey's window, "you can fertilize this here pavement all you please but there ain't nothing gonna grow worth a darn."

"Wha', what do you mean?" Aubrey responded.

"I mean this here machine that you're so busy pullin' is engaged. In fact, it's doin' a real fine job, but I figgered you'd be a whole lot happier if all this here fertilizer was to go on your field."

The expletive that came uncalled for to Aubrey's lips was the four-letter word at the top of Sabine's banned list. He jumped out of the truck and accompanied the man to the back of the spreader. Sure enough, Mister Congeniality, distracted by the foreman from his too casual conversation with Aubrey, had failed to disengage the machine after his demonstration to Aubrey. There were more heartfelt expletives from Aubrey, and more heartfelt mirth from the toothless one, before the problem was corrected and both went on their separate ways.

Aubrey's adverse experience with the spreader did not end there, however. Once home, he got it all hooked up to the tractor and proceeded to the front forty. Very methodically, he engaged the drive as the man had shown him, reduced the setting from 120 to 110 pounds to make up for what he had spread on the road, and then did a trial run of fifty feet before getting out to check the spread. Oh it was good, he was good, what else now mattered? He hopped back into the tractor, cranked up the country music, and got down to wailing with Willie Nelson, growling with Johnny Cash, and tripping along with Dolly Parton. Five lengths of the field he went; it was so easy in that the field was regular in shape and his lines were clear to see. He never really felt the bump, nor even the clattering afterward, because he was down at Folsom Prison with Johnny Cash. But he did see Sabine stop on the road the other side of the fence, saw the hands gesticulate a message something akin to "What the heck do you think you are doing?" He turned to look behind. The spreader was not there, gone, *disparu completement* as Conley would say in what he called Jean-Claude's "Canadian Chinese". Once again, that same expletive that topped Sabine's unwanted list burst forth from his lips. He turned down the volume of the music, only then hearing the one half of the spreader's pto shaft spinning around uselessly. He stopped the pto, switched off the engine, and then spotted the spreader squatting like an abandoned duck at the far end of the field. He had popped the hitch-pin when he had hit a rut. Farmers have to develop a capacity to laugh at themselves, Aubrey thought fleetingly, knowing at once that this was a weak attempt to explain away his complete lack of attention to the task at hand. Sabine was already consumed with hysterical laughter, could not help it really, knowing also that her turn was sure to come. Laugh when you can, it's your turn next, was her motto.

The learning curve was just as steep when it came to the manure spreader, and the after-effects of the mistakes were more lasting. He bought the machine at Rimbey, the same day he bought the "donkey tractor", later christened "Big Bertha". He had gone to Rimbey, with his buddy Pete, to a mammoth machinery auction with the express intention of buying a disc. One of Murphy's Laws as applied to auctions postulates that if one attends an auction to buy a specified item, one will inevitably return with something other than what one intended.

The "intended", a disc, a sixteen-footer with offset scalloped discs, went way beyond Aubrey's pocket book. But at the time, he would have had no way of knowing that his competition would turn out to be two of the area's well-known characters whose primary goal in life was to plunder the adversary's bank account by bidding him up at the auction.

Since both were very well endowed in the treasury department, also in the victuals department judging by their girth, to compete against them would have been folly. Besides, and the Rimbey auction site always did this to him, Aubrey was freezing to the nethers because of what Pete described as a "lazy wind".

"Lazy?" quizzed Aubrey. "Seems very industrious to me."

"Nah, it's lazy. It can't be bothered to go round you, so it has to go through you." What Pete could have added was that it had a tendency to ice up its victims' brains.

The tractor looked innocent enough in its faded coat of harvester red. Big and squat, she sat there; her rear dual wheels making her look like a broody dinosaur waiting to devour prey or to give birth. Officially, the label attached to the door proclaimed her to be an International Harvester model 1566 Turbo, 160 horses. Copies of a couple of invoices taped to one side window indicated that a local repair shop had recently fiddled around with her innards to the tune of three thousand dollars, which was probably the reason nobody seemed interested in making a bid.

"C'mon boys," pleaded the auctioneer, "she's here to sell and we've got a ways to go yet before the day is over. Somebody please give us a start. How about nine thousand?"

Silence.

"Eight. Eight anywhere? Seven, seven, seven then? Okay, somebody give me six."

Silence again.

"All right, let's start out on the floor. Five thousand? Five thousand anywhere?"

Maybe it was the cold and the shivering. Maybe it was Pete's whispered counsel. Maybe Aubrey was just thirsting for action, any kind of action. "Fifteen hundred," he said in a monotone, barely audible because he was feeling so guilty at making such a ridiculous offer.

"I have fifteen, fifteen hundred," shouted the auctioneer, not about to let any offer pass him by and relieved that all he had to do now was to coax the price upward. But no matter how hard he tried, whining and cajoling and carrying on like a wounded waterfowl, it was a bust, a lull, a stall in life. He tried every trick in the auctioneer's book and nobody was impressed. Aubrey got the beast for the fifteen hundred.

"Holy smokes," said Pete, "you bloody well stole it."

"I did so," said Aubrey grandly. "Trouble is, my dear wife is sure to have a very different point of view." That different point of view would not have been expressed so forcefully if Aubrey had come home only with "Big Bertha". It was not that Pete actually coaxed him into buying the manure spreader; he simply commented how his own, by some coincidence the same model, was so useful and had paid for itself many times over. Not only did you save on corral cleaning, he said, but also you could cut back on expensive chemical fertilizer by substituting good old-fashioned manure. "Besides, this baby here hasn't done too much work. Just look at the paint".

"Sold!" crowed the auctioneer, now back on a more triumphant track. "To buyer number 146," he added for the benefit of the sales clerk who wrote Aubrey's number into the records for the second time that day.

Aubrey's reasoning with himself began right there. He had set out to spend up to ten thousand dollars. He had spent only six and a half. He had intended only one single purchase. He was coming away with two. Even if he had got the disc he so wanted, the old Massey tractor would have surely expired trying to pull it. They needed a bigger tractor. Well now they had it, even if they did not have a disc for it to pull. Yet! And he, correction, they, needed a manure-spreader to get rid of all their "bovine guano" as Sabine liked to call it. Well, now they had one, a good one, one that had not seen too much work. If Pete's had paid for itself within a year, there was no reason in the world why theirs should not do so either.

Pete was busy while all this deep thinking was going in Aubrey's mind. Good neighbor that he was, he had found Aubrey a trucker before they even left the sale. Both items were delivered the very next day. Sabine's caustic verdict was delivered within minutes of their arrival. "You boys are just plain nuts," she said. "Let you both loose at an auction and you're no better than a couple of spoiled kids in a candy store." Wisely, Aubrey said nothing, self-righteously abstaining from listing the number of times Sabine herself had been the kid in the candy store when she was at an auction. Ah, but her purchases were always in the hundreds, *never in the thousands,* she would have yelled back at him. He didn't need the yelling right now.

Thankfully, Murphy must have died before he came up with a law for absolutely everything. Common sense is supposedly so obvious there is really no need to codify it. For example, common sense would tell you that an inexperienced farmer should never try two unfamiliar machines at the same time, even if his most experienced neighbor had told him what to watch for.

The "new" tractor was huge, compared to the Massey that is. Aubrey felt as if he was the captain on the bridge of an aircraft carrier. Driving first around the yard, he almost felt as if he should call a pilot to navigate around the shoals especially after one of the rear duals clipped the back wheel of Sabine's bike leaning against a tree at the side of the driveway. Neither Aubrey nor the tractor even felt it, but it was enough to persuade Aubrey to go and play away from the yard. Just as well Sabine had gone over to Jeannie's. He hid the bike, planning to buy a new wheel the next day. Yet the tractor surprised him with its maneuverability; so much so that he felt right at home in it within an hour, steering it, that is. He still had to get used to the hydraulic controls and the power takeoff mechanism and how all these things interconnected. But at least the radio worked. After that, he attached the manure spreader. Using a rope tied to a lever and running through the back window of the tractor, he figured out how to stop and start the floor chain, realizing that the pto must be engaged to do all this. The floor chain moved the manure slowly backwards to the beater. A second rope, again running through the window, activated the beater, the monstrous great flail that did the spreading. He fooled around some more and decided he could handle it. It was child's play really. He should have known better. When something can be so easily dismissed as "child's play", Aubrey was likely to make the typical child's mistake. So pleased was he with himself, he forgot to disengage the floor chain lever before he shut down.

Sabine's job, when she finally made it back, was to drive the loader tractor and load him up with manure from the big corral. He had no inkling of what was about to happen because a) he was so coolly in command, and b) the pto was disengaged even if the apron chain was not. So at ease was Aubrey that while Sabine was loading the spreader, he was tinkering with the radio, suddenly getting it to catch his favorite country station. It was in the middle of his loud accompanying of Kenny Rogers' knowing when to hold 'em and when to fold 'em that Sabine hooted to let him know he was loaded. Great! He started up the tractor, unthinkingly engaged the pto and set off past the corral and down the full length of the thirty-yard driveway, crooning mightily along with Mr. Kenny.

He heard her before he saw her; her high-pitched shriek was probably the only thing that could pierce his *basso profundo.* He did not even have the time to turn around before she appeared running alongside the tractor. "Shit," she was shouting, "you're dropping all your shit." If only she had selected the word "stop", he would have stopped immediately, but he rumbled confusedly onwards wondering why she was using one of her own banned words with such vehemence. Finally, he had the presence of mind to look behind. What he saw brought him to a halt immediately.

Sabine was panting so hard because she had been compelled to abandon her tractor up in the corral and run after her husband's machine, trying desperately to alert him to the fact that he was laying down a thick aromatic carpet of prime manure all the way down the driveway. When Aubrey turned in his seat, he was stunned. Although the tractor was now stationary, it was still running and so still piling manure out of the back in a heap because the floor chain was engaged.

"Shit," Aubrey yelled as he shut down. "Shit, shit, and double shit!"

"More like quadruple shit," said Sabine breathlessly.

There and then, Aubrey resolved first to ration his access to any and all radios, second to give his undivided attention to what the current machine might be doing at the outset of any job, and third to buy his wife a bouquet of flowers in an attempt to allay her displeasure at the mess, worse yet the stink on the driveway. Of course he knew it was far too good a story for her not to tell the neighbors. Nevertheless, in hopes that she might see fit to temper the tale somewhat, he offered to run the loader tractor and clean up what he could. But she was on the warpath and did it herself, doing a better job of it than he could ever have done, he had to admit. Even so, there were still globs of plop and clumps of sodden straw bedding that escaped her; Aubrey was assigned to deal with them using a pitchfork and a pail.

Sabine's self-righteousness was almost insufferable, her moral superiority prompting her to name Aubrey "Captain Whatashitzu" until her own hubris struck her down. She too had developed a soft spot for the radio—not for Aubrey's country and "whining" station, but for the good old CBC: Shelagh Rogers in general, and Stuart McLean's "Vinyl Café" in particular. She had also developed a taste for opera, something that her husband never really knew. Something else he did not know, either, was that his darling wife was a "closet diva", prone to harnessing her lungs in tandem with whatever aria was being played, even if she did not know it or the language. Aubrey loved to sing in the tractor, in the corrals, and pretty well anywhere else too, but he never thought his wife had the same proclivity.

It was soon after the manure incident. The haying season was off to a flying start. Haying was now very much a team affair with Sabine running the old haybine and Aubrey doing the baling. Being the attentive husband that he was, he jumped on the quad to escort her and her tractor up to the field to begin the day's cutting. Why she chose to adjust her radio just as she was approaching the gate was a mystery. Unfortunately, too, the gate was shut. Aubrey saw it all unfold as if in slow motion; the steel gate first wrapped itself around the front grille of the tractor before the hinges broke out of the post. Her look of utter consternation was something to be both savoured and later mimicked, especially when she veered too closely towards the tale of "Captain Whatashitzu". Of course he did the right thing and calmed her down with a "There, there my dear, shit happens to you too, you know," before he sent her off on her haybining way, the tractor now sporting a few more scars of war.

It was later in the afternoon that he went back to the field to see how she was making out. Sabine being Sabine, and one who could lose herself so quickly in a world of her own, had no idea he was even there, chugging alongside the rig on his quad. And Aubrey was concerned. There was an alien, erratic sound, maybe the telltale sound of a bearing about to give up the ghost and disintegrate. He speeded up to get ahead of the tractor and get a better listen. The moment Sabine saw him, the whining noise ceased. He signaled to her to keep going. Seconds later the sound recommenced. Aubrey listened with all his concentration. It had to be a bearing that was on its last legs, but he could not make out why the sound was so variable. He had to know; he had to isolate the source before the damage was compounded and maybe a shaft was destroyed. He continued to follow her between the swaths. The sound began really pulsating. Sabine turned, saw that he was still there, and the sound stopped. He signaled her to a halt, went over to the tractor and opened the door.

"Are you, er, are you, uh, singing?" he asked hesitantly, the slightest trace of a grin beginning to crease his face.

"What's it to you?" she responded coolly, only then turning down Verdi's "March of the Toreadors".

"Just answer my question, why don't you?" he said. "Were you singing?"

"Well yes, as a matter of fact I was singing," she said way too aggressively.

"Loudly? Like very loudly?"

"Yes, loudly, like very loudly," she responded even more aggressively. "And why do you have to know all this?"

"Oh, it's okay. It's just that I could have sworn you had a blown bearing. But I guess it was nothing more than Mrs. Pavarotti *in flagrante inflecto*."

Sabine resorted to a phrase involving sex and travel that she had sworn never to use, and Aubrey went on his way, his grin as wide as the gate she had destroyed.

Possibly because he had not been a full-time farmer all of his life, and probably because he cast himself as "mechanically challenged", Aubrey fell into the trap of according his machines their own personality, and much like with his cows, that personality conjured up a name. The manure spreader, for example, had already proved that it had an excess of attitude when the slip clutch started playing games with him. When it stopped the unloading process prematurely, vindictively, contemptuously jamming half a load of wet muck up against the rear beater requiring Aubrey's physical presence to fork out the whole stinking mess, the spreader became known thereafter as Mrs. Schitzburger. True, there was not much original about the name, but trying to fork out the contents with the ammonia doing its very best to put him down was a chore not to be contemplated too often, and yet the clutch made him do it six times in two days before he got it licked, er, under, let's say "under control". The big tractor was aptly named "Big Bertha", a gentle workhorse who always started no matter the weather, and who was always obliging as long as her filters were changed and her batteries kept topped up. On the other hand, the swather had been demented from the moment he had bought it. Aubrey had been inclined to name it "Jack the Ripper" because of the

Hutterite incident. Sabine settled on the more benign "Evil Knievel". When Pete discovered this penchant for naming things, he said he hadn't realized the Hanlons were such simple peasant folk, likely pagan and undoubtedly superstitious.

"Don't talk like that," said Sabine. "It's a full moon tonight."

Chapter Three
A SENSE OF EXTREME WELL-BEING

*E*very walk of life has its own share of "characters". But sad to say, fraudsters abound: the con artists, the smooth talkers, and all of the others on the look-out for a sucker. Today's agricultural world unfortunately is no exception. Farming by its very nature attracts the independent-minded and the free-spirited people who do not always recognize accepted conventions. These are the hardy souls who seal a deal with no more than a handshake, but also the sort who might reach for a rifle if ever they are double-crossed. The trouble is that today many ordinarily honest folks have been forced to become not so much con artists as withholders of critical information. Certainly in the farming sector, margins have become so tight, every single transaction teetering between profit and loss, that people are compelled to hold back crucial information if they wish to hold on to their economic shirts. They will go ahead and consign a murderous bull into the sale ring as "a good breeding bull" when they know full well that any buyer will probably need to run fast or shoot straight to survive. An observer might see parading through the ring cows with everything from "hardware disease" (the poor girl swallowed the owner's vice-grips perhaps), to fallen haunches, to nigh terminal inertia or dementia. Aubrey had already keyed into this and was very cautious about the "real bargains" that slipped through his fingers. Overly cautious, he sometimes got to reflect later in the day. So he developed his own "Hanlonic Protocol for Buying a Cow".

Aubrey was by now an auction aficionado; he loved auctions, adored them, and was addicted to them, the thrill of the chase, the feeling of triumph when he got what he was after. When it came to livestock, the "Hanlonic Protocol" came into play. Basically, it postulated that the buyer has a 30 to 60 second window to:

(1) Do a visual check of all character defects of the animal on offer.

(2) Do an instant and searching conjecture about potential past criminal activity that might influence future attitudes and behaviors.

(3) Do a full visual, including feet, hips, tits, etc, "of everything that any red-blooded male might want to check out on a prospective date," as Dick Conley put it before the legendary Sabine slap put a stop to such nonsense. Part of the check would naturally include the number of brands evident on the animal's hide. Three to five would indicate that it had only ever had visitor status on every spread it had lived on.

(4) Do an estimate of age more number-specific than simply "indiscriminate".

Every farmer has to address the issue of how not to be too influenced by the pitch and patter of the auctioneer. Aubrey was, by now, an experienced enough buyer to treat much of what he heard with a pinch of salt and a dab of vinegar. He had been caught too many times before by an auctioneer stroking his ego; "good eye there," or "you sure know how to pick a winner" were comments he barely registered any more. He had very soon come to the awful truth that the auctioneer knew just about as much as he did, maybe less. How could it be any different when all the man was doing was passing on whatever information he could read off the sales docket or whatever the seller might have chosen to tell him? His job, the auctioneer's, was simply to render it all into "sale-ring poetry". The only person who truly knows what is up for bidding is the seller, and all too often he ain't telling because then there'd be no selling. *Caveat emptor,* or "buyer beware" was the mantra of the mart, had to be so. The buyer must always listen to what is not being said as much as to what is.

It was maybe a full month after all the financing for the expansion had been approved, by which time Aubrey and Sabine had carefully begun gathering a number of flyers and brochures about impending cattle dispersal sales and auctions, when the phone rang just minutes after they had finished their supper one Friday evening.

"It's for you," said Sabine handing the phone over to her husband and heading for her favorite reading chair.

"Well now, Mister Hanlon, and how're you doin' this fine evenin'? My name is Quincy, Quincy Klug". The gravelly voice pronounced the last name "Kloog" and then proceeded to spell it out, K-L-U-G. "Say, I hear tell you might be looking around for a few cow-calf pairs. I've decided to have me a bit of a dispersal sale, mini-dispersal you might say, because I need to cut down on my herd. How many critters might you folks be lookin' for?"

Aubrey knew he was being drawn into a conversation he did not feel much like having, but maybe it was just good conmanship on the part of Mr. Klug, reeling a sucker in. Or had he, Aubrey, been a policeman too long? Was he just too suspicious? He had always believed in the old saying, "If it's too good to be true, then it probably is."

"Ugh, well, I'm looking for around thirty pairs. That's thirty cows with calves at side," said Aubrey, his mind already hard at work wondering how on earth the fellow had even got his name.

"Well, whaddya know, that's just about the same number I'm lookin' to unload. Mebbe you and I could do ourselves a real sweet deal 'cos I'd sure like to dump, er sell off that is, thirty pair out of my eighty. I'm gettin' too doggone old to be chasin' after these dang critters anymore." The pseudo-cowboy accent, if that was what it was, had really begun to grate on Aubrey; he had dealt with too many such talkers in his time.

"What sort of animals are they, like what breed I mean?" Aubrey knew he sounded distrustful, but that came with having been a cop all of his working life.

"Oh, a bit of this, a bit of that, like most folks around these parts. Why? Are you holding out for a particular breed?"

"Well, I have quite a few Red Anguses in my herd, so I…."

"There you go now! Wouldn't you know it, a fair few of mine are Red Angus types, too. I knew we had something in common as soon as I heard your voice. Tell you what; I'll even give you choice. You take the critters you want and I'll keep the rest. Couldn't be a whole lot fairer than that, now could I?"

"Well, I, er, well that's very generous of you. How much are you asking for them?"

"Tell you what. Why don't we talk about that when you come over to my place and see 'em for yourself. I know you're gonna like what you see." Every time Aubrey heard that line he cringed; it usually turned out that he detested what he saw.

"Excuse me for a moment," he said. "I've forgotten your name already."

"Quincy. Quincy Klug. Most folks just call me Quince."

"Quince, forgive me for asking," Aubrey felt compelled to pursue him further, "but how did you find out that I was in the market for cows?"

"Oh that's easy. See, I ran up against my old pal Stan, Stanley Himilton. He was tellin' me as to how you were buyin' his place and said you'd probably be lookin' to buy some more cows. I guess he was right on the money, eh, good old Stan."

"Yeah. Yeah, he was right," Aubrey said just a little too heavily.

"You don't sound too darn thrilled about it," the voice came back soothingly. "But see, I want my girls to find themselves a good home. Stan tells me you folks take real good care of your animals, treat 'em like pets."

"Oh I'm sorry. It was just that we were not quite ready to deal. So here's what I suggest. My wife and I will come out with a good buddy of ours, and we'll take a look at what you've got. But I'm warning you ahead of time, I won't be buying anything I don't like. Just as long as you understand that." Aubrey needed to get at least one cautionary out there so the fellow realized he wasn't about to be a total pushover, as he felt he had been for most of the conversation.

"Aw shucks, you're gonna like what you see, that I can tell you for sure. Phone me when you're ready to come on out and I'll give you directions how to get here. I live just to the west of Cow Lake."

"What was all that about?" quizzed Sabine, looking up from her reading. "Someone already knows we're in the market for cows?"

"Yup. Courtesy of the Stanley Himilton Telegraph Service. What the heck, we'll go out and see what he's got, but I'll get Pete to come out with us."

"Well you two can go. Leave me out of it."

Pete happened by the next morning before they had even had a chance to phone him. He came to borrow some engine oil and scrounge a coffee, not necessarily in that order he said.

"So tell me, Pete," said Aubrey. "Have you ever come across some joker by the fancy name of Quincy Klug?"

"Quincy? Sure. Lives out near Cow Lake. They all call him Glug because he's famous for his love of the whiskey. Why do you ask?"

"Well, he phoned us last night. Wants us to buy some of his cows from him. Cow/calf pairs that is."

"And?"

"So I said the wife and I and a buddy would come out sometime and take a look."

"I'm not going," said Sabine defiantly.

"Oh, hold on now," said Pete. "You have to come. Experience of a lifetime, I'm telling you. He's one of the last of a dying breed, certifiably wild and western and as mad as a hatter, all in the same package. He's the sort of cowboy that probably wears his cowboy boots and his hat in bed. But he's got quite the operation out there. You have to see it to believe it. Makes your place look so high tech and modern that Aubrey could even convince himself he's a progressive farmer. He's the real thing, a real character." Sabine's mind was changed instantly; she had always been a sucker for "characters".

"But don't go out there with a closed mind about buying his stock. He sure knows his cows, even if he does things a whole lot differently than regular folks." Pete refused to elaborate any further, other than to say that when you buy a bottle of wine, you should always hold it up to the light.

The appointed day arrived, with Pete's urging that their visit to Quincy's be scheduled for after lunch. "He's very hospitable, old Glug is, but you don't want to eat with him. See, he's a bachelor, has been for twenty years, so hygiene is not his strong point. Let me put it this way. If you eat there, you'll know what his two previous meals were just by looking at the plate he puts in front of you. But then again, I did see him bid on an old dishwasher at Cole's Auction last week. Got it too, for a full three dollars, so it probably doesn't necessarily run like it's supposed to. You're going to love his cowboy architecture, too: Baroque Western." Pete grinned, enjoying playing up the mystery. He had Aubrey and Sabine actually looking forward to the visit.

On their way out, in Aubrey and Sabine's pickup, Pete suddenly redirected the conversation from typical farmer talk to the subject of Quincy. "There's a couple of things I want to warn you ahead of time about Quincy. He's a real smart cookie, but he can be quite offensive if you don't know him. Not intentionally, you understand, that's not his style. But his language can be pretty, let's say raw. Just try and take him as he is because he won't give a tinker's fart if you don't. And by the way, just so as you know, his best friend in the whole wide world is a horse that goes by the unlikely name of Screw-U. You're both forewarned now, so I refuse to tell you anything more. You can find out for yourselves. Forewarned, yes. Expectant, for sure!"

When they arrived at Quincy's driveway, Pete said it was at least another mile to the yard. There was a faded sign, "S-U Acres, Q. KLUG," in black letters on a peeling white background. Leaning as if off the post was the now ubiquitous black metal cutout of a cowboy in silhouette, the head tilted forward as if in slumber. All of the yuppie acreage types were buying them, a wistful longing perhaps proclaiming who they thought they were or wanted to be.

"So help me, but I hate that darn cowboy with a passion," muttered Aubrey thinking how a novel idea picked up by too many unimaginative people soon becomes tawdry and overdone. "If I had my way, I'd shoot a hole in the ass of every one of them."

"Well you'd best get used to them because you're about to see a few more," warned Pete. "But take a look at his bandana, isn't that something different?" Somebody had apparently wrapped what were clearly a pair of women's fishnet tights, puke pink at that, around the poor dude's neck.

When they came up to the first bend in the road, there was the cowboy again, only this time a pair of large scarlet bloomers hung beneath his chin. Bend number two and there he was once more. Hanging from his neck was one enormous cup that must have come from a truly outsize-bra, a blue gauzy thing with "…enough mesh on it to trap a school of sardines" commented Aubrey. Bend number three and Macho Man was clad in a baby doll nightie, the canary yellow contrasting savagely with the matt black of the silhouette.

"Is this fellow Quincy a bit sick or what?" asked a now slightly perturbed Sabine.

"I doubt very much if any of it is his doing," Pete replied. "But knowing him as well as I do, he wouldn't bother taking the stuff down either. You know how some folks love to razz an eccentric."

The last cowboy, the one at the front gate, had no article of clothing as such, but someone had contrived to paint a light green polka-dotted thong in the appropriate location.

As if all of this was not overwhelming enough, the farmyard itself was quite unlike anything Aubrey and Sabine had ever seen. If one was seeking out a visual history of rural Alberta from the early days of homesteading to the technology of today, this was the place to be. Machines of every vintage and from every decade going back to the turn of the century—horse-drawn to spiked wheel to rubber-tired—were here. Roccoli, Minneapolis-Moline, Allis-Chalmers, Massey-Harris, Fordson-Major, David Brown, John Deere, all the names were here. Not in neat viewing rows mind you, but emanating outwards from the yard like ripples in a pond: the oldest on the edge, the more modern in the inner circles. A huge Quonset type building dominated all, with a large John Deere tractor housed inside, this year's model Aubrey noted. Sheds and lean-tos, some not too clear which structure was supporting which, were dispersed among the piles of junk, themselves full of junk.

"Don't go calling it junk, now!" hissed Pete. "It's pastoral treasure, the supreme collection of agricultural necessities."

That was when the man appeared out of the clapboard shack, so utterly nondescript in appearance that it was lost among the gaggle of other buildings about the place. He was a big man, huge in fact, and craggy, John Wayne craggy, sporting the largest pair of cowboy boots the Hanlons had ever seen. The uniform, the jeans, checkered western shirt, cowboy hat stained with sweat, was exact right down to the belt and buckle: a rodeo buckle of course, a cowpoke bulldogging a Longhorn calf. He was John Wayne with a droopy moustache, his bottom lip distended outward with a plug of chewing tobacco. But it was the eyes that grabbed you and held you, steely blue and piercing, proclaiming an indomitable character however much anyone chose to label him spinny or eccentric.

"Howdy folks," came that same lilting voice that Aubrey had first heard on the phone. "And a mighty fine day to come and buy some good ol' bovine mamas, right Ma'am?" Quincy tilted his hat to Sabine in good old-fashioned cowboy courtesy.

"Yes, right," she responded gallantly.

"Say Quince, Aubrey here wants to know what's with all your boys down the driveway wearing all those pieces of women's clothing?" Pete asked. There was an immediate howl of laughter.

"Some damn fool is tryin' his doggone best to piss me off," Quincy chuckled. "Either that or there's one helluva woman somewheres who wants to get her claws into me. Quantity on top of quality, wouldn't you say Ma'am?"

Aubrey was now praying that Sabine's feminist streak was not about to immerse Quincy and the entire male gender into the fires of hell and damnation. He need not have worried. She had noted the gruff politeness, had been charmed by it, had intuited that there was a real gentleman behind that gruff exterior, had even acknowledged that here was a man trapped in a time gone by, yet a man who was as much a straight-shooter as any man she had ever met.

"She's sending you a pretty strong message, fellah, that's for sure," she said, delighted to play along.

"That she is," Quincy shot back, "that she is. You know, I was gonna put me up one of them new-fangled cameras they have nowadays just to find out who might be lusting after Quince the Prince. But you know what?

That'd spoil the fun. Damn it to hell, but it sure is something for an old piece of rawhide like me to feel wanted. Every time I get to takin' the stuff down, more of it goes up. Sheesh, I bet I got more ladies' underwear in my shop than you've got in your closet. What d'ya say, Ma'am; nothin' wrong with a bit of hot romance even if it's only in the mind?" Clearly old Quincy was as much impressed with Sabine as she with him.

"Better it stops in the mind before it finds its way to other places," she said. There were a couple of seconds before Quincy burst out laughing, his hands slapping his sides in unrestrained mirth. Whatever ice there had had been was now broken completely.

"You know what, Ma'am, you're one helluva woman," Quincy said when he finally regained control of himself, wiping the tears from his eyes with a handkerchief so filthy it could only have been described as a mechanic's rag. Then he strode forward and shook Sabine's hand in introduction, firmly but not crushingly as she would have expected. "Quincy. Quincy Klug, Ma'am. Pleased to make your acquaintance."

"Sabine. Sabine Hanlon. And this is my husband Aubrey."

"Pleased to meet you," said Aubrey offering his hand and ready to endure the bone crushing that never came.

"Ah, so you're the ex-custodian of the law of the land, or so my friend Stan tells me. Why in hell did you guys decide to go farming? Are you plumb crazy or something?"

"Some would say so," said Aubrey.

"Hi'ya Pete. Haven't seen you in a coon's age."

"Been in jail, Quince. Serving my sentence, condemned to hard labour in the field."

"For a crime of fission, no doubt, an old fart like you." Quincy's comeback did not take a second. He turned to Aubrey. "Did this here old fellah tell you what kind of bulls I run?"

"No," said Aubrey dubiously, surprised he had never thought to ask for himself.

"Texas Longhorn," Quincy pronounced grandly. "Angus-Longhorn cross, best damn cross you'll find anywhere."

Sabine could not help herself. "You mean those pretty, little, spotty cows with curly horns? Oh they're so beautiful. Now I can't wait to see your cows," she gushed. Her enthusiasm only confirmed Quincy's adoration; this gal was as smart as she was beautiful. Aubrey on the other hand was totally deflated and convinced that even if Quincy's patter didn't take him in, his wife was now a lost cause. He would never have agreed to the visit in the first place had he known about the Texas Longhorns. Why had he not thought to ask? Why had Pete not told him, deliberately it would seem.

"What on earth made you cross Texas Longhorn with Red Angus?" he asked, hardening his decision that he would not be buying any animals here and concluding that the afternoon should be written off as no more than a sight-seeing tour of the local fauna and flora.

"Son," Quincy sighed as if talking to a child, "I like my animals with a bit of spirit; you know, a bit of get-up-and-go. I hate them tame little dogies that have a hard time getting up and have the same top speed as a three-legged stool. 'Sides, the boys and me, we sure like 'em for a bit of roping. But then again, when a young fellah gets up to my age, why, his body makes sure he cuts back a little. You know how it is."

"Let's go and see them," Sabine intervened, nipping in the bud any further objection or expressions of disinterest on the part of her husband.

"Screw you!" Quincy roared.

Sabine would have slapped him right there and then had she not been taken so by surprise. She was searching for the right response when Quincy roared again.

"Screw-U, get your sorry dumb ass over here right now." Only now did Sabine recall the name of Quincy's horse. A whinny made them all turn. Sabine gasped. One very large bay mare ambled into view. In her own equine way, the horse exhibited the same characteristics as her owner, the same shambling gait, the same indicators of age and the same twinkle in her eye as if she, too, shared his sense of humour. She was all saddled up and ready to go with a look that seemed to say, "Here we go again, about to put on our grand parade."

"You folks mosey on down to that corral down there, why don't ya? I'll spin around the back on my old nag here and bring 'em all in." Old, certainly older than their audience they may have been, but horse and rider were clearly born for each other and the saddle. There was none of the usual rider cajoling horse to stand still and behave, none of the high-strung antics of a filly playing hard to get, no standing on ceremony. Both had business to do and they set off to do it. Sabine was especially fascinated. She had always been terrified of horses, seeing them as ever bad-tempered and always unpredictable.

The corral was like something one would associate with a set used once in a B-western movie and then left to decay. Basically constructed out of poles, many stayed in place only because of the abundance of baler twine wrapping them to the posts. Obvious holes where perhaps a flighty Nellie type had exited in too much of a hurry had been plugged up with an assortment of boards, an old set of bedsprings, and in one corner the hood of some cast-off pickup truck. The visitors lined up behind what appeared to be a more robust section of the fence and waited.

They heard Quincy's whistling and hollering before they actually saw the herd appear at the bottom of the hill sloping up to the corral. Moving slowly, the cows were cooperating very nicely Aubrey thought wryly, his mind casting back to his efforts to contain his own herd for Peter Walshe. That is until the lead cow, halfway up the hill and approaching the gate to the corral, stopped dead the moment she spotted strangers. The herd came to a halt behind her. The cow, clearly the matriarch of the herd, her ribs all apparent as if to declare her age, shook her head in a show of great indignation, as if to let it be known that she for one was not up for sale. It was more by good luck than by good management that Quincy urged some of those in the rear to push their way through. This in turn bumped granny cow into moving again and the herd wheeled into the corral, evidently to granny's profound displeasure. Doubtless she would have turned and bolted, but Quincy and Screw-U were right there and she knew better than to joust with Quincy.

The calves, anywhere from two weeks to two months old, were stunning, even to the negativistic Aubrey bound and determined to shoot down any makings of a deal. The array of colours—brindle reds, spotted grays, shining blacks, roans and brockles, all in contrast to the solid reds of the cows—rendered the calves even more striking to the eye. And they were so full of life. The cows were suspicious, wary, but the calves were like a bunch of kids let loose in the playground, tearing up and down the corral, tails up, and screeching to a halt alongside mom for a quick nip of refreshment.

Sabine, poor Sabine was in love. For an ex-manager of a women's boutique, an ex-yuppie addicted to café lattes and Gucci, she had traveled a long and tortuous road in the country to arrive at where she was at this precise moment. The calves positively vied for her attention, particularly one—a younger heifer calf that was the most audacious. It came forward to check out the entire audience before deciding to ham it up for all. An exquisite composite of reds and blacks, it had the eyelashes of a model, with deep black streaks beneath the eyes as if the mascara had run. The instant his wife began her "ooh-ing and ah-ing", Aubrey knew he was done for; they would be going home with at least one cow and calf. Where he always tended to focus supposedly on the practicalities, saleability of progeny, average daily gain, that sort of thing, Sabine was a romantic all caught up in aesthetics and image and how well an animal might dance and sing and paint pictures. But the agricultural dimension of their relationship was one of give and take; it had to be, for Sabine was too strong-willed to be in the ranks of the meek and humble. She was not, nor ever would be, a silent partner who could be dismissed lightly. Besides, Aubrey had to confess, she had been proved right just a few times too many, womanly intuition he had to suppose. What irritated him right now though was that Quincy had perceived right off that Sabine had a power base of her own, and Quincy was playing up to it unashamedly. What made it even worse for Aubrey was that he knew his good friend Pete was enjoying every minute of Quincy's stellar performance, Aubrey's acute discomfort, and Sabine's unbridled enthusiasm. Indeed, Pete was not above doing a little stirring of his own.

"Damn nice cows, I have to say", he told Quincy.

"Damn right," the cowboy replied. "I've been at this game too doggone long not to know what I'm doin'."

"How saleable are the calves?" Aubrey had to make at least an attempt to deflate the balloon.

"Why, look at 'em," retorted Quincy. "How saleable do you think they are? Lean beef on the hoof is what they are. Buyers can see exactly what they're getting, right Ma'am?" Of course he just had to appeal to Sabine. Of course she just had to agree. Aubrey had to try to get a last word in before she struck out on her own and bought them all.

"Tell you what, would you let us pick out five? That'll give us a chance to try 'em."

"Try 'em? What, like testing out a new bicycle? Sure, sure, I'll let you pick five but you must understand that if somebody else comes along and wants the rest while you're busy tryin' your five of 'em as you call it, why, there won't be none left once they're gone. Right, Ma'am?

"Right," came the echo. But Sabine had already conceded in her own mind that her husband's caution might be well founded.

"Okay, so we pick five," Aubrey plowed on. "At what price? Cow and calf as a pair?"

"Make me an offer," said Quincy smoothly, giving the response that Aubrey dreaded, but one he had to know was coming.

"Well, at the auction marts, cow-calf pairs are selling anywhere from nine hundred to fifteen hundred dollars."

"Okay, so they are," said Quincy. "So what's your offer?"

"How about we pick five first and then go from there?" suggested Sabine coming to the rescue and slowing things up.

"Suits me," said Quincy. "I'll just move 'em around a bit so's you can see 'em good." Quietly, without fuss, he got his cows circling around the corral.

"Fifty-six," said Aubrey eyeing up a big red mama with a hefty dark steer by her side.

"Twenty-seven," said Sabine making sure to have her turn. Twenty-seven was a young roan cow with a gorgeous roan heifer calf by her side, the calf very lively and only about two weeks old.

"Take a look at that one forty-seven," offered Pete. "Look at her bag and the milk she's carrying. Good feet, too."

"One forty-seven," Aubrey and Sabine cried out in unison.

"What about that mottled-colour cow, the one over to the left of one forty-seven?" suggested Sabine.

"Take her," said Pete. "She's young and she's got a dandy bull calf."

"Mottled one," Aubrey yelled out.

"Mottled? What the hell's that?" bellowed Quincy.

"Spotted cow," said Pete. That one, over there."

"Spotted cow? That's number sixty-two," said Quincy without even looking.

There was a pause as the herd moved off to the far end of the corral before being persuaded back to where the prospective buyers were standing.

"Seventy-nine for sure," shouted Aubrey. "That's five, Quince, that's five," he said making sure that Sabine did not try for a few more yet. "That's all we want."

"But what about my calf? Who is the mother of the calf I pointed out when we arrived, the one who came to entertain us, the one that…there she is, there's little Miss Prissy."

"Oh, you probably won't want her when you see her dam. She's an old girl that goes by the name Elvira. About twelve years old I reckon. Good cow in her time though, damn good cow, one of the best. But a mite old and ornery, now, and a bit flat-footed. There was a time you could pet her. Not so sure any more."

"Cost. Let's talk cost," Aubrey cut his wife off at the pass.

"Fourteen hundred apiece, each pair," was Quincy's instant response.

"Thousand," responded Aubrey, fearful he might offend the old cowboy but trying his luck nevertheless.

"Thirteen," said Quincy without batting an eye.

"Eleven," said Aubrey.

"Come on, honey, don't be so mean," Sabine could not help herself. "They really are nice cows."

"Now there's one lady who knows where it's at," commented Quincy. "Twelve twenty-five. That's bottom."

"Deal," said Aubrey with evident satisfaction." Now what do you want for the calves?"

"Eight hundred apiece," Quincy responded without missing a beat. "You're gettin' a deal whichever way you cut it."

"Done," said Aubrey.

"But what about my calf? What about Elvira?" wailed Sabine, akin to a small child who had just been firmly denied in the candy store.

"What about her?" asked Aubrey, too implacably. "You heard the man. She's old."

"You're old…"

"You know Ma'am. You sure are one spirited lady. I ain't dealt with a woman like you for years. Tell you what, five hundred on the top and at least a couple of whiskies with this old cowboy and you can take her home with the calf. How's that?"

"Deal," snapped Sabine.

"So here's how we're gonna do it," Quincy took charge. "Me and old Screw-U here will split 'em out for you one day next week, you choose the day. You bring the money then, and you'll have another whiskey of course."

"Of course," said Sabine, a little too unthinkingly.

"Do you need a certified cheque?" asked Aubrey, wise to the ways of old folks wary of being ripped off from their money.

"Oh shit no. How fast do you think you can run anyways? You go back on a deal with ol' Quince here and he'll hunt you down, boy, cop or no cop. If you can't take a man's word then what the hell is left, right Ma'am? 'Sides, your old woman ain't gonna let you get away with any fancy footwork, that I can tell. Right Ma'am?"

"Right! But you leave off the old woman bit if you want to stay on your two feet."

"Ooh, she's a feisty one right enough. Come on now, enough of this gum-flappin', it's time to wet the old whistle. Buyin' and sellin' is thirsty work. You folks make your way up to the house while me and the hoss put these critters back where they came from. I'll see you up there."

The house. Shack perhaps, but "house" was pushing it. The glass-paned front door was so grimed up, it was impossible to see in, or out for that matter. They decided to wait. Quincy, quick in arriving probably because for him whiskey tasted best in a party, hitched his horse up to a tree and showed them in, initiating a full-frontal assault on their olfactory senses. The smell—or more charitably put, the aroma—was not so much antagonistic as musty, not toxic so much as wilting. The odour of unwashed laundry grappled with the aroma of left-over food and dishes that had been dirty for a week or more. The only table in the kitchen that masqueraded as dining room-cum-sitting room was littered with dirty crockery, a few tools, a sample of barley, a biography of "Dief", and a few other assorted objects.

As if Sabine was not already enough in shock, Quincy first ordered them to keep their footwear on, that same footwear that had trudged around the yard and the corral picking up whatever might be attracted to their boots. But then her guilt turned to gratitude as they ventured into the room; walking on that floor in socks would have been akin to walking about in the corral without shoes. Indeed, the corral might well have been cleaner!

More shock and awe was generated by Quincy's next move. Picking up a large cardboard box half-full of papers, "my filing cabinet" he called it, he turned and dumped the contents in the corner of the room. Then, holding the now empty box at the end of the table, he swept everything into it, breaking a glass in the process.

"There, now we can start again," he announced. "Pull up a chair, folks, and sit yourselves down. I don't get good company like this every day." He put the box down on top of his papers, walked over to a cupboard and pulled out two china mugs and two glasses. "That's all I got left that's clean," he said. "The rest is in that dang dishwasher I bought me at the auction last week. Thing's no darn good. Spits the soap out all over the doggone place." He placed the two glasses in front of Aubrey and Sabine "as guests of honor" he said, keeping the mugs for Pete and himself. "Clean" for Quincy was obviously very much a relative term, judging by the film that coated both glasses and mugs. Pete urgently signaled Aubrey and Sabine to keep their mouths shut as he steered the conversation to safer waters.

"What do you mean the dishwasher spits soap all over the place?"

"Well, so help me, that's what the damn thing does. It spits the soap all over, bubbles pouring out of the door and all."

"Does it actually run?"

"Near as I can tell."

"Have you got it on the correct cycle?" chimed in Sabine getting all technical.

"Well, I read them there destructions and did what they said I should do."

"Hold on a sec," said Pete. "Sabine's got something! What are you using for soap?" Pete was the ultimate pragmatist.

"Soap? Why, washing up soap, right? You know, Sunlight or some darn thing. Like you use for washing dishes in the sink. Filled up the little soap gizmo thing like the book of words told me to."

"Aha!" Pete pounced before the others could get a word in. "You can't use that kind of soap, Quince. Filled the gizmo, you say? You must have had bubbles coming out everywhere. You have to get yourself some proper dishwasher soap."

"You're kiddin' me."

"No I'm not. Right, Sabine?"

"He's right, Quincy," said Sabine.

"Look, I'll bring some over for you," said Pete. "And then we'll test it out. How much did you pay for it? The dishwasher, I mean?"

"Three lousy bucks," replied Quincy, still very much unconvinced he had any sort of a bargain.

"Three bucks," yelped Sabine in astonishment. "You paid three dollars for a complete dishwasher? My friend, you'd better not be complaining if it works."

"So how much would I pay for a new one then?" asked a man whose grasp of the domestic had never extended beyond buying basic toiletries.

"Three fifty or so, that's three hundred and fifty, and that's the most basic," Aubrey threw in as his contribution.

After that came the whiskey, very generous amber servings of Crown Royal. The two male visitors were barely comfortable about the volume but Sabine was horrified. She looked at the glass before her and asked in a despairing voice, "Do you have anything to go with it, like soda or ginger ale or something?" She dared not ask for water, not in this house.

It was Quincy's turn to be horrified. He looked her up and down with all the solemnity of a judge about to pronounce sentence on the felon before him. "Ma'am, the Scots will tell you that whisky cannot swim. They're right. I'm telling you they're right. Crown Royal does not go well with any traveling companions. Now, I may not know a whole helluva lot about them dishwashers and soap, but believe me, what you have before you in unadulterated form is the best medicine a man or a woman could ever swallow." He raised his mug to set seal on the pronouncement. "Here's to us and all who sail with us. And to hell with all the rest of 'em."

Sabine had never been a serious drinker. Now she had a choice to make; sink or sip, get it over with in two swallows or prolong the agony and drag it out. She picked the former and upped the glass. To the astonishment of all three men, the contents virtually disappeared in one shot. The aftershock was instant. Her eyes bulged in burning disbelief, her breath came in short gasps, her hands gripped the table and her face flushed scarlet.

"Now there's one helluva woman," roared Quincy, downing his glass in full support. "You boys had better drink up unless you're gonna let yourselves be outdone by a woman."

Naturally they did their manly duty, Sabine still hanging onto that table for dear life, and still speechless. Quincy only did the obvious; he poured another round, even more generous than the first one. This time Sabine determined to stretch the thing out, to nurse her glass until they could get out of there. Either that or they would have to carry her out. But then again, this Crown Royal stuff was not half bad.

Pete took the pressure off. He turned to Quincy and asked him what he thought of the latest government initiatives to help the beef industry.

"You mean that BSE testing program of theirs, do you?"

"That, and their so-called income insurance program."

"Well that BSE program is a start, but that's all it is, a start. See, us boys have got to go for full testing, right across the board, not this pissy-assed stuff of having some overpaid vet come out and shoot a downer cow so he can send off a chunk of her brain to some lab in Winnipeg. All animals should be tested, without exception. But shit, Pete, let's not even talk about it. See, I was born a Yankee down in Montana. But I'm so pissed off with them Yankees right now with their closing of that dang border, my so-called country. Why, I would pee on their flag if I could find one." He turned to Sabine. "So what do you think of my cows, Ma'am?" Sabine's face was positively glowing with, was it happiness, perspiration, or a sense of unqualified well-being?

"I love them," she yodeled. "Especially the calves, especially Elvira's calf," she smiled benignly. "Do all your other cows have names?"

"Only one other one, and you bought her. Number twenty-seven, the roan one with the little roan heifer calf. Bought her from a lady up in Rimbey. It was her pet. Called her Babe. She's a real sweetheart too, but remember to stay away from her for a day after she has calved; she can be a mite feisty. Okay, of course you love 'em, so bottoms up and let's have another to keep you out of the ditch on the way home." Old world courtesy dictated they do as they were told, with Sabine's first panic now turning to a wondering whether they really would have to carry her out.

"No more for me," said Aubrey. "I'm driving." On the other hand, Pete had no such excuse and no qualms, either, if truth was to be known. Sabine hesitated then realized how disappointed Quincy would be if she failed him now. Up went the glass, down went the whiskey. Once more those sweet eyes bulged, once more the doll face flushed, this time with tears running down her cheeks. Once more her glass was filled. She would later admit, she did not recall too much after that: a bit of singing here, some rowdy laughter there, lines from a ditty about Elvira to which Quincy was giving full operatic treatment.

Chapter Four
PARTY TIME

In the intervening days between their visit to Quincy's and S-U Acres, Aubrey and Sabine took in a couple of dispersal sales, and failed to bag a single animal. Oh, there was plenty of opportunity, but at the auction mart in Red Deer, prices for cow/calf pairs were stratospheric and far beyond anything that thrifty Aubrey was prepared to pay. After all, he knew what he could get at Quincy's, and at a far better price. Then at the Gelbvieh dispersal sale they attended somewhere near Hanna on somebody's farm, the animals came into the ring and they were all "heads-up" as Pete called it, "fighting wild" to Aubrey, more of the layman. Both Aubrey and Sabine suggested they abandon the sale and indulge themselves in a good lunch back in Red Deer.

Both Aubrey and Sabine felt deeply indebted to Pete for all his help; while Sabine now saw in him something of an accomplice, her partner in crime in their recent carousing with Quincy Klug when dear old Aubrey simply had to steadfastly maintain his stick-in-the-mud posture of "designated driver". What would one expect of an ex-cop anyway? Not that she or Pete could remember much of Pete's rambling attempts at "cowboy poetry" or Sabine's high-pitched rendition of "Oklahoma" complete with dance routine, her response to Quincy's rousing version of Elvira. Their finale in trio—Sabine, Pete and Quincy—was a chorus line rendition of "The Farmer and The Cowman should be Friends". Their partying and carrying on left them with enough of a gap in the memory to wonder how badly they had compromised their dignity. In a sense, then, the lunch was intended to give them all space and the moral courage to go back out to Quincy's and pick up their six chosen cows. Pete, as Sabine had hoped, indeed had conspired and offered them the use of his stock trailer together with himself as driver, all part of Sabine's master plan.

It was a glorious morning when they headed out to S-U Acres, with Sabine excited about her new "babies", and Aubrey feeling very apprehensive that he would find their picks substantially less impressive when he saw them again. When they arrived, Quincy and his horse were just finishing up sorting the animals. The "Hanlon Selects" were confined to a small holding pen next to the loading chute; the remainder of the herd moved back into the large corral where the Hanlons and Pete had first seen them. Aubrey was relieved to find his fears were unfounded; the animals were better, far better, than he had recalled. Sabine was ecstatic, yet the ecstasy was somewhat muted as she appraised the animals in the main corral as if expecting to find another honey of a calf that she should not leave behind.

"Howdy folks," Quincy's voice boomed over them as he approached and tied up his horse. "Remember, you can't just up and haul 'em out of here like you're stealin' them in the middle of the night. You gotta stop for a bit of refreshment."

"No whiskey," Sabine put her foot down.

"No whiskey," Pete echoed.

"Hell, you folks gone and joined The Mothers of Temperance or something? Okay, okay, a cup of coffee it'll have to be then. Come on, I'll leave the horse here for half an hour."

The state of the house was the same, the same mess on the floors and the windows. But the coffee mugs were sparkling clean so that nobody had to steel their nerves before drinking.

"Thanks again for putting me straight on that there dishwasher, Pete. Take a look at these doggone cups now. And look at this here glass." He held a glass up to the light. Not a trace of grime anywhere. "I never realized they were so darn dirty until that machine showed up." The gratified Sabine blessed Pete for being the good neighbor that he was, the sort of Good Samaritan who never sought glory when he helped other people. The coffee took time to perk, even though Quincy had set it all out beforehand, knowing that he would insist on a visit. They were chatting once again about all the usual stuff, weather and so forth, when a somewhat preoccupied Aubrey suddenly turned to his wife and said, "Do you know what I'm thinking, dear?"

"Yes," she said. "I know very well what you are thinking, and let me tell you I fully agree."

"What am I thinking?" Aubrey continued, although he should have been well used to his wife's extraordinary intuition.

"That it might be better…" she replied.

"Depends on whether…" Aubrey came back.

"Say, do you people always talk Greek among yourselves?" said a bemused Pete.

"That ain't Greek," interrupted Quincy, now up and serving the coffee. "That's shorthand for 'I'm thinking that because prices were so high at the sales that it might be better for us to buy the other twenty-four cows here, depending on whether the senile old bat gives us the same dang deal as last week." He chortled.

Both Aubrey and Sabine were crimson.

"The answer," Quincy went on quite unabashed, "is yes. The old bastard will give you the same price, but only if you agree to a gate-run."

"Gate-run? What on earth is a gate-run?" queried Sabine.

"Aubrey, I'm sure, will tell you. Ain't that so Aub?" Quincy was enjoying their discomfort.

"Aubrey, being the retired cop that he is, has no idea," said Aubrey.

"First twenty-four through the gate, cows that is. One-legged, one-eyed, one-eared, certifiably insane, ancient bag o'bones, it don't matter. Besides, you folks already got the oldest cow in the herd, you got Elvira."

"Fine by me," agreed Sabine.

Aubrey, trying his pathetic best to picture the other cows, was not so sure. "What if there's one of them I absolutely hate?" he asked.

"Too damn bad," responded Quincy. "That's gate-run. It was her destiny to get married to you, in a manner of speaking of course."

"How, how will you get them to run through the gate in pairs?" Sabine asked naively. "Like every cow coming through the gate might not have her calf by her side."

"That's why it's the first twenty-four cows through the gate. So do you folks trust me or what?" Quincy challenged them.

"I trust you," responded Sabine instantly.

"It's not that we don't trust you, Aubrey floundered. "It's just that…"

"Look, here's how we do it. We run them all, the whole shooting match into the sorting alley. When I say 'we', I mean me and your friend Pete, here. You trust Pete, right?"

"You I trust," Sabine jumped in again. "Pete, no. You forget. I've seen how badly he misbehaves on your whiskey."

"We trust you," said Aubrey earnestly.

"Then me and Pete will pull out the first twenty-four cows that head for the gate back into the corral, okay?"

"Make it twenty-six," said Sabine. "If you can."

Quincy looked over at Aubrey and arched his eyebrows.

"Twenty-six", Aubrey said heavily.

"Boy, you folks are goin' all out today," said Quincy. "That's four trips, for sure, for ol' Pete here and his trailer."

"Can you manage three more?" Aubrey turned to Pete. "I'll fill up your tank when we're done."

"More to the point, have you got time for four?" asked Sabine

"For you, my dear, I'll always have time. But we'd better push it."

"Whoa there, whoa! Hold yer horses some. Will ya? There's one more condition."

Here it comes, Aubrey was thinking. The deal was too good to be true.

"What's the condition?" asked Sabine so innocently.

"The party afterwards," said Quincy. "We all gotta have us a little celebration, no?"

Sabine's heart sank. She might have guessed. Aubrey simply looked into his cup. Pete, dear wonderful Pete, saved the day.

"Just as long as this party gets to be at my place," he said flatly. "So it's not too far to my bed. Next Thursday. We're starting a tradition, Jeannie and I: an annual summer get-together for all the folks that matter. You're all invited."

"Well I'll be damned," said Quincy. "I ain't been to a party for years. What all should I bring?" He was clearly thrilled to the core.

"Just you bring that wrinkled old carcass of yours," said Pete. "We'll supply the food and Aubrey'll bring the whiskey. By the way, you might need a pair of swim shorts."

"Swim shorts? Why in the name of tarnation would I be bringing swim shorts?" Quincy was genuinely puzzled.

"Because Pete and Jeannie have a swimming pool. You might want to go swimming."

Quincy's roar of laughter stopped them all dead. "Can you folks imagine my wrinkled old cadaver in swim shorts? I mean, can you? Damn it, underneath I look like a piece of burned bacon still with the hog's hide attached. Besides, I'd have to spend all my time fighting off the chicks with a tan like mine, right? Swimming pool, my ass! Now that's a good one. Too darn bad I can't swim."

"And if you go and drink a little too much of Aubrey's whiskey, we'll make sure you get a ride home," added Pete just in case the man needed any further convincing.

"Pete, you don't have to go to all this trouble just for us," Sabine was now very concerned that somehow she and Aubrey were not pulling their weight.

"Oh, don't think I'm doing this for you, not for one second. I'm doing it with you, not for you. Actually, truth be known, I'm doing this for me."

"How do you figure that," Aubrey chipped in.

"Well, see me and Jeannie would like to borrow that boat of yours and do some salmon fishing."

"Done," said Sabine immediately.

"Done," echoed Aubrey. What else could he say?

"Ah, but there is one small catch," added Pete grinning widely. "The crew has to come with it."

"Done," said Aubrey automatically.

"Done," echoed Sabine.

"Good. Then drink up that coffee and let's get to sorting and loading, right Quince?"

"Right."

The sorting done by experienced cattlemen was quick and almost effortless. When they saw their new collection, both Aubrey and Sabine had to acknowledge that they could not have done better at any sale. Besides, as Sabine pointed out, these animals were all from one home, reducing greatly the chances of their picking up some exotic disease or rare strain of scours. Moreover, having been together as a group, they could seek safety in numbers when the inevitable challenging for status came about after their merging with the herd at home. Nellie for one was sure to contest the right to her title of the Hanlon Sacred Cow atop the manure pile.

The party, ah the party, the one that Quincy christened as "The Night of the Sloppy Dives". It began, as all such parties do, very innocently. People began arriving at five o'clock on a glorious June evening, dressed not so much in finery, image not being a paramount consideration among farming folk, but neat and scrubbed and brimming with the goodwill bequeathed by a warm summer's day. Aubrey and Sabine were on hand with Pete and Jeannie to act as hosts, along with their old friend Dick Conley, joker extraordinaire, who had come down from the city especially for the occasion. Sabine, as her wisdom dictated, had pleaded with him to be on his best behavior and, above all, to keep his waggish tongue still. Aubrey had remained discreetly silent, knowing that when it came to his old friend Mister C, it was a lost cause entirely, no matter that he was the only person at the party wearing a tie. The barbecues were on, the Italian sausages were sizzling, the chicken wings were disappearing as fast they were charred, kids were tearing around the large garden with custodial siblings in tow, cold beer and chilled wine were flowing, and the odd eligible girl was playing coy with the odd available lad; all was as it was supposed to be. The pool, indoor and fenced off, had been declared off limits for now to prevent any unwanted mishap.

By the time everybody had arrived, there were about thirty adults on hand, all locals except for Pete's two brothers and their spouses who farmed somewhere out east near Three Hills, where the family had grown up. The neighbours east of the McBains, Pete's folks, were an English couple, the Brinkworths, with three strapping daughters: twins Priscilla and Peony, and the youngest Penelope. "King George's Dragons of the Moat" Pete used to call them when they were growing up. Then when he saw how quickly Priscilla and Peony had conquered his two older brothers' hearts, he knew that the Brinkworth campaign would only be deemed complete when he had been subjugated by the formidable Penelope. He did the only thing he could think of at the time; he bolted into the construction industry in Red Deer where he met and married Jeannie, and "lived most happily ever after," he said. Penelope, perhaps taking Pete's hint, also took off to become a welder in the booming oil patch. From the euphoric look on their faces, this was as near to a night out on the town as the McBain boys had made in a long time; and with both Joe and Bert in the company of the likes of Dick Conley and Quincy Klug, they were happily pushing the limits. Appropriately overdressed in high-end western gear, they began the night immaculate, becoming more and more disheveled as the devil in the drink and the evil in the company loosened their constraints, much to the displeasure of their "better halves". The latter nearly as burly as younger sister Penelope but more femininely refined, were preening around in their royal robes, yards of diaphanous creation yearning for the ballroom of Calgary's Palliser Hotel. People from around were simply too nice and too accommodating to freeze them out, so there they were, half out of their element, sashaying together from group to group, two women-of-war, their sails full of wind, one in powder blue, the other in honeysuckle yellow.

The meat—beef of course, and Pete's own as one would expect—was as good as one could buy anywhere, triple A for sure. The food in general—the salads and the breads and the bowls of pasta-ed glory, the plates of potato-ed heaven and zucchini marinade, the desserts configured to ensure multiple returns—all ensured an ambiance and contentment worthy of the best French cuisine. People loosened up, the serious talk of economic insecurity finally moved off from weather and cows, horses and pigs, wheat, barley corn, weeds, dismal prices and so forth. Earnest exchanges slipped effortlessly into exaggerated yarns and the kingdom of the tall tale. Yet everybody remained well behaved, even Quincy whose loud guffaws were heard only occasionally. Youngsters were eventually ferried home or harbored safely downstairs, chaperoned by a succession of movies, and all was right with the world upstairs—until Dick Conley started the riot by speaking up over everyone's head to Pete.

"Hey Pete, old son, when are you going to show the folks the pool?"

What could Pete say? Realistically, that is? That he would prefer to leave the facility closed? Not with Dick Conley around. Ever the good host, he could only hope his guests would preserve their decorum.

It was an indoor pool, glassed-in and heated, built with money from a generous legacy left to Jeannie by an eccentric uncle. Jeannie's passion had always been swimming; indeed, she had once been on the Canadian Olympic team, so the chance to have her own pool in her own backyard had been too good to miss. And to be sure, she used it every day, winter and summer.

"You're not thinking of actually going in, are you?" Pete asked Dick as they filed into the building, Pete turning up the lights.

"Would sure like to but I don't have any gear," Dick replied ruefully. "I would go in without gear but these good ladies would probably report a sighting of the Ogopogo and we can't have that. They might want to kill it."

"They might," Pete concurred shepherding his guests around the pool so that they could "ooh" and "ah" and generally compliment their hosts on such a wonderful facility. Then came the moment when, Conley, down near the entrance spotted his new friend Joe McBain at the far end, near the one-meter board.

"Joe, bet you ten bucks you're too darn chicken to dive in," he yelled. Everyone paused in expectation.

"Ooh, but you're such a despicable little man," Peony turned on Conley. "You leave my Joey alone, you hear me?" She turned to see her husband hop up onto the board as if in preparation to do a dive. Another hush, some there would have described it as a "heavy hush", descended on the guests.

"Joseph G. McBain, you will have to deal with me if you go in and wreck those dress pants and that brand-new shirt, you hear me?" She was shrill because she was uncertain.

Joe looked up, the most serene of grins on his face. Almost as if in slow motion, he began a slow run, hit the end of the board, and achieved a mighty belly flop into the water, his black leather shoes coming adrift and floating off in the process. Silence reigned supreme as he surfaced and looked about for Conley.

"Mister Conley," he said, "you owe me ten dollars." He turned to his wife. "You should come in, dear, this is really nice, I mean really nice."

If others were amused, Peony most certainly was not. "You stupid bleep-bleep bastard," she was yelling at the top of her voice, her finger actively remonstrating at the impudent little boy in the pool. "You're so bleeping stupid, you'd do anything for ten bucks if some crazed fool told you to do it, now wouldn't you?" She was so angry the words barely made it out coherently. "I've got a good mind to put you over my knee this minute and give you a darn good spanking," a most unfortunate comment judging by the titters in the crowd. "Now you listen up, you dumb bleep, why on earth did you have to listen to that crazy fool of a man? Can you at least explain that to me?"

In the attendant hush, nobody seemed to register "that crazy fool of a man" moving up behind Peony. She herself was so full of outrage and so busy glaring down at her man, sister Priscilla standing tall next to her as righteous back-up, that neither of them noticed what was happening behind them. It did not take much, indeed Peony barely felt the push, but there she was, flying through the air, arms flailing wildly until the mighty splash that indicated she had joined her husband in the water. There was a great howling of laughter when Peony's head came up spouting virulence. They say of soldiers and sailors that they curse the best, but then they also say of farmers and ranchers that headstrong cows and uncooperative machines make them the champions of them all. Vintage cow-woman that she was, Peony certainly had the gift when it came to creative cussing. It was a stellar performance. Spontaneous and uninterrupted, she let loose a torrent of invective that left the onlookers spellbound, every word directed at describing the utter stupidity of her spouse and of men in general, with a goodly portion reserved for a reflection upon the illegitimate ancestry of Mr. Dick bleep the bleep Conley. As was to be expected, as soon as her twin sister in the pool had run out of breath, Priscilla felt compelled to take up her cause from the side of the pool, proving to them all that she was every bit as good as her sister when it came to carrying on a scene. The mistake that she made, however, was to turn towards Pete to launch into a full-scale dressing-down for associating with such riff-raff as "that Mr. Conley and the likes of that hillbilly in the cowboy hat." Then having done her duty, she summoned husband Bert to her side.

"You get your sorry ass over here," she commanded, "and help me get my sister out of the pool." Bert could not understand why Peony did not think to make her way over to the ladder, but he meekly obeyed. Together, husband and wife embarked on their rescue mission, ready to pull poor Peony out.

"So help me God, I just could not resist," the hillbilly in the hat recalled later. He came up behind the pair of them, and all of a sudden they too were in the pool.

It was Joe who started to laugh first, a deep belly laugh that immediately infected brother Bert. This deflated the tension only momentarily before the two Three Hills galleons made their way to the mid-pool ladder and climbed out, only to begin ranting and raving about whom would pay for their dresses.

"**Diaphanous**, n. 1. Allowing light to shine through, transparent or translucent. 2. Characterized by delicacy of form, says an old high school dictionary". It should have added, "When wet, such properties may be magnified."

What happened next was a modern-day variation of the fable of "The Emperor has no Clothes". As the two still fuming sisters began making their way along the side of the pool, the light made it more than clear to the people watching that even if the two ladies did not show much delicacy of form, their forms were very much on public display: more so than they had ever been in their lives, heavy-duty under-armour notwithstanding.

"Mommy, Mommy, I can see that lady's knickers," a small voice shrilled in one of those inexplicable momentary silences that can occur during a general hubbub. The two galleons came to an abrupt stop. Both ladies looked down. One shriek later and they were back in the water.

Often adults do not recognize it, but anger is a choice. It can take you down a particular road far enough that you cannot make it back to where you first started. Fortunately for all the guests, Priscilla chose another road, she began to laugh, a loud, hysterical cackling. Peony's eyes bulged in momentary fury at her sister before she too let loose. The place erupted. The folks in the pool were soon egging-on the others to come and join them. It was inevitable that Pete was compelled, or rather propelled, to join his brothers. Then Conley pushed Aubrey in. Aubrey retaliated by signaling to Sabine to push Conley in, but Conley outsmarted her with an unexpected sidestep and she went in under her own steam. Conley's triumph was short-lived, however, because the hillbilly in the cowboy hat appeared out of nowhere, hoisted Conley up like a sack of potatoes, and heaved him in. Quincy turned then to find Jeannie standing next to him. "Get me outa here," he said hoarsely, "I can't swim."

"Too bad old man," came the response, "this here is the shallow end." With that the diminutive Jeannie pushed the cowboy into the pool, hat and all.

And so the party came alive; in danger of coming to an untimely and rancorous end, it turned into a memory, a night never to be forgotten, and a party to be emulated but never matched. Soon everybody had a need to go and get dry. Dick Conley, once again the architect of divine comedy, notched up another two "critics" in the two diaphanous twins but made fast friends of their mild-mannered husbands. Yet the saga was not over, at least not for everyone.

Quincy, soaked through and vulnerable to cold, insisted that it was time to go home, but he was much too full of whiskey to get behind the wheel. On the other hand, young Kevin Hopcraft who had a thirty mile drive home past S-U Acres, had steered clear of alcohol altogether. He offered to run Quincy home, but Quincy had no dry clothes, and since the diaphanous sisters had laid claim to the dryer, there was no way of drying them. Worse yet, nobody in attendance was anywhere near as big as Quincy, so there was no chance of borrowing anything appropriate. That was when Jeannie remembered the frilly pink nightgown in the closet, a tent-like thing that had been left behind by a guest many years ago. It did not bother Quincy though, not a bit. He was not in the least put upon to wear such a female accoutrement. Foolishly, he even allowed Jeannie to take his picture, and became part of recorded legend, before he set off with young Kevin, his cowboy gear in a plastic grocery bag behind the seat. They left long after the sun had gone down.

Murphy's Law, somewhere in the section dealing with "Fortuitous Circumstances", states something to the effect that "if there is any chance that somehow, somewhere, you will be compromised because you are doing something ordinarily outrageous, it will surely happen."

And it did!

There they were, Kevin Hopcraft dressed like any normal young man of these parts, and Quincy Klug, dressed in a frilly pink robe and looking like a haggard old reprobate being transported off to some mental institution. Quincy, being a naturally gregarious fellow, was chatting away to a reserved Kevin, so neither of them saw the partially concealed police Check-stop before it was too late. Not that Quincy was bothered. But poor Kevin! How was he going to explain his passenger to the officers on duty?

Two officers approached. Kevin's driver's side window went down. The lead policeman shone his flashlight into the cab and knew the answer to his question before he even asked it.

"Good evening, gentlemen. Have either of you been out drinking this evening."

"Only a few Cokes, sir," said Kevin hesitantly.

"Yup", said Quincy grandly before burping.

"May I ask both of you to step out of the vehicle," the policeman said in a tone not to be challenged. His partner took up a position to cover for any extraordinary happenings on the passenger side where Quincy got out, a stupid grin on his face. The first constable found he had no further need to shine his flashlight on the apparition that moved into view; the headlights of a logging truck that showed up and stopped behind them did an admirable job. In the meantime, the officer on the driver's side had seen at once that Kevin Hopcraft was as sober as a judge. Morally derelict he might be, judging by his company, but sober nonetheless. He ordered him back into the pickup before signaling the truck that had pulled up to keep on going. But the trucker was slow to act, mesmerized as he was by the unreality before him. Finally he slipped his rig into gear, giving a couple of shots on his air-horn at the creature in the nightgown as he did so. That creature, clearly appreciative of all the attention, bent over and hitched up the gown to expose a derrière that any orangutan in the zoo would have been proud to possess.

"You! Get in your truck, and get the hell outa here before you cause an accident," roared the policeman, who promptly bolted to his cruiser where he remained doubled up in laughter for a good two minutes.

Chapter Five
ONE IN THREE

*N*umbers.

Numbers have significance. They imply all sorts of things: volume, density, speed, things that are definitive and significant. They also imply risk. The hobby farmer who aspires to be the real thing has to think volume and reduce unit cost of production, all according to the doctrines of fiscal wellness. The more cows that Aubrey and Sabine purchased, the more pasture they would need in the summer, and the more hay they would need in the winter to see them through. But volume can be a two-edged sword. For sure, the farmer getting bigger and expanding the empire might mean more bushels harvested, more bales baled, more calves marketed. Yet in a beef operation such as the Hanlons', more numbers meant more manure, initially in such volumes as to assault the senses: an assault made more fully frontal when Aubrey picked up another twenty-eight bred heifers at a disaster dispersal in late summer. It was Dick Conley who summed it up in his own unique way. When people happened to ask Aubrey what he did for a living and Mr. Conley was around, Mr. Conley would tell the questioner, "Mr. Hanlon is a pilot."

"A pilot?" would be the puzzled response.

"Yes, a pilot. He piles it here, he piles it there, he piles it every bloody where."

"Mr. Conley, you're so full of it," Aubrey would have to reply.

The trouble with farming, though, is that over time, you really only get out of it what you have put into it, and even that is a gamble. In the first place, you have to spend money if you want to make money, the precise point where those dread terms "capital outlay" and "input costs" raise their ugly heads. Tractors, balers, combines, barns, fences, waterers, all have capital costs that can swamp the ship, especially when they get older and nickel and dime you to death with their constant need for repairs. All of them in combination are key components of the so-called industrial model of agriculture.

To start with, Aubrey could never see himself as an "industrialist". As time went on, he preferred to characterize himself as "a man of the soil". But soon after their expansion, he very quickly came to appreciate how the land, his "sacred soil", his own special place on God's earth, was fast becoming no longer mystical but a chunk of real estate, just another commodity to be bought and sold like any other piece of merchandise. Indeed to Aubrey, land was fast losing its sanctity, inevitably so with real estate prices at an all-time high in oil-rich Alberta. This in turn tended to eliminate from the equation the notion that soil is a non-renewable resource. The idea that a farmer's ground was in some way sacred, well that was now passé, quaint and old-fashioned: an idea that belonged back in the days of the early homesteader or resonated only in the wacky world of tree-huggers with bandannas wrapped around their heads. So it was that Aubrey and Sabine looked on as numerous small farms passed into the hands of non-farmers, people who had made their pots of money elsewhere and then bought land as a long-term investment or for recreational purposes. To a bona fide farmer, there is something wrong—even immoral—about somebody who buys a quarter section to pasture a pair of aesthetically-pleasing horses, especially when so many people in the world go hungry. Moreover, some of these people posed as farmers: "posed" because profit and loss were never critical considerations in what they did. Others, in keeping with the mercenary values of the marketplace, rented out their land to the highest bidder, not much caring what the farmer did on the land, nor how it was done, just as long as the rent was paid. Others again cast themselves in the mantle of a newborn "landed aristocracy", building the finest of mansions. For the latter group, their sense of entitlement extended not just to the dollars for rent but to having the renter do all of the "grunt" jobs like refurbishing the fences and tilling the soil. Pete loved to recount the story of one of his landlords who had phoned him up a couple of summers previously.

"My wife just woke me up to tell me that three of your cows are out," said a male voice, trying to strike a note of authority not to be trifled with. "They are in the garden, apparently."

"Yes, and there's cow poop just everywhere," echoed a shrill voice in the background. "Honey, you tell that man to get his sorry ass over here right now."

The second voice irritated Pete immensely. "Tell your wife that this sorry ass will be over just as soon as it has deposited its breakfast," he said.

"Please hurry," the male voice was now conciliatory. "The wife, she's terrified of cows, you know."

"And she doesn't like their poop either," screeched the falsetto voice. "They're such filthy beasts."

"Tell your dear wife that cow poop is no different to any other fertilizer," said Pete drily. "We'll be over within the hour," and he hung up.

With renting, Aubrey and Sabine found themselves in a whole new world, two new worlds to be exact: the world of the landlord and the one of the renter, and they were inexperienced in both. Their first move was to rent out the Stanley Himilton mobile home. Immaculate as it was, the surrounding garden too, it was still a smaller and an older two-bedroom home. Nevertheless, the cash rent would sure come in handy to offset the rent paid out for pasture. Aubrey should have known, being an ex-policeman and all, that low-end rents tend to attract low-end renters. It was not that people drove into the yard proclaiming themselves "trailer trash," it was just that people who could only afford four hundred dollars a month were likely limited in their resources and therefore lacking somewhat in a sense of responsibility. Or else they tended to spend their money elsewhere on more grandiose purchases. Yes, Aubrey and Sabine were judicious in assessing the responses to their ad in the newspaper, but then what did they know, however much Aubrey insisted that he was a better judge of character than Sabine? Wisely then, she deferred to him in his first choice of an older man verging on senior citizenship who phoned to co-rent the place with his cousin in BC. The fellow looked respectable enough when he turned up, giving no reason to the Hanlons to disbelieve that he was the retired government botanist that he said he was. "I'll sure enjoy the garden and the greenhouse," he said.

It could have been all right if he had not appeared the very first week "to borrow a spot of gas" because he had not realized his car had run so low, and he did not think he could make it to town. And if he hadn't immediately begun a practice of mowing the lawn clad only in orange jockeys and green sandals. Unfortunately he was fully visible from both field and road where he was offensive to all eyes, although offering a public spectacle could have been his intention all along. However, the sight did nothing for Sabine who was busy harrowing in an adjoining field. She crested the hill, harrows in tow, and there he was: a mobile peeled potato in all its jockeyed glory. Worse still, he had the nerve to wave at her! Her eyes, once they started to believe what they were seeing, forbade her to look any longer, even to go on working there. She found the highest gear and abandoned her chore, never again able to look at a peeled potato without conjuring up that most bizarre of sights.

And then he seemed compelled to "borrow" gas twice more that first month. "I am getting so absent-minded, you understand," he told Aubrey and Sabine. The latter had to seek immediate refuge in the house because the image of a peeled potato was still too fresh in her mind.

Then the second month's rent was a week late because, explained the renter, "My money from Prince Rupert hasn't come in yet."

Almost the final straw was the cousin from BC: a vast lady who decided to emulate her relative by gardening unrestricted by a conventional dress code, save for a nigh invisible thong and a halter top that had to have been manufactured by KingSling Cable Company, patent pending. It was apparent it did not have much capacity, either, if you looked that long! Certainly there was not much traffic on the road and few people to see her, but she was such an arresting spectacle that more than one passer-by took an unscheduled detour through the ditch. In addition, once word had got out, the Hanlon's renters undoubtedly became part of a "scenic route", if the increased traffic was anything to go by.

Happily, it was the renters themselves who solved the problem. In talking to the botanist, the *bottom*ist as Sabine liked to call him, Aubrey had let slip that he and Sabine were going away for a few days. Only they arrived back a day or so early. They drove into their yard and there was Mr. Bottomist and his cousin borrowing a spot of gas from the farm fuel tank. The successive pleadings of poverty, sickness, and injustice could not mask the fact that the car's fuel gage read full. Aubrey's policeman-on-the-beat demeanor took charge.

"I'll give you a choice," he said, "a simple choice. First of all, you know I'm a policeman so I know the ropes. So either I prosecute or you vacate the mobile home in the condition you found it, by this coming Sunday night." They were gone by Friday.

"Dancing with wolves, that's what renting is, dancing with wolves," chuckled Pete when he heard all about the Hanlon renting woes. "You can expect one renter in three to be a good one, maybe one in four."

"Dancing with wolves?" said Sabine as if incredulous. "That was more like dancing with peeled potatoes."

Back to the drawing board they went, back to the local weekly paper. Affordable housing was already becoming a serious issue in Alberta with the oil-patch heating up and oil workers snapping up anything even half decent. Those not fortunate enough to have an oilfield job had to compete for the scraps or set up squatter camps at the river.

The second renter Aubrey settled on was a single woman, a twenty-something with pretty fancy wheels, a recent model Toyota Avalon, and a small dog. Oh no, she had never smoked, filthy habit that it was, and yes of course the dog was house-trained.

That the dog was house-trained turned out to be true; it was trained to pee specifically on the carpet and to crap on the linoleum, if later stains were any indication. The woman herself did not smoke, either—outside. The vilest sins of your renters are the ones you discover when the renter has gone. As if it was par for the course, she too had trouble paying the rent. "My job at Smitty's doesn't pay well," she said. She neglected to say that she only worked a fifteen-hour week, by choice. Once again, the stars in the firmament came into alignment for the Hanlons. After Sabine had gone up to the mobile home to pursue the second rent cheque, some starry-eyed tree-faller arrived on the scene. Not only did he pay the woman's outstanding rent then and there, he also whisked the woman away into his mountains, where she mined as much of his gold as she could before moving on.

Clearly it was Sabine's turn to conduct the interviews. "I can't do any worse than you," she reminded Aubrey, after a new carpet and new linoleum had been installed on the floor of the home.

She hit on a couple—or at least a "couple" was how they presented themselves—even though Sabine was not quite sure, which should have raised a red flag in her mind.

"We could not live anywhere else but in the country, right honey?" said the man, Roy Mudd, a thirty-year old trucker driving in and out of province for a well-known local company. Coming across as both serious and upright, he would surely be dependable even if he seemed a little bashful.

"Oh for sure, we love it in the country," echoed the wife, Elinor, also thirty-something and in need of a diet, an exercise plan, or just a bicycle.

"That's good," said Sabine, taking the first rent cheque and the damage deposit before they moved in. "I hope you really enjoy yourselves here."

"We might like a dog, like later on," Roy added before Sabine could get away. "Would that be a problem?"

"Let me talk to my husband about that," said Sabine ducking the question.

"And we'd like to ride around on our quad when we get one," said the woman continuing to lay the groundwork.

"No problem, just as long as you stay off the hayfields," said Sabine, already anxious to run the cheques to the bank to see if they would bounce. They didn't.

The first hiccup occurred when the couple moved in with two children: not children, exactly, but budding adolescent girls both seemingly hooked into the latest trends in body-piercing, heavy war paint, and undergarments worn more on the outside than on the inside of their clothing.

"Oh, we thought we mentioned to you that we had two kids," Elinor said when Sabine commented to her that the home really was not big enough for the four of them.

"Oh, we'll make it work," said the woman. "Besides, Roy will be away for most of the time because his job takes him all over the place, particularly up north."

First, the TV dish went up. Then a new suite of furniture was installed, rockers, recliners, you name it. The schools went back in, yet everyone in the home continued to sleep in, that is all except Roy who was not there. Elinor did not work, not formally, not informally, not even sporadically; there was clearly too much of interest on TV. Apparently, the daughters did not work either—not on schooldays, holidays, any day.

This bothered Sabine greatly, so she raised the issue with Elinor. "Oh, the girls are in school. It's just that they keep sleeping in and missing the bus." "They were not about to miss their shows," she should have added.

Then one afternoon, Sabine's phone rang.

"Hello, I'm looking for a Mrs., a Mrs., Say-Say-Bean Hanlon," said a man's voice.

"Sabine Hanlon. That would be me," Sabine responded.

"Oh, hello there. My name is Doug Johnstone. I'm the manager of Econo Furniture and Appliances of Red Deer. I'm calling about a lady whom I understand rents a mobile home from you."

"Well, we do have renters, but what does this have to do with me?"

"Well, when the lady applied for credit, we naturally asked for references, not that we always check on them when we should, you understand. She gave us your address and phone number."

"I see. Well, I hate to tell you this, but I barely know the lady, and she certainly never said anything to me about using my name as a reference."

"Oh dear. You see, she is now delinquent on her furniture payments. She is still living on your property, isn't she?"

"You haven't given me the lady's name yet," said Sabine, "so I don't even know if we are talking about the same person."

"Oh, oh, pardon me. The name is Elinor Mudd. That's E-L-I-N-O-R, then M-U-D-D."

"Yes, she's still with us. But I hope you don't think you can hold me liable for her delinquency when I never ever gave her permission to use my name as a reference."

"Oh no, no, we would never do that, Mrs. Hanlon. We are just trying to cut our losses. If you don't mind giving us directions to your farm, we'll just come out and pick our stuff up."

"So you're about to repossess their furniture, is that what you are saying?" Sabine had to be sure.

"That's exactly what I'm saying. They have only made one payment in four months."

Sabine gave him directions; there was little else she could do. She did not want to bring Aubrey into the picture, not yet anyway, because he would give the renters notice on the spot and, truth be known, Sabine was feeling a little sorry for them. By giving the store manager directions, she felt she had betrayed her clients in some way. In a sense, she realized that she had bought into country ways too far; she was particularly reluctant to kick people when they were down, as long as they made every effort to pay the rent at the end of the month. She would have liked to talk it out with Roy but he was home only sporadically, especially at this time when he was assigned to Prince Rupert for most of the coming winter, or so Elinor had told her. Did he know what was going on, she wondered.

Once again, events took a further twist. When Sabine drove up to the mobile home to collect the October rent, there was a half-grown and very boisterous Black Labrador pup tied to the step of the small outside deck. It was just on eleven o'clock in the morning when she knocked on the door. No response. She tried again, louder and more insistent. No response. She tried one final time, more of a thumping than a polite knocking. Somewhere inside, a door opened and closed. A face appeared at the window before the main door opened. There was Elinor Mudd in her nightclothes, a ship in full sail.

"Oh, it's you," said the tired voice. "What do you want?"

"I've come for November's rent," said Sabine flatly.

"Ah yes, of course, the rent. Well, er, see Roy doesn't get paid until this coming Friday, which is when he is coming down." Elinor moved her considerable bulk to try to ensure that Sabine could not see too far into the living room or the kitchen. Too late, Sabine had already spotted the wooden crates serving as seats or tables and the old model fourteen inch TV that sat on the floor in one corner of the living room. So too, her eyes had already registered the ashtray overflowing with cigarette butts, her nostrils had already twitched to the reek of stale tobacco smoke. "Would it be okay if we pay you on Monday?" The voice drew her back to the business in hand.

Again what could Sabine say; there were now so many issues to contend with. "I suppose," she said. "But what's with the dog? I thought we had agreed with you and your husband that you would ask when you were ready to get a dog."

"Oh, oh yes, yes that's true, but you see, we, we were given this one by er, by a friend in town. She had to get rid of it. If… if we had not taken it, they would have put it down." Sabine could feel Elinor's fabrication gathering steam. "We, we just thought we should help out. If you don't want us to keep it, we'll have to put it down ourselves, I guess." The attempt to impose a sense of guilt on Sabine was masterful, though only partly effective because Sabine knew what was happening.

"That won't be necessary," she said. "But you'd better make sure you keep it under tight control because if it gets to chasing livestock anywhere around here, somebody will shoot it dead, no questions asked." There was nothing else she could say. She was soon to discover, again, that no farming couple should keep critical information from each other. "You'd better not tell my husband you have the dog," she was compelled to add as she left. She would tell Aubrey when the time was ripe.

The Hanlon phone rang shrilly at four in the morning, strident, persistent, slicing into Aubrey's sleep like a surgeon's scalpel. Aubrey knew Sabine had heard it, knew also that she would feign deep sleep so that he would have to take the call, so that he would be the one who had to crawl out of bed and shuffle into the kitchen to answer it. Farmers' phones don't ring at four in the morning unless there is a crisis or a drunk dialing a wrong number.

"Aubrey Hanlon," he gruffed into the phone.

"Hey Aub, Bill here, Bill Martin. Say, there's a bunch of heifers on the road out here, say about thirty or so, only fifty yards off Highway 22, and I don't need to be telling you how busy that is even at this time of day. Pink tags. Most of 'em red, with a couple of white faces. Could they be yours by chance?"

Aubrey went from irritability to panic in a heartbeat. "Sounds like they could be mine," he said. "We're on our way." Sabine was not happy, not happy at all at being woken up, then hauled out and coerced into the truck all within the space of one minute.

Yes, the heifers were Hanlon heifers. And yes, the Hanlons were very lucky indeed that they had not made it to the highway. But how on earth had they had broken out of the corral where they had been penned for the night? He, Aubrey had wired the gate shut. "We'll have to run them into the pasture field alongside the road," he said taking charge. "Honey, would you drive ahead and open up the gate and then block off the road with the truck so they don't decide to go exploring. Bill and I will come up behind. I'll walk behind 'em, while Bill, if you can be ready for any that try to double back on us, that'd be dandy, if that's all right with you Bill?" It was. He was already late for work, and besides he did not much want to get out of his nice warm truck if he did not have to. Anyway, what would an extra half hour matter?

Moving spooked heifers in complete darkness is not so much of a chore but a challenge, in some ways akin to chaperoning a bunch of teenage girls who should never be let loose. If they were not trying to sneak back, they would be scattering like buckshot over the gravel road or bunching up behind the illusory sanctity of a willow bush in the ditch. Aubrey fell headlong not once but twice— the second time into the soggy ditch—and scratched himself on the barbed wire several times when an animal sought to reroute itself that way. And his language was not pretty, much to the amusement of Bill Martin who had always thought of Aubrey as a gentleman. Finally, after an hour, they had done it. The heifers were locked away in a small field, and they could go back to bed. Or at least Sabine could; Aubrey had to scrape the mud off and take a shower before he would be allowed anywhere near the bed.

At first light, and quite unable to sleep, he had to get himself up and go check the corral to figure out how the heifers had got out of their corral. The gate must have come undone or something. Not at all! There, plain to see was an entire stretch of plank fence that had been utterly trashed. Jagged pieces of planking hung off posts or lay on the ground. What could possibly have happened? Had a moose or an elk got in there and panicked the girls? What on earth would cause them to burst through the fence like that? It had to be a stray moose, surely, but then they were not usually around at this time of year. Maybe it was the cougar people said hung around two miles to the east, in the bush bordering the Clearwater River. Oh well, these things, the inexplicable, always happen with farming he consoled himself. He went back to the yard, gathered up the appropriate tools, loaded up an assortment of planks into the pickup and headed back to the corral. Thank heaven nobody had bid him up on the planks at the last auction or he wouldn't have had any on hand. Of course, Sabine had harassed him at the time. "Why are you wasting money on planks when you don't even know where you're going to use them?" she had whined. Naturally the answer was also suitably vague, more of a grunt into the shirt really.

By the time he had patched up the corral, Sabine had left for town to do some grocery shopping, so he made himself a belated breakfast before going back up the hill to move the heifers back into the corral. Although skittish after their night's adventure, they cooperated and soon he had them back where they were supposed to be. He then went back to the yard to change the oil in the loader tractor, never his favorite job because whenever he did it, he always managed to get dirty black oil wherever it was least required, in his ear, in his hair, and naturally all over his hands and his coveralls. That was why he had stripped off and put his clothes aside before getting back into his coveralls with nothing on beneath them. So what if there was an expanse of bum cheek visible to the world, it was not as if he had an audience.

He was almost through this most detestable of chores when he heard the commotion up on the hill. There was the unmistakable sound of a dog barking, and then some bawling from what he was sure were the heifers. He leapt onto the quad and tore up to the corral. What he saw initiated the sort of anger spasm to which every livestock farmer is prone, the kind of anger that makes the so-called Latin temperament look benign. There was his problem—a half-grown Black Labrador chasing the heifers around the corral and having a great time doing it. Aubrey yelled, screamed at it to no effect; the animal was enjoying itself just too much. In desperation, he picked up the large rock that happened to be lying at his feet and hurled it at the beast. It was a fluke of a shot, to be sure, but it caught the dog on the rump. Instantly it spun around howling and came face to face with a man howling just like he was. A momentary pause, and then it was off like a startled rabbit, off towards the mobile home.

"Those freakers have got themselves a freaking dog," Aubrey found himself yelling at nobody in particular, not realizing at the time how his commitment to Sabine to give up swearing was altering the very nature of the English language. "They were supposed to ask for freaking, snooking permission, were they not?" he continued. Realizing at this point that his heifers were either not listening or not interested in what he had to say, he spun on his heel, jumped back on the quad and headed for the mobile home. Sure enough, there was the dog, now cowering inside a homemade monstrosity of a kennel. Aubrey rapped on the door; surely somebody had to be up and about at ten-thirty in the morning. No response. He tried one more time, more of a heavy-duty thumping than a polite knocking. Somewhere inside a door opened and closed. A face appeared in the window, and then the door opened. Aubrey's tirade launched itself.

"I thought we had agreed that you would talk to us before you got yourselves a freaking dog," he fired off at the apparition before him, for apparition it was, voluminous, and utterly uncomprehending.

"Ugh?"

"Dog," said Aubrey. "Whose is this freaking dog?"

A second apparition appeared alongside its mom, this one only half-dressed according to accepted convention, but what did Aubrey know anyway. "The dog is ours," said the second creature, the black lipstick making it seem positively ghoulish.

"Well, that freaking dog had better be tied up away from my corrals because if I catch the sucker loose anywhere on this farm, I'll shoot the thing on the spot."

"You'd better not," said the girl. "Or I'll shoot you." Her eyes blazed defiance.

"Hush now," said the mother showing her first sign of life.

"No I won't hush. Our dog has the right to run around like any other animal. That's why we live in the country, yes? Who is he to tell us that we must tie up our dog? Would he like to be tied up all day?" She adjusted a wayward strap not so much for the sake of decorum but for support.

"Look here, young miss," said Aubrey, now suddenly acutely aware that he was standing there talking to two women dressed in non-daylight clothing, "the dog stays strictly under control or the dog dies. Simple, yes?'

"I'm very sorry," said the mother.

"Get a life!" spat the girl.

Aubrey could not help himself. "I'll get me a life if you get some clothes on," he retorted as he turned to leave. Too late, he realized his cheek was on full Technicolour display, like a butt roast at the butcher's shop. He heard the giggling which prompted him to reach down and endeavor to hold the cloth together, which only made the spectacle worse.

"You're the one who needs some clothes," spat the girl, slamming the door.

Aubrey was beyond furious, he was apoplectic. He jumped back on the quad and roared back home just as Sabine drove into the yard. He attacked.

"Did you know that our illustrious renters have got themselves a freaking dog?" he not so much said as yelled before a word of greeting could be uttered.

"Well yes, yes I did," said Sabine sheepishly, very much aware that her husband was on the deep edge. "I was meaning to tell you, but I thought you might decide to shoot it then and there and it's such a nice dog."

"Oh, it's such a nice dog, is it? Let me tell you something. Your 'nice dog' was responsible for our heifers being on the road. Your 'nice dog' was responsible for the trashing of the corral. I went up and found your 'nice dog' chasing the heifers an hour after I put 'em back in the corral. 'Nice dog' or not, I'll shoot the bloody thing dead if I ever find it chasing the bloody heifers again." He knew his voice was rising but he could not help it.

"Language, honey, language. You promised me you'd clean up your language."

As Aubrey walked away into the house, all he could say was, "Let's go get ourselves a coffee. I just had a talk with the lady of Mobile Mansion and that freak of a teenage daughter of hers. Now there's a fine piece of artwork, may I tell you."

Sabine, following along behind, had to ask the obvious question. "You didn't go up there dressed like that, did you? You surely realize you have a whole ham hanging out of the back of your coveralls? What did you do with your clothes? You had them on this morning."

Aubrey stopped then, compelled to give a full accounting of the morning's happenings."

"You know," said Sabine in response, "I think we could save ourselves a whole lot of grief if we give them notice. Like, today."

"Maybe. Let's give 'em one more shot to see if the rent comes in on time." Aubrey surprised himself at his own generosity. Or was it that he just did not feel like playing policeman anymore?

The rent did not come in.

The dog was also loose, but with a bruise on its backend it was not inclined to chase cows at the present time.

And once again, the renters' complete lack of understanding of the ways of the land was expressed in the starkest of terms, and once again Aubrey had to deal with them.

Sabine suggested that Aubrey should go up and try for the rent, seeing as she had come away empty-handed twice in a row. Reluctantly he agreed. As he came out of the house, he heard the din; a barely mufflered quad was screaming down the road. He was just in time to see it zip past their driveway, the two renter kids on board doubtless heading down to the river. So much for school, thought Aubrey sourly. Still, the mother might be at the home, and at least her two daughters would not be around to add colourful commentary to whatever was said.

For once, the woman came to the door immediately, clearly dressed to go out. Clutched in her hand was a sheaf of dollar bills, the rent in cold hard cash. "Roy came down this weekend," she gushed in an attempt to cut off any hostility. "We are so sorry it is late. And as you can see, the dog is tied up."

What could Aubrey do but take the rent? "Thank you," he said. "Try to get it to us on time in future. I'm glad to see the dog tied up, for his sake as well as yours. May I suggest you tell your girls to lay off full throttle if they don't want to get hurt? Without helmets they are tempting fate, you know." Aubrey had dealt with too many accidents in his former life.

"I can't tell those girls anything," Elinor snapped. "Their dad went and bought them the quad, and now that's all they can think about. That and beer." She turned her back on him, a clear indication she had no desire to hear anything he might say in reply. He heard the quad as he was leaving, close by it seemed. Oh well, he had done it so many times before, picking up the bits of those who thought they were invincible, the ones who ran out of road or refused to wear seatbelts. He turned the corner to head home and there they were, blasting around the field, his field, *the hayfield!* Damn it all, did these people not know anything, not care about anything? He sped into the field in his pickup and signaled them over.

"Who the hell said you could ride that thing in my field?" he roared at them. They were clearly taken aback at his anger, but the older one was her usual defiant self within seconds.

"It's only grass," she said sourly.

"Only grass," roared Aubrey. "Only grass! It's my bloody hayfield. It's my freaking livelihood. It's what I have to feed to my cows every year, and here you are wrecking it all. Now you girls stay out of my fields, you hear? Stay off my entire farm, for that matter. Go down to the river and stay there. Go somewhere far away."

"Whatev-er," said the older one, before starting up and blasting off.

Any satisfaction Aubrey may have felt was short-lived. Barring the kids from his fields merely forced them to roam the roadside ditches, and not just the girls, mama too! People in the neighborhood began to talk about near misses with a quad bearing two screaming girls who would suddenly come bombing out of a ditch on a flight path that acknowledged no possibility of traffic. For sure, when big Elinor was aboard, the quad had to work that much harder, which in turn meant that she was not quite as crazy as her progeny.

The year wore on and the weather turned cold. The rent came in only once in full and on time. Every other occasion saw excuses and installments, but still Aubrey and, more so, Sabine could not bring themselves to turn out the family, with the husband and father Roy being such a decent type and trying so hard to make it. Sabine advised Elinor to fill up the propane tank so it was ready to heat the home when the full brunt of winter decided to announce itself. Elinor insisted she could not afford it "quite yet", what with apparently another suite of furniture to pay for and a plasma TV the size of a house.

As invariably happens, the first really cold snap arrived unexpectedly and then chose to hang around for a while. When Sabine took herself up to the mobile home to collect the October rent it was two in the afternoon, so surely everyone would be respectably dressed. Elinor was—in full Arctic getup, inside the fridge of a house. Since it was so cold outside, she could not just leave Sabine standing there; she had to invite her in, especially as it would take time to tell her latest long-winded story, "The Saga of the October Rent Money". Sabine glanced into the kitchen. The oven door was open, the grille full on with nothing cooking.

As Elinor handed over one-third of the rent, the rest to come next week, when they promised Roy he would get his overtime pay, Sabine had to ask, "And how are you heating this place?"

The woman could hardly deny it. "Well, when it gets real cold like today, we have to use the oven a little bit," she said. "But, like, we do have electric heaters in every room."

"But what about the furnace? Isn't it working? Did you not order propane?"

"Oh, it's all fine and dandy for you rich people to talk," Elinor pouted. "People like us have to spend most of our money paying rent just to have a roof over our heads and trying to stay alive."

"But you do understand that if you heat with only electricity and use the oven as well, your utility bill is going to go through the roof?"

"Well, what are we supposed to do?" Elinor pouted some more.

"Do?" asked Sabine. "Why, use propane of course. Do you have any idea how much propane costs?"

"No."

"Have you even called a propane company?"

"No."

"So how do you know you can't afford propane?'

"We can't afford anything." The woman was in a downright sulk now.

She could not help it. Sabine's eyes took in the new furniture and the new 27-inch TV set, but it was probably on credit like last time. She felt little compassion or even sympathy when she handed the rent money back to Elinor. She just could not imagine how they could survive if the weather continued to be so brutal. "Here, take the money back and order propane now; right now, while I'm standing here. Then I know you won't be spending the money on the cigarettes that you don't smoke."

"Look, you would smoke too if you got as depressed as I do," Elinor snapped. But Sabine held her ground while Elinor looked up the number for a propane supplier and ordered their product.

"Now you'll find life a lot more livable," Sabine added. "And I'll look for the rent money next week when Roy gets his overtime pay."

"Okay." No smile, no gratitude, just a "get-out-of-my-life" face and a scowl to match.

It was all too late. Towards the end of the week, the utilities company called, a delightful lady on the line. "Mrs. Hanlon? I guess we need to talk. You know when you waived the usual deposit that we ask from renters…"

"Oh yes, they couldn't afford the deposit at the time, what with the damage deposit and a month's rent all at the same time…"

"Well, unfortunately that makes you as the landlord responsible for their electricity bill which is now closing in on a thousand dollars…"

"A thousand dollars," Sabine heard herself almost squeak.

"Yes, a thousand dollars. I keep calling the lady and she keeps telling me she'll be in next Monday or Wednesday or Friday but she never shows."

"What on earth are they spending all their money on then?" Sabine burst out. "They have never been on time with the rent either."

"Well, when I told her that we are about to switch the power off, she then said there is something wrong with the electrical system at the house that you people refuse to fix so she will contest any bill."

"Well, that's the first we've heard of it," said Sabine. "I suppose there *could* be something wrong. What do you think?" she finished up innocently, wondering where she and Aubrey might free up an extra thousand dollars to meet this bad debt.

"Well, I had our man check out the power pole and the transformer and everything looks fine there. But there is no doubt their power bill is very high and they seem to consume an awful lot of power. I hate to say this, but you might have to get in an electrician to go through the house. It can be quite expensive."

"Wait a minute! You know how they were heating the house during that last cold snap we had? They were using electric heaters in all the rooms and the oven full-on with the door open in the kitchen."

"They *what?*"

"That's right. She was using the oven with the door wide open. I saw it with my own eyes when I went up to ask for the rent. Plus she told me she had an electric heater going in every room. You'll think I'm crazy, but here's what I did. I gave her the rent money back and made her order propane with me standing there."

"But I hate to say this, there's still a bill of close to a thousand dollars that has to be paid. You see, company policy tells me I have to switch off the power if the bill goes over a thousand, which it will by the end of the week. So, maybe you need to talk to your renters one more time."

"I can sure try," Sabine replied heavily. "And thank you for your patience."

It is always bad enough when renters don't pay the rent, but when they run up additional expenses on your account, then as a landlord your options become stark. Sabine freely conceded that her judgment of people was no better than her husband's before handing over the whole problem to him for resolution. He had had enough, and steeled himself for a full frontal assault, heading up to the home that same evening. Great, the lights were on, all the lights inside and out, all burning his electricity. He rapped on the front door, wondering if anyone could possibly hear him above the blare of the TV going at full blast. To his surprise, the door opened almost at once, and to his further surprise it was Roy who stepped out and shut the door.

"Hello Roy," said Aubrey. "Boy, am I ever glad to see you."

"Oh," said Roy affably. "Why's that?"

"What are you folks doing about your electricity bill?"

"Electricity bill? What electricity bill?"

"The one that is now up to a thousand dollars. The one my wife and I were stupid enough to guarantee to give you people a break on when you first moved in."

"How can it be a thousand?" Roy was clearly both perturbed and resigned. "I've been sending the money down to cover both rent and all utilities."

"Then that's a question you need to ask your wife. But we've had enough. We think it would be better if you folks moved back to town, so I'm giving you notice as of now. Besides, you've got to get those girls of yours back into school."

"What do you mean, back into school? They go every day...don't they?"

"Do they? You need to find that out too."

Roy sighed, knowing that once again he had been undercut by his wife and his kids. "Okay, okay, we'll be out. I can stay with my sister until we find another place. I hear where you're coming from. It's not the first time this has happened. You don't owe us a living." He turned to go.

"One more thing, Roy," said Aubrey, determined to make the separation final, however reasonable Roy sounded. "Here's the deal. If you can be out in a week, we'll forget the rent owing as long as you pay the power bill and clean the place up. If you leave the bill unpaid and the place in a mess, I'll come after you and I'll make darn sure every landlord in the area hears about your history. You don't need that with the housing shortage that's on right now. I hate to be such a shit, but you're the one who said it, we don't owe you a living. We have to work too darn hard ourselves to survive."

What had Pete said? One in three? Well, here they were coming up to number four. But at least the power bill got paid and the premises were left reasonably clean.

Chapter Six
THE SYSTEMS APPROACH

Somewhere in Canada, in some faculty of agronomics or in some college of agriculture, there is probably a little man at his lectern counseling his students that "bigger is better", "bigger is the modern way to go", and "bigger numbers force efficiency because they lower unit cost". Yet, it was no little man at his lectern that taught the Hanlons the reality of that last bit about numbers; it was day-to-day experience. No matter if you had only ten cows or five hundred, to be on top of herd health and, therefore, maximum productivity, you had to follow some sort of standardized program: cows had to be routinely vaccinated, calves needled, all at the appropriate time of the year. The little man at his lectern would doubtless talk of "systems", about how all businesses, agricultural or otherwise, would be vastly more efficient if they practiced a systems approach. When talking about reducing the sacred unit cost of production, time had to be factored in. Aubrey and Sabine, like so many beginning farmers, tended to think of their time as "free", that as long as the job got done, then who cared how long it took to actually do it? The weather was the first to disabuse them of this naiveté. Then the issue of numbers drove the message home. Now currently in possession of sixty bred cows and then the thirty bred heifers Aubrey had picked up, they had to bring the notion of management to the table. They decided to sign up for the "Herd Health Program" at the local veterinary clinic, where the vet sat down with them to review their herd health practices and recommend what should be done to every animal and when; "preventative maintenance" he called it. The Hanlons were compelled to get with it and learn, indeed practice, the difference between subcutaneous, intramuscular, and intravenous. They had to learn that "hardware disease" amounted to a foreign object swallowed by an animal—a nail or a piece of wire, not some sexually transmitted disease suffered by a computer. They had to become familiar with dosages, with calculating ml. of vaccine per kg. of body-weight, with estimating an animal's weight with some degree of accuracy because, like most small farmers, Aubrey and Sabine had no scale on the farm. Was a cow eight hundred, fifteen hundred, or two thousand pounds? Aubrey had some inkling, Sabine none, so they set to, making a point of sitting at the auction and guessing the heaviness of animals against the weight shown by the scale.

"I take it you have a squeeze at home?" asked Gordon Clark, the old Scottish vet, soon to be retiring said the rumor mill.

"Aye, and I brought her along with me," Aubrey responded, mimicking the man's accent in an attempt to lighten up the process, learning on the spot that trying to humour a dour Scot is akin to separating him from his malt.

"No, I'm talking about a restraining squeeze for cows," he snapped, making it abundantly clear that herd health was not something to be joked about.

"Well, actually no, we don't have a squeeze at home," said a chastened Aubrey.

"Then you'll be getting one I'm sure," said Mr. Clark. "That old head-gate you've got out there is just not good enough any more. And a crowding alley would also be a good idea, as well as a small sorting pen. You people are going to have to be a lot more systematic about things. It'll be quicker and a whole lot safer. You're both getting too old to go chasing after cows. If you want to get bigger, you've got to take it seriously." It was in fact a speech the Hanlons needed to hear.

Squeeze, sorting pen, crowding alley. This called for a serious sit-down with Pete and Jeannie: a cup-of-tea sit-down, not a box-of-beer jaw session. There at the kitchen table, they designed a corral system on paper, one that partly incorporated the tumbledown setup already in place.

"Ideally," said Pete, "you would do better to get yourself some fellow with a Cat to knock the whole darn mess into a big hole, then start again."

"First off, we're not idealists, and second, we're not rich," said Sabine hurriedly, afraid that her headstrong husband might decide to pick up that particular expensive ball and run with it.

"Which means you do what every other small farmer in Western Canada does… you start off with a mess and then you keep adding to it. But you folks had better figure on doing a bit of hurrying because it isn't going to be long before the ground is frozen. If that happens, you won't be pounding in any posts until next spring."

Posts were no problem; Co-Op delivered them the next day, a hundred of them in two bundles, seven feet long at $3.75 apiece.

Rails were a problem. The price of lumber was soaring out of sight thanks to the hurricane down in the States, Cindy or Sidney or some such thing. Around twelve dollars a plank for two hundred planks was not a price Aubrey wanted to pay, he found himself saying to his friend Gene at the Co-Op fuel depot.

"So use bull rails then," said Gene. "Tell you what, I get mine from a friend who runs a small sawmill down in Caroline. 'Big E' they call him, or 'Eric the Red'. I'll give you his number. His real name is Hank Snow, not the fellah who used to hurt country music for a living, another Hank Snow. Hank Eric Snow. Tell him your friend Gene sent you, otherwise he'll want six bucks each. I got mine for three and a quarter."

Gene was right; Hank Snow, Big E, Eric the Red, asked for six.

"My friend, and I guess your friend too, said you'd probably give them to us for three and a quarter," responded Aubrey hoping for a better quote.

"Give 'em is right," said the voice on the phone. "So who is this friend of yours and mine?"

"Gene, at the Co-Op gas bar in town."

"Oh Gene, that Gene, well darn Gene anyway. You know what? If you're a friend of Gene's, I should really be charging you ten dollars apiece, but I'll let you have 'em for four bucks because the price of diesel has gone up since I sold to Gene. How many are you looking for?"

"Two hundred."

"Wowee, a big spender is coming into town, eh? Okay, for that number you can have em for three and a half, but only if you come and pick 'em up within a week and you load 'em yourself. If we have to stop and load 'em, they'll be up to six again, you hear me?"

"It's a deal," said Aubrey.

"You'd better take my old three-ton truck," said Pete who knew Big E. Pete knew everybody. "She's old but she's yours once you get her going. But watch the brakes; they're a bit soft. In fact, when you take her, drive a couple of times around the field so's you get a sense of how she handles. And if Sabine is fool enough to go with you, tell her to watch where she puts her feet. The floor's a bit ragged. You know I'd come along with you, but I've got to be in Red Deer that day."

Pete's truck, *the truck,* was quite unlike any other vehicle Aubrey had ever seen. The front grille said it was a GMC. The insignia on the hood said it was a Chev C65, whatever that was. The hood itself was maroon. The driver's door was not quite fluorescent orange while the other door was olive green. The rest of the bodywork was a faded banana yellow. Other than the extraterrestrial colour scheme, the rest of the vehicle seemed ordinary enough. It had a steel box on the back; and the aged wooden floor boasted a hole here and there, the result of a losing campaign against rot and an owner who clearly had a penchant for transporting things that scraped, pierced or penetrated. Aubrey should have postponed to a day where Pete could have accompanied him. Being as stubbornly independent as he was, he did not, and so began an escapade he would long remember, and one that Sabine would remember longer yet, she being the nervous passenger type and a lady blessed with an acute sense of smell.

Aubrey climbed into the cab without ceremony and set out to discover the more important controls: the choke, broken; the hand-brake, could be broken; the activators for the hoist; the accelerator, now just a piece of shaped rod that had long since parted company with its foot pedal. He heard rather than saw his wife open the passenger door.

"Oh," she said. "Oh dear!"

He looked across. There was more "stuff" on the floor and on the seat than they had in their entire garden shed; clearly Pete's claim to being a tidiness freak was very suspect. Bits of rope, a long tow chain, a pair of hammers, a hacksaw, a couple of coiled hoses, two containers of engine oil, an empty two-gallon plastic gas can made the cab look like a hippy junk pile, and that was what he could actually see. He was debating whether to get out and go round to the passenger side and help his wife in because he so wanted her to accompany him, but his wife was nothing if not courageous. She took a deep breath and clambered aboard, making a sort of a nest for herself amongst all the junk, just enough to connect rump to seat.

"What's that smell?" she released her breath.

The thing about any bad smell is its ability to creep up on you, to envelop you with its stealth, until suddenly you discover yourself smothering in pungency.

"I dunno," said Aubrey. "Musty grain, maybe?"

"Pooh! Oh my, it's, it's disgusting…, it's…" a mouse had appeared on the dashboard, seemingly wiping its whiskers after a good feed below decks. Sabine had become inured to mice on the farm, but only at a distance if her piercing scream was anything to go by. The mouse paused long enough to look her over, and then like a denied panhandler on a city street, it scampered away; it had no desire to hang about where it was not wanted. What Sabine could not know was that this was the prelude to an experience to which the wafting stench of stale mouse droppings merely added savour.

Surprisingly, the truck roared to life as soon as Aubrey turned the key, and it even ran quietly. He slipped it into reverse and astounded himself with the ease with which he backed out onto the gravel road past Pete's place; there were plenty of obstacles both to the left and to the right that could have got in the way. Buoyed by his competence, he slipped into first gear and pulled away.

"Watch the brakes, they're soft," Pete had said.

Okay, so Aubrey decided he should test the brakes. He pushed the pedal almost to the floor. Nothing. No slowing down, nothing. *Rien, absolument bloody rien,* as his buddy Jean-Claude would say. Panicked a little, Aubrey's foot pumped the brake frantically, and this time the brakes took hold, listlessly perhaps, unwillingly maybe, but yet something of a hold nonetheless. He pumped with more gusto. This time, the wheels locked solid and they skidded to a halt in a cloud of dust, Sabine's head straying dangerously close to mouse territory.

"What the hell are you doing?" she screamed at him at the same time as trying to unearth a grimy seatbelt.

"Brakes," said Aubrey. "Pete said to test the brakes."

Finally, Sabine broke her belt free from the debris around it and she put it on with a shudder. "Ugh," she said, her jaw set as if to endure whatever torture came her way.

They made the three or so miles up to Highway 22, The Cowboy Trail, waiting for all traffic to pass before venturing out onto the pavement. The severe jolt as Aubrey changed clumsily to third gear—coupled with the unscheduled reappearance of the mouse—caused Sabine's voice to find wind and her one foot to kick out. As the mouse ducked back into safety beneath the dash, there was a loud clattering noise as the tow-chain, followed with great gusto by the two hammers, the hacksaw and the two-litre containers of oil began gently sliding through a hole in the floor, and onto the road below. Happily, the gas container was a little too big to follow suit, and that prevented all the rest of the junk from making a quick exit. Aubrey braked. Nothing. Nada. *Rien, absolument bloody rien.* By this time, Sabine was yelling at the top of her lungs, "Stop. Stop now." Aubrey's wild pumping of the brake finally had the desired effect, and they ground slowly to a halt.

It was at that precise moment that the mouse chose to check out the situation one final time. Sabine's reaction was instinctive; she grabbed that unfortunate little creature off the dash and hurled it out of the window. Aubrey was already out of the truck retrieving what he could of the stuff on the road before it caused an accident, something he was terrified of, he being an ex-RCMP officer and all. Sabine had gone out on one of those days where she would have done better to have gone home, gone to bed, and waited until tomorrow. She bent over and picked up the hacksaw and the hammers, the two containers of oil being next on the list. She had seen the approaching car, but the occupant, ear and most of his mind glued to mobile phone, had not registered her presence even if he had seen her. Sabine could only leap onto the shoulder of the road just as the car beetled on by, squashing both containers in succession and squirting the contents all over the unfortunate Mrs. Hanlon. The language that ensued, involving a sharp critique of cell phones and all who used them in vehicles, included most of the top ten of Sabine's banned word list.

"Please let's go back home, Aub," she pleaded, trying her very best not to sob as Aubrey came up dragging the heavy chain behind him.

"We got this far, damn it," he growled panting mightily. "We're going on, even if you are well-oiled."

"Up yours!" Sabine was not gracious as she used her very last tissue to wipe the gobs of oil off her face.

They piled all of the junk back on the floor only after Aubrey had scouted out a piece of plywood out of the ditch. It covered enough of the hole in the floor to allow the re-piling, less the two containers of oil of course. He was muttering away to himself about how here he was, an ex-cop, and a good conscientious cop at that, out on a public highway driving one of the most derelict and hazardous vehicles he had ever seen. Sabine, indulging herself fully in her own misery, knew enough not to pester him when he was in ex-cop mode. Luckily, the next twelve miles down to the sawyer's were uneventful.

The sawmill was quite unlike any place the Hanlons had ever been. It went far beyond the simple notion of untidiness; this was environmental anarchy. Abandoned vehicles and discarded machinery competed for space with the dozen or so wooden shacks, most of them in the terminal stages of leaning and collapsing, that housed piles of lumber of every possible dimension. Quincy Klug's place was positively immaculate compared to this. A huge pile of sawdust announced the location of the mill, so Aubrey chose one of the muddied tracks leading in that general direction. As they got closer, they could hear the infernal noise of a busy woodlot. Slowing down to a crawl, Aubrey nosed around a bend to pull up behind a parked pickup truck. He applied the brakes. Nothing. Nada. *Rien, absolument bloody rien.* His truck slithered to a sudden, unengineered stop when nose to tail contact was made with the pickup.

"Oh no," groaned Sabine, sinking herself from view below the level of the dash. "This is just tooo much!"

Aubrey backed up as the noise subsided and a giant of a man with unkempt red hair, no shirt and soiled jeans, sauntered around the pile of sawdust, followed by a gang of four other men, not one of whom would have been out of place as a "baddy" in any western movie. They converged on Aubrey and the three-ton as Aubrey climbed out.

"Geez, I'm so sorry," he began in confession to the giant. "I'll be happy to, to pay for any damage."

The giant, totally inscrutable, came to a stop four feet away. He looked first at the pickup and then at Aubrey's truck. The posse of four fanned out behind him, hardy and unsmiling.

Finally the man spoke. "That ff…ing Pete never did fix his damn brakes, now did he?" It came out more as a flat statement than a posed question.

"Oh, so you know this is my friend Pete's truck?" asked Aubrey, easing gently into what could turn out to be a costly conversation.

"Do I know Pete's truck? You bet I know Pete's truck. Pete and me go back a long ways, a long ways," he mused. "You know what? You stopped that damned thing the exact same way as he did the last time he was down here. You just added a little more to the dent he put in. You're the fellow for the bull rails, am I right?"

Aubrey nodded. Hearing no major commotion, Sabine's head now popped up above dashboard level. When she saw the men, she knew her husband was doomed, she too in all probability. What on earth would she do if they decided to take him apart for smacking their pickup? Fighting the huge temptation to slide back below sight, she watched, trying to pick up the snatches of conversation.

"Who did you bring to help load the rails?" The giant moved beyond the accident.

"Er, my wife. I brought my wife."

"You brought your wife. So you're gonna load a hundred bull rails with your wife?" The man was still utterly inscrutable.

"Two hundred. Two hundred is what I need," said Aubrey.

"You'll only get a hundred on a load," said the man. "And you're gonna load a hundred with your wife?" There was maybe, just maybe, a glimmer of amusement playing on the man's lips.

"Why? Is there something wrong with that?" Aubrey was completely out of his depth and he knew it.

"Not unless your wife looks like Godzilla, there isn't." Then a thought struck him. "You do know what a bull rail looks like, don't you?"

"Well, er, no, not exactly. Pete told me…"

Deciding to risk it, Sabine very self-consciously opened the passenger door and climbed out of the truck. Even though she was dressed in her work clothes, even though her work clothes were blotched with great blobs of oil, she could still attract undivided attention—as the five pairs of male eyes drawn to her made obvious.

"Mornin' Ma'am," said Eric the Red. "The man here says you're his helper. That right?"

"Well yes," said Sabine. "He's my husband." Once again, she felt her terror creeping up now that she was in such close proximity to the most thuggish-looking lot she had ever met.

"I see." Smiles were evidently on some sort of a quota for this Neanderthal. "Come with me and I'll show you the pile."

A "bull rail" is nothing more nor less than a sixteen-foot chunk of tree trunk sawn flat on two sides, Aubrey and Sabine discovered when Eric pointed out the rails to them. How the hell was his dear wife going to lift even one end, Aubrey found himself wondering.

"How the hell am I going to lift one of those things?" said Sabine out loud. "They're bloody enormous." There was subdued laughter among the posse.

"Do you bake?" Eric turned to her.

"Do I bake?" Sabine was incredulous. "Like, you mean, bake cake?"

"That's what I mean. Bake, like bake cake."

"As a matter of fact, I do," she said, thinking that this whole adventure was becoming a bit too surreal.

"Good. Me and the boys here will load up your hundred rails. When you come back for your second load, you're gonna bring us a great big mother of a cake. Yes?"

"Chocolate cake," stipulated the meanest-looking of the crew, the scar across his face giving him a permanent leer.

"With two feet of icing," added his mate, nearly as scary of visage.

"But, but what about the tailgate on your pickup?" Aubrey had to ask in a bid to bring order where there was only chaos.

"What about it?" said Eric.

"Well, I need to compensate someone for the damage."

"Let's put it this way. Your good friend Pete started out on that dent before you ever got to it. All you did was to gussy it up a little. Don't worry about it. Me and Pete, we go back a long ways. Why would a perfectly sane-looking fellah like you be driving Pete's three-ton heap of scrap metal anyways?"

The question prompted a telling of the full story, upon which all of the Hanlons' misgivings were blown away in gusts of unrestrained laughter.

Within half an hour, they were loaded and pulling out of the yard, the load cinched down tight on the truck with a chain and come-along loaned to them by Big E because Aubrey had never thought of such needs. What astounded both Hanlons, indeed had unsettled them completely, was the degree to which they had misjudged, prejudged their benefactors. These people, as scary and as thuggish as they looked, could not have been more helpful to them, and yet they had expected so little in return. Sheesh, their looks alone would have caused the most intrepid of souls to detour to Saskatoon to get around them.

"That darn cake had better be the biggest flipping cake you've ever made," said Aubrey. "And the best."

It was. In fact Aubrey had the easy job, unloading the truck. All he had to do was to find the right spot, loosen the chain, and let the truck and the hoist do the rest. Sabine bolted into the house and baked a monster cake: chocolate, with icing an inch thick, fresh cherries, and a great big "Thank You Boys", in white lettering. Then, on their way down to Caroline for the second load, they stopped at a liquor store and picked up two dozen cans of Molson Canadian; "maternal tit of the Canadian Redneck", Pete always called it. On their arrival back at the sawmill, Big Eric shut down the mill as before, but this time there was no holding back the posse behind him. Sabine presented them her cake, which apparently exceeded all expectations even if the whole thing was gone in under three minutes. Not so the beer.

"Might surprise you some," said Big E, "but nobody on site touches a beer while we've got work to do. No way. It'd be just too easy to slice off a couple of your fingers, or worse yet someone else's. But thanks anyway. We'll shut down ten minutes early at the end of the day and toast the baker."

So it was that the Hanlons took yet another new message to heart. The sweetest oranges do not necessarily come in the most unblemished skins.

Now for the corral, Pete came over with his post-pounder, a thoroughly evil machine as far as Aubrey was concerned because it was so overtly dangerous. He had to force himself to think where his hands were every single time he was set to pull the lever that dropped the massive hammer onto a post with a mighty whump. How many people had left a hand on top of a post to steady it and unthinkingly dropped the hammer, he wondered aloud. "Quite a few," said Pete, whose "agricultural idol" status in Aubrey's eyes had taken quite a knock after the adventures with Pete's truck.

"Oh, and by the way, that Eric says you and he go back a long way," said Sabine. "How's that?"

"I went to school with him. One of the smartest men you'll ever come across, let me tell you. Could'a been a lawyer or an accountant or anything he chose. Probably one of the strongest men I've ever met, too. But he's a genuine bush pig. He lives for the bush. He was born in it and he'll likely die in it. That independent woodlot of his allows him to do what he pleases. He does it all himself, he and the boys, all relatives of one sort or another. They go out into the bush, fell their trees, transport them home and saw them up, and make a damn good buck doing it."

Within a week, the setup was ready, squeeze and all. The squeeze came from the unlikeliest source, old Art Zimmer, the Hanlon's neighbor to the east. If Quincy Klug was a redneck, then Art Zimmer had to be The Scarlet Pimpernel of all Rednecks. As usual, Pete, the fount of all local knowledge, knew Art had a squeeze that he had not used in years. "It's a bit of a heavy hitter," he said, "but see if you can get Art to part with it. It'll probably cost you as much in time as in dollars, but I'm sure it'll be worth it." It was, but that was another story. As they surveyed their finished handiwork, Pete pronounced that they were just in time. "See, it's about now that you should be vaccinating your cows with 8-way and scours vaccine."

"Oh, oh dear," said Sabine. "I forgot all about checking the Herd Health Calendar. I'm sure that has to be in there." Yes it was, in black and white and a wake-up call not to store the binder in the "inconsequential pile" downstairs.

"I'll even come over and help you, Jeannie too, just to make sure you're off on the right track," said Pete. "Just as long as you return the favor and help us do ours in a couple of days."

"Done," Aubrey and Sabine were in unison.

When Sabine took on a job, she took charge. She was by nature far more organized than Aubrey, and he was smart enough to give her precedence when she embraced a particular role like Captain of Herd Health. He was quite content to be First Mate, forgetting too often that First Mate was the captain's understudy, that he should know what vaccine did what and when and in what dosage. In this he was a little lax, which prompted the vet, Gordon Clark, to regard him more as Sabine's Cabin Boy than First Mate. It became customary then for Sabine to conduct all dealings with the vet clinic, and it was only natural that she became fast friends with a number of the ladies working there. So too, it was Sabine who drove into the clinic on the Tuesday to pick up the requisite vaccines, syringes, and needles. Thursday was to be the day of reckoning, the day when they would find out just how well their corral system would work. Pete was committed to spending the morning in Red Deer on business, but the plan was for him to drive directly out to the Hanlon place for a quick lunch and a one o'clock start. Jeannie would come over on her own, in her own time.

At eleven o'clock on the day, Sabine and Jeannie, who had just arrived, decided to set everything up, preloading syringes and that sort of thing, while Aubrey set off on the quad to bring the cows into the field next-door to the corral. It was Sabine who suddenly realized they were way short on 8-way vaccine.

"Darn it all, I seem to be missing a box of vaccine. They've charged me for it but that new girl must have forgotten to put it in."

"Call them up and ask," advised Jeannie, ever the pragmatist.

Sabine did just that and was lucky enough to connect with her good friend Gail. After the preliminary hello, how are you routine, Sabine continued. "Gail, I've just checked the package of drugs I bought for the cows on Tuesday, and I find I'm a box short of the 8-way vaccine, even though I was charged for it."

"Aha, so it's yours! You see, we found the box on the counter and figured somebody had somehow left it behind. Now we know."

"Well, it was that new girl who served me. She was reading the directions off the box when we were working out what we needed. She must have forgotten to put it back in the bag."

"When do you need it?" Gail cut to the chase.

"Well, we are supposed to be vaccinating in an hour. Aubrey has just gone to bring in the cows."

"Okay, no problem, I'll jump in my car and bring it out to you." Gail was always so obliging.

"Drive it out? Oh that's so awfully sweet…"

"Don't get her to drive all the way out here," Jeannie interrupted. "Tell her to meet up with Pete at the weigh scale on Highway 11. He's in our red GMC pickup. She can give him the drugs on his way home."

"Here's the deal, Gail. Jeannie has just had a better idea. Pete is on his way home from Red Deer. We'll get him on his cell phone and tell him to stop off at the scale. If we don't get him, one of us will come up instead."

"Sounds good enough for me," said Gail. "I've got a couple of customers. See you later."

Aubrey burst into the house at that precise moment. "Hey ladies, come and look at this," he shouted before dashing outside again. The two women followed wondering what could have caused Aubrey so much excitement. There, high up in a tree at the far side of the corral was a magnificent Bald Eagle. The Hanlons had certainly never seen one this close, never one gracious enough to sit there and allow Sabine to rush back inside for her camera and take a series of pictures. Finally, as if to say "that's your lot, folks," he spread his wings and flew nonchalantly away, secure in all his majesty.

"You'd better be phoning Pete, or he'll be past the scale before we get to him," Jeannie prompted Sabine while she was still waxing enthusiastic about bald eagles outside. "Here, use my cell phone. The number is 403-844-4014."

"Why do you need to call Pete?" asked Aubrey, causing Jeannie to explain their predicament and distracting her from Sabine. The latter pressed the numbers and a voice answered right away.

"Hello, is that you?" said Sabine.

"Sure it's me. Who else would it be?" the voice laughed just like Pete.

"Oh good. Look, we're short on the drugs. Gail is going to drive out to the weigh scale in her car. Can you meet her there? She'll be in a little blue Ford Focus."

"To pick up the drugs, you say?" said the voice, now very serious.

"Yep, the drugs. We didn't get them all when I picked up on Tuesday. Blue Ford Focus, okay?"

"Got it," said the voice, now not sounding too much like Pete at all. "Blue Ford Focus." The phone went dead.

Gail was glad of a break from the hustle and bustle of the clinic on a busy day made worse because there were not one but two new people on staff, which of course explained why the problem had occurred in the first place. Oh well, it was a nice day, the sun was shining, the music on the car stereo was easy on the ears, and she deserved a breath of fresh air. When she pulled into the scale, located in a dedicated spot just off the main highway, the place was deserted, probably because the scale did not appear to be functioning. Okay, so she had made it before Pete. No worries, she tilted back the seat and lost herself in the crooning of Diana Krall.

Two of them appeared, jumped her really, one at the driver's door, one at the passenger door. The one in uniform, older and kinder looking, signaled her to get out of the vehicle. The other one, younger, decidedly pushy and immaculate in uniform, yanked open the passenger door with a flourish and grabbed the plastic bag on the seat. The older officer, also in uniform but not so spiffed-up, took her gently by the arm and steered her over to a police cruiser parked discreetly at one end of the scale lot. It was at that moment she spotted Pete driving by in his red GMC pickup. She did the logical thing; she began jumping up and down and waving at him. Pete drove on by, not even looking at the weigh scale. If the older policeman was a little bemused by Gail's behavior, the younger one certainly was not. Within seconds he had handcuffed her hands behind her back. There would be no more signaling to accomplices this day, no sir! Even if her accomplices had got away, at least she would have a hard time trying.

Back at the farm, Sabine had just uttered the statement, "you know, come to think of it, that didn't really sound like our Pete on the phone. Has he got a cold or something?"

"No," said Jeannie. "But here, I'll phone again and see where he has got to."

"Hello", Pete's voice answered after the very first ring.

"Hi, honey. Where exactly are you?"

"About three miles from you folks and lunch. Why?"

"Did you pick up the drugs?"

"Yes Missus, these ees Pablo. I meet with Pedro at the aeroport. He geev me de drogs."

"Will you stop joking around and listen to me. Did you pick up Sabine's drugs?"

"Huh? Drugs? What drugs?"

"The drugs you were told to pick up from Gail at the weigh scale. Don't tell me you forgot and drove right on by."

"What on earth are you talking about? What drugs? What weigh scale?"

"Oh, so it wasn't you that Sabine talked to on the phone?"

"Honey," Pete was now getting exasperated. "I'm pulling off the road. Then you can tell me your story from the beginning."

"Okay. First question. Did you or did you not get a call from Sabine fifteen minutes ago?'

"No."

"Second question. Would you mind turning round and driving back up to the weigh scale on Highway 11? Gail from the vet clinic should be there waiting for you. She has some vaccine that somebody forgot to put in Sabine's order. Otherwise we won't have enough vaccine to do all of the cows."

"Thees ees Pablo. I go now to peek op de drogs." Pete rang off and headed back up to the scale to find Gail mired in an extreme turf war, not with an older man in regular police uniform but with a younger officer so spruced up he looked as if he was off to the Commandant's Ball. It was clearly his show. He was the one who had taken the criminal down, who had handcuffed her to prevent her diminutive five-foot, one hundred pound frame from being any further threat to society. He took the plastic bag off the roof of the cruiser where he had left it and looked inside, knowing that he would find some illegal substance for the purpose of trafficking. How many times had they been told in training and retraining that it was the most innocent-looking of faces that posed the greatest menace? He knew, oh he could sense a criminal type when he saw one, and this was one who would not be getting away. No sir, she would have to do her time like all the rest of them. Inside the bag was a green box, fifty doses of Express 5 / Somnugen "for Bovine Rhinotracheitis-Virus Diarrhea-Parainfluenza-Respiratory Syneytial Virus, Haemopholus Somnus Bacterin", none of the words he had studied in crime school.

"So, what's this stuff?" he sneered, uneasy that he might be cheated of his prize.

"Drugs," said Gail, an impish smile playing on her face.

"Drugs," repeated the man. "Drugs for whom?"

"For what, you mean," Gail corrected. "For cows. I'm guilty, officer. I am a courier of drugs for cows." Gail was enjoying herself hugely. So was the man in uniform.

"We've made a mistake," he said quietly.

"Hold on now," said Mr. Young and Very Restless. "Don't be letting her go until I've checked out her vehicle." The man in uniform sighed and rolled his eyes. Gail simply grinned. Just as the man playing detective got into Gail's car, Pete arrived. Gail held her hands up in the air to greet him and so that he could clearly see the handcuffs.

"'Ey kiddo," Pete said, rolling down his window as he came alongside." You got de drogs? Hey Jimbo, what the hell are you doin' arresting our mule? What are my cows gonna do without their fix? Goldarn it, they're gonna need a fix PDQ." Jim, the uniformed cop and Pete the uniformed farmer played on the same old geezers' hockey team.

"Sorry guys," said Jim. "Mister Keen in there intercepted a call that said there was a drug drop going down at the weigh scale. I guess he was right, eh?"

At this point the younger man got out of the car. "Nothing. I guess we owe you an apology, lady," he added.

"Just let her loose and go back to real life," said Pete. "And stop wasting a person's time."

"And who the hell are you?" the young cop asked belligerently as he released his prisoner.

"Just one ornery SOB type farmer you don't want to tangle with."

Chapter Seven
COLLECTIBLES AND SUCH

*T*ending to a few cows as a glorified hobby farmer was one thing, dealing effectively with ninety head was quite another. This was the message brought home by the Hanlons' foray into mass vaccination. Both were quick to realize that even if you had a decent corral system, efficiency did not happen by itself; you had to make it happen. Had they simply gone ahead and done the vaccinating on their own as they had planned to do, the day would have been tortuously long, and fraught with danger. With Pete and Jeannie on hand, however, things went very smoothly—insofar as anything can go smoothly when you are stabbing a twelve to sixteen hundred pound creature with a huge great needle. Cows, no less than people really, are not pro-choice when it comes to inoculation. They balk, they toss their heads, if they have horns they do their very best to horn you, they back up at speed, they jump up and ride the animal in front of them in a last bid to find the exit, and they would love to stomp on both the doctor and the nurse. Big E's bull rails were perfect for the job, stout and unyielding, so there were no worries about the crowding alley holding up. Nonetheless, the first animal into the squeeze made an untimely escape because the inexperienced Aubrey swung the head-gate the wrong way and a prospective Matilda got out, prospective because at this point in the exercise, Sabine had clean forgotten that she was going to tag every one of them with a name. A twenty-five minute sideshow ensued with all hands taking time to cajole the nervous mama back into the holding pen with the others. Then, once the first cow was trapped in the squeeze, the others were lined up behind her, the holding gate was shut, and seven cows could now be vaccinated in one sweep.

Pete and Jeannie were a joy to watch because they worked so smoothly together. Each seemed to read immediately what the other was doing, or was about to do, and would complement the action accordingly. Jeannie took it upon herself to show both the Hanlons how to administer a subcutaneous shot of scour vaccine with a minimum of fuss; the key word here was "minimum". Aubrey had given such injections before, it was true, but his bedside manner had been sadly lacking, hence the "maximum of fuss" whenever he did it. Using the multiple-dose syringe, Jeannie had dosed the first batch of cows in about a minute. Then it was husband Pete's turn to show off his technique for intra-muscular shots. Again using a multiple-dose syringe, he would clench his fist then pound on the animal a couple of times before plunging the needle into the neck, the conventional inoculation site these days. The pounding on the neck seemed to somehow mask the shock of the needle's entry into the animal's body.

"With you two, we'll be finished in no time," said Sabine ecstatically.

"Maybe," said Pete a little too knowingly.

They brought in the next seven. Jeannie took her syringe and handed it ceremoniously to Sabine. "You're doin' it kiddo," she said. "They're your cows.

The initial shock on Sabine's face was instantly replaced with the demeanor of the go-getter that she was.

"It's much better to be firm than gentle," counseled Jeannie as Sabine was poking energetically but ineffectively at who else but Elvira, the cow's skin bunched in her hand. A more resolute effort convinced Sabine she could do it and the deed was done, four others in quick succession after her. The next one in line, however, decided to take exception to all that was being done to her and for her; the head rolled this way and that, and then the cow put her head below the rump of the one ahead and there it stayed. Sabine could feel the frustration bubbling up inside her.

"This is the moment when you learn to keep your cool," said Jeannie quietly. "Animals will sense your anger and will misbehave even more if you let them get to you." It was the perfect advice for the moment. Sabine took time to pause, the cow's head popped up to take a look at what was going on, and in one fluid motion she had been inoculated. "Now that, my dear, was impressive," added Jeannie, as Sabine finished up the last in line. "Now it's time for the cowboy himself to have a go."

Basically, all Aubrey had to do was "to stab and run," said Pete. But after he had done the first two, he got air in the line running from the plastic container to the syringe. Once he had purged it, he ended up holding the bag of vaccine clenched in his teeth allowing gravity to assist the flow of the vaccine. Primitive it may have been, but it worked. Then he went and got the line stuck between the bodies of two cows and all but landed on top of them in his efforts to prevent syringe and vaccine being pulled in too. Finally the deed was done, Aubrey's efforts having taken noticeably longer than his wife's and with noticeably more puffing and panting. Seven cows out, another seven in, with Pete and Jeannie now doing the leg-work and the Hanlons doing the vaccinating. The second batch went smoothly, deceptively so.

"Change-over time," yelled Jeannie as the next group was brought in. "Sabine, you're on the intra-muscular, Aubrey you're on the subcutaneous." It was time for them to repeat each other's mistakes and learn from the process so that by the end of the afternoon, they had accomplished what they had set out to do. More importantly, they could adjourn without guilt to a well-chilled bottle of wine and the Beef Stroganoff that Sabine had simmering in the crock-pot. What the Hanlons had taken to heart, though, was that in farming one must never be afraid to pick the brains of another and never be afraid to learn from the experience of others without having to suffer through the same experience themselves as a prerequisite. In this regard, Pete recounted how he had cracked a rib the previous year while trying to insert a post behind a cow in the crowding alley at the same moment that it chose to go full speed backwards.

"Always have a healthy respect for an animal so much bigger than yourself," he said over his glass of Chardonnay. "By the way, what are you going to do about ear tags? You know you have to have them, right?"

"Tags!" yelped Sabine. "I forgot all about the *bleeping* tags! You're talking about the CCIA buttons, right? And I want to give all our cows brand new name tags so I'll always remember who's who."

"Use numbers," said Pete. "In your case, numbers one to one hundred. Your dear old Nellie can be number one, I'm thinking."

"Numbers?" Sabine reacted in mock horror. "This is not some scientific experiment in the laboratory. Where's the poetry? Where's the music? You can't sing numbers. You can't have a warm cuddly relationship with a number. How would your wife like it if you called her number ninety-three?"

"What's so wrong with that?" Pete came back with a straight face. "A good ol' country crooner would probably love to sing about the ride he took on good ol' ninety three with all of her huffin' an' puffin'."

"Is that right," Jeannie interrupted. "But in our case, he'd have to sing about poor ol' ninety-three having to drag along this big-ass caboose all her dang life."

So deteriorated the evening, but such decadent togetherness inveigled Pete and Jeannie into helping out the following week when the tagging was done, just so that the decadence was not wasted.

Tagging a cow in and of itself is not too burdensome, but when an old tag first has to be removed from a cow's ear, she generally sees the procedure as no reason for enjoyment. Some cows will thrash this way and that, others will endeavor to bunt the invader into eternity, while others again will simply stand there and take what is coming with the stoicism of a monk. At the end of two hours, every Hanlon animal sported a CCIA tag, a small button in the left ear with an identifying number and square pale green tag in the right ear proclaiming Sabine's chosen name and number for that particular cow. Of course Nellie was H1 Nellie. Elvira was H32 Elvira, Babe was H33 Babe, and so forth. There was H42 Matilda, H56 Bubbles, H72 Sweetpea, there was a Pepperoni, a Honey, and, Jeannie's favorite, a brockle-face by the name of Gorgonzola.

"Why would you want to call a cow H40 when you can call her Gorgonzola?" Jeannie heckled Pete.

"Why would anyone name a cow after a food that is half-rotten and stinks as bad as a skunk?" Pete retaliated.

"You knew, I'm sure," said Jeannie to Sabine, "that this is the year of the 'P'?"

"Just had one behind the barn," Aubrey interrupted facetiously.

"Come again?" said Sabine.

"I've just had one behind…," Aubrey started again.

"Not you, you fool, I'm talking to Jeannie."

"This is the year of the 'P,'" Jeannie repeated.

"I shudder to think what comes next year," Aubrey continued his nonsense in an aside to Pete.

"What do you mean?" asked Sabine of Jeannie.

"Every year there is a designated letter of the alphabet for naming your animals. 'P' tells you that any animal with a name beginning with 'P' was born in 2003."

"Oh, oh, so now you tell me," laughed Sabine. "Well that's just too bad, although I do have a Peony, a Priscilla, a Peppermint and a Pancake.

What Aubrey and Sabine learned was that the more they handled their cattle, the more the cows got used to their style. Not that this necessarily signaled a new era of bovine cooperation nor anything close to it, not with dear old cantankerous Nellie assuming the role of Big Boss Mama. Nellie had always made a point of doing just what Nellie wanted, but then again, and thankfully, Nellie could always be bribed with a bucket of chop.

That year, winter descended upon them like a giant, fluffy blanket. Then a prolonged cold spell in late October saw the cows constantly munching on the bales Aubrey put out for them in the steel bale feeders. "You know, they eat and eat and waste so much," he found himself lamenting to Pete.

"Maybe you should get one of those bale shredders like mine," Pete responded. "Plus, you can feed your cows back out in the field where their manure does some good. The machine lays the bale out in a long line so that the younger cows don't get booted out of the way by aggressive bigger ones." Then he added a significant comment that ordinarily Aubrey would probably not have dared to pick up, not with Sabine looking over his shoulder.

"Say, did you see that ad in the paper about the snap farm sale out at Lacombe. It's a sale conducted by Montgomery Auctions. Machinery, collectibles, household, the whole nine yards. They say the old boy just up and pulled the plug. A bit too much of that sort of thing these days, but that's what happens when old people cannot see their way out. Anyway, there's a Balebuster 256 Plus Two on the sale. I'm going up to look at a round bale mover, carries fourteen bales. Why don't you come up with me and take a look yourself?" Aubrey agreed he would, the focus on the bale shredder diverting his thoughts from the more sobering comments about suicide.

Sabine should have gone along with them, not simply as a chaperone but because she was always more observant than her husband. But on this particular day, she could not face the idea of standing there twiddling her thumbs on some windswept farm out near Lacombe, not with a wind chill of minus sixty-five, (people exaggerate as they get older), percolating through her skin and into her bones. Besides, she did not really think they should be spending money on yet another machine, no matter how logical it might be to buy it. No, the men could go, and anyhow it was time she caught up with the paperwork. The price would surely go too high if the machine was as good as Pete said it was. And Pete would hold her husband in check like he always did. To cap it all, there was nothing that interested her. "Antiques and collectibles" too often turned out to be a couple of dented milk churns; a handmade dresser constructed out of a packing crate; a couple of hundred assorted jars, dusty and with a pile of non-fitting rusted lids; a washstand without its basin; a prehistoric clothes wringer; and twenty or so eight-track cassettes of Hank Williams and The Mormon Tabernacle Choir and such. No, the "collectibles and the antiques" could collect dust in somebody else's house, not hers.

Emergency "snap auctions" do not attract huge crowds at the best of times. Snap auctions in winter are worse still. Never fun, they amount to a form of self-inflicted torture, an endurance test of a different kind. The sparse crowd fulfilled expectations; everyone who showed up was there for a specific item, not for a joyride. That was especially apparent when Pete and Aubrey merged into the outside ring, where the general consensus seemed to be that the auctioneer should darn well hurry up and get to the item the individual had come for: the seed drill or the combine, the fancy-schmancy four-wheel drive tractor, or the antiquated

Minneapolis-Moline. The ring dealing with the household and collectibles was in a heated Quonset, and by all accounts the crowd was just as sparse. The machine that interested Aubrey was, of course, the Haybuster 256 Plus Two. What a stupid name, Aubrey was thinking when Pete said to him, "you look over yours, I'll look over mine. This thing is going to be over pretty darn quick. Too damn cold for people to be standing around."

Aubrey's machine looked relatively new; the paintwork was largely unblemished, suggesting that it had probably not done a huge amount of work. Yes, he decided, he would take a chance on it; eight thousand max, he was thinking, as two other interested types converged on it. He moved away, affirming to himself that perhaps seven thousand should be his maximum even if he had never seen one in the newspaper ads for under nine thousand dollars. So it was that he did not see the young fellow try to turn the main shaft by hand, did not see him discover and point out to others coming over to take a look the burn marks indicating failed bearings at both ends of the shaft. He did not hear the old grizzled farmer, dressed like an abominable snowman, saying "what a swine of a job it was to change those bearings and someone else could have it."

Realizing that he had at least fifteen to twenty minutes to kill, Aubrey headed over to the Quonset to get out of the wind. Judging by the number of people now inside, others had had the same idea, their primary aim in life being to stay warm and to heck with tagging along behind a spouse or friend fanatical enough to brave the elements outside.

Apparently the bidding inside was just as sluggish as it was outside. Aubrey craned to see what was currently on the block: some kind of antique phonograph in a wooden cabinet, announced the auctioneer. Bidding had started out at fifteen dollars and stalled at twenty, so the young auctioneer did what he had seen more seasoned auctioneers do. He sweetened the pot by throwing a pile of long-playing records into the bargain; "Some Beatles and such," he said, and started the bidding over. This time the bidding went up to twenty-two dollars before stalling once more.

"Twenty-five," yelled Aubrey from the back.

His opposite bidder's interest had obviously been only momentary, or maybe he did not need a stack of weighty vinyl because the bidding died for good and the auctioneer knocked the deal down to Aubrey.

"Number?" called the clerk at the front.

"Seventy-four" yelled Aubrey, coming forward to claim his prize. As soon as he saw it close up, he knew he had scored. The thing was exquisite; the turntable nestled in a glorious cabinet of carved oak. The records were simply a bonus. Very carefully, he picked up the cabinet and was at once surprised by how heavy it was. This was not one of those pressed board creations covered with veneer; this was the genuine article. How it had made it this far without a scratch was something that puzzled Aubrey for the rest of his days. A gray-haired granny in winter boots and fur-lined parka offered to carry the records for him. They went to the back corner of the Quonset where Aubrey set his load down on a rickety table. He was about to relieve the lady of the records when she stopped him.

"You know, if I was you, I would not leave this stuff alone. You do realize that you have something very special here, don't you?"

"I know. But I really have to put a bid in on a machine outside," said Aubrey. "It should be up any minute."

"Tell you what. I'll look after the stuff for you," was the good lady's reply. "I can watch what's going on up front from here. Not that I want anything, anyway. My husband is busy messing around outside too. You men are all the same." She smiled.

"Thank you so much," said Aubrey knowing how pleased his wife would be. "See you in a few minutes, I hope."

The moment he exited the Quonset, he saw the auctioneer was already parked beside his machine, and darn it all, he was already taking bids. He heard the "fifteen hund'ed, fifteen hund'ed, going once, going twice…"

"Seventeen," Aubrey hollered. Twenty pairs of curious eyes turned to appraise this late arrival.

"New man in," yelled the auctioneer gratefully. "And thank you, sir. Seventeen, seventeen hund'ed." No matter how much he cajoled and begged and sang the praises of such a wondrous machine, he could not squeeze out another bid. Aubrey's opposite bidder walked away in disgust. So the auctioneer took the last resort, he actually broadcast the deformities of the machine. "Fellahs, there's a pair of main bearings that need replacing, but they can't be more than a couple of hundred bucks apiece. Where are you gonna find a better deal than this one? Take a look at any paper. These babies sell for around nine thou'. So let's get serious, or am I missing something?"

On a normal day in summer, the ploy would have worked marvelously. But the wind had got up and people were making it very clear that it was time to move on to the more important stuff, the combines and the tractors. Aubrey bagged the machine for seventeen hundred dollars.

"You stole it," said the auctioneer. "Number?"

"Seventy-four," said Aubrey, anxious now to get back to the Quonset. Pete, on the edge of the crowd, gave him a thumbs-up when Aubrey signaled that he was going back inside. Pete's bale mover came up three items later. He had to work for it, unlike Aubrey, with three other interested parties in the hunt. He got it in the end, but not at a bargain basement price, not that Aubrey had fully registered what a steal he had.

Back in the Quonset, there was his old lady all wrinkles and smiles, the sort of woman anyone would be blessed to have as their granny. "You know what?" she said. "You'd better get this thing out of here right away. I've had three people offer to buy it, one at a hundred, another at a hundred and fifty, and the last fellow at five hundred, would you believe?"

"Well, thank you so much for not selling it and skipping off to Florida with the loot," said Aubrey.

"You know," she added as if imparting a confidence, "I think you really have something here, something very, very valuable. Gosh, even this pile of records would fetch a decent price all by themselves in the right place at the right time."

"Here, I hope you'll accept this twenty dollars for looking after it when you didn't have to," said Aubrey feeling that he had taken advantage of her.

"Oh no, I can't possibly do that. I'm just happy to help. But I do think you should get it out of here, and I'm happy to help you do that. You see, my husband is still outside, no doubt waiting to buy his beloved tractor."

"Oh, that is very sweet of you. But I've just realized, I'll have to go back out to get the keys to the truck from my buddy."

"You go do that," smiled the lady. "I'll be right here when you get back."

By the time he did get back, there was a man standing next to the woman, his fingers tracing the outlines of the carving on the cabinet. Aubrey disliked him the moment he saw him, the sallow mustachioed face topped with a fedora and the heavy luxuriant overcoat making him resemble a 1930s Chicago mobster. The man reeked of money, most of it assuredly ill-gotten. Aubrey was glad that to all appearances anyway, he, Aubrey Hanlon, was just an anonymous Canadian farmer in his anonymous Canadian winter coveralls. The man wasted no time.

"Say, my friend, I'd be happy to give you a thousand for this here phonograph." It came out more as a statement than an offer, and was backed up with a handful of bank notes already counted. "You see, I know how little you paid for it," he added conspiratorially as if he was trying to make Aubrey feel somehow guilty.

"It's not for sale," Aubrey said flatly.

"See, I told you," said the lady triumphantly, needing to do her part in putting down a man she clearly had no time for. The man ignored her; she simply did not exist in his world.

"Fifteen hundred," the man said, not quite scowling.

"Forgive me, sir, but it's not for sale," Aubrey said quietly.

"Look fellah, my daddy had one of these back in the days when I was a kid in Saskatoon. He gave it to my sister who went and sold it when she moved to New York. See, for me this thing has great value, sentimental value you understand. That's why I'm prepared to pay a whack more dollars than it is worth. So, final offer, three thousand." The old lady drew a sharp breath and held on to it in her suspense. Aubrey was thinking that with a face like his, the man could not have known the difference between sentiment and sauerkraut. Besides, he resented the implications of his little speech.

"You deaf or something?" Aubrey heard himself reacting like the cop he used to be. "It's not for sale."

The man was evidently hard of hearing. "Well, what'll you take for it?" He shifted his weight to the other foot as though beefing up his attack.

"Come on, my dear," said Aubrey to the lady, so patently enjoying the man's discomfort and Aubrey's brusque manner towards him. "Let's get this out to the car before anybody else takes a shine to it." The man actually found a cooperative thought at this juncture.

"Let me carry these here records for you," he said, almost pushing the old lady out of the way.

"There'll be no need for that," she responded. "Us dumb old farmers are tougher than we look, and maybe a mite smarter too." With a sweep like the Duchess of Dovercourt, she picked up the pile and cruised past him, a galleon in full sail. Aubrey picked up the phonograph and followed. The man made as if to pursue them then apparently thought better of it, much to the relief of the old lady who had already decided that if he saw which vehicle they put the stuff into, he would be tempted to come and steal it. So once they had placed the records on the back seat of the truck and covered them over with Pete's old raincoat, they wrapped the cabinet in the two blankets and the tarp that Pete always carried with him in winter, gently securing it with tie-downs in the bed of the truck. At this moment the lady's husband appeared, grinning from ear to ear.

"I got it, Luce! I got the son of a bitching thing. For less than I thought we would."

"Well done, honey," she said. "And boy, have I ever got a doozy of a story for you." They ambled off hand in hand, the only two people in the world as far as either of them was concerned.

"Thank you so much," Aubrey had to yell after them as they headed back towards the machinery to inspect their new treasure. He made his way back to the Quonset to settle up. There at the door was the man. Of course the grin was forced as he handed Aubrey his card.

"I'm an antique dealer from Vancouver. I got here a little too late. If you ever decide to sell it, give me a call."

"Thanks," said Aubrey as graciously as he could, pocketing the card without even looking at it, resisting the temptation to grind it into the dust. The man walked off, and Aubrey joined Pete in the lineup to settle their bills.

What Aubrey had never appreciated was that Sabine was becoming more than a little apprehensive about the wisdom of their expansion. Now here was her husband out on the spending trail, buying another blessed machine that might or might not make their lives better. Oh sure, it was his money, their money, but it wasn't unequivocally theirs. The bankers had too great a hold on their credit. It would have felt a whole lot different had the money been theirs outright with no strings attached.

So when Pete and Aubrey drove into the yard with this great big, yellow monstrosity in tow, Sabine was not exactly overjoyed. She could not even pluck up her usual enthusiasm to go out and greet them, preferring instead that they find their own way into the house for a coffee, as was the custom. Her heart sank even further when she caught snippets of their conversation coming out of the boot-room as the two of them removed their footwear.

"...so I'll pick up a couple of bearings in Red Deer...something...something...help you put 'em in if you like...something...something...only if your dear wife makes us beef olives, and only if," Pete talking

Aubrey's response was muffled but seemingly enthusiastic.

They came into the kitchen.

"Beef Olives is it, Petey-boy?" said Sabine as brightly as she could.

"Yep. Your husband has had too good a day for you two to get off any lighter than that."

"Okay then," agreed Sabine with a joviality she did not feel. "How did we do? Or rather, what did you boys buy that we don't need?"

For once, Aubrey sensed the unease, sensed the putting on of a brave face, so he took the obvious choice of handing her the bill for the day's purchases. She put on her reading glasses and began to read, looking at the figures almost with incomprehension they seemed so low. "Hold on now!" she said breathlessly, "you paid only seventeen hundred dollars for a machine you told me would cost about eight thousand? What's wrong with it?"

"Two main bearings," Pete chipped in, feeling too much like an accomplice in crime, "which is why he got it for the price he did. Nobody, or at least nobody with their sanity, likes the idea of installing bearings into a machine in the dead of winter, right?"

"Right," echoed Sabine, barely registering such excuses from criminal minds as she continued to look over the invoice. "But tell me, what's with these forty long-playing records and a phonograph? Sure we like our old LPs, but do we really need another forty? This is the era of the CD, or have you forgotten that?"

"They're not ours," said Aubrey. "They're yours. All yours. Now, will the judge and jury please pour us a coffee before resuming her inquisition?"

"While she's doing that, I'll go one better and fetch the records," said Pete, bound and determined that Sabine's famous Beef Olives would be on the menu that week. The silence that ensued between the Hanlon couple was evidence of Sabine's apprehension and of Aubrey's backing off from a fight. But the instant that Pete got back inside and plonked the pile of records on the kitchen table, Sabine's girlish curiosity could not be restrained. From then on, the conversation was one-sided.

"Ooh look, here's a 'Sergeant Pepper'. And 'Bridge over Troubled Water' by Creedence Clearwater, and, blow me down, here's that James Last record we like so much. I hope it's not as scratched up as ours. Holy smokes! There's a couple of Joni Mitchells, a Tom Jones and a Judy Collins. This is amazing! These are all from our time! She rattled on, essentially talking to herself in her excitement. When she got to the bottom of the pile, and unearthed Percy Sledge's 'When a Man Loves a Woman', she let out a wild whoop of joy, dropped everything and gave her husband the sloppiest kiss of their matrimonial history. Now there was no stopping her. She had to see the phonograph "this instant". With all this sudden enthusiasm, the men were easily persuaded to put down their coffee and lead her out to the truck. Pete climbed in the back and removed the tie-downs and the tarp, and still she had to wait because the treasure was swaddled in blankets. When they were carefully removed, Sabine all but swooned in delight. That was the moment Aubrey chose to hand over the antique dealer's card. **Gilbert A. Wheatside, Art Collector and Antique Dealer,** with an address on Seymour Street, Vancouver.

"So what's this for?" asked Sabine a little perplexed.

"If you want to sell it, he'll buy it," said Aubrey.

"I wouldn't sell it even if he offered me a hundred bucks," she said looking at the auctioneer's invoice again: One phonograph in wood cabinet and records, $25.00.

"Well actually, he offered three," said Aubrey.

"Three hundred bucks," Sabine's breath drew in sharply.

"No, three thousand."

"Three *thousand?* You're kidding me."

"No, no kidding. Three thousand smackeroos," said Aubrey.

"And you didn't grab it?" asked Sabine stressing the "you".

"Obviously not. Should I have?"

"Oh, oh it's so beautiful. But…but…but why didn't you take it? I mean, you'd sell your dear darling wife for three Gs, now wouldn't you?" she winked at Pete.

"Wouldn't get three Gs. Two maybe. I thought you'd really like it, but then if you don't want it…"

The conversation was terminated abruptly by the second sloppiest kiss of their shared history.

Chapter Eight
GUERILLA TACTICS

The next hurdle after herd vaccination was the calving season itself: ninety-one "preggies" were due to start calving on February 7, if the gestation tables were anywhere near right. But the projected dates could only be applied to the Hanlons' original herd. The cows they had bought from Quincy "should start a-poppin' by the middle of February," he said. As for the bred heifers, Aubrey would have to rely on the inexact science of a vet's thirty-second exploration conducted when they were brought into the auction mart. For cattle folk the world over, calving season is the reason for their existence. If the calving season is plagued with problems, you can bet your boots the entire year will follow in the same direction. And so the people in the business look forward to calving with both trepidation and excitement. They know how, once again, they will marvel at the miracle of birth; but they also know they will come face to face with death, sometimes inexplicable, sometimes the consequence of their own wrong decision. With a problematic birth, there is rarely time to second-guess. The decision to intervene and to help has to be made sooner rather than later, and that decision should be based on more than just an impulse. The only true teacher, tried and tested time and time again, is experience itself, something that Aubrey and Sabine still lacked to some degree…but then at least they were smart enough to admit it. Moreover, having hospitable neighbors like Pete and Jeannie, and good old John Upham, even Art Zimmer if it came right down to it, they were in good hands because all of them had spent years in the corral.

"Don't you hesitate to call us," said Jeannie, "even if it's two in the morning and minus thirty degrees outside. I might not come but I'll sure be happy to turf my Pete's bum out of bed and get him over there right away." Jeannie was doing what so many farming wives do naturally, putting her husband directly into the line of fire, Aubrey was thinking.

"Whatever you do, make darn sure you get your girls in at least a week early so's you can watch 'em closely. There are always a couple of early birds, young un's who decide to take the Ejection Express. Anyway, we don't know if old Quince's bull got out early and made a charitable contribution, do we? And one more thing; no stories about how you didn't know where your calving chains were because you had forgotten where you put them after last year. Say, you do have a calf puller, you folks, don't you?"

"We have one," responded Sabine, "but we've never used it."

"Well, this is the year you may have to," said Pete.

"Why's that?" asked Aubrey.

"Because ranching is no longer the call of the range, it is agri-business. It'll cost you around three hundred bucks to have the vet do a C-section, and that's only if you drive the cow into the clinic in town. It'll be a darn sight more if he has to come out to the farm, and that's assuming he'll even agree to do that."

"Three hundred bucks?" cried Sabine in alarm. "Jeepers, that's as much as some of our older cows are worth right now."

"Precisely, my dear lady, precisely. I know of quite a few farmers who will just up and shoot the cow if they get into a situation where they can't get the calf out themselves."

"Shoot the cow? Shoot their own cow?" Sabine was aghast. "You mean that rather than save the lives of two animals, they would destroy them both? That's so wrong! How can a person even think like that?"

"Put it this way," said Pete stoically, "a lot of people in the beef industry have their backs so hard up against the wall, they can't turn right or left. They certainly can't afford a C-section for a cow, so rather than see her suffer, they shoot her. What choice do they have?"

Sabine was speechless. She knew things were bad, but not this bad. And to hear Pete tell it all so matter-of-factly, that was an eye-opener; the same Pete who would go the full mile to save one of his animals.

"Let me give you two a piece of advice," Pete persisted. "Don't either of you be too trusting of your new cows, Quincy's and the heifers. You never know how they're going to react when they have their very own newborn baby on the ground right in front of them, and you arrive on the scene to check it out. Me and that Jeannie-girl of mine have gotten used to all that free food and drink we get here, so we need you folks to be around a lot longer."

Sabine was appreciative, always amazed at the lengths country folks would go to help each other. "Well, thanks to your help we have a corral system that we know will work for us. Aubrey has set up floodlights in all of them so we can see what's going on more clearly than if we just use a flashlight. We've put twenty or so girls in the small corral, thirty in the medium corral, and the rest in the big corral. Like you suggested, we've mixed heifers in with cows so hopefully the young ones will see how the older ones go about their business. Aubrey has fixed up the old barn so that we can put a couple of mamas and babies in there when we need to. We've also put in that system of gates we talked about, so if we need to work on a cow, we can get to the head-gate without too much fuss." Clearly, Sabine was proud of what they had accomplished: justifiably so, as they were soon to find out.

February 2, at 3:00 AM. The previous day at lunchtime, they had said on the radio that the weather was to turn decidedly miserable during the night: barometer falling, winds gusting, that sort of thing. Aubrey did not like that particular message, so he phoned the Environment Canada weather line, and be darned if they didn't just go right out and agree with the radio. Okay, there was no other choice but to resort to the news channel Sabine liked to watch on TV at six. Maybe he was getting too old or something, but he found that weather hostess insufferable. Somebody higher up must have told her to make the weather entertaining. That was certainly the message of her attire, what with the huge pendants dangling like wind chimes from her ears, gold charms glistening around her neck, and the silly tuque to complement the gaudy woolen suit sponsored by Skunkleby's Womenswear of Edmonton, where you own your image. And that was before her pitch: a shrill voice and counterfeit humour mixed into an introductory segment so tweet and full of small talk that Aubrey could only dismiss it as "squirrel chatter". The segment was introductory because it was designed to heighten expectations and force you to sit through another batch of banal commercials until the heavy-duty forecast itself hit you right between the eyes. The weather was about to be grim and vindictive, end of story.

"Why do you always have to shoot the messenger?" Sabine always asked when her mate reacted so churlishly to a forecast. "The poor woman is only doing her job. Besides, I really like her outfit today. I could be seen in that myself."

"Oh yeah, well here's one for you, my dear. You can always take the woman out of the boutique, but you can't take the boutique out of the woman." Aubrey was wise enough not to let the reference to his wife's ownership of a womenswear boutique in Edmonton hang too heavily in the air, so he carried on. "Look at her, for heaven's sake. She's taking absolute delight in the story of snow and blowing snow and wind chills of minus forty with exposed bits of flesh falling off in five seconds."

February 2, at 3:00 AM, Aubrey awoke with a start. Maybe it was the wind that woke him, for it was sure conducting its own little sing-song outside. But he was inexplicably uneasy, so much so that going back to sleep was out of the question. Well fine, he would get up and brew a mug of tea and settle into his book. Soon wide awake, yet somehow still too unsettled to pick up his book, he put on his winter gear and set off to the barn. He almost turned back. The wind was downright hostile, lashing out at him in vicious bursts, driving snow pellets horizontally into his face. He got to the power box just inside the barn door and switched on the corral lights. Man, was he ever proud of those lights, even if they had tended to spook the cows when he switched them on for the first time. His practice of leaving them on for a few hours the next five days after he had installed them solved that problem; now the cows barely looked up at the ghoulish creature that seemed to appear every time the lights went on. Aubrey also made a point of doing his "more-song-less-dance" routine to assure them that yes, it was their lovable cowherd himself. They were serenaded with all of the old favorites: "Blue Suede Shoes", "Great Balls of Fire", Sweet Caroline", later complemented by his current favorites of "Danny Boy" and "Guide Me Oh Thou Great Redeemer", thanks to his new CD "Welsh Choirs, A Selection Of Magnificent Choral Music".

He checked the small corral first and then the medium-sized one adjoining it. He was just at the point of imploring The Great Redeemer to "feed me till I want no more" at full volume, when he spotted Babe over the plank fence in the big corral. What was that mess hanging from her derriere? The famous hymn stopped abruptly. "Damn it all, you've gone and popped one, haven't you?" he yelled. He climbed over the fence and began running towards her until Pete's caution echoed through his mind: "Whatever you do, never panic your mamas. Suddenly rushing madly about will put any mama on edge, and she might suddenly prefer that you and she not share the same planet."

He slowed to a walk. Yep, there it was, fawn-coloured and almost buried in the straw bedding. At least she had had the sense to have it there and not in the snow bank, building up against the fence. But the calf was tiny. It looked pretty much dead, too, until he saw an ear twitch. It was alive! The little fellow was alive! He went over to it. Oh yes, he was alive for sure, but he might not live much longer unless he got warmed up. The tips of his ears and the bottom part of his tail were already frozen solid.

"Don't go work a cow in the middle of the night by yourself unless you have to. It's always better to have someone with you". Another of "Pete's Principles" flashed through Aubrey's mind as he galloped off to wake Sabine. Already psyched up for calving, she was up in minutes but almost balked when she stepped out of the front door.

"Now I can see why you have a hate on for your tweety forecaster," she commented, as she put her head down and they plowed into the wind together.

Babe looked up as soon as they got into the corral. Aubrey was carrying the shiny, new, blue plastic sled that had been on sale for $25.00 at Peavey Mart the last week of January. Much to Babe's alarm, they loaded up the tiny baby into the sled. Sabine serenaded her through the whole process with "googy-gaga" noises that Aubrey could only surmise were her form of encouragement to Babe to get on with the natural bonding business. It was as they moved off toward the barn that she tripped on something solid in the straw. She looked down to discover the body of another tiny, fawn-coloured calf lying comatose, completely covered over by the bedding.

"Aub, oh Aub, here's another one!" she stuttered. The whole operation ground to a halt. "It's a twin. Oh Aub, Babe has got twins. Isn't that wonderful?" But when Sabine took a closer look, her excitement died in her throat. The poor thing seemed awfully dead. Aubrey hunched over it and picked it up. The head moved weakly.

"It's alive," he muttered, "but only just. You pull the sled and I'll carry this little guy." They made their way to the barn, Babe tagging along anxiously as though full in the knowledge that these were preferred humans who were trying to help.

In order to minimize winter forays down to the bathtub in Sabine's prize bathroom to warm up frozen calves, Pete had built them a hotbox to which Aubrey had added an electric-powered construction heater. Both Babe's calves went in, with Babe looking on uncertainly. Then, as if sensing that somehow her babies would be all right, she munched contentedly on a couple of wads of fresh hay that Aubrey placed before her. Sabine went back to the house to heat up two of the small pots of colostrum that she had saved the previous year and placed in the freezer. Aubrey did a slow check of all the other cows; nothing but looks of bovine boredom. By the time Sabine arrived back with two feeder bottles of milk, each with an outsize orange nipple comparable to the teat of a cow, there were all sorts of thumping noises coming from inside the hotbox. Aubrey opened the lid. One calf was standing there as if demanding to know what the heck was going on and why was he being kept in the dark. The weaker one was still lying down, but at least he was holding his head up as though he had some purpose in mind. Aubrey lifted B.B., Big Boy, out of the box and introduced him to the nipple. He latched on with gusto for this is what he had been waiting for. Naturally, Sabine was down to mothering L.B., Little Boy, who was still contemplating the meaning of life from the hotbox. Yet he too latched onto the nipple immediately and was soon guzzling the milk with evident pleasure, his tail flicking madly from side to side in glee. Sabine could almost feel the strength flowing into that tiny body, and she reveled yet again in that respect for life that caring for animals can so often bring.

Once Aubrey and Sabine had established that both babies had no trouble sucking, the next challenge was to get them sucking from their mother, which meant coaxing Babe into the head-gate. Surprisingly, Babe cooperated and was quickly restrained so that Aubrey and Sabine could put the calves to her.

B.B. was no problem because he could stand already. With the bottom half of the restraining gate open, Sabine directed the calf to a tit. He was so small, he had to look unnaturally upwards to reach it, but once he had it in his mouth, he was not about to let go, sucking noisily and then bunting his mother as his instincts kicked in. L.B. was altogether another story. Still too weak to stand on his own, Aubrey draped him over a square straw bale, feeding a rear tit into his mouth and holding it there. At first L.B. insisted on chewing it, and made it clear he was becoming tired and frustrated. Aubrey forced his mouth open and squirted some milk down his throat. L.B. responded with great enthusiasm, suddenly convinced that sucking rather than chewing was the way to go. Both calves were so small that their bellies could not hold that much before they were full, so the feeding routine would have to be planned very carefully. Babe was freed from the head-gate, and at once she went to her babies and began to love them, with L.B. in the nest that Sabine had made for him in the straw, and B.B. settling down right next to him. Babe would have said her thanks if she could; she did the next best thing, intimating to her human benefactors that she could handle the situation now and that they could leave any time they chose. They did; they had to because they realized how cold they had become having spent nigh on an hour and a half since the drama began. Time was always gobbled up on such things—gobbled up and masticated and digested so that being awake simply meant showing a slightly higher level of consciousness than being asleep.

All that day, Aubrey and Sabine worked not so much with Big Boy who was mobile enough to find his own groceries, but with Little Boy whose back feet were unable to bear his weight long enough for him to address his needs. This of course meant getting Babe back into the hated head-gate five more times, and every time she made clear her increasing displeasure. Yes, Aubrey had to phone Pete and tell him of the goings-on and how he had come to dread putting Babe in the head-gate.

"You need to go watch the Titford boys," he said, "Garth and Gary. They never carry a cane or a stick; they just smile and talk, and nudge and talk some more, and walk around in circles with the cow and eventually the cow figures she ought to do what they want her to do. Stand back, give her some time, don't make her feel threatened, don't force the pace. Have yourself a gentle talk with her and see what happens. Oh, and one more thing, don't try this out on a cow you know is rank and miserable. She'd probably enjoy redesigning your facial features if she thinks you have gone soft in the head."

Yeah, yeah, all this sweetness and light, Aubrey was thinking, but then again his mind was open enough to put Pete's advice to the test. First he isolated the two calves on the outside of the head-gate. Of course B.B. had to do some wandering about of his own accord, but L.B. was still too wobbly on his legs so he was not about to venture off some place he did not have to go. Babe was interested in helping for sure, but not enough to go into the head-gate on her own. Besides, she made it clear that Aubrey was now in the barely-tolerated category, even if he was without his customary cane, as the "Titford Technique" designated. Her flanks were trembling, but she listened nonetheless, tilting her head as if to question all these sweet nothings from a man who had shown little patience with her before. Aubrey could have been reciting *The Communist Manifesto* for all that it mattered; it was the tone that was important. Soothing, caressing, soppily schmoozing, she could stand it no longer and entered the head-gate on her own, even waiting for Aubrey to close it while she munched on the grain mix that Sabine had put out for her. All through that day and into the night it was the same procedure: B.B. directly at the tit, L.B. across his bale, both calves gaining enough strength to deal with the bitter cold. At five the following morning, Aubrey roused a lethargic Sabine out of bed, even going so far as to brew a fresh pot of coffee before he did so to sweeten her mood. Then they trooped up to the barn together, ready to begin the feeding performance one more time. Aubrey opened the door and there they were, both calves sucking energetically from an unconcerned mother. L.B. was unsteady on his legs it was true, but clearly he was willing to contest with B.B. for his share of the spoils. Sabine was ecstatic; never in her life had she experienced that sort of high. Two more days and they could let Babe out of the barn.

And so on to the morning of day four. Aubrey finished his pre-dawn check and then poked his head into the barn as he usually did. There was B.B. at the buffet but no sign of L.B. He moved further into the barn, and that was when he saw it. The utter shock of expecting to see an animal full of life and then finding its corpse in full rigor mortis instead is a farmer's worst nightmare. The body was flat out in the bedding, where his mother had lain on him. Aubrey was at once sick and angry, frustrated that death is so starkly final, and so irreversible. He resented the fact that there is no dignity in death, the once-pulsing corpse now so pathetic, so small and stiff and meaningless. His fist impulse was to beat the living daylights out of the mother, the more so because she was just standing there so contentedly, chewing her cud while B.B. bunted her for his breakfast. Then the guilt feelings and the second-guessing began to overwhelm him. What if they had put her back into the corral where she would have had to be more protective with the other cows about? What if they had given her less bedding so that she would have felt her baby struggling beneath her when she lay down? But still it all came back to one of the inescapable realities of farming; death is a part of life. You win some, you lose some; this was one they lost. Life has to go on for the living. The dead are hopefully an anomaly, an aberration, a slice of bitter experience soon to become a scar on the memory. Slowly, he reached down, and grabbing the cadaver by the back feet, he dragged it out through the door, resentful that Babe gave him a dismissive look before continuing on with her chewing. Slowly, he trudged back down to the house and broke the news to Sabine who had just risen to make the coffee. As he knew she would, his wife burst into tears, refusing even to go up to the barn until Aubrey had taken the tiny body away and disposed of it on the edge of the muskeg, a skinful of veal and bones for the coyotes. The birth that afternoon of two more babies, one to Nellie and one to Jemima, made up for the loss, layering the story of Little Boy into the folds of time. The later drama of "The Loader Ballet" pushed the story back even further.

It was one of those spells where the weather had everybody fooled again, when it was blizzarding one minute and balmy the next, a series of sporadic bouts of cooperation with all those ranchers watching their calf crop come into the world. When he entered the big corral just after sunup one morning, Aubrey noticed a Quincy cow eyeing him up for size, and by the look on its face, it was more likely to be for a coffin than a suit. It was back down to minus eighteen, again, so any newborn not quickly up on its feet was liable to be well on its way to freezing. Quite apart from the physical discomfort to the animal, buyers always discounted any calves with frost-chewed ears and tail; it didn't do well in the feedlot, they said. They said a whole lot of things if they could find a way to take down the price, Aubrey thought sourly. He took a couple more tentative steps before the cow signaled to him that he had come far enough. At her feet lay a very still black blob, hoar frost dappling its coat. Clearly something had to be done, and fast.

Now among men, there are those who will never let themselves be intimidated. Aubrey was such a one, which might have explained his career in the police force. Even the most belligerent of criminals, the very worst of the bottom-feeders who mooched their days away in a life of crime, never saw fit to take him on. And as of this minute, he was not about to surrender meekly to some damn brown cow, no sir, not Aubrey Hanlon. He strode towards her, his cane raised to show her that here was a man not to be trifled with. Unfortunately, Honeydew, for that was the name on her tag, was unilingual, and evidently her language was not the same language as the cowman with whom she was having her current dealings. She charged. Not a fake run, not a three-yard, nice-to-get-to-know you dash, but a full-out, unequivocal charge. At times like these, cowmen are invariably astonished that their muscles react faster than the brain. Aubrey was over that plank fence and out of the corral in a split second, but not before a sharp horn had torn the seat out of his coveralls and his sweat pants beneath, exposing his pallid pink buttocks to the elements. Now he was mad, consumed with fury, especially when he saw Honeydew amble nonchalantly back to her blob with what he could swear was a grin on her face.

"I'll show you something, Missy May," he yelled at the top of his voice, "and it won't be my sweet pink cheeks either."

"Pardon me?" said Sabine, who had arrived on the scene unexpectedly. "Who is about to show what to whom?"

Not even bothering to reply, Aubrey turned around and displayed the damage to his coveralls and sweats. Sabine was horrified. "What happened?" she asked tremulously. Aubrey told her. "Then we'd best leave her alone," she said.

"And lose a perfectly good calf? Not bloody likely!" Aubrey growled, his machismo driving him on towards showdown. "You go bring the pickup. We'll drive up beside the calf, I'll jump out and huck it into the cab, and we'll get it into the hotbox. The bloody mother can stay the hell out until the baby is warmed up and we get some colostrum down its throat." Sabine knew enough not to say anything; dubious about the whole operation, the lack of militarily precise pre-planning and intelligence gathering, she dutifully went off to get the pickup. Aubrey went looking for the pitchfork, a better weapon than the cattle cane in this instance, his mutterings about Honeydew's ancestry only serving to stoke up the drama because the cow knew that he was up to no good.

Sabine arrived with the truck; Aubrey tossed the pitchfork in the back and then went to hold the corral gate open for Sabine to drive through. He closed the gate and climbed into the cab beside her. Potential problem number one: once they had the calf, he would have to get out of the truck to open the gate for Sabine. Potential problem number two, and one that had not yet become evident; Aubrey would have to pick up a calf likely to be very slippery with the fluid from the birthing process.

Mama cow was probably not going to be smiling benignly at him as he did so.

Sabine was on the ball. She drove up to the calf, nosing the mother to the driver's side with the truck. Aubrey was almost as brilliant, almost. While Honeydew was contemplating what sort of modification she was about to make to a beat-up 1975 Chevy half-ton, he opened the passenger door, jumped out and attempted to press-gang the calf into the cab. Like a rookie quarterback in the Manure Bowl, his move had merit but the execution fell short. The calf slipped out of his hands and finished up under the truck. If Aubrey's offense was well conceived, Honeydew's defense was no less so. She was at that passenger door in the blink of an eye. Aubrey's slithering underneath the vehicle to join the bewildered calf was dictated simply by the instinct for survival. Honeydew's taking up a hostile stance alongside was dictated simply by the killer instinct. And so now an impasse occurred, with poor Sabine inside the truck not daring to go forwards nor backwards because she knew her man and the calf were somewhere under the truck. Eventually, Aubrey was able to crawl to the far side of the truck away from Honeydew's legs, and there he made a bolt for it. Honeydew's immediate impulse to give chase was happily tempered by the stronger instinct to stay with her baby. Aubrey, now on top of the fence and seeing that the calf was so placed that Sabine would not run it over, signaled her to back up slowly, and Honeydew triumphantly reclaimed Blob.

In the military, troops are always encouraged to regroup, never to surrender. Aubrey was now fired right up. Like a general planning the full-frontal, winner-take-all assault, he told Sabine to drive the truck out and come back with the loader tractor. He would, he explained, pick up the calf and put it into the loader bucket, then he would get in next to it in case it decided to get up and fall out. She would close the grapple so that the steel fingers would offer him some protection from the Bitch Boss from Bonnyville, and voilà, they would drive the baby over to the barn. The strategy was solid: unrehearsed yes, but logical just as long as the enemy was logical, and it was achievable just as long as the execution of the plan occurred enough in sync that neither of them got their signals crossed.

"Let battle commence!" shouted Aubrey after making sure that Sabine knew exactly what was expected of her, and not appreciating that he was now as far away from the gentle-as-she-goes "Titford Technique" as he could get. Once again, he opened the corral gate for the tractor to pass through. Once again he had to shut it because he did not want the thirty or so others in the corral to make an early exit. Not that they would have, being bunched up in the far corner in silent bovine awe at what was going on before them.

Armed with his untested pitchfork, Aubrey climbed into the loader bucket, Sabine hoisted it up in the air, and they set off for mother and calf. Honeydew was courageous; she stood her ground, shaking her head defiantly. Aubrey was perplexed. Why did the noisy mechanical monster before her intimidate her not the slightest bit? Was it because she knew her nemesis Aubrey was up there in the bucket? If she showed no hesitancy, was he doomed to fail as before? Any manual on guerilla tactics would surely suggest staging some form of diversion at this point in the operation, but what? It was not as if he had any other troops at his disposal, and no amount of urging would ever convince Sabine to step out of the tractor and sprint across the corral as a decoy. Then he had it, and it was so simple!

He mouthed the words "Be ready!" to Sabine, who was secure in her cab. Then he threw down his tuque as far from the tractor as he could, his favorite rainbow-coloured tuque, the one with a splendid tassel hanging from the crown. Honeydew fell for it, pouncing on that tuque and stomping it into the ground with gusto. The tassel seemed particularly offensive to her because the more she stomped, the more that tassel stuck out of the cow mess in which it was mired. Aubrey motioned Sabine to drive forward, separating mother from baby with the tractor. He then signaled her to lower the bucket and open the grapple. Panicked, she got the first part right but left the grapple fully closed, which may have saved Aubrey's skin. Too late to re-communicate, Aubrey was out of that loader in a flash, latching onto that calf and hustling into the bucket with unnecessary difficulty because the grapple was still shut. In the meantime, Honeydew's passionate affair with the tuque suddenly ended when she clicked onto what was going on; she made for that loader and the man inside it like the wild beast she had become. Had it not been for the closed grapple, Aubrey would have had the pleasure of her company in the bucket. Gesturing madly at his wife sitting there transfixed in the tractor, Aubrey finally got her mind to engage and she hoisted him and the calf high over raging mama. So quick was the hoisting, with Sabine not much concerned with leveling the bucket as it went up, Aubrey landed in a sprawled heap over the sticky wet calf, but at least he was now safe—all gooey, but safe.

Honeydew, on the other hand, was either very impressed or very puzzled, and as Sabine backed over to the gate, mama cow reverted to frantic circling around where her baby had been lying. This gave Aubrey the time to get out of the now lowered bucket so that he could open the gate. He got it open, yes, but as Sabine was reversing through, the calf raised its head up in the bucket and let loose a mighty bawl. Honeydew spun around as if stung, and with a loud snort she left her station like the fabled Bullet Train to Hokkaido or Someplace Else. Aubrey did what he had sworn he would never do, something the Titford boys would never ever consider; he thrust that pitchfork into her chest as she came. It was an epiphany for the cow. It was the one moment in her life when she knew not so much that she had been bested by a very undistinguished-looking man, but that humankind in general, and this human in particular, should never again be challenged because humanity had access to WBDs,— Weapons of Bovine Destruction. She took off down the sorting alley that led off both the big corral and the barn, and took up a position at the far end. Aubrey felt bad, really bad, but self-defense is rarely a premeditated choice, regardless of what the animal rights folks might say. Besides, how would any of them handle a similar situation? What if a wild mama confronted them head on? Would they leave the calf to die in deference to mama's wishes? Or would they run, only to be trampled underfoot or tossed out of the corral? Aubrey now had time to shut the gate and open the barn door. Carefully, he picked the calf up out of the loader and took it inside. Honeydew was watching but without intent, seemingly mulling over her newfound respect for the main man in her life. And she stayed there for a couple of hours while her baby was warmed back to life in the hotbox.

Both Aubrey and Sabine never ceased to marvel at the effect of warmth on a comatose calf that any layman would have been quick to pronounce as dead. By the time they had let him out, him because he turned out to be a little bull, he was raring to go. Aubrey opened up the barn door; immediately, the calf spotted his mother and let loose a hungry moo. Honeydew's ears pricked up; she was into the barn in an instant and her baby's troubles were over. He was licked and fussed over like a long lost son, which in cow terms indeed he was. Interestingly enough, from that day on, Honeydew while not always friendly was at least respectful. Surprisingly, though, there are still those who insist cows have no memory.

Dramas never come singly down on the farm, but then "Murphy's Book of Abstract Farm Laws and Probabilities" could have told Aubrey that. This time, at least the weather was benign at a balmy minus eight. Sabine had noticed the heifer, the one she had named Papadum, off by herself in a corner of the corral. At two in the afternoon, the timing was a bonus, too. She urged Aubrey to put her in the barn. Aubrey protested. There was no need to panic he said, but then, as he often had to do, he acknowledged that with Sabine as the power behind his throne, he might have been quite happy sitting under the North Saskatchewan River bridge sipping on a bottle of red grape juice in a paper bag with a few buddies. So, largely for the sake of peace, he caved in and they walked her quietly into the barn. An hour later, ignoring her husband's very voluble opinion that Papadum had at least two weeks to go before she calved, Sabine walked up to the barn to check on her. The water bag was out but poor little Papadum, totally confused about what was going on with her body, just could not settle. Sabine played it by the book and decided to give her some more time. She returned to the house and informed her husband that the heifer that had at least two weeks to go was in the early stages of calving. He looked up from the paper, muttered some inanity about wifely intuition, and buried his face in the sports page.

The next time Sabine went up to the barn, she knew they were in trouble. There were no legs protruding where there should have been two, and Papadum herself was decidedly unhappy. It was time to put Aubrey's nose to the grindstone. He was only too happy to oblige, no doubt in some hope that his wife would not crow too loudly about his underdeveloped cow sense. Together, he and Sabine coaxed Papadum into the head-gate.

Then Sabine had him put on the usual vast plastic "surgical sleeve" that reached all the way to his armpit. Aubrey was thinking at the time that if the gloves came any bigger, he might just as well have climbed into one and crawled his way into the cow. Once Sabine had lubricated his arm with mineral oil, he launched himself on his voyage of discovery, reaching deep into the cow's vulva and feeling his way over the calf's rump and up to its rib cage. This prompted Papadum to resume her contractions. Aubrey was astounded at the force, his arm crushed severely as the heifer endeavored to expel both him and her calf. He pushed in further after another mighty contraction and rectified the problem, pulling the two back legs out from underneath the calf's bum and realigning them.

"The little fellow is alive," he shouted exultantly, now pulling on the two legs in time to Papadum's contractions. Sabine insisted Aubrey attach the calving chains, one to each leg, double looping them as Pete had shown him in order to spread the pressure on the legs. With him on the end of one chain and Sabine at the end of the other, they both began pulling downwards. They kept the pressure on as slowly a black rump broke through, then the whole body. The calf dropped with a thump into the straw, its eyes wide open as if trying to memorize this unorthodox entry into a foreign world. Without waiting a second, Sabine had bent over him and was sticking a piece of straw first down one nostril then down the other, prompting the tiny beast to take great gulps of air. They then dragged the baby over to a neutral corner and let the mother out. She took one look at this alien creature that she had brought into the world, took one hesitant sniff as if trying to determine what connection it might have to her, and retreated to stand as far away from it as she could possibly get. Aubrey was wondering what to do next when Sabine suddenly went out, only to come back a few seconds later with a coffee can half full of chop which she proceeded to scatter over the calf's body. Papadum could not resist; she moved in and began to lick the chop off the body of her calf. This initiated the natural bonding process and within an hour or two, cow and calf were inseparable.

"Where did you learn that?" asked Aubrey, grateful that nothing more would have to be done.

"I read it in the 'Calving Special' of *Cattlemen* magazine, last night. The farmer who sent in the tip says it works for him ninety per cent of the time."

"Okay," said Aubrey, "finally I have to admit that you're good, very good."

From there, the calving season morphed into an out-of-body, out-of-mind experience where hours melted into days, daylight seeped into darkness, and legs extended mechanically to carry Aubrey or Sabine out of the house and up to the corrals and the barn for yet another check. Stitched sometimes too boldly into the interminable hours was the weather, naggingly long days of cold with Aubrey praying for the warm caress of a Chinook wind. How the hell did those folks ever survive where there was no Chinook, he wondered. There were brief moments of triumph when pallid frosted sunlight gave way to a full burst of warmth, but then not despair so much as resignation snuck right back in when the warmth lapsed into uncompromising frigidity. Sleep was sporadic; snatched and deep as the body ached for peace, only to be disturbed again because Sweetpea was birthing in a snow bank or Mirella looked like she might have a problem. The mind gave up on thinking, was incapable of thinking. It floated on remote above those trudging feet, not bothering to focus on anything any more.

At least we only have ninety head, Sabine was thinking.

Thank heavens there are only ninety head, Aubrey was thinking.

Chapter Nine
PERFORMANCE DATA
AND LAWN CLIPPINGS

Spring, that time of year when a bovine gal's thoughts turn to … well, not romance, exactly; there is none of the "fluff and stuff" of romance when it comes to animal courtship, cattle courtship, anyway. There are no Hallmark cards, no sweet nothings on Valentine's Day, no kissing beneath the mistletoe—just a hustle and a tussle in the meadow, a bump and a grind by the pasture gate. There is no denying Taurus, no playing hard to get, for he has been genetically engineered or better yet, genetically designed to be single-minded about his business. If he is not, he is quickly consigned to the dog food trail.

As far as Sabine was concerned, with her history of urban living and conventional niceties of flirtation and amour, when it came to the basics of cattle breeding, everything had been reduced to dry clinical science. Bull sellers sold bulls touting their virility, their masculinity, their libido and capacity. All sorts of numbers might be provided to claim a particular bull had this or that fine trait; they even trumpeted the size of the animal's scrotum, for heaven's sake! There was no doubt about it; it was a darn good thing humanity had evolved beyond the cow pasture, Sabine was given to thinking. Not to downplay these things, all of the science and of course all of the numbers; she would never do that. Carrying capacity and conception rates were as important to her as to the next livestock producer, had to be if the Hanlon operation was to remain viable. But then again, all this circling of the bulls and the cows, was it all *that* different from the singles bar or an Internet dateline? Had the so-called "party animal" of either sex evolved that much further from the bull and the cow? So much for the romance, then, when it was all so scientifically and biologically predictable.

Not that Sabine saw the need to share such thoughts with her spouse. Why would she? He was a bull, unlikely to understand the nuances, the finer points, of playing the game. No sir, all he was interested in was scoring a goal and retiring a winner. Men were like that. But, as in all business agricultural, she began to take a keen interest, no longer content to allow Aubrey to choose the bulls they needed for breeding on his own. And as with so many other things, not only did she read extensively about breeding and genetics, but she also proved she had a keen eye and an open mind. So it was that the first bull Aubrey found himself closing in on during a visit to an Angus breeder was rejected by his wife out of hand.

"Look at him, Aub, he's way too feminine," she said, not quite believing that she was actually saying it. Aubrey looked first at her in disbelief and then a seventieth time at the bull, and now he could see it. The smaller head and finer bones would probably not give them the heavy, chunky calves they were looking for. They needed more weight on their calves, and this bull was not going to provide it. The bull seller, believing that he had pretty much clinched a deal, began grasping at straws.

"He would sure make a dandy heifer bull," he almost pleaded, inadvertently admitting that the bull was indeed deficient in the masculinity department, as Sabine had said he was.

"Yes, but we won't be breeding many heifers," said Aubrey. "We know where he is though, so we'll keep him in mind." This was the line that told the seller that the deal was as good as dead. Know-all women, the bull man was thinking. Too feminine...as if! But he knew in his heart of hearts that she was right.

The world of bulls and breeding is a world apart, the Hanlons discovered. First of all, and predictably, every breeder made the claim that his or her breed of cattle was the chosen one; the one that would give you the perfect cross with the cows you presently owned. If you went a progressive step further and bought some of their high-priced heifers that just happened to be available for sale, then you would upgrade your herd immeasurably. Second, no two producers saw the exact same things in a bull, nor in a breed for that matter. Charolais, Galloway, Gelbvieh, Angus, Welsh Black, Hereford, Blonde d'Aquitaine, Limousin, ("don't forget Limo!" that old reprobate Ernie Campbell would start whining); every breed had its distinctive features, with every breed association trumpeting their own breed's particular virtues while trashing the opposition.

"If you think that's bad," said Pete to Aubrey, "try joining one of the associations. The people in them are more often than not worse than their animals for fighting and farting and generally carrying on, let me tell you! Mix a bunch of blue-rinse, old time matriarchs with a couple of born again cowboys, throw in a couple of college types, a hustler or two, a dumb old farmer like you and me, a pair of techno-nerds, three mavericks, four bullshitters, a partridge in a pear tree, and you get the kind of love-in that makes a Conservative convention in Calgary look like a tea party. So my advice is, by all means, buy purebred bulls, but stay the hell away from the purebred business."

"Oh, and one more thing while I'm up on my soapbox, always remember that buying a bull is nothing more than an unlicensed form of gambling. You never know what you've got until the calves start hitting the ground. Treat everything you hear with a grain of salt because there's a whole lot of mythology being peddled out there. People will tell you Limousin are ornery, Charolais are hard calvers, Blondes have no hair and no bags, Maine eat too much. Most of it is stuff and nonsense. Sure, there's a bit that might be true, like Angus can be feisty. So if you're interested in a certain breed, I'm telling you to check with folks who've used the breed commercially. Ask to see the calves if you can."

Sabine did not hear this. As she was always wont to do, she went her own way and fell in love with the so-called exotic Blonde d'Aquitaine, a lesser-known breed in Canada. Her interest was heightened by the fact that with their expansion, the Hanlon operation was in the market for two new bulls. Both Aubrey and Sabine had read all about hybrid vigor, and both acknowledged the urgency of putting more weight on their calves. So once again, they found themselves traipsing around a variety of farm and auction bull sales in a determined effort to research for themselves what was out there. Many times they were astounded at what people paid for a bull, and did not pay, which bulls were sold, and which were passed over. They heard the fantastic claims from Stetsoned auctioneers who then went on to make the same claims for every bull that walked through the ring. They watched people stampeded into buying when they would have done far better to wait, and they saw others who waited too long only to curse themselves for being overly cautious, too stingy or too much asleep at the wheel. The Hanlons learned their lessons well. They settled on a bull-buying procedure that would work for them: not a sophisticated scientific process that charted EPDs (Expected Progeny Differences) and other such data, but a procedure that would work for them within the confines of their own knowledge base, a procedure without the danger of information overload.

Whether they were looking at bulls lined up in sales pens at an auction mart or gathered in groups in some farmer's corral, they would list their preferences individually, neither one of them letting the other know what he or she was thinking. Then, if they were looking at a private deal, they would establish the price a breeder was hoping for, without giving away their selections. Invariably, the breeder would then say that price depended upon the bull selected. Of course, if that information was given away, the seller would say something like, "you people have a good eye; you picked the best animal in the string." To dampen down a breeder's ardour for a deal, Aubrey would announce beforehand that no decision would be made on the spot. It was his way of lowering the potential of their being seen as shark bait. Only when they had gone through the offering independently would Aubrey and Sabine compare notes, and the more they got versed in the process, the more their choices were unanimous.

"Ach, man and wife in this game should always end up thinking as one," said Jeannie, "with the odd exception, of course."

One spring Saturday, Aubrey and Sabine decided to attend the annual "All Breeds Bull Sale" at Cole's Auction Mart in Rocky Mountain House to see if anything might take their fancy. On this particular day, a Blonde d'Aquitaine breeder from New Sarepta had brought in a string of breeding bulls that he had on offer. If any one of them fetched a price above his reserve of sixteen hundred dollars then he would accept the bid and let the bull go, although such intentions were kept to himself. How else was one to get an unknown breed more accepted into the mainstream of the commercial cattle business, particularly at a time when the market was so flat? What Aubrey saw was a distinguished-looking gentleman, older and bearded, the gray lending him the air of a Socrates or a Methuselah, a face seemingly steeped in both wisdom and knowledge. He was inside one of the pens grooming a big tan yearling bull by the name of Amber Nero, so the placard tacked onto the pen gate proclaimed.

"And how are you folks today?" the deep melodic voice greeted them, the eyes twinkling either with amusement or a deep zest for life.

"Fine, thank you," said Sabine demurely, hoping at the same time that her standoffishness would deter any major assault.

"That's sure a nice bull you have there," Aubrey felt compelled to add in an effort to counter the effect of his wife's cold front.

"He is nice, isn't he? Actually, he's a real pet. I'll be sorry to see him go, eh big boy?" The man rubbed the bull fondly on his massive neck.

"Are they always this quiet?" Sabine found herself asking in spite of herself. "I mean he seems so gentle."

"Mine are generally quiet. But it all comes down to how you handle your animals, doesn't it? Treat them like rodeo stock and they'll act like rodeo stock, right?"

"Are the other bulls all as gentle as this fellow?" Sabine persisted, really struck by the animal's passivity.

"Well, I have to say this guy has always been the friendliest. But yes, they are all quiet, all halter-broken, but they'll react like any other bull if you do something to annoy them. Say, why don't you come on in and have a talk with him?"

Now here was a challenge Sabine had never anticipated, and one she could have done without. Conventional wisdom had always told her that animals could detect a person's fear and would likely react negatively to it; and here she was, about to step forward and pet a seventeen hundred pound bull in an enclosed space. All she could do was walk forward, holding out her hand tentatively as if she was about to greet a dog by holding its paw. The bull turned, looked at her in appraisal, sniffed her hand, and then licked it as if to say she was all right and that she had passed the test. Emboldened with delight, the fear still there but in check, Sabine took another step forward and patted the bull on the shoulder. The bull shivered momentarily and then went on chewing his cud, totally unconcerned. Sabine knew at that precise moment that she was in love. Aubrey knew that Sabine was in love. Stewart Anderson of Amber Blondes, New Sarepta, knew she was in love, but he did nothing to take advantage, much to Aubrey's relief. Finally Sabine withdrew, silently making a prolonged assessment of the five other bulls in the string before coming back to study Nero some more.

"I hope you make a bid on him," said Mr. Anderson, handing her a sheet of the bull's performance data. "I really want him to go to a good home," he added, finding the one sales pitch that would reach into Sabine's heart. Aubrey mumbled something appropriate, and off they went to look over a large batch of Charolais; some Horned Herefords; a couple of Pete's feisty Anguses; a huge, five-year old Limousin; and a six-pack of Shorthorns for a total of thirty-five bulls up for sale. Aubrey was not gung-ho about any of them, and while he had to admit he was impressed with Sabine's new heartthrob, Nero, he was wary of getting into a breed most people had barely heard of. How was it, then, that he and his wife circled all of the pens only to end up back where they started, at the Blonde pens? Mr. Anderson was in deep discussion with other potential buyers down the alley, and there was nobody at Nero's pen. Sabine stopped at the gate.

"Come here, big boy. Come and see mom," she said sweetly.

Aubrey could not believe his eyes. The huge animal turned and gave her a look as if to say, "and where'd you get to?" before ambling over to the gate, once again sniffing then licking Sabine's outstretched hand.

"Let's get out of here, the sale is about to start," said Aubrey too hurriedly, clearly loathe to allow Sabine to get too involved with the bull. Sabine, on the other hand, sensed that their destinies and that of the bull were to be linked somehow, but she dared not risk a total rejection of Nero by a husband who was too obviously holding back.

They entered the tiered sale hall and found a seat high above and to one side of the sale ring, Sabine getting the distinct feeling that Aubrey had deliberately made for a spot less visible to the auctioneer and the ring man soliciting bids. The sale began with the usual bevy of goats, a dozen or so weaner pigs, another dozen feeder pigs, two gigantic mama sows close to farrowing, and a lone donkey, someone's discarded pet it seemed. Finally the bull sale itself was announced, with Clayton Cole, the ultimate in auctioneers, playing up to the crowd by pandering unashamedly to them, telling the folks how very soon they would be into some of the best bull power they had ever seen, and all produced right here in our own backyard.

"Folks," he carried on, "a lot of us may not be that good-lookin', but we can sure produce a bull or two that can stand up with the best anyone has to offer, and I mean anyone." It was a masterful performance that left the crowd warm and fuzzy, and hopefully prepared to open up their wallets.

First up was the supposed centerpiece of the sale, the batch of Charolais. To the Hanlons, prices soared or dropped for no apparent reason until eventually they were all gone. Then in came the two Horned Herefords, massive beasts with horns so intimidating to the uninitiated. Both went for around three thousand dollars apiece, near double what Aubrey intended to pay for any bull he bought. Next up were the Blonde d'Aquitaine; Aubrey did not even need to look over at his wife to know how she had suddenly tensed up. The first two Blondes came in as a pair. Majestic they were, as if above all this clamor of humanity conducting its commerce at their expense. They stood aloof, and to the surprise of many, they sold as a pair for a total of four thousand dollars. Then a single came in, but even though he was as majestic and as well behaved as the others, he did not attract any excitement so he was passed out as a no-sale. The next two came in, again as a pair, but with the auctioneer calling "choice".

"Bid on the one you want boys," announced Clayton Cole. "If you want 'em both at the same price, take 'em both. All right now, who'll give me twenty-five, twenty-five hund'ed, twenty-five per bull…?"

Bidding climbed erratically to eighteen hundred and stalled. Clayton Cole switched off the microphone, leaned over his counter, and consulted with the breeder parading his animals around the ring. Back to the microphone he went. "They're here to sell boys. Real dandy bulls. Come on now, you want to put meat on them calves; well now, here's your chance."

Clayton's patter squeezed another two hundred from the dubious crowd, with a buyer taking his choice of the bulls for an even two thousand. Bidding recommenced on the remaining animal. Back up to eighteen hundred it went before petering out.

"Sold. Eighteen hundred," yelled Clayton enthusiastically, knowing that he had done better than the breeder had hoped for.

Sabine hardly dared to look as Amber Nero was led in. Aubrey had to again confess to himself, he liked the bull best of all the bulls he had seen, but then if his wife liked him as much as she claimed, then she would undoubtedly go ahead and bid on him. Clayton Cole had to work hard to get things started. The bull was so massive for a two-year old that he seemed to scare people off. Maybe that was why bidding died at a measly sixteen hundred. Sabine saw Mr. Anderson look up to where they were sitting, saw him turn away in resignation. This would be another bull he would have to take back home.

"Stewart would like eighteen hundred," announced Clayton. "If you can use him for that and you change your mind, go out back and talk to him. He's easy to get along with." And Nero was gone.

"You didn't bid," Aubrey said flatly to his wife.

"I thought you didn't want me to," Sabine replied.

"I thought we had agreed. You get to buy one that you like. I get to buy one that I like."

"Why didn't you say that before?" Sabine was as angry with herself as she was with her husband.

"Well, if you want him that bad, let's go and talk to the man out back." It was Aubrey who was clearly getting off the fence and making the decision to buy.

"Oh do let's," Sabine suddenly came alive, uncaring that they had to endure all the stares and good-natured grumbling as they pushed their way out of the packed seating. When they got to the pens, Stewart Anderson was in a somewhat heated discussion with a giant of a man trying to bully him into taking sixteen hundred dollars for Nero.

"I mean, look at it, why don't you? And look at the bull. There's no way you'll ever get more than sixteen for him, no way. He's got a sway back, and his feet are no screaming hell either." The man rested his hands on his hips like a gunslinger about to conclude unpleasant business. Sabine had heard enough to know what was going on, and Sabine was desperate.

"Eighteen hundred," she called from down the alleyway.

"Sold to the lady with the gorgeous smile," shouted Mr. Anderson. "I wanted to be sure he was going to a decent home," he added for good measure.

"Humph, too many foolish folks around with money to burn," grumped the pseudo-cowman. "Okay, I'll give you two thousand for him, no more."

"Maybe you didn't hear me," said Mr. Anderson, all but gloating. "The bull is sold. You, sir, could have bought him in the sale for two thousand, sway back and all."

"And so could she," thundered the man in disbelief. "So could she. Tell you what, I'll give you twenty-three; that's two thousand three hundred."

"My friend," said Mr. Anderson as if he was lecturing a rebellious schoolboy, "I said the word 'sold', and that's what I mean. The bull is sold. Now, may I wish you a good day?" He turned his back on the man, the cue for the man to move off muttering some inanity about "dumb blondes anyway."

"Actually, she's a brunette," Aubrey called after him, determined to have the last word, much to Mr. Anderson's amusement. Thus, a bull was bought and a lasting friendship born; the bull was destined to be a mainstay of the Hanlon spread for as long as the Hanlons were farming. Not that they were to know this at the time.

Now it was Aubrey's turn to buy a bull, and he was more enamored of Gelbvieh than Blonde at this point in time. Much more common than Blonde d'Aquitaine, he had a much bigger field from which to make his selection, which meant that he and Sabine took in more farm visits and sales than ever. Ironically, the bull Aubrey finally settled on was no more than thirty miles from home. He was another "N" bull, Narcissus.

"What a lovely name," gushed Sabine. "Does he like the look of himself or what?"

The breeder, a soft-spoken older man with decades in the cattle business, seemed to hesitate, but only for a moment. "Let me tell you a little story about him. If you choose not to take him after I tell you, why that'll be all right too."

Their curiosity was piqued.

"See, I had this, this ... I'm gonna call him pretend farmer come into the yard last week, looking to buy a yearling bull. He pulls into the yard and says, 'You got any yearlin's for sale?' No greetings, no how's your father, nothin' like that. Sure thing, says I. It so happens I've got ten of them in the field over there. 'Let's go take a look at 'em,' he says. 'Sure thing,' I say, expecting him to get out of his shiny new truck and walk. No such thing! He's one of them hotshot oilmen with a shiny black oilman's truck, all fixed up with chrome and lights and what-not."

"I know the style," said Aubrey, egging him on.

"So he tells me to jump in and we head down to the field. Now, it so happens those bulls are down at the far end, about a hundred yards down the field. 'We'll drive over there', he tells me, 'if you care to open the gate.' So that's what we do, we drive over. We get out. The bulls come over for the bucket of grain I brought with me, and that fellah, he starts yakkin' ten to the dozen. The more he flaps his gums, the more I realize he ain't got a clue about cattle. Just then his cell phone goes off. Well, he makes it clear he ain't about to have some dumb old farmer listenin' in on his oilman conversation, so he walks off a-ways so I can't hear what he's sayin'. While I'm standin' there, I see where a staple has popped out of a fence post. Seein' as I always carry a couple of staples with me in my pocket, and I happen to carrying a hammer, I go on over to fix it. Meantime, the bulls have finished up the grain and they're makin' out like they're friskier than all get out. I fix the fence and turn around. The fellah is still yakkin' away on his fancy phone, and that's when I see this bull standin' there, lookin' at his reflection in the truck door, it bein' so clean an' shiny an' all. Well, next thing I know, that young stud, he took after that door, givin' it a darn good butt with his head. I guess he thought he was lookin' at the competition. Well, that oilman, he goes ballistic, drops his phone, and runs after that doggone bull like he was his very worst enemy. Damn but it was funny to watch, put me in mind of a great big bullfrog thinkin' he can run. Pretty quick he's out of breath and comes back to tell me I'm gonna be payin' for a new door. 'Nah,' says I. 'Not me. See, you could've walked down here in the first place, so you're plumb out of luck.' So now he's real pissed off. He gets back in his truck in a hell of a hurry, starts up mad as hell, then spinning his wheels like a young buck, he does a racing turn to tell me what he thinks of me, and be damned if he doesn't go and run over his phone, not that he realizes it right at that moment. So there he is heading over to the gate when he remembers his dang phone. He does a fancy turn and comes screaming back to where he dropped it. It's still there all right, in a thousand little pieces. Well now, you should'a seen the look on that man's face. He gives me the sex and travel sign, screams a bunch of stuff about me and my ancestors, jumps back into his truck, and takes off flyin'. But now he's so darn stoked up, he doesn't even see the gate before he has driven through it. It was one of them wire gates we all have; you know, four strands of wire held up with four or five sticks cut out of the bush. Well, that's okay by me cuz I can sure rig up another gate in a hurry. Problem was, though, all the wires broke 'cept the top one. That top piece of wire, why it just lifted up some, scraped over his hood, up over his windshield and sheared all them fancy little clearance lights off of his roof. So that's why I had to call that bull Narcissus."

"We'll take him regardless," said Aubrey immediately. "I like his history."

"Just don't go parking your fancy truck too close to him, that's all I ask."

"We don't own a fancy truck. Besides, our cows have already put enough dents in our old truck, so it would not make any difference," added Sabine laughing. And so it came to pass that Narcissus joined the Hanlon family, although it was clear from day one that he did not see things this way himself. As soon as they got him home, Aubrey realized Narcissus' problem; he was full of adolescent aggression. Billeted in a corral with Nero and an older Angus named Hobo, all Narcissus wanted to do was to fight. Bellowing and snorting, he first decided to take on Hobo. It did not take Aubrey long to conclude he had to get his new bull out of there before he got himself killed, but how? Exactly how was he to persuade two nearly one-ton meaty monsters to cease and desist? Hobo solved the problem for him. Tired of the young Gelbvieh usurping his afternoon siesta, he suddenly spun around like a ballet dancer and caught Narcissus in the mid-section, literally bulldozing him through the plank fence before going back to his corner where the planks trapped the warmth of the sun. Aubrey was not quick enough. Narcissus made it back through the ragged hole in the fence before he could get his mind in gear. Only now it seemed that he was all of a sudden deeply respectful of Hobo. He decided he would challenge Nero instead, his second big mistake of the hour. Nero was both taller and heavier, and clearly intolerant of fools. Almost with clinical calculation, he maneuvered the Gelbvieh into a corner and then knocked him down, pinning the aggressor's head to the ground with his own massive head. Aubrey could have sworn he heard Narcissus say "uncle" before Nero released him and walked off to the bale feeder. The young bull had learned the lesson of hierarchy; from now on, although he was the one full of baloney and bluster, never again did he take on his two corral companions.

The Hanlons had advertised for pasture all spring and very little had come up for offer: a quarter section with no fences, another with no water, an eighty-acre "gem" that turned out to be mostly swamp, and a barren half-section that showed no evidence of grass whatsoever. They were on the verge of panic when the phone rang one evening. Aubrey answered to hear a man's voice saying he had a quarter section of pasture for rent at a good price, provided the caller could pasture ten of his own cows there as a part of the deal.

"So what breed of bull are you running?" asked the voice.

"Gelbvieh, Blonde, Angus, take your pick."

"Gimme the Gelbvieh and two thousand and the place is yours. But you'd better come on out and take a look first. I don't want no bullshit later on, if you get what I mean." They exchanged names and Aubrey took down the directions.

Aubrey and Sabine went out the very next day. The yard was immaculate, the driveway graveled in red shale, outdoor lights everywhere around a house that was not a house but a mansion.

"Oil money," Sabine huffed as soon as they pulled in.

"Oil money," echoed Aubrey looking at the company logo on the over-muscled pickup, parked outside the three-car garage.

A man came out of house; the sort of man to whom Sabine took an instant dislike, the sort of man who only acknowledged a woman as if she was an appendage of the husband or a piece of steak depending on the circumstances. He was dressed like the ultimate urban cowboy that real cowboys loved to hate: big black Stetson, oversize to match his belt buckle, his pickup and his ego; stone-washed jeans; checkered cotton shirt; and a belt big enough to corral a whole team of horses, yet probably necessary to keep an expansive belly from straying southwards. The graying sideburns and the droopy moustache together with the shiny western boots completed an image of counterfeit cragginess.

"Sam Sloan," said the man shaking Aubrey's hand and trying his best to break it.

"Aubrey Hanlon, and my wife Sabine."

Sam Sloan tipped his hat presumptuously and nodded over at Sabine, as if approving of a good man's horse. Then he launched straight into business, making it somehow clear that this was as close to his castle as these shit-kickers were likely to get.

"If we take a ride in your truck, I can show you around the place so you folks know what all is here. You'll have to do a bit of fencing, I'll tell you that now, so the critters will all stay in. Good thing the neighbors all have crops on all our boundaries."

Not a good thing at all, Aubrey was thinking as he pictured his cows breaking out and chewing down the neighbor's bumper barley crop.

Sabine did the subservient thing and got into the back part of the cab, not for the sake of subservience but because she had no desire to be in close proximity to a cologned John Wayne look-alike. Besides, that left the passenger side free for his considerable bulk.

The "bit of fencing" that needed to be done was an understatement of epic proportions. A full day's work would have been more like it, morning clear through until night. "I'll make sure you get all the posts and the wire you need," Mr. Sloan assured them. He was as good as his word, but only after a half dozen calls from Aubrey put him in the mood. As for his ten cows, they were run-of-the-mill; no better nor worse than the renters', but you would never have known that after hearing Mr. Sloan talk of them.

"You know, for the kind of real quality cow herd I'm building up, I think a Gelbvieh bull is the answer. Looked into buying one of them myself, a Gelbvieh bull that is, but I figured hell, for ten cows, I might just as well see if I could get a renter's bull to do the job and save a few dollars."

When they had done their tour of the place, much of it bush and muskeg, Sloan said they needed to come back to the house and meet the woman.

"See, me, I'm just a little old consultant in the oil patch. I'm always either on the road or in the damn plane. She's the one who holds the fort while I'm gone."

When they pulled back into the yard, Sloan said, "You folks wait right here, and I'll go get my Ethel."

At least Sam made some effort to be personable: Ethel did not even try. Bearing her wrinkles like the scars of battle, the nearest she came to a smile was a scowl. All decked out in her Eddie Bauer gardening gear, she could not even remove the gloves when it came to shaking hands with the people. "As long as you folks keep your animals in, you and I will get along quite fine, I'm sure," she growled her warning flatly. "And by the way, we expect payment in advance. I have no desire to chase after people who think they deserve something for nothing."

"You see...," Sam began his effort to soften the landing.

"That'll be quite fine," Sabine smiled back using Ethel's words of two seconds previous. "I just happen to have a cheque in my purse. Who would you like the cheque made out to?"

"Ethel Sloan," Ethel's response was instant. She was probably already calculating the number of bags of steer manure she could buy at Home Depot with the money, Sabine was thinking unkindly. "Oh, and by the way," Ethel saw fit to add, "I'm sure you won't have any objection if I take the grass clippings and throw them to the animals when I'm done mowing the lawn."

"That shouldn't be a problem," said Aubrey automatically. How sweet was his innocence!

When it came time, the first day of June to be precise, Narcissus was sent to Sam Sloan's along with twenty Hanlon cows, most likely to have been bred by this time because Narcissus had been with them since the third week in April. So the ten fresh Sloan cows were an added bonus he had not counted on. Never a bull that was lacking in libido, he acquitted himself with gusto as the days slipped away into a lazy warm summer.

The call, the famous call came on June 30 at one o'clock in the afternoon, just as Aubrey and Sabine were finishing up lunch. How could they ever forget it? No greetings, no how are you, no conventional niceties, just a "Get your sorry asses over here right now. Your bull is in my garden and he is defecating everywhere." Ethel's voice was barely a voice at all; it was a screech, something akin to the noise emitted by an alarmed African Hornbill when its nest is under siege. Such things happened. But how on earth had he got himself into the garden? He could not have pushed his way through the chain link fence, could he? Maybe he had somehow popped the gate latch? At any rate, both Hanlons were overcome with extreme guilt when they arrived at the Sloan's; they were just in time to see it all happen.

The Sloans had a large glassed-in solarium on the southern side of their mansion, home to Ethel's prize collection of exotic plants. Standing outside was the bull, shaking his head in agitation. Ethel was inside doing much the same thing and gesticulating frantically in her bid to make the bull go away. Any normal bull would have probably wandered off without further ado, but this was Narcissus, over-zealous, feisty Narcissus, who had a thing about his own image—leave alone any competition. When he had spotted his own reflection in the glass, it wasn't his image he was looking at, it was a mean SOB'ing bull come to lay claim to his babes. Things might yet have been okay had Ethel's wild movements on the inside not convinced him that the bull in the reflection was in fact challenging him directly. For Narcissus, the best mode of defense was offense; he charged.

"Oh Lord, have mercy on us all," Sabine whispered to nobody in particular.

"Oh dear," said Aubrey, getting out of the truck.

It was Ethel's great good fortune that the sturdy wooden bench loaded with all sorts of plant life toppled over, presenting Narcissus with a solid obstruction if he chose to go forwards. Not that the showering of glass had done anything to improve his mood, but then somehow, he was not quite sure how, he must have vanquished his challenger for his challenger had vanished. With slivers of glass needling him all along his back, and hearing from the inside a stream of invective akin to the skirl of poorly played bagpipes, he did the smart thing and departed, casually shaking off the glass as he made off through the open gate back into the pasture.

The bull's retreat may have been reasonably graceful in the circumstances, but that only made room for Ethel to fill the gap as it were. She was beside herself with fury, hysterically spewing profanities like the most seasoned of troopers, cussing cows and bulls and all people associated with animals so filthy that they shat in their own food, and who was going to pay for the mess, that's what she wanted to know. Barely pausing to take a breath, Ethel had simply lost it. While Aubrey could only stand by in awe, Sabine tried her best to reach out by talking softly, but it was a fruitless effort, Ethel's tongue was amok. Finally Sabine had had enough.

"Madam!" she screamed.

There was a momentary glitch in the spate of colourful language before it deluged on as before. It was time for Sabine to go into action. She climbed over the debris, spotted one of the coffee cans, half full of water, dotted about the place to provide humidity to the plants, and threw the contents directly into Ethel's face. The torrent of words stopped abruptly, Ethel's eyes wide and uncomprehending.

"Now," said Sabine softly. "Let's talk about this like normal people, shall we?" There was no mistaking the steel in her voice, no point in Ethel re-launching her attack on a foe so unintimidated. "You left the garden gate open, didn't you?" Sabine continued.

"Ugh, me? No, no, I was in here." Ethel was groping for words now, her brain trying to grapple with this new problem, how to deal with her own mistake without admitting to it. Droplets of water were coursing down her cheeks. "I was in here all the time," she added.

"Does your husband happen to be around?" Aubrey intervened.

"No, he's over in Kazakhstan," said Ethel. "He comes back next week."

"So you're the only one around?"

"Yes, me and my two little dogs that your stupid bull has so badly traumatized they'll probably never get over it."

"Probably not," said Aubrey flatly.

"Did you leave the gate open?" Sabine persisted.

"No. I just told you, I was in here."

"So how come there are fresh lawn clippings in the pasture, just the other side of the gate?" Aubrey picked up the interrogation.

"They, er they're from yesterday." Ethel obviously sensed she was floundering, but she was not about to cave in to a bunch of cattle herders.

Aubrey walked not through the gate to the clippings but to the riding mower parked to one side. The engine was still hot.

Ethel now found herself in the same predicament as the bull ten minutes before; her only mode of defense was offense. Her voice rising, she attacked. "I want you to know, one way or another, you people are going to pay for this, all of it. My husband won't like this at all. I mean, you can't have other people's animals just wandering into your yard and trashing your house. My husband is very good friends with a lawyer by the name of…"

"Honey, have a talk with this lady and see if you can get her to make sense," Aubrey interrupted. "I've got the camera in the truck. I'll go grab it and take a few pictures, just for the record."

This clearly disconcerted Mrs. Sloan. "You can take all the damn pictures you want, Mister. It won't change the fact that it was your bull that trashed my home," she yelled after him.

"Mrs. Sloan," Sabine said quietly, "no matter how clever our bull happens to be, he is not clever enough to open a gate latch like yours."

"Oh, so now I'm a liar, is that it?"

"Mrs. Sloan, maybe this is the time for you to tell the truth. You see, my husband is a retired police officer. If in fact you were cutting the lawn, then you would be wise to say so. If you took the clippings out into the pasture and forgot to close the gate when you came back through, you need to say so."

There was no doubt about it, Ethel and the bull had much in common. "You had better get the hell off my property, you and your so-called retired police officer. And by the way, I'll be phoning the RCMP if you don't leave now."

"The number is 845-2881, area code 403. Or you can call 911 if you like," said Aubrey, hearing all this when he came back with his camera. "I'll just take a few pictures, and then we'll be delighted to leave your property." What could Ethel do but retreat inside. Aubrey took his pictures. The incident was over, for now!

Chapter Ten
STAND UP AND ASK THE QUESTIONS

Pete and Jeannie had always said that when you rent property, either as a renter or as a landlord, the strangest things can happen, things that even a wild imagination could not conjure up. "No matter what sort of agreement you have, written or verbal, you can never make provision for changing circumstances," said Jeannie. So it was that Aubrey and Sabine awaited the fallout from the Narcissus incident, and waited.

It took a full two weeks for the bill to arrive. *For damages incurred while renter's bull was on the rampage in landlord's domicile...$2000.* If the bill was short and to the point, so was the accompanying letter signed by Neil Symington of Symington and Dodd, Barristers and Solicitors, Red Deer. An iron fist in a velvet glove, it suggested tersely that Mr. Samuel A. Sloan would seek legal recourse if Mr. And Mrs. A. Hanlon did not see fit to settle the matter within thirty days.

Sabine was highly perturbed, Aubrey not in the slightest. "Let 'em go for it," he said. "They haven't got a leg to stand on." He was right—as the call from Sam Sloan exactly a month later attested.

Evening time. It was always evening time when the dramatic calls came through. Sabine answered the phone.

"And a good evening to you, Mrs. Aubrey," purred the man's voice. "Say, is that man of yours hanging around by chance. I'd sure like a word or two with him." Recognizing the voice, Sabine did not even bother asking him to hold on. She just yelled for Aubrey.

Aubrey took the phone. "Hello. Aubrey Hanlon here."

"Ah, Aubrey ol' buddy. Say, we got ourselves into a bit of a misunderstanding over that darn bull of yours. I gotta admit, that wife of mine did not handle things very well. Got herself all worked up, but you know how these women are, God love 'em." He paused for Aubrey's comment, which did not come. "So I'm saying that we both went a little overboard. So I'm gonna suggest you folks throw a thousand dollars our way, you know, to help with the repairs, that sort of thing. Then we can put this whole business behind us. What do you think?"

"You know what, Mister Sloan? If you people had reacted this rationally in the first place, we would have gladly come up with a thousand dollars." Aubrey spoke very precisely, making sure that he would not have to repeat himself. "But let me remind you that first it was your wife and then you who decided to take the high road, doing your very best, you and your lawyer, to railroad us into paying for your wife's mistake."

"Aw, shucks, the old gray mare was upset. Can't you accept that? We all say and do dumb things when we're upset, and don't say we don't. Come on, buddy. Let's settle this thing man to man. Let's leave our crazy womenfolk out of it. Hell, you and I don't need no catfight on our hands, now do we?"

"Sir, you could quite easily have settled this business before trotting off to your high-flying lawyer and threatening us with legal action, which, by the way, I might just enjoy. And I'll thank you not to refer to my wife as crazy. So, unless you are willing to back right off, we have nothing more that we can say to each other. Which means, I presume, that once this season is done, we won't be renting your place next year?"

"You got that right, skunk-head," shrieked Ethel standing next to the phone and listening in. Sam Sloan hung up.

In the affairs of the land, the farming community shares a certain solidarity. News travels, stories grow in the telling, and one farmer's bad experience is viewed as potentially one's own. The Hanlons came to understand this when Sloan's next phone call came late in the fall, catching them off guard. Their advertisement soliciting pasture for the following season had only been in the paper a week. Once again, Sabine took the call.

"Say Mrs. Hanlon, Sam Sloan here. How the heck are you?"

"I'm fine, Mr. Sloan, thank you for asking." Sabine answered in that clipped tone she saved for fools, jesters, and telemarketers.

"Say, is that upstanding pillar of the community around, your husband I mean? I'd sure like a quick word with him."

"I'll go get him."

"Aubrey Hanlon here."

"Say, Aubrey, ol' buddy. I've decided to let bygones be bygones and I'm offering you my place for next season's pasture if you want it. No hard feelings and all that, eh? I'll even wire that darn gate shut so's neither the wife nor the bull can open it, heh, heh."

"Same rent?"

"Same rent, same deal, different bull mebbe? Anything you like."

"Why the change of heart? Nobody else interested?"

"Kinda like that, I guess. You farm folks must do a lot of talking among yourselves. We learned our lesson, I guess."

"I'll let you know in a week, if that's okay."

"Take your time, Hanlon, take your time," and he rung off. What Sloan did not know, and Aubrey had seen no need to explain, was that Narcissus had ended his own saga in life. Having apparently satisfied himself that he had bred all of the cows in his harem, instead of taking time out to laze around as any normal male of any species would do he answered the call of wanderlust by exploiting the weaknesses in the boundary fence to the west of the Sloan property. Aubrey was well aware at how bedraggled it was, but he had hoped it would suffice given that it ran through such an inhospitable terrain of muskeg and brush that even a moose might feel challenged. Ah, but there was no stopping this boy! Narcissus was cut from the mold of David Thompson; he had to go exploring, had to expand on his horizons, had to check out if there were any cow *belles* to the west. It was the Brand Inspector who phoned the Hanlons to tell them of Narcissus' travels; the message he left on the answering machine stated, "Mr. And Mrs. Hanlon. A Gelbvieh bull bearing your brand is currently trapped in the corrals of Mister Fred Busch, west of the Sloan place. Please check it out ASAP and phone me to confirm the bull is yours. If it is, Mr. Busch has asked that you pick him up immediately as there is no feed in the corral, and Mr. Busch has been called away to Edmonton on business."

Aubrey and Sabine hardly needed to check it out; they just knew it was Narcissus. They borrowed Pete's truck and trailer and headed out to the Busch farm. Sure enough, there was Narcissus by himself in a corral, and by the shaking and bellowing going on, it was clear he was being held against his will.

"What's the matter with his *thingy,* his willy?" Sabine asked in shock as soon as she saw him. "It's all covered in blood and hanging out."

"Oh hell," said Aubrey. "He must have damaged it on his travels. We'll load him up and take him into the vet clinic right away."

Easier said than done. Unfamiliar truck, strange trailer, and almost no experience backing up to a chute, Aubrey had a miserable time, made no easier with Sabine's unintelligible hand signals. Finally, after a brush with the side of a granary, he was in place, sort of, enough to get a bull on board he figured. He hopped out of the cab and went to fetch the bull himself; the rule on the Hanlon ranch was that Sabine, on the advice of Pete and Jeannie, was never to be involved where bulls were concerned.

Now a bull with a sore *thingy* is not going to be a cooperative beast. Moreover, this was not just any old bull; this was Narcissus, and he was in the sourest of moods. Back and forth he and Aubrey went before he elected to go down the alley to the trailer.

Sabine was standing alongside the trailer ready to kick the door shut.

For whatever reason, the bull decided to put down his head and bunt the trailer before getting in, which would have been all right if Aubrey had remembered to leave it in gear with the handbrake on. The truck rolled forward far enough for Narcissus to stick his head around the trailer and give Sabine the evil eye. Thank God for Sabine's voice, Aubrey thought afterwards. If she needed to, she could "out-shrill" any woman on earth. She rose to the occasion, and Narcissus turned and ran back into the safety of the corral. Had he gone the other way, the Hanlons would have been looking for him to this day.

Both Hanlons knew how lucky they were. Aubrey knew that it would have been a nightmare chasing after an enraged bull; Sabine knew that her legs would not have carried her fast enough had Narcissus made the decision to "rumble". Aubrey returned the trailer to the original position, this time ensuring that the brake was full on and the truck in gear. The time it took allowed Narcissus to cool down slightly, though not enough to make him amenable to anyone's wishes. The tango recommenced, with Aubrey ready to bolt over the fence in an instant. Once again Narcissus played hard to get until finally he tired of the game, shot down the alleyway, and lunged into the truck. Sabine was nowhere to be seen, having decided to take refuge in the cab so there was nobody on hand to kick the door shut. No sooner did Narcissus feel himself confined than he spun around and charged out, missing Aubrey by inches. That was the very same moment that Aubrey recalled the statistics that he had read in the "Safety Supplement" in *Grain News*; six livestock operators killed by livestock the previous year, four by bulls. But to Aubrey, sweet-talking this guy was akin to saying his anger was not legitimate, and Aubrey was now seething with anger. He happened on a short piece of two-by-four lumber, and he took after that bull with a face fearsome to behold, accompanied with language which would have cowed even the most dedicated of linguists. This time it was the bull that was surprised. He had never seen his master act like this, never. He took off down that alleyway and lunged aboard the trailer, and came to a halt in the front section shaking with trepidation. Aubrey, wishing to avoid a repeat performance of the last charge out, slammed the sliding door shut with all his strength, and caught his index finger in the process. It had to be said, the blood squirting from his finger was as colourful as the language spewing from his mouth. Sabine or no Sabine, there were no proscribed words on this occasion.

Poor Sabine! Much as she would have liked to help her husband out, she was not about to drive another man's truck, pulling another man's trailer containing an enraged bull with which her apoplectic man now had something in common. She watched in horror as Aubrey pulled out a cotton handkerchief from his pocket and wrapped it tightly around his finger. Filthy, stained with oil from when he had wiped the dipstick of the tractor, it was all they had. "Ach, the bit of oil and grease is probably as good as any antiseptic or better," he winced as he got his wife to tie the corners.

They were lucky, extremely lucky for Aubrey because there was room to park the whole darn rig on the street just outside the hospital. It was as Aubrey had suspected in the hospital; however, on every single occasion he had been compelled to present himself with an emergency medical problem, a large number of people in the community also decided to have a similar crisis at the same time. There were mothers with babes, mothers with toddlers, limpers, pukers, shirkers and shakers, the walking wounded among the walking dead; all were there. Even the new vet from the clinic, Kenneth Petrie, was there nursing a dislocated shoulder and waiting patiently in the lineup.

"I'm very sorry, sir," said the frazzled receptionist registering Aubrey's particulars. "The place is a complete zoo today, and we only have one doctor and an intern on call. You're going to have to be very patient."

Aubrey mumbled his thanks and he and Sabine moved over to the vet who stood up to greet them.

"And what happened to you?" asked Aubrey feeling some solidarity with him.

"Had me a little argument with a cow, and the cow won," he replied ruefully. "You?"

"Had a little argument with his bull, and the trailer won," Sabine interjected. "Actually, we were just about to take the bull down to your clinic when Aubrey slammed the trailer door on his finger."

"Ouch," said the vet. "What's the bull's problem?"

"Well," Aubrey picked up the story, "he broke out from pasture, did some serious cross-country hiking and finished up on Fred Busch's place. When we went to pick him up, we found he had seriously damaged his what-do-you-call-it. It's all bent and quite bloody."

"Sounds like a broken penis to me," said Dr. Petrie, D.V.M.

"A broken penis?" shrieked Sabine. "Did you say a broken penis?"

Every male in the place flinched first then looked across at Aubrey and the vet, no doubt searching for evidence of this terrible calamity. Several just shook their heads in sympathy. The only thing Sabine could do was to bolt out to the truck where she stayed the full hour and a half it took before Aubrey showed up, his finger all stitched up and neatly bandaged.

At the vet clinic they were lucky, their luck perhaps being a reflection of a depressed livestock industry. People just could not afford the rising costs of veterinary medicine, many choosing to let their livestock live or die as the animal in question chose. So although there was no waiting and the diagnosis/prognosis was severe, the proposed treatment was even more dire as far as they were concerned. "Yes, he hasn't completely wrecked his penis," said Dr. Clark matter-of-factly, "but he has lacerated it very badly. I can give you some ointment. You'll have to tether him up somewhere; better yet, put him in a squeeze, and then hose off any dirt with cold water before rubbing some ointment into his wounds. Three times a day for three days should do it."

"Excuuuuse me!" Sabine could not help herself. "We're talking a one-ton monster here. And you're asking us to rub ointment into his thingy-majig three times a day? Three times? Oh, he'll like that so much, he'll lie down and let me rub his tummy too, I'm sure."

"You heard right, my dear," said Dr. Clark quite unperturbed by Sabine's outburst. "Rub ointment into his thingy-majig three times a day. Even twice might be enough. See, you folks have to decide how important this bull is to you. He's out for this season, that's for sure. If you don't feel like treating him, take him into the auction market tomorrow. The packers will buy him but you won't get very much. So the choice is simple I'm afraid. You treat him or you sell him."

"We sell him," Aubrey and Sabine crowed together.

They got twenty-two cents a pound for a bull of 1,818 pounds in weight—$399.96 for a bull that cost them two thousand dollars, three months previously. Okay so these sorts of accidents happen, right? They do in other walks of life, no?

"You know what?" said Pete when he and Aubrey were driving back from Red Deer after having dumped Narcissus and three cull cows that Pete wanted to get rid of, "it's time that you and Sabine got yourselves your own livestock trailer." Aubrey immediately concluded that Pete was telling him nicely that they had "overstayed their welcome" in borrowing Pete's rig every time they needed to move an animal or two. Until Pete went on to explain his reasoning.

"See, in this farming game of ours, you've got to spend money to save money. Now if you folks were to get yourselves a stock trailer, we could work together. You could help me truck my critters out to pasture, I could help you move yours. First off, you'd save all that money you've been paying out for trucking. Better yet, when you need to take an animal to the vet's or the auction, you just hook up and go." Aubrey had no trouble accepting the argument; it was the financial outlay he was worried about. For her part, Sabine was downright dubious. She was starting to believe that there were a few too many plunges and not so many rises in this roller coaster of expansion they had embarked on. Without actually being able to articulate her thoughts yet, she knew that, nonetheless, she was somehow succumbing to the blues that were really starting to take hold in the country's agricultural sector, at least wherever the small family farm was involved. In a perverse sort of way, those blues were pretty much articulated for her in what was billed as "probably the last farm auction sale of the year" on a farm west of Sundre, in the golden days of fall.

Unusually late for a regular farm auction, local scuttlebutt had it that the older farmer and his wife took such a beating on the recent sale of their calf crop, they up and called it quits. Apparently, they were so distressed they could not even face attending their own sale, so kindly neighbors pitched in to help, which explained why there were so many cardboard boxes of "miscellaneous" in the household line and why the machinery was unwashed and not lined up in any logical order. Worse still, there were not that many quality items to draw a crowd and rescue the sale from a seemingly endless line of junk. The crowd was both sparse and morose. As if to add the *coup de grâce*, the day itself was overcast, making for an atmosphere that was steeped in an almost eerie gloom.

Even the seasoned auctioneers out of Olds had to work twice as hard as normal to eke out a respectable price for anything, and they were not always successful. Not that Aubrey should complain. He was able to pick up a twenty-foot stock trailer, in excellent condition, for a mere half of what he had come to pay. Yet, and strange it was too, there was no sense of euphoria. Indeed, Aubrey and Sabine both felt decidedly guilty, as if they had made an undue catch by fishing in troubled waters. Sabine was unusually subdued as she watched box after box of household treasure go under the hammer at ridiculously low prices. At times, she even caught herself bidding just to help things along, which was how she got stuck with a large cardboard box of "miscellaneous" for eight dollars. When she stepped up to the auctioneer to claim her prize, she could not believe how heavy it was for a box that the man helping had said contained a bunch of tablecloths and napkins, stuff like that. She did what she always did on such occasions; she hustled it over to the truck so that she did not forget it or leave it somewhere for someone more unscrupulous to pick over. Having then decided that she had done her bit of community service, she headed over to the second sale ring at the machinery to join up with Aubrey and Pete. She was just in time to hear the auctioneer knock down the white Ford three-quarter ton diesel pickup to buyer number 59 for five thousand dollars even.

Fifty-nine? Fifty-nine! Hey, wait a minute, that's our number! Somebody must have the same number as us! Wait a second, that's Aubrey picking up the slip from the clerk. Had he come unglued? Five thousand even! Five thousand. What, did he have a money tree she did not know of? They didn't even have five hundred in their main account right now, and he, buyer number fifty-nine, had just committed to pay up five thousand. Well, he was about to get a piece of her mind, a blunderbuss loaded with salt and vinegar, five thousand indeed! She watched as Aubrey made his way back to his new truck, no, their new truck dammit; a beautiful machine, it had to be said, if it were to be placed alongside their old clunker for which no dealer would give more than five hundred on trade. It turned out that this was the truck that was used to pull the trailer, so all the fifth-wheel towing apparatus was part and parcel of the deal. Her anger died on her lips. She knew they would find a way to finance it, but at the same time she suddenly felt sick, sick as if they had been picking over the corpse of one of their own. The truck was worth triple what they paid and everyone knew it. The men, she discovered to her surprise, felt no better. All they could think of doing was settling up at once and getting the hell out of there, Aubrey sweet-talking Pete into covering the payment until he could get to the banker. Pete, bless his heart, even offered to drive the new acquisitions home and so they departed "Gloomsville Farm" as Sabine christened it. Normally, Aubrey and Sabine would have been exultant. Instead the trip home was decidedly subdued, neither one of them willing to share with the other the black thoughts clouding over the mind. Had they gone out and expanded in defiance of all reality? Could this sort of crash happen to them? Sabine dared not ask how they were going to drum up the five thousand they now owed Pete. Aubrey would have to deal with it, seeing that it was he who had put them out on a limb in the first place. Aubrey, it turned out, had gambled correctly. The bank, awash in the largesse of the superheated oilfield economy, was only too happy to throw some of the pickings their way. It was only a piddling five thousand after all.

When they arrived home, Sabine had Aubrey carry in her box of goodies into the house. She put on a pot of tea for the three of them and sat down to go through the treasure trove of miscellaneous, the "bunch of tablecloths and napkins" announced by the auctioneer's helper. It was a treasure trove beyond belief. Buried deep beneath the tablecloths and napkins were half a dozen flat boxes, each one bearing the logo of the Franklin Mint. Sabine opened the first one to find an exquisite collector's plate, part of a series of six entitled "Adventures down on The Farm". This particular one boasted a great big mama sow, identical in every way to Sabine's fabled Miss Piggy, lying on her side, eyes closed and ten piglets guzzling their way to glory. The second one showed a beef cow and calf, appropriately not a Nellie nor an Elvira but a perfectly correct Shorthorn mama and calf. The third one presented her with that old spotted mare and her foal, the fourth a ewe with three fluffy lambs, the fifth a nondescript brown duck with a flotilla of yellow ducklings, and the last a bearded nanny-goat with a couple of tri-coloured kids trailing behind. Clearly the plates had never been hung, never been out of their boxes. Sabine could not help it, she burst into tears. If it had not been for Pete, wise as he was to the ways of the farming world, then and there she would have located the owners' phone number and asked if they wanted them back, telling them that there must have been some mistake. At the same time, she was wondering why she could not be like other normal folks and be glad that they had "scored".

Pete merely laughed at her, calling her quaint and old-fashioned, and then he went on to tell the Hanlons that he had it on good authority that the farmer and his wife had been the recipients of a very large sum of money, approaching the million mark, from an oil company that had seriously contaminated their land some years back. Animals had taken ill and expired, plant life downwind had sickened and died off, and the couple themselves had taken sick. Their problems were traced to some sort of waste pit that the company had operated illegally and then abandoned. Faced with a potentially damaging lawsuit, the company had concluded an agreement spiced with many dollars provided the couple sealed their lips. That way, the company could plead ignorance and the farm couple could get out with some dignity.

"But what if someone comes along and buys the land without knowing the history?"

"Buyer beware, I guess," said Pete. "Besides, you can bet they will have covered it all up by now." This prompted Aubrey to give voice to his gopher analogy.

"You know, Pete," he said, "sometimes I get the overwhelming feeling that we small-time farmers are like a bunch of gophers, with every family down their own little hole. We look out at the world, and the view is always limited to our immediate surroundings. We never scurry very far from that hole; we certainly never see the full horizon, and so we rarely see disaster coming until it's right on top of us. Just like gophers, no?"

"But aren't we happier that way? Think about it. There are so many variables in farming, we're always just a couple of steps away from disaster at any given time. That's why they call us folks 'next year's people.'" Pete the philosopher-optimist was ever a good person to talk to, ever a soothing influence, ever one to reposition the stars into a more positive alignment. But even Pete had to call on Aubrey to help with his next predicament. Even he was so shaken that he actually admitted that most small farmers could only survive if they denied reality to some degree.

The whole thing began when Pete drove into the Hanlon farmyard at high speed one day at four in the afternoon. "Drove" is the wrong word. He burned into the yard in a cloud of dust. He was in luck; Aubrey and Sabine were just on their way into the house for the afternoon cuppa, as Pete knew they would be.

"Get in!" he yelled. "Both of you!" he barked. The Hanlons did as they were told, never having seen their Pete in such a state.

"What's up?" Aubrey asked quietly, the policeman in him taking control. All Sabine could do was to stare incredulously at the speedometer and pray.

"You know that young couple, good friends of ours, out west, by the name of Delamere? Jim and Sonya Delamere?"

"You mean the couple with those darling twin girls?" asked Sabine, the question relieving some of the strain of watching a speedo needle with an alarming tendency to go way beyond a hundred kilometers an hour, even on a gravel road. Not one to forget a face, Sabine's mind pictured an earnest young man with a bubbly slip of a wife at some community function at the local hall: the picture-perfect young farm family.

"They're the ones. Well, turns out that sometime back they applied for an interim payment out of that new government program that's going to lift all us poor farmers up by our bootlaces and keep us out of the poor house."

"You mean the CAIS program?" queried Aubrey, still trying to put the name Delamere to a face he could remember.

"Well, it seems they got thirty-five thousand dollars of help out of it. That's thirty-five grand they needed and could put to good use right away. Jim, being the cautious fellow he is, phoned up his banker and his accountant and his granny and even the people who run the program itself. Every darn one of them told him that if he had bills to pay, then he should go ahead and pay them and not worry. The person in the government office in Lacombe told him that the program was designed for folks like him and that the payout probably only amounted to fifty per cent of what he might be entitled to later. Now like everybody else in this game, he had a pile of outstanding bills and a mob of creditors on his back screaming for their money. So he pays 'em all off, at least most of 'em. Me, I figured on waiting a while before I applied for any kind of payment because I wasn't too sure those bureaucrats knew what they were doing up there in Lacombe. Turns out I was right."

"How so?" said Aubrey who had enrolled in the program but had been frightened off by the paperwork involved, even though he and Sabine could have used all the help they could get. He had talked to too many old-timers like old Art Zimmer who had no intention of signing up to a program that promised the world and "smelt like a dead skunk".

"Well, seems everything was going along fine and dandy for the Delameres until today. Jim opens up a letter from our guardian angels up there in C.A.I.S.P heaven, only it turns out it's a bill not a letter, for an overpayment of thirty-five thousand dollars that he now has to pay back in full. He panics and phones them up there in their air-conditioned offices. You know what I'm going to tell you, don't you? Jim finally gets to talk to some head honcho on the phone and he suggests there has to be some mistake. 'No, no Mr. Delamere, there is no mistake; your inventory is too this, your income is too that, your reference margin is too something else, your allowable expenses are this way,' you know how these folks talk. Sonya said he was blown away, absolutely devastated. Who wouldn't be? So without saying a word to his wife, he puts down the phone, grabs his rifle, jumps into the pickup, and takes off. That's when Sonya read the bill and called me. She's terrified he's about to pull the plug and commit suicide. I remembered you saying how you had experience with this kind of thing, so I took a chance on finding you home. Jeannie is down in Calgary right now visiting her sister; so I hope you, Sabine, can hold Sonya's hand while we try to figure out where Jim was headed. I just hope we're not too darn late."

When they arrived in the Delamere yard, immaculate down to the white picket fence, Aubrey realized they were dealing with a "tidiness freak", someone who would not be able to take the disorder of the Hanlon yard for example, someone whose affairs would be meticulously ordered. Sonya Delamere answered the door, her face puffy and red.

"I hope, I hope we're not too late," she stammered before breaking down. Sabine stepped forward to hold her, giving her enough strength to say, "I think. I think he may be up on the hill, at the old barn on the east quarter. He often goes up there, up there, when he needs to be alone." At that, her will broke. Sabine signaled to the men to get going as she quietly led Sonya Delamere back inside her home.

Pete could not have made a more inspired decision than calling in Aubrey Hanlon. Aubrey had been the point man in the resolution of half a dozen suicide situations in his last year on the beat. He seemed to have an uncanny ability to read how to reach into a distraught mind, how to massage it enough to reduce the tension enough for his colleagues to do the rest. But this was different. His companion was untrained—well-meaning, maybe, but still untrained. And their "target" had a weapon. An agitated mind could just as easily turn on its benefactors as turn on itself. How well did Pete actually know Jim Delamere? Would Delamere see Pete as a do-gooder interfering where he had no business? In an instant, all these questions became academic as they spotted Jim's truck parked outside the old barn, just as Sonya had hoped. They stopped some distance away and approached on foot.

Jim Delamere had made his way into the old tack room, sitting down on an upturned chop pail. His mind was reeling, seething, a cauldron of images and thoughts and hopes and despair all bubbling up together. Visions of his treasured little girls fought with the stark image of those numbers in print, "$35,000 overpayment", only for them to be overwhelmed by a heavy swell of profound anger and desperation. How would they ever make it now? How could they? How could he care for his cherished wife and his angelic twins when he had so patently failed them? He should have known it was too good to be true. How could he crawl out of the hole he had dug for himself and his family, a hole he had dug so deep? God knew how hard he had tried, and for what? So many in the neighborhood said what a good farmer he was, and a good man, but being a good farmer and a good man did not seem to put much bread on the table, let alone buy a couple of new dresses for his girls. Sonya had to make them, had to make all of their clothes pretty much. Why? Good farmer, my ass. He was a failure, couldn't even provide the basic necessities for his wife and kids.

As for that government official on the phone, the one who blithely assured him there was no mistake, that he now owed the government $35,000, what was in his bureaucratic mind? Did he think that he, Jim Delamere, had somehow defrauded the government? Could the man not see? Did he have a wife and kids? Oh probably, and a fancy house with a two-car garage and a shiny new SUV parked outside. How could it all have gone so wrong? How could somebody, somewhere, miscalculate so badly that they could award him so much money and then six months later take it away, just like that? What about his banker and his accountant, the ones who said to go ahead and pay his bills? Would any of them miss any sleep over him, or miss out on even one paycheque? Not bloody likely! They would simply shrug their shoulders and move on to that next bit of paper. It really wasn't their problem; they would never mortgage their lives to the whims of a government flunky, now would they? But then again, if he went ahead and did what he had a mind to do, if he went ahead and pulled that trigger, who was he appeasing? What was he leaving behind? Pain. Mountains and valleys of pain, and incomprehension. How could he *choose* to abandon the love of his life, how could he *choose* death over his soul mate, how could he leave his darling little girls without their father, leaving them with worse yet, the memory of a father who was a failure, somebody who could not cope? Oh God, but he needed help. It would be so easy, too easy to end it all. He looked down at the gun, slipped a shell into the breech. It could be over in a minute, in seconds, and at least for him it would be so clean…

"You call out to him," whispered Aubrey to Pete. "You know him, he knows you, let's see if there is any response."

There was none.

Quietly they padded round one corner of the barn, Pete calling out softly, "Jim. Say Jim, we need to talk."

Silence.

"You got too much to lose old son," said Pete, a note of desperation shaking his voice. "Way too much to lose over some lousy scrap of paper that says you owe a bunch of money. What if they're wrong? What if some clown in some office some place has made a dumb mistake?"

"There ain't no mistake." The answer was muffled, coming as it did from the inside of the barn. The two men edged though the main door. There was nobody in sight.

"Say Jim, I'm Aubrey Hanlon. Pete and I are long-time buddies. And I'll be darned, but I'm in the same boat as you with that darn government program. Can we come in and talk without you trying to blow off our tootsies?"

"What the heck, come on in." The voice was resigned, echoing out of an old tack room in one corner of the sagging barn. Maybe it was the touch of humour, maybe it was the two friendly voices, maybe it was nothing more than farmer solidarity or perfect timing, but the man they called J-D put down his gun and stood up as they entered. Pete's first move was not thought out; it was instinctive. He stepped forward and embraced Jim while Aubrey went straight for the gun, picking it up and unloading it. And Jim broke down, his great strong body shaking with anguish.

"How…How'm I…ever…ever gonna…pay back thirty-five thousand… how?" The words tumbled out almost incoherently.

"You're not going to pay it back," said Pete, now holding him up. "Just let it all out, all of the bad stuff."

"We're here to help you sort it all out," said Aubrey. "Just as long as you take us down to that lovely lady of yours and get her to give us a cup of coffee. Too many darn spiders around here for my liking."

That was all Jim needed to refocus. But now he was too clearly embarrassed and ashamed, which was why Pete said what he did. "No need to feel embarrassed by the way, not at all. Aubrey here, he's the ex-cop that farms down the road a little ways. He's been through this kind of thing before a number of times. It's just that sometimes we need a friend around to talk us through a mess like this."

"That's for sure," added Aubrey ramming the point home.

"Thanks guys," Jim mumbled, still feeling shame but stepping forward to shake first Pete's hand then Aubrey's.

"Mind if I hang on to this old blunderbuss for a couple of days?" said Aubrey slinging the rifle over his shoulder and posing the question in such a way that it was not a question.

"Go ahead. But you know what? I couldn't have done it anyway. I could not have left Sonya to pick up the pieces. But I have to tell you, I was scared to death."

"Scared us a bit too," said Aubrey taking the lead. "You go down with Pete in his truck, and I'll follow you in your truck."

Their arrival back at the Delamere house was the most fulfilling moment of Pete's whole life. Sonya literally burst out of the front door and threw herself into her husband's arms, the two of them utterly oblivious to the rest of them in their relief.

"You two lovebirds can hang around outside if you want to," said Pete finally. "We're going inside to put the coffee on." The Delameres arrived a couple of minutes later and better composed.

"So where are the girls?" Pete popped the question they all needed answered.

"Oh, they're down in Lethbridge with Jim's mom, thank God," Sonya replied. "We're going down tomorrow to pick them up."

"Would you mind showing me that evil piece of paper saying you were overpaid?" asked Aubrey. "Nobody I know has figured out how this flipping program works. It's my guess that the folks who administer it and those who work with it every day are only half a step ahead of us. That's why we must never take no for an answer." And there they were— the numbers! In black and white, so innocent and so threatening, carrying with them a significance that could reach so far into people's lives and literally destroy everything they had worked for. The words, too, seemed vindictive; especially that one word "overpayment", sending the message that the virile young man for whom they were intended could, if he so wished, actually contemplate his own self-destruction, leaving behind useless and unnecessary tragedy.

The analogy of the small-time farmer as a gopher bound by limited horizons returned to Aubrey ever more forcefully. Who knew what calamity was about to be visited on any of them? Not simply calamity brought about by weather, drought and flood, and the like, but contrived calamity: man-made, ill-conceived plans and programs directed by people who perhaps dared not be too connected to the havoc they knew their little bits of paper could cause. There was nothing malevolent or sinister in what these people did for their living; but there was no real understanding that, as if embarked on gopher control, they were blowing the poor and the innocent off the farm. Aubrey saw that the answer to the problem lay in those overused words of business; they needed to network, to "interface", with those in authority. He and Pete and Jim would take them all on, face to face, not via the 1-800 number with a squeaky voice prattling on about how "your call is important to us so please hold the line for the first available agent…blah…blah." No, they would demand to see with their own eyes, they would demand an appointment with a real live person, a bureaucrat with a face and a voice, and hopefully a heart. As Aubrey had anticipated, Jim Delamere was highly dubious about the idea. He had never ever spoken up like this. To him, this was defiance of the authorities, civil disobedience, a sort of communistic revolution. But he agreed to go along for the sake of Sonya and the kids. He could not do any worse, could he? And so he authorized Aubrey and Pete to speak for him, to set it all up: an exclusive meeting with someone who could walk them through Jim's file.

Aubrey's first phone call to the program's head office in Lacombe was telling.

"Can your questions not be settled over the phone?" said a lady's voice a little too archly. "It can't be that complicated, can it?"

"Madam, you are not listening to me," said Aubrey. "We need someone to walk us through this whole application that I'm talking about. We are trying to understand the program that is designed specifically for us."

"Well, my instructions are to inform callers that all our analysts are extremely busy. We can't just jump up and assign their time to one individual farmer who is upset with the program. We are working on behalf of all the farmers in the province."

"Exactly," said Aubrey, wondering how it was that such people seemed to think they were somehow defending their territory. "So would you mind putting me in touch with somebody who has the authority to set up an appointment seeing that you are not allowed to do so."

"Please hold the line, sir," the voice was suddenly deferential. One whole minute went by, then another before the voice finally came back. "How about two o'clock next Wednesday?"

"It's a deal."

"Very good. You'll be seeing a Mrs. Greta Helwig, one of our senior analysts. And this is on behalf of...?"

"Jim Delamere, D-E-L-A-M-E-R-E. Pin number 018462769."

"Thank you Jim. Have a good day."

The whole experience from there on, the trip up to the government offices in Lacombe, the readjusting of a slew of numbers, of Jim's overvaluations and under-valuations, the review of and subsequent tinkering with reference margins and year-end inventories, the recalculations of feed consumed and not consumed, the reconfiguring of "transfers in" and "transfers out" convinced all three of them how quickly numbers can just as quickly betray you as vindicate you, which made them so much more fickle and untrustworthy than words. The "senior analyst" as was her official designation, was pure delight. Down-to-earth yet thoroughly professional, she won over the hearts of the three farmers with her frank commentary about a program that was experiencing not just "teething troubles" but full-blown design problems too. Better than that, she was a farm girl herself, born and raised on the family farm near Carbon. Rather than approaching the program and Jim's figures from the outside, as it were, she went at it from the inside, showing them how everything was interrelated. The bonus came with the fact that she explained why it was best to do something one way and not another. It was less a manipulation of Jim's numbers and more of a reconfiguration, with Jim sitting there feeling like a schoolboy who had done a poor job on his math assignment.

"Actually," she said, "you have done a better job on your submission than a lot of farmers. It's clear that you did not know what all we were looking for. Now you do. Just let me double check your livestock ins and outs, and we're done." Down went her hand, the fingers on the calculator working as if independent of the brain. "Voilà!" she said. "The whole thing balances and, you know what, these figures tell me you must be a darn good farmer even if the paperwork doesn't come easy. My dad is just the same. I have to do his, too, you know."

"Thank you," said Jim bashfully.

"Now I am sure that with all the revisions we have made, you will regain some peace of mind. The whole thing now has to go through a verification process, but I foresee no difficulties. You'll get a revised assessment in the mail, for sure within six weeks. If you don't, here's my card. Call me. Oh, and I don't think you'll have to pay much back, if anything. As for you boys, Pete and Aubrey, I hope this has helped."

"Oh, beyond all expectations," Pete answered for both of them. "And thank you."

"Can you think of any other questions," she added, leaning back on her chair and looking quizzically at them over her glasses.

"Well, actually I do have one," said Aubrey very carefully. "Have you any idea how many farmers have been caught in the same predicament as Jim here, you know, with a massive so-called overpayment?"

"Now that I do not know … other than to say, more than just a few. You see, you've got to remember that the government was trying to get dollars into the farmer's pocket as quickly as possible because of both the drought and then the BSE crisis, all while they were trying to cobble the program together."

Pete was compelled to butt in and pose the question that had brought all three of them up to Lacombe in the first place. "Given that, in your words, more than a few farmers are suddenly being told they have to pay huge sums of money back to the government, has anybody given any thought to how this could be so devastating to a farmer that he might be tempted to take his own life?"

The silence that ensued was telling, and the good Mrs. Helwig had not failed to see young Jim tense up instantly. Finally, she moved uncomfortably in her chair. "I can only answer a question like that personally," she said. "Let me put it this way, a farm gal's view of the world you might say. Government and government programs are a machine, like a round baler if you will. They are run by bureaucrats like me it is true, but we have to stay utterly impersonal or else we would all go insane. Besides, if you're working for Revenue Canada for example, you rarely get a sense of the human drama that goes along with the figures in front of you. Now you as farmers know that for any piece of equipment, you should familiarize yourself with the Operator's Manual. But beyond that, you still have to learn by doing, by direct hands-on experience. You have to learn as much about what you should not do as what you must do. This program is no different. Jim, here, and you boys as well, have seen now how your information needs to be presented, and to a degree, how it should not be presented. In Jim's case, the information, even though it was all pretty much correct, was presented in such a way as to give a completely wrong picture and that caused him a huge disadvantage. So, in answer to your earlier question, as an individual running the program, yes I have agonized many times over how a farmer might take bad news, but, fundamentally, all I am is a little cog driven by the big wheel of government. I have to remain impersonal; otherwise, I would never sleep at night. I would go insane. By the same token though, farmers have to learn not to take these things personally. They have to do what you boys did; they have to stand up and ask questions, yes? When all is said and done, farmers do what they do for the lifestyle, no?"

Chapter Eleven
LIFESTYLE

*L*ifestyle. The word somehow evokes the goings-on of the rich and the famous, "celebs" and all, where money and survival are never in question. In resource-rich Alberta, it was increasingly applicable to the "high-risers"— the consultants and the engineers, the geologists and the drillers—who were busy buying up country acreages and building themselves not houses but mansions, no expense spared. Stories circulated of heated driveways even, where the resident excellencies would never have to shovel that damnable snow like peasants; of fridges that made the bed and put the dog out before chilling the beer and lighting the barbeque; of re-renovation because some Queen of Alberta did not much care for the newly installed oak cabinetry in the kitchen and decided polished birch would be better instead. Maybe this explained, in part, the number of television programs today where foppish "home interior stylists" explained their makeover of the latest victim's evident lack of imagination coupled with a readiness to throw cash at "a fresh, new look".

"You know," said Sabine, "I am starting to hate these people with some passion," and Sabine had never been the sort of person to hate anyone with passion. "Why the hell don't these people do a makeover of a normal person's house, the kind of house where people spill an occasional cup of coffee on the carpet or knock over a bottle of red wine? A house where the inhabitants actually live in the rooms, instead of flitting in and out of them like bloody mosquitoes?" Clearly, an ageing Sabine was a Sabine having a hard time holding onto her sanitary language resolutions; that, or Sabine was genuinely troubled. Aubrey could only grunt his affirmation, as he always did when such conversations arose; they were conversations not worthy engaging in, not when he was so content with what he had. Nevertheless, Sabine's outburst was food for thought. The more that the economics of farming impinged on them, the more the oil-rich seemed to flaunt their wealth while those in the farming sector scrambled ever more desperately to make a living, and the more profoundly Aubrey began to reflect upon the notion of lifestyle itself.

In underdeveloped countries, as for example in many African countries, lifestyle is primarily more of a struggle and less of a choice. In developed countries, as in Canada, generally you are free enough to make choices; the more that you are lucky enough to be on the upside of the economy, the greater the range of choices you can make. By the same token, people on the downside of the economy do not go out and choose poverty. In a perverse way, the economy chooses it for them, just as farming at this moment in time was putting pressure upon so many. Yet with farming there are always so many intangibles, benefits that one can enjoy, revel in, without worrying the mind as to how much they might be costing. As the agricultural sky continued to cloud over, Aubrey and Sabine found themselves taking solace in those intangibles that gave them and so many other small farmers strength in adversity.

When you have a half-section, a full three hundred and twenty acres to yourself, you have real space—private and uncluttered—where ownership becomes a distant legal term that has to do with what Dick Conley called "man's obsession for possession". Technically, the Hanlons owned the trees and the woodland, the creek and the slough; but these were what they were no matter who owned the land, well to a point. Of course there were those who were forced to cave in, to surrender sovereignty as times got tougher. These were the ones who devastated their woodland because some roving lumberman offered them a quick dollar for their poplar or their pine. These were the same folk who went on to lament the mess that was left behind, who missed the bird life and the deer, only factoring in the full cost after it was way too late. For Aubrey and Sabine, their trees were sacred; that giant Colorado Spruce down at the creek could never be an economic commodity of "x" number of board feet of lumber. It was the home of a Depilated Woodpecker and, later on, of Mtata's favorite family of squirrels. The willow bush and the lowland was not wasted space; it was a haven for the deer and the odd stray moose—and yes, for the coyotes too. Okay, it was true that on occasion, the privacy afforded by all of this space could clash with the conventions of civilization as Aubrey's incident with the coyotes attested.

One of those lazy summer evenings and well after dark, Aubrey was turning in. Sabine was away in Edmonton for a couple of days, so he was a bachelor with a "pink ticket", free to do whatever he pleased. He had enjoyed a fabulous BBQ supper over at Pete and Jeannie's and was feeling thoroughly replete when he arrived home. Their sampling of an array of British Columbia red wines had convinced him that Canadian vintners had come of age, and the whole experience had left him at peace with the world. With the world maybe, but not with coyotes! He came out of the bathroom as naked as the day he was born and ambled into the sitting room to pick up the new issue of *Country Guide* to read in bed. There is nothing in this world like an article about spraying entitled "Pick Nozzles That Get Product to Target" to get a person to slide off into dedicated slumber. He glanced out of the big bay window and there on the lawn was a large coyote, clearly devouring something feathered and white.

"Damn and blast it, I forgot to shut the *bleep bleep* chickens away," Aubrey yelled, making absolutely no impression on the coyote enjoying his meal out on the grass. Instinctively he went for his gun, a sixteen-gage shotgun, and his gumboots. He slipped quietly out of the back door and began creeping around the side of the house, hoping for at least a sporting shot at the intruder. The very instant he showed only the tip of his nose, the coyote had seen him and was gone, taking his chicken dinner with him. Ah, the privacy of the countryside. Still dressed in no more than a pair of gumboots, still armed with the shotgun and muttering darkly about the onset of Alzheimer's, he made his way up to the chicken house. He could hardly believe his eyes. There, exiting from the open gate of the chicken run was a second coyote with another of Sabine's large white chickens flapping in its mouth. Blind fury consumed Aubrey. He fired a random shot that was way off the mark, even with a shotgun, and then took off after the animal in hopes it would drop the still live chicken. Of course, the coyote took the unimpeded route and headed straight down the driveway towards the road, Aubrey in hot pursuit. So full of impotent anger was he that he did not see approaching headlights flickering below the hill, to the west. He was fully focused on that shadowy coyote, that was all there was to it. As if in deference, and surely not because it felt threatened, the coyote decided to drop the chicken where the driveway merged with the main road. And the lights of the oncoming vehicle that crested the hill illuminated for the Reverend Cecil Baldwin and his wife Gertrude the spectacle of a naked man in gumboots, endeavoring to catch an apparently distressed white chicken running around in circles in the middle of the road. It was not a heavenly sight, even if it was mesmerizing. Aubrey was so angry, he was past caring. He straightened up, the flailing white chicken hanging from his right hand, just as the Baldwin car pulled up alongside.

What else would a good man say? "Glorious...glorious...night... out, isn't it?" Aubrey managed as the driver's window came down.

"Are you all right?" asked the man's voice from inside, a man whom Aubrey had never met in his life, thankfully. "Do you need any assistance?"

"Not the sort of assistance any normal person can give," said Aubrey.

"Well, if I can offer you any spiritual guidance, I shall only be too pleased to do so," the unctuous voice came back, clearly expressing the man's concern for Aubrey's moral condition.

"Thank you all the same but I'm quite beyond that," said Aubrey just as the chicken gave up its unequal and inverted struggle to live.

"I think your chicken has just expired," said the reverend.

She never knew why she said it nor what prompted her to say it, and certainly she was berated by her husband over and over for doing so, but Gertrude Baldwin said it anyway. "It's not only your chicken that's gone limp," she said. Her husband had to pull away then, had to, leaving Aubrey standing in the road, staring down at his nether regions, the words resonating incomprehensibly in his mind. "It's not only your chicken that's gone limp."

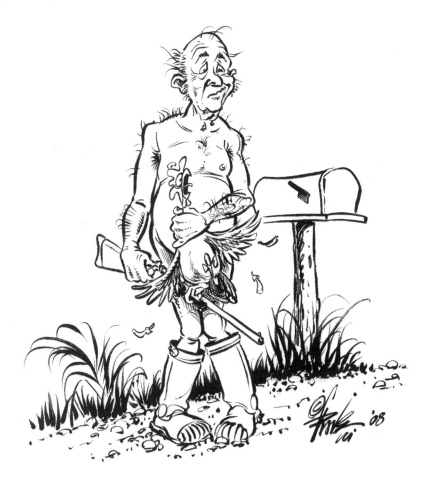

Fungula! he roared at the departing taillights and the sliver of a moon.

Privacy and space, get real! How could a story like that not get out, a story that inadvertently added to the mythology of Mister Big of *Footloose in the Front Forty*. The trouble was, Norah Barker and Sarah Campkin were also staunch Anglicans and when Gertrude told the story of the naked man in gumboots, explaining where it occurred, Norah was compelled to jump in with the words, "That's him, that's our Mister Big. Isn't it Sarah?"

"By Jove, I believe you are right." This meant that the story of Aubrey peeing on an overheated bearing in his baler and then falling off had to be recycled, always with additional trimmings, generally twice. Larger than life characters are created not born.

Trouble may also arise when ownership of space is interpreted too loosely by others and viewed as a legal term so distant that it has virtually no meaning. Aubrey and Sabine came to dread the opening of the deer-hunting season in the fall. Oh sure, they understood the dynamics, the need to keep a burgeoning deer population in check, and the fact that most hunters "used respect" as the posted signs asked, and sought permission to hunt on one's land. But as the Hanlons quickly found out, their whole attitude towards hunters was soured by the occasional bad apple. The final straw came when Sabine, standing by that same bay window from which Aubrey had spotted the coyote eating the chicken, actually saw a hunter bag a deer in the front field by shooting it from the road. She watched as two men got out of their pickup, climbed through the barbwire fence, and hauled the still twitching animal back to their truck all in the span of ninety seconds. She was furious. It was as if she had been watching herself being violated. Calls to the police and to Fish and Wildlife were fruitless as Sabine had no real details to give, no license plates, no names, only a vague description of what the men looked like. More signs went up that very afternoon. "No Trespassing". "No Hunting".

A week later, while he was checking out the fence in the southeast corner of their property, Aubrey came upon a massive bloodstain in the fresh snow. His heart skipped a beat. Somebody had shot one of their cows! Then he saw the quad tracks and the traces of deer hair on the ground. Hunters! Did anyone respect the law these days? This fellow, assuming it was a fellow, had driven right past a "No Hunting" and a "No Trespassing" sign. Now Aubrey was angry, really angry. Nothing was safe: not the wildlife, not the cows, nothing. If only he could catch one of those hunters on his land, he would prosecute; he would avail himself of every inch of the law.

The following Monday, he was in Co-Op buying some screws when he bumped into Pete. "Say, old man," said Pete, "you posted your land, right? Like you don't allow hunting, right?"

"Right," said Aubrey. "Why?"

"Because that guy who lives in the shack across from Bill Edgson's place was apparently in the bar last night bragging about a mega-Whitetail buck he shot on your place."

"So it was that SOB," Aubrey erupted, going on to tell Pete of his discovery. "How do we ever put a stop to this sort of thing?"

"Put a stop to it? We don't," said Pete in resignation.

"What do you mean, we don't? We can't just sit back and let it happen, can we?"

"Let me put it this way. A high-powered rifle with a scope does not know the difference between a Whitetail, your cow, and your dog. Maybe even you, for that matter. And to some, it does not matter either."

"What do you mean?" said Aubrey, not quite willing to believe what Pete was actually telling him.

"I mean these people live in our neighborhood. They are your neighbors and mine. If you choose to go after them, they will turn against you and you will certainly end up paying a far higher price than if you had left them alone in the first place. Like for them, respect for the law and for ex-cops only goes so far."

"You are not saying they might shoot…," Aubrey began in disbelief.

"That's exactly what I am saying. In today's rural world, you have to learn to live and let live. Let these people take the odd deer if that's what they feel they really have to do."

What astounded Aubrey was that about a week later, the guy who lived in the shack showed up at the Hanlon yard asking for Mr. Hanlon. He was not at home at the time, so it was up to Sabine to drop her baking and deal with him. She found herself face to face with what Aubrey and his police buddies used to call a "likeable rogue": the kind of fast-talking huckster with a talent for convincing his target to be an accomplice in his latest scheme, the sort of person whose very appearance struggled to be a cut above that of a ruffian.

Sabine disliked him instantly, even before he opened his mouth, and her body language showed it. Once his mouth opened, she found him smarmy, what today's young would call "slimy", talking away as if it was truly a blessing for Sabine to hear his words of wisdom. The most oily of introductory chatter dispensed with, the man popped his question. "Do you suppose you could give me free access to your land? You see, I am making a documentary video about nature and wildlife and I happen to know there's a helluva Whitetail buck that lives in the muskeg between your two quarters. I would sure appreciate a chance to see him close up."

"What? So you can blow it away like you did the last one?" Sabine responded tartly. Neighbor or no neighbor, she had no wish to have this Hickory Bill mooching about the place with a gun, pardon me, camera slung over his shoulder. He could go out and buy his own place.

The man hesitated as if trying to comprehend such belligerence, then a lopsided grin creased his face. "Aw shucks, so you folks got to hear about that. I kinda forgot where I was that day, the heat of the chase and the size of the trophy, you understand."

"Uh huh."

"But that's okay. No offense. I can take an answer of 'no', if that is your final answer."

"That is my final answer," said Sabine stonily. "And one more thing. You should know, if you don't already, my husband happens to be a retired cop who is getting more than a little tired of people poaching on our land. So be warned, if he catches someone doing what that someone should not be doing, then that someone will be put through the wringer."

"Okay lady, okay, I get your message loud and clear," and he backed away from Sabine like a duck that had mistakenly taken on a wolverine. "Have a good day, eh?"

"Same to you," said Sabine turning. "Same to you, eh!"

Pete expanded on his "neighbors" theme the next time the Hanlons went over for a visit. "What you have to realize," he said, "is that the more us farmer types are forced to subdivide chunks off our land to make enough money to survive, the more we are going to let folks into our countryside who really have no idea how to conduct themselves. Some of them genuinely believe they have some sort of natural right to all of the space around them no matter whom it actually belongs to. A fair number of them truly do not know any better. To them, it's just open space. Think of those renters you had with their bleeping dog running loose all over the place."

"So much for one's own space," said Aubrey bleakly.

If the farming lifestyle was blessed with space, it was also blessed with time, at least on the surface. Yet time was not dictated so much by the clock as by the seasons. However, it was not as if the seasons were independent in their own right. Oh no, the weather always saw to that! The weather extended the winter and shortened the fall, sanctified the spring and glorified the summer, only to do an about-face the following year. Always, the weather contrived to remind you what you should be doing and had not done. Sometimes it could be downright vindictive, sometimes graciously benign. There were those awful years where the weather deliberately ran one season into another so quickly you could find yourself on the combine after the second big snowfall of winter, or on the tractor seeding at the tail-end of May and praying that the growing season would last long enough to let your barley crop survive. Maybe it was the phenomenon of global warming that the gurus were so busy propagating or denying, maybe it was El Niño or La Niña, or pollution, or all that hot air from all those politicians preaching Kyoto and carbon credits and an environmental review or two depending on what the polls were saying. One thing was for certain, the weather had never been this unreliable, antagonistic, fickle, and worst of all, unreadable. Aubrey and Sabine became slaves to the forecast; often it was dead right, but equally often it was dead wrong. The meteorologists with all their isobars and their warm fronts, their thermal casts and computer spit-outs, were still often only as adept as Farmer Joe reading his tealeaves.

"You want a forecast?" Quincy Klug asked Sabine the one day. "Take a look out of the bloody window. You'll be right every doggone time."

"You want a better forecast?" Dick Conley would ask. "Change the dial on your radio until you find a forecast you like."

"You don't much like the weather?" Pete would climb on the bandwagon. "Wait six hours, or go live in the Arizona desert—either there or in Winnipeg."

The basic message, then, was that when it came to the seasons, time simply involved taking advantage of any window you were given: raking or swathing, combining or baling, working the long mindless hours to get it all done. There is a certain smug satisfaction in watching it rain after your hay is up, and you know that the know-all down the road—the self-styled country sage who lectured you about getting your sweet ass in gear, the same fellow that had the one hundred per cent calf crop last year and the year before—is now whining that his hay is turning black in the swath because he slipped off for a break in Idaho.

Other than that, the Hanlons quickly learned that down on the farm, the machinery of time is measured by jobs and activities, and also by what is convenient to other people. It might only take ten minutes to bring a herd of cows into the corral, or it might take four hours; it depended on the mood they were in. And to some extent, the mood you were in. It might take an hour to remove and replace a bearing in the baler, or it might take a day; much depended on whether the machine's designer intended the repairman to be a contortionist or whether the remnants of the old bearing insisted on staying put. Then the parts you needed might take a day to come in from Vermilion, or they could take a week to come from Illinois. And even then, everything was contingent upon who was having a statutory holiday or long weekend, or on who had gone AWOL or on strike for more pay or shorter hours. The organizer in Sabine had to give up holding her husband consistently accountable when a job took six hours instead of the anticipated one only because she experienced for herself how time was simply unknowable down on the farm. As she said to Sybil, the hippy-type wife of Sigmund the musician, "you only have to unblock a combine or a haybine once before you realize that you cannot hurry that which refuses to be hurried, a bit like our Nellie, really." And so for the Hanlons, even their "free-time" jaunts on their holidays were never held to coincide with some specific hour in the day. If the fishing suddenly came alive on Vancouver Island, why, they would stay an extra day or two. For those urban types pursuing their nine-to-five jobs and their fixed paycheques, time had to be regimented and committed. For them, breakfast is usually snatched, lunch is on the run, and dinner or supper is curtailed so that other things can be done: the kids taken to hockey or ballet practice, and so on. On the farm, however, breakfast can be leisurely, lunch can be paced, and supper unhurried, a prelude to downtime. No wonder, then, that for the circle of friends the Hanlons had left behind in Edmonton, the farm provided an escape from the grind, a sanctuary away from the bustle.

Sigmund, a professional trumpet player with the Edmonton Symphony Orchestra, would endeavor to come down from Edmonton at least once a month for a drive of whatever self-propelled machine was in action. He simply had to have a regular fix of diesel fumes. His wife Sybil loved the farm for a different kind of freedom; in her case, it was to wear clothing creations that would be deemed inappropriate in most urban settings. Add to that her taste for all things hippy, and her "co-workers" were blessed with fleeting visions of her bits and pieces straying in and out of view as she helped with the chores, picking up square bales from the field or gathering the eggs, for example. For the men it was delightful, but nothing more arresting than that given Sybil's innocence.

Then there was Ernie, Ernest the mechanic, whose mission in life was to tinker with all things designated as a machine. If something needed resetting, readjusting, lubricating, Ernie was there. He was the man to keep the Hanlon machinery "regular", maintained and functional. He loved welding too, but unfortunately his best efforts were not much better than Aubrey's "turkey droppings", so that welding tended to be a bit of a hit and miss affair. His wife Mavis, the resident bookworm, also designated herself as "Custodian of the Cellar" and chief wine consultant, not that much in the way of consulting was ever effected. That she took her offices with a commendable gravity was evidenced by the glass of wine almost always in one hand, the other clasping some unabridged literary classic of never less than seven hundred pages.

To add to the cosmopolitan atmosphere and the pool of cheap labour, Jean-Claude and Pierrette Moreau were also regular visitors. All of the others liked to coordinate their visits with the Moreaus because Pierrette was a gifted cook, chef, a gastronomic wizard. When she was down at the farm, she knew she was free to experiment with her wildest gourmet fantasies and get away with it because the open air activities going on always made her "guinea pigs" famished and ready to eat anything. Besides, any *faux pas,* and there were very few, could be masked by the wine tastings that Mavis had planned. Pierrette's husband, Jean-Claude, would remain ever famous for his encounter with Porky Pig in *Footloose in the Front Forty*.

Rounding out the "frequent caller" list was the ineffable and sometimes insufferable Dick Conley, the life and dread of any party, the wise man with the wisdom of the fortune cookie. Unmanageable and therefore unmarriageable, he was embraced by all because of his heart of gold and his utter irreverence for sacred cows and the niceties of convention. Sig and Mavis made a point of keeping his wine glass always full in their constant endeavour to get him to take flight in song. He had one of those rare voices that if unleashed *au naturel,* would send frissons of awe down the spines of his listeners, even if he were giving vent to some low-brow English rugby song from a misspent youth. If he needed to be nudged from there into Tom Jones or Rodgers and Hammerstein, or better yet from Sig's point of view, into Bizet's *Carmen* and "The March of the Toreadors", the wine was an investment well spent. Needless to say, Pete and Jeannie came to insist on a standing invitation when "the crew" was down. As philosopher Pete put it, "what makes a lifestyle a lifestyle worth having is the company you keep."

However, what Aubrey and Sabine also discovered when they expanded their operation was that time is money, just as it is in the industrial sector. Jobs not done, whatever the reason, and there was always a reason, remained undone at a cost. Grain unharvested in the swath because the combine broke down deteriorated in quality, even if one finally did get to it. Hay that had to be raked a second and third time before being baled because Aubrey decided to quit earlier than he should have one evening, cost additional fuel and was vastly poorer in quality owing to the rain that fell during the night. Oh sure, he could and he did blame Dick Conley because he was the one who had dropped in unexpectedly, armed with two bottles of *Chateauneuf Du Pape* that he insisted needed airing this very instant. Above all, time was the unknown in every equation; it was a continuum of separate experiences simply because no job turned out or could be done the same way twice, which is certainly why the faint of heart never lasted at farming. Indeed, time became bound inexorably to character, linked to a person's persistence and staying power. All too often, if you were fool enough to surrender, problems compounded themselves. If you had spent a fruitless hour in trying to catch that calf that needed treatment and you had given up, the odds were that it would be dead on the morrow, and another sick from the same contagious bug. If you did not get around to repairing the baler, the haybine, the rake, the weather could happily sneak up on you and teach you a lesson. Moreover, unlike in most normal jobs, if you were not feeling up to par, you could not just up and take a sick day. No matter how Aubrey and Sabine might be "dragging butt", cows still had to be fed, hay had to be baled, or fields seeded. Aubrey was one of those many males prone to assume the demeanor of a martyr when he was sick. For sure, he never neglected his chores, even when they took him twice as long as they should, but then he would collapse pathetically into the chesterfield and expect his wife to minister unto his every need.

"You're the classic wimp," she would say.

"At least I'm a classic," he would respond weakly. "And anyway, I don't recall you out there helping to feed the girls."

Then there were the days he was not sick, as such, but days where the body still claimed frailty from shoveling grain or snow, from forking manure from the barn into the loader, or from stacking square bales. Once again, the chesterfield was Aubrey's preferred refuge.

"Honey, would you care to massage my legs?"

Naturally when Sabine was sick, she had to make it on her own, more or less. It was not that Aubrey was not caring enough; it was just that he was blithely incompetent. If she wanted a couple of Advil, he could rarely find the bottle. If she asked for a massage, Aubrey thought he was being given a license to explore other forbidden territory.

For those like Aubrey and Sabine who liked the outdoors, time and space combine to form the perfect work context, except in those inevitable and unrelenting cold snaps of minus thirty Celsius. But then it had to be said that the beloved Chinook kept such snaps reasonably short, except when the barometer indicated plus thirty-four Celsius with Aubrey raking hay on the cabless tractor and not daring to remove any more clothing for fear of delighting the neighborhood with another tale about Mister Big.

Still, the whole issue of farming as a lifestyle presupposes one basic fact; that you can make enough to more than just barely survive. Aubrey and Sabine both began to appreciate that because of their expansion, their whole existence had become more tenuous, more contingent upon the goodwill of outside institutional players like the government and the banks, for there was no such goodwill in the marketplace. They began to feel as if they were beggars in some way, and they did not much like it. This realization was not instantaneous, not some sudden revelation on the road to Damascus; it was gradual. They found themselves going through what so many farmers were going through: lean years, several in a row, years when talk was cheap and despair widespread but hidden.

The Canadian farmer is by nature an independent sort, tough and relatively uncompromising, has to be to endure the vagaries of the climate let alone the machinations of the markets. Nonetheless, spiraling input costs and sliding returns put many of them into the hands of the bankers and their collection agencies. An occasional trip to the local Food Bank was never an option for these hardy souls; it would carry too much stigma, too much shame. No matter how human the face at the bank or the credit union, these farmers would have far preferred to tough out the worst of blizzards than wade through the numbers detailing their own failing operations. When it came to paper, and numbers, so many of them floundered in their own self-described stupidity, unable to concede that it was not stupidity at all but unfamiliarity with another world—that baffling world of numbers which could be made to say all sorts of things, depending upon who was doing the packaging and what they wanted said.

Very early on in their joint enterprise, Aubrey and Sabine had concluded that truly the farmer had to be a Jack-of-all-trades. Mechanic, plumber, welder, vet, trucker, you name it, but most of these trades, if not all of them, were hands-on. The bankers' world was an abstract one of spreadsheets and data, of computers and laptops spitting out the too often sordid story of your financial woes when you never knew it was actually being written. How could you know, too, that as far as one or more of the readers was concerned, your story was a comedy of tragic proportions, or a tragedy of comic proportions? Aubrey was told by a succession of bankers in suits that he was overcapitalized, underfunded, overextended, undermechanized; he tended to remain underwhelmed. Other than Peter Walshe, in Red Deer, whose outlook was sympathetically agricultural, not one of the financial gurus ever saw fit to look above the paperwork and congratulate him on the immense progress he and Sabine had made in spite of all of them, certainly not because of them. As Clayton Cole once told Aubrey, "You tell them bankers that you and me'll still be around long after they're gone." To a large degree, he was right.

However, as the Hanlons gradually discovered, they had thrown themselves into an occupation that was in deep trouble the world over. The federal and provincial governments in Canada were forced to find creative ways to bail out their farm folk; but creative too often meant convoluted and cumbersome, and besides, compared to the USA and the EEC countries, Canadian governments refused to have deep pockets when it came to the folk on the land. For many farmers, accepting government help smacked too close to the notion of them taking charity. Aubrey had heard the same old story many times; that every time a Canadian farmer was buried in a cemetery, one hand would extend upwards for a handout. Both he and Sabine found themselves getting angry, angry and frustrated that, by and large, the average Canadian consumer could care less where food came from as long as it was cheap enough not to erode the rest of their disposable income available for things like entertainment and play. Compared to most other developed countries, Canadian consumers spent less of their income on food, and clearly they wanted it to stay that way so they would vote accordingly come election time. Aubrey had a new hobbyhorse!

Outwardly, the agricultural lifestyle seemed as it had always been, but there were major fault lines developing as smaller farmers became increasingly marginalized. One up-and-comer in the banking world, bright as polished brass and lusting for promotion, told Aubrey "the government and the taxpayer do not owe the farmer a living, you know. It was their choice, your choice to do what you do." Would the man's "I'm all right Jack" attitude come to haunt him later on? Aubrey could not say, but that did not mute his response.

"Abso-bloody-lutely, I was the one who chose to go into farming. But then again, if our government wants the small farmer to fade away into the sunset as some kind of anachronism, then the government ought to say so. And please remember something else. It's poor suckers like me who are actually paying your salary so that you can sit up high on your horse and preach your gospel and conduct your so-called 'annual review' of my finances. So go easy on the banker's wisdom, if you don't mind." Once again, another beautiful friendship foundered on the shoals of the banker's shore.

Still, farming had to go on, and the business of making a living on the land called for greater and more varied sacrifice, which in turn brought into question whether lifestyle was the primary attractant for getting into agriculture. Young people, potential farmers themselves, were deserting the agricultural sector in droves. Many of them had grown up on the farm, grown up with the grunge, the grind, the chores. They had witnessed first-hand their parents struggling to stay afloat, had seen so much of their pastoral dignity stripped away by their having to re-mortgage the farm and undermine their equity, their retirement, so who could blame them if they wanted none of it? At least in the oil patch and the wide world of trade and commerce, you could make an assured living. If the consumer needed food, some other sucker could toil away to produce it. It did not matter any more how good was the crop you harvested, how great a calf crop you raised; the market always found a way to render the farmer into a "price-taker". Spiritual satisfaction, yes; economic satisfaction, you've got to be joking! Why hadn't Aubrey seen it before? Over time, he knew the answer to that, too; he and Sabine had expanded, gone further into it because they thought they could not get out of it. Getting out was too much like an admission of defeat. Besides, they had come to enjoy the lifestyle!

Chapter Twelve
OF MUTTS AND MORE

"We need a dog," Sabine said suddenly over breakfast one summer day.

"What for?" mumbled Aubrey not even bothering to look up.

"Every farmer has a dog,' said Sabine. "A dog is part of the agricultural lifestyle."

"We're not every farmer," Aubrey was doing his mumbling best not to engage in the conversation. "Pass the milk, please."

"That's true. But that does not mean we should not have a dog."

"Dogs shit on the carpet and eat the flowers." Aubrey was not sure he could face the whole business of house-training a puppy, and if it was a cattle dog Sabine was after, well she had better think again. Knowing his dear wife, she probably thought all you had to do was to command the dog to "go get them there cows" and hey presto, there the critters would be, filing serenely into the corral with the cattle dog behind them; all you had to do was shut the gate and go and have a cup of tea.

"Dogs keep undesirables away from the property," she said.

"Dogs don't stay home and end up killing the neighbor's cat." Aubrey knew already from the length of the discussion he was "in tough".

"Besides, when did we last have undesirables on the property?"

"There's always a first time," she replied smugly. "Anyway, I'd feel a whole lot safer if we had a big dog around."

Oh, so it was going to be a big dog and an issue of safety, was it? He knew as soon as the question was out of his mouth that he was losing the latest verbal tug-of-war. "What sort of dog are you looking for?"

"A big one."

"A big one? Like a Doberman or a Pit Bull? Or a hulking Great Dane?" The sarcasm was necessary as far as he was concerned.

"A chocolate Lab would be nice."

"Well, if you have to get yourself a dog, then so do I." This last volley would surely put all this silliness to rest.

"Fine," she said. "What kind of a dog do you want?"

Oh, okay, now she's into the sneak attack, Aubrey was thinking. "A small one," he said.

"A small one? Like a poodle or a sausage dog? Or a Chihuahua? Or a pug? A Pug would suit your looks. You, my boy, are joking. You always said you'd never have a dog in the house."

"I would train it," he said.

"Oh, you'd train it! Like to crawl into bed with us and watch football on TV and all. Meanwhile, we could both lie there on a Sunday morning and watch the fleas playing hop-scotch on the bed clothes."

"Your sarcasm is not good enough for an Oscar, my dear," Aubrey said drily.

"Okay," she said as if finally making up her mind. "You can get yourself a small dog as long as I can have a yard dog. But let it also be very clear that your dog does not get any farther than the boot room when it comes into the house." Sabine knew she had to lay down the law right from the start.

"So when are we getting these mutts?" Aubrey asked, thinking he would still have some time to talk her out of it.

"I'm getting mine tomorrow."

"*Tomorrow?* You mean you have already set it up?"

"Yep. And you're coming with me to get it, right?"

"I guess."

Some people should never be allowed to keep dogs just as there are some people who should not be allowed to keep any animal, not a cow, not a dog, not a cat, not even a guinea pig. The Lauterbergs, west of the village of Caroline, were such people. First off, the "chocolate Labs" were Labrador crossed with mongrel, chocolate Labs dressed in some other breed's clothes.

"I thought you said they were purebred," said Sabine to Mrs. Lauterberg who answered that Mr. Lauterberg would be along any minute, and if she had any questions she should ask him. "He'll be here just as soon as he has figured out how to open the outhouse door."

"All the same, I was looking for purebred Labs," Sabine protested, forcing a further response from a lady best described as "grimy".

"Purebred, bah! Look at 'em close. They're just the same as any other chocolate Labs you will ever see. Now how many are you folks looking for? We'll give you a real good deal if you take more than one. We'll give you the deal of a century if you take 'em all, including the mother. We've had enough of 'em. They eat too much and they're always crappin'."

The pups, four of them, were in a makeshift run; an upturned steel half-barrel with a door cut out of it served as a kennel. The ground was littered with dog feces, and even with the wind, the stale smell of canines was almost overpowering. As soon as there were signs that humanity was approaching, the mother took refuge in the kennel, only emerging when she heard Sabine's "oohs" and "ahs" and the kind words being spoken to her babies.

"Well, what d'ya think?" a male voice boomed behind them. Instantly the mother bolted for her kennel, three of her pups right behind her. Mr. Lauterberg was a bear of a man and as grimy as his wife, and he reeked of unpleasantness.

"Well, we were actually looking for purebred Labs," Sabine was determined to hold her ground.

"Purebred? Purebred? What the hell is purebred? Are we not good enough for you or what? These are damn fine puppies, Ma'am, let me tell you. You won't find better any place you go." His wife now hung back, cowering in the same manner as the dog in the kennel.

"Who was the sire, the father?" Aubrey interjected. If Sabine was about to succumb because she was feeling sorry for the animals, at least he would make this unsavory character work for his money.

"The father? Looked like a German shepherd sort of style. He was kinda passing through; roaming around, you might call it. I come around the corner one morning and there he is, having it away with my dog. I shot the SOB right there but it was too late. There's a few too many of these dogs runnin' loose these days, a few too many."

"You shot him?" Sabine was incredulous.

"You're darnn right I shot him. Don't need a new batch of pups every time I turn around, now do I?"

"Why don't you get your dog fixed, spayed?" Sabine pursued him.

"Not everyone in this world is rich like you folks, you know. Runnin' off to a high-priced veterinary every time an animal farts ain't how we do things around here."

"C'mon dear, it's time we went," said Aubrey putting his foot down.

"Where, where are you goin' to?" said the man. "You can't leave without taking a pup or two. Take 'em all. I'll throw the bitch in too if that's what you want."

All the animals were still in the kennel except for the one pup playing with a piece of bone. The man made as if to pick it up. Immediately the pup turned tail and fled to its mother. The man laughed, a sadistic mirthless laugh. "If you folks don't want them, then I'm of a mind to put the whole darn lot in a sack and drown 'em at the river. The bitch too."

Aubrey knew the man was testing out the sensibilities of Sabine, but he did not know Sabine. She reacted, but not in the way he had hoped for. "You know, Mister, somebody like you should never be allowed to keep a dog. You have already ruined these animals. They're terrified of you, terrified of people. So no, we are not going to take any of your animals because we have no wish to buy a dog with lifelong psychological problems. In fact, what I am going to do is to call the Alberta SPCA to come out and take a look."

The man was stunned, had never been talked to this way before, least of all by a woman. He took a long hard look at Sabine, seemed to hesitate a second, then backed right down. "Aw shucks, lady," he said, "there's no need to get all uptight. I'll give 'em all to my neighbor for fifty bucks. He's always wanted them. Always harping on at me, just like you, come to think of it. Damn it to hell, anyhow, women and dogs should all be kept on a short leash, what d'ya say Ira?" Ira had retreated into the house. Ira knew what was good for her.

"So, who's your neighbor?" Aubrey cut in.

"Archie Phelps. Everyone knows Archie cuz he's got a dragon of a wife."

"Here's fifty bucks for the dogs," said Sabine. "You get them over to this Mr. Phelps by the end of the day. I shall phone him tonight. If he doesn't have the dogs then I will bring the SPCA down here myself." Sabine's anger was evident but controlled, and the man knew that she had backed him into a corner because he had accepted the money.

"Okay, okay. Now it's about time you people got the hell off of my property because I'm about ready to call in the cops." The man felt he had to get in one last shot of belligerence, if only to salvage a bit of dignity.

"I'm a retired cop," said Aubrey quietly. "So if you want to make an issue of things, then you go right ahead and call, and I'll call the SPCA at the same time. They might as well all come down and take a look."

A prolonged silence ensued as the man was figuring out what he should do next. "Oh yeah," he said finally. "Well, if you folks would not mind leaving us poor folks in peace, I can get on with my business."

"It'll be a pleasure to leave," said Sabine, turning and walking off to the car with Aubrey following. "And don't forget, I'll be phoning your Mister Phelps tonight," she said over her shoulder.

"Humph," was all the man could muster, taking a kick at an empty beer can lying on the ground.

Sabine was as good as her word. She phoned Archie Phelps that evening, right on seven o'clock.

"Archie here. Archie Phelps," said a kindly older voice.

"Mr. Phelps, my name is Sabine Hanlon. Listen, did your neighbor bring his dogs over to you by any chance."

"Well, as a matter of fact he did. Why do you ask?"

She told him the story, sparing no detail.

"Ah," he said with a sigh, "that man is something else. May I salute you for putting him on the spot. We've been trying for weeks to get the dog from him, even before she had her puppies. Had to pay him a hundred bucks, though. Not that I mind because at least all of them have a good home now."

"A hundred bucks," squealed Sabine. "A hundred bucks? I already paid him fifty and he agreed that was enough. He's nothing but a scoundrel."

"Scoundrel is right, but he's the kind of scoundrel you should leave alone. So let's not worry about it, shall we? I mean, he is my neighbor and you know how neighbors have to get along with each other in the country, much more than in the city. Hold on a second, my wife would like to have a word with you."

"Hello there! This is Sherry Phelps speaking. I don't know what all you said to that awful man, but it sure put him in his place. I thank you for it. I hope you don't mind but I was listening in on the other line. He truly is an awful creature. So I have to thank you for our new dog and her four beautiful puppies."

"Well, I hope for your sake and theirs they are not too psychologically damaged," said Sabine, now feeling a degree of guilt for not taking at least one of them home.

"Nothing that a good dose of TLC cannot cure, and Archie and I certainly have the time to give them that. Besides, my son who farms out west is going to take a couple of the pups once they've settled down. Now, any time you pass this way, you be sure to drop in for a cup of coffee. We would sure like to meet you."

"We shall make a point of it," Sabine replied.

"We've got to make good and sure that we get the dog that we want, not some mutt that somebody else wants to offload on us. When all is said and done, the dog we choose should be our companion for many years, God willing," Sabine said to Aubrey when she put down the phone.

"I can't argue with that," he said, wondering whether his wife would actually honour their deal or welsh on it as soon as she got her own dog.

The following week, the weekly paper, *The Mountaineer*, contained not one but two adverts of interest. One of the ads stated: "Australian Red Heeler pups. Great cattle dogs. 3 male, 2 female. $150each." The number was a Condor number, about fifteen miles from the farm.

"Let's go and have a look," said Sabine. "I'm not sure what a Red Heeler is supposed to look like." She said nothing about the second advert, leaving Aubrey to find it for himself: "Jack Russell Terriers. Must have room to run. Tails docked. 2 male, 3 female. Available now. $250 each." The number was an Eckville number, probably a good half hour away. Had Sabine not seen the ad, Aubrey was thinking. Or did the price put her off? Or was it that she was simply not going to countenance a small dog in the house? Maybe she had no idea what a Jack Russell terrier looked like.

"I'll come with you only if you agree to go and check out the Jack Russell pups for sale in Eckville."

"Okay," was Sabine's guarded response with no real enthusiasm but no real negativity either, whatever that might mean. Of course she had seen the ad.

It turned out that both dog sellers were located on farms, as Aubrey would have hoped given that the one lot were "good cattle dogs" and the other lot had to have "room to run".

The first stop was at the place with the Red Heelers. Sabine was a conquest the moment she saw them. Like the "chocolate Labradors" of Caroline, they had their own run, but here all similarity ended. The run was pristine; the kennel was actually a kennel, not an upturned barrel, and there was a large tree offering shade. As for the animals themselves, they were bouncing with health and happiness. The issue came down to choice; which one to take? The farmer and his wife were a middle-aged couple who obviously took pride in putting their dogs to work. If the farmer himself had not finally pushed Sabine into taking the male pup he had picked out, she would have stayed there until nightfall humming and hawing and cavorting with the pups.

"See, this here dog has markings on the roof of his mouth. That tells me he's going to be a great dog with all sorts of personality," the man had to clinch the argument.

He'll need a strong personality if my wife is going to be his trainer, Aubrey found himself thinking a little uncharitably.

"Should be a fine cattle dog too," continued the farmer. "But then again, I can't make any promises. See, we've had some that couldn't figure out the front end of a cow from the back no matter how hard we trained 'em. It's there or it's not there, game over. But for most of 'em, it just comes naturally."

A coffee, further conversations of discovery about red Heelers, and the Hanlons went on their merry way—made the merrier by the antics of one very cuddly, supercharged reddish-brown puppy—and down of course by one hundred and fifty dollars.

The second farm, when they eventually found it, was equally pleasing, not as organized as the first one but pleasing nonetheless. As soon as they arrived, the patchwork pups came tumbling off the raised deck, their curiosity restrained only by a garden fence of chicken wire designed no doubt to keep them from heading off to Saskatoon. Sabine was shrieking with delight when a lady came out of the house, a smile of genuine amusement on her face. Neither Aubrey nor Sabine had ever had any direct experience with Jack Russells, but they were captivated immediately, Sabine especially. So at least there would be no problem with his bride, Aubrey thought smugly. As they watched the show the dogs were putting on, one little pup decided that it was time for him to display a little defiance. Golden brown blotches on a coat of snow white, he stood alone, endeavouring to show some muscle while his siblings tumbled around after an old tennis ball.

"Is that little fellow a male?" Aubrey asked of the lady.

"As a matter of fact he is," said the woman, clearly much in love with all of her animals. "We call him *Kali,* Swahili for 'fierce' because he always decides he has to protect the others from strangers."

"He's the one," Aubrey said immediately. "We'll take him."

"Hold on a second," Sabine interrupted. "You haven't even looked over the others and you've already picked one." It was then that her agenda became evident to her husband. "How about that little fellow over there, the little one with black spots. He's a blast."

"That's also a 'he," said the woman. "We called him *'Mtata'* because he's always the first to get into trouble. *'Mtata'* means 'trouble' in Swahili."

"Isn't that a coincidence? We have a cow called *'Mtata'* and does she ever live up to her name," gushed Sabine. "But you've already given them names and then you put them up for sale. Isn't that, how can I put it, very difficult for you when they go?"

"No, not really. You see there comes a time when we need them out of here. It's kind of like having a house full of your own rambunctious teenagers. You love 'em dearly, but boy you're glad when they're gone. You don't have to go with our names, you know. Feel free to choose your own. Naming them helps me and my husband to remember which is which."

"Why Swahili?" asked Aubrey.

"Why Swahili? We immigrated to Canada from East Africa, from Kenya to be exact. We used to raise Jack Russells out there. The mother you see here, *'Malaika',* was actually born in Africa. We brought her with us and put her to stud."

"Can we come through the fence and play with them?" Sabine could not hold herself back.

"Oh sure. My husband was on the phone when you arrived. He'll be out any minute."

Sabine was over that fence in a flash. She then let herself go completely, clowning around with the gaggle of pups, the mother right in there and having as much fun as the unrestrained adult. Aubrey hung back, trying to second-guess himself on his choice. He couldn't. The little character he had chosen was right in the thick of it with the rest of them until it seemed he suddenly remembered his self-appointed role of protector, whereupon he would disengage and attempt to bark at Aubrey. Finally Aubrey walked over and picked him up. The little dog growled once then licked his hand.

"That's the star," said a man coming out of the house. "That's our *'Kali'.* You won't find a better guard dog anywhere."

"Charlie, we both agreed we'd stay away from advising people," his wife scolded him gently.

"Yeah, yeah, but this man has a keen eye. That's all I'm saying." He came over to Aubrey and pumped his hand in greeting. "Charlie Hainsworth is the name."

"Aubrey. Aubrey Hanlon."

"And my wife Cheryl," he signaled his wife to come over.

"That overgrown kid in with the dogs," now somewhere around the corner of the house, "that's my wife Sabine."

"Sabine? What a lovely name," said Cheryl.

"That overgrown kid" reappeared laughing hysterically, the dogs chasing her, the ball, each other, probably wondering why all the other humans standing there were not as playful as this great big human puppy in their midst.

"Sabine, come on over and meet these people," Aubrey shouted in hope of bringing at least some decorum back into the scene.

Suddenly subdued, Sabine made her way over, embarrassed as adults often are when they have been caught reverting back to their childhood.

"Sabine, this is Cheryl and Charlie Hainsworth."

"Pleased to meet you," Sabine said sheepishly.

"You know what?" said Cheryl coming to her rescue. "It's so lovely to watch an adult lose all inhibition and just play. Thank you for making my day."

"Will you both come on in for a coffee?" Charlie asked.

"Well," said Sabine hesitantly, "we've just bought ourselves one pup and had to stop and have a coffee there, but yes, we'd love to stay and have another."

"What did you say? You've just bought a pup? Another Jack Russell?" asked Cheryl.

"Actually no. A Red Heeler."

Naturally they all had to go out and meet the Red Heeler and shake paws and gasp with all the appropriate trimmings.

"His name is "Chippy," Sabine suddenly announced.

This of course prompted suitable comments from all except Aubrey who had been thinking along the lines of "Prince" or "Duke", even "Simba" if he had to be in keeping with the African theme they seemed to have adopted. By then it was time to withdraw to the house to talk of Africa and lions and snakes and Jack Russells. The coffee was duly taken, two cups all round, before Aubrey launched into the dealing; it was, after all, to be his dog.

"So I'll take the dog I picked out at the very beginning, the one you named Kali, a name I really like by the way."

"Fine by us," said Charlie.

"So, how much did you say you wanted for him?" Aubrey continued, hoping the couple might do better than the $250 in the advertisement.

"Two fifty," said Cheryl gaily.

"Hold on a sec," Sabine came in from nowhere. "Honey, are you absolutely certain about the one you picked because I sure like the one Cheryl says is called Trouble. He's so cute!"

"Take 'em both," said Charlie, as if $500.00 should be no great sacrifice.

"How much did you pay for the Red Heeler, if you don't mind my asking?" Cheryl chipped in.

"One fifty," said Sabine.

"Okay then, how about four hundred for the pair?" said Charlie.

Aubrey was always a sucker for bargaining. Forgetting the fact that he was only interested in one, he blurted out, "Three fifty."

"Done," said Cheryl. "Only because we know they're going to a fabulous home." Whereupon she burst into tears, mumbling something about losing her babies to such nice folks and causing a similar reaction for Sabine who felt so guilty about taking the babies away.

Dogs on the farm added a whole new dimension to life. Because they were introduced to each other so young, they flourished together; although from the very beginning, it was clear who was boss. Kali took no guff and gave no quarter, although it was a source of great chagrin to him that Chippy was outgrowing him so quickly. Yet Chippy never ever took advantage of his size, at least never with his two buddies; they were his playmates and his brothers, and he had far too gentle a personality to challenge the inner hierarchy. Which may also have explained why he was such a useless cattle dog; of that there could be no doubt, he was hopeless. If he needed to go to the left, he would go to the right. If he needed to get behind a bunch of cows and push them forward, there he would be in front of them and causing them to back up. If he needed to sit quietly, he would take to running madly about and barking incessantly. On the one occasion when he got too exasperated, Aubrey put the dog in the tractor cab and shut the door. It took him only minutes to complete the particular task he was doing before he came back to let Chippy out, only to discover that Chippy had first chewed the knob off the gear shift and had then been working assiduously on the padding around the cab, put there to reduce engine noise. Aubrey was furious; Chippy just wagged his tail, assuredly seeing himself as "Achiever of the Month". When Aubrey communicated his utter displeasure with her dog to his wife, it was she who brought perspective.

"You know, dear," she said, "in all honesty, Chippy is about as trainable as you are."

"Meaning?"

"Meaning that both of you are completely untrainable. Leave him be. Let him be the guard dog he's supposed to be. If you want to work with cows, shut him in the granary."

"Guard dog, my foot. He would smother any burglar with love."

Then there was Sabine and her Golden Rule that Aubrey's dogs were not to get beyond the door of the boot-room. Within a day, she had those two butterballs in the sitting room, and within a week they had somehow found a way to curl up in her bed. It was true that Mtata puddled once, only once mind you, in the bed. Their subsequent banishment lasted a full forty-eight hours before clemency was granted, possibly because Mtata had been smart enough to pee on Aubrey's side of the bed when he did it. Within a month, they pretty well had the run of the house. Being the quick learners they were, they soon preferred to cock their legs and do their constitutionals in Chippy's territory. The house remained clean from there on.

Jack Russell terriers are known for their boundless energy and over-abundant enthusiasm, spiced up with a go get 'em attitude. Stray cats soon learned to give the Hanlon yard a wide berth. The squirrels, on the other hand, developed a special relationship with the dogs. As nimble as they were, they reveled in teasing the two Jack Russells. Coyotes were always a danger, but as long as Chippy was around to protect his companions, they never ventured too close. But then again, no dog world can be definitively serene; there are always those occasions where the world is turned upside down.

Mtata was the inquisitive one, the one with the nose that could leave no scent unexplored. He conducted his business with all kinds of creatures, mostly to their peril: voles, field mice, a stray rabbit that was too frustratingly fast for him, a mama goose with a temper, even a wandering toad. But the porcupine was the first creature to teach him the essence of respect. Indeed, it was Mtata who led his two partners in crime, into a new understanding of pain and the respect that came after.

Sabine and Aubrey had gone for a walk in the treed portion of their land; both scenic and tranquil in autumn, it was a haven of peace. The dogs were running ahead as usual, with the two Jack Russells serious about noses to the ground, and Chippy trailing first one and then the other as if it was the job of the terriers to serve up the most interesting of scents for his predilection. By the time Sabine had spotted the animal, it was too late. Mtata was already in attack mode and already had a face full; Kali decided he had to take over, and the porcupine gave him the same treatment as his brother. Chippy hesitated but must have concluded that he could not hang back, and he too got whacked across the muzzle for his efforts. Having put all would-be predators to flight, the porcupine waddled off to a swamp willow that he proceeded to climb to get out of the way of pesky canines.

Aubrey and Sabine were now faced with what, to them, was one of the hardest decisions a farmer has to make. Should they shoot a porcupine that was just going innocently about its business, in case the dogs happened on it again? And what if it got in among the cows, what then? The live-and-let-live school of thought was all very nice, but how expensive would it be in vet bills? They would soon find out since it was to the vet's they were now headed. Worse yet, since it was evening, they would have to call him out after hours and pay for his inconvenience. "Robber's wages," Aubrey called it sourly. Sabine suggested they phone Pete and Jeannie first to see if they had ever had a similar experience.

"Oh my dears, don't even think of running to the vet; it'll cost you two of your arms and a leg. Three dogs? My goodness, you'll be paying enough for the man's whole family to go on a Caribbean cruise. Pete and I will be right over. We'll get the spines out; we've done it before. Whatever you do, though, don't follow that old wife's tale of cutting them so they fall out. They don't and they won't. We'll be there in fifteen minutes."

Mtata was the first up; so chosen because Sabine knew he would be the toughest to deal with. Pete and Aubrey wrapped him tightly in a towel, a sort of doggy straitjacket, and Sabine and Jeannie set to with needle-nose pliers, removing a total of 25 spines, with Mtata all the while determined to get at least one bite into a helping hand. Once he was done, he was let loose out of the towel and he took off around the room in "happified" dementia. But as soon as Kali was brought in, Mtata decided the best strategy was to take refuge under the bed in case of revisitation.

It was uncanny how differently the two dogs behaved. Kali seemed too know he was being helped. In fact, they did not need to wrap him up in a towel because he conducted himself like an old soldier having his war wounds dressed on the field of battle: "stiff upper lip, boys, I can take it." When he was done, he went to sit beside the fireplace as if to weigh the gain that comes from pain.

Chippy was altogether a different proposition. Now near fully-grown and a solid fifty pounds, he was not about to lie there and take it, nor could he be wrapped in the towel like the others. Aubrey finished up lying across him on the boot-room floor while the ladies did their work. Between all three dogs, they counted 63 spines, and they knew they had got them all after rubbing their hands over the dogs' muzzles checking for anything that might have broken off at skin level. They let Chippy outside as soon as he was done, and he went and lay beneath Pete's pickup to lick his wounds and sulk a bit. Half an hour later, porcupines were no more than an experience layered in the dogs' memories as creatures to be avoided. Further encounters with porcupines produced only frantic barking; there was never any further engagement with the enemy.

The skunk was another story; largely because it was Sabine and not one of the dogs that took the first direct hit. She had gone up to the chicken house one Friday evening to put the chickens away for the night. The dogs had gone off with Aubrey for a walk in the woodland. Sabine actually saw the skunk picking its way across the big corral. It was arrestingly beautiful, majestic even, with its black and white business suit shining in the sun. She stood and watched in utter fascination; the only skunk she had ever seen close up was a dead excrescence that was lying in the road. Of course the animal had seen her, but it came on with an arrogance born of glandular power. What did it care about the laws of property and title that these humans liked to weave around themselves? Such laws had no application to its natural world. Only it suddenly dawned on this particular human where the animal was going: to her chicken house. Unthinkingly, she grabbed a stick and took a run at it to chase it away. As if in slow motion, the animal turned and gave her the full treatment. Sabine had never experienced anything quite so disgusting and so vile in all her life. The odour—no, the stench—was indescribable. Nauseating, it was so overpowering it dropped her to her knees, allowing the skunk to make a deft turnaround and find a hole in the building that led it to safety beneath the chicken house floor. Sabine rose unsteadily to her feet. She was screaming in anger, howling with anguish, and weeping in frustration, all at the same time. Oh God, this was absolutely unbelievable, beyond awful, beyond catastrophic. She could feel wetness seeping into her clothes so she did the only thing she could do in the circumstances, she stripped down to her underwear. Even her gumboots were tainted, she realized as she kicked them off. So there she stood, the Lady of the Manor, barefooted, clad only in undergarments, contemplating life in the raw.

Ah yes, her undergarments. That very morning it had so happened that she had run out of clean, farm-duty underwear; even her emergency drawer was empty, so she had been compelled, therefore, to throw her entire collection first into the washing machine and then into the dryer where it now sat. Forced to root around in the back of her closet, she had found one of those sexy sets(the kind that only a man might buy for his wife at Christmas time and then expect his woman to wear daily throughout the year), a low-slung lacy bra, in screeching "La Senza crimson", with a thong-like thing to match. The moment she had pulled it out of her stocking, she had told Aubrey very forcefully that Santa should never again spend hard-earned dollars on such follies because she would refuse to wear them. So here she now was, marooned up at the chicken house, all set to hobble her way back to the house in her socks, and still good-looking enough to be "Mrs. October" in the "Mobile Mamas of Agriculture" calendar for 1974.

Halfway to the house, and panic! She could not run: not with the rough ground assaulting her feet. She heard the car slow down to turn into the drive where she would be in the direct line of sight, and she also knew who it would be. Dick Conley had invited himself down for the weekend, and wouldn't you know it, it had to be Dick Conley of all their friends who was now about to see her *in extremis*. The urge to increase speed led only to a stubbed toe. Mr. Conley drove sedately down the driveway, and there she was, doing her very best with her diminutive hands to cover the too much territory that the La Senza designer had deemed should be available for viewing. Conley was Conley: inimitable, irreverent, not one to let an opportunity pass him by. He was certainly not the kind of man who would look away in false modesty, preferring to stare with admiration at such unexpected exposure. Worse yet, he switched his headlights on bright and activated one of those novelty air horns that played a spirited rendition of "Oh Canada". The racket brought first the dogs and then their owner out of the trees. Aubrey's eyes nigh popped out of his head when he saw his wife clad in a get-up that he had long assumed she had burned. Then he saw her distress, as did a now contrite Mr. Conley who was now getting out of his car to be of assistance. But chivalry can never triumph over skunk. The aroma did not merely arrest the noble crusaders, it repelled them with gusto. Conley yelled at his hostess to go and take a bath in tomato juice, which she did. Twice. And when she had exhausted Mavis' entire supply of juice for her Bloody Marys, she tried tomato soup, and still she reeked. A soak in Epsom Salts, another in water and milk laced with something labeled "Fragrances of the Canadian Shield", Santa's offering of four years ago, and she was prepared to face the world. But even after all of that, she could still smell skunk. The men said that she was "tolerable", but Aubrey still could not bring himself to share the matrimonial bed that night.

Ah, but the saga was not over with, not yet. The next morning, following their usual routine, Aubrey let the dogs out for their morning pee on the flowers. He put the coffee on and waited for the dogs to come back and scratch at the door. And he waited, and some more, but they did not come back. Worried now about coyotes, he changed into his work gear and headed outside. That was when he heard the furious barking, and he knew; oh yes, he knew. He knew they had cornered that skunk. As he neared the chicken house, the stench was so thick, he found himself virtually gagging. Being a man of immense courage and fortitude, he plowed on. There they were: Chippy, a wise spectator to this canine "Wide World of Sport"; Kali, too fat to fit down the hole, was barking at one side; and Mtata, rump outwards, halfway in the hole and chastising that skunk for all he was worth. This skunk had to die, and quickly, had to—however much of a conservationist and animal-hugger Aubrey thought himself to be. That was when he spotted the hose still attached to the nearby water hydrant. Time for action!

He switched the water on, turning the setting on the pistol to jet stream and attacking the skunk from the opposite side to the dogs. He knew he must have flushed them all judging by the heightened cacophony of barking, but perhaps it was the memory of the porcupine that held back the dogs from a full frontal assault. Aubrey just caught a glimpse of the enraged skunk burrowing into a small stack of straw bales near the barn. This time it was Kali who took up the challenge. Hackles up, a no-nonsense militaristic demeanor, he went in. Aubrey heard a noise akin to a spray can going off. Kali appeared in "reverse express"; he began rolling frantically in the grass at the same time as furiously wiping his muzzle on the ground, on the straw, on anything. Mtata hung back in awe with Chippy. Aubrey had just made the decision to go and fetch his shotgun when Kali's fury apparently got the better of him. Growling angrily, he stormed back into those bales, only this time he reemerged with the sunk twisting and turning in his jaws. That dog's fury knew no bounds; the poor skunk was shaken to death in seconds. So began a second nightmare of "de-skunkification", made all the worse because the dogs were wet from Aubrey's hose attack. Chippy was not so bad, but the two terriers were both repulsive. Conley refused to help unless Aubrey got right down to sexy underwear as his wife had done.

Chapter Thirteen
CAUTION, DETONATED DRIVER!

"Sabby, my dear girl, you've gone mad, completely bloody mad. Certifiably insane!" Stella proclaimed. "Look it, getting married to your dreamboat of a husband is one thing, but deciding to get down and work alongside of him every hour of every day, just you and him, how on earth will you ever manage? I'm telling you here and now, you won't be able to stand it. Now, your desire to escape to the country, that I do understand. The hustle and bustle and the glare of city lights get to me, too. So why not just go out and buy yourselves some acreage or a cabin at Pigeon Lake? Keep a cow and a goat, too, if you have to. But this going out and buying a whole damn farm; to me that does not make any sense at all. As if that's not bad enough, you and hubby-boy are going to work with a few cows. Why cows? A couple of horses, maybe, but cows? Don't you remember where the word "bovine" comes from? Besides, cows are such dirty animals; they're probably the only animal that has no problem shitting and eating simultaneously. Don't you folks realize how much you'll be getting yourselves into, and I do mean that literally?"

Sabine was to recall that conversation with Stella many times. Stella was her best business friend and confidante in Edmonton before they moved. She was a self-made lady, a career woman who had long since dispensed with the excess baggage of her husband: "A useless appendage whose only thought upon waking was the next boy-toy he should go out and buy with the money I earned."

"Think about it, Sabby. In five years you'll have scabby hands, skin like a dinosaur, and a body thick enough to be a freakin' coalminer. And there'll be cow poop permanently under those fingernails. Your going-out dress will be a pair of jeans and a checkered blouse, and you'll be wearing cowboy boots of course. You'll come out with words like 'shucks' and 'aw' and 'howdy', and you'll keep a nag called Blue in the barn. Is that what you want, really want? Worse yet, you'll get to cussing like a trooper and swilling your coffee like you're at the trough." Stella always expressed herself in Technicolour and without reserve, which was why Sabine so enjoyed her.

Oh yes, Sabine remembered that conversation, every bit of it, as if it was yesterday, and she was determined to prove Stella wrong. But then again, when Sabine first metamorphosed from city slicker to country bumpkin, she realized that she too harboured a whole range of stereotypes as to what made up the average farmer's wife. As with all stereotypes, they were created more by a lively imagination than by any resemblance to reality. In her own muddled way, she saw herself as a modern-day Bo-Peep, skipping about in the meadow with her lambs. There were never any cows. Aubrey and five years down on the farm had changed all of that, erasing all her idealized fantasies forever.

The whole thing came down to a series of recognitions, she decided. The first of these was that for the family farm to truly flourish there had to be an equal commitment to the enterprise from both husband and wife. If there were any kids around who felt like doing their share, well, that was a real bonus, especially when most kids quickly realized they could do far better with their working lives if they were off the farm permanently and far enough away that they could not be press-ganged into helping with the harvest and such. Moreover, any commitment had to be as much mental as physical; it had to be so because a second recognition was that spouses were never as physically strong as each other, wives generally being regarded as the weaker sex in the physical department. What was so refreshing was that there was no stigma attached to stating such a recognition, no rabid accusations of chauvinism or sexism or discrimination; it was just plain obvious! Sabine, therefore, made no apologies that she did not shovel grain, preferred not to huck square bales off the field, and never could have stomached cleaning out the chicken house. Those were all designated "Aubrey jobs". After all, he was the one who liked to think he was pectorally well endowed. Oh sure, she would carry a couple of pails of chop if she absolutely had to, but it stopped right there. However, it also had to be said that what she lacked in the physical dimension was more than made up for in the managerial one. Custodian of all bills, accounts and all things paper; dispenser of drugs, vitamins, minerals and TLC; and quartermaster for home and yard, she was indispensable, even if she had to remind her husband occasionally that this was so. She had her role in life, as did he. Far from being "stuck " with Aubrey day in day out as Stella had predicted, she and her mate learned to work as a team; they complemented each other, and thus the team was formidable. Even the animals knew this and respected it, although good old Nellie did seem to get a perverse enjoyment in making them run for their money now and again. Rarely did the cows balk if Aubrey and Sabine chose to take a stroll among them, but let a stranger tag along and that was altogether a different story! Bring in that buffoon Conley, and they would be instantly primed to take the gate; shut or open, it mattered not.

Sabine also found her rural female neighbors to be more upfront and genuine than her previous urban counterparts. It was easy to see why. There was little need for airs and graces for there was rarely anybody around to be impressed. Image, for example, made no great splash here; stonewashed jeans were nothing but presumptuous in a world where jeans got genuinely stained with everything from battery acid to transmission oil. This is not to say that Sabine found rural women not to be fashion-conscious; it was just that they had other priorities on their minds. Take the fabulous story Maisie Browlee told her; "Irrepressible Maisie" Aubrey liked to call her. It helped that the story put Sabine's "La Senza incident" into a wider perspective.

Maisie was one good-looking woman, thirty-something, who farmed with her husband Roman out towards Strachan. It was the height of the calving season, said Maisie. For the Brownlees, this was their time of stress—overseeing the birthing of about 250 calves. There was just Maisie and her husband with no outside help, so stress was the order of not just the day but also the season. There were no two ways about it; that couple put in their time even if they were highly organized. Maisie usually took the night shift, 10 p.m. to 4 a.m., which allowed her husband a minimum of six hours straight sleep, assuming there were no crises. Roman would rise at four and go at it. On the particular day in question, he was very busy. A heifer had just calved in a snow bank. So with Maisie helping, he had to rescue the heifer's newborn and walk her into the barn, he carrying the calf, Maisie shepherding the mother behind. Maisie then went off to bed, while her mate continued on. One sick calf had to be "hosed" or tubed: force-fed its milk because it was too weak to suck. Another had to be reintroduced to its mother's tit, and reintroduced again and again because it just could not figure out how to recapture it after it had slipped out of its mouth. Two more cows beginning their labour had to be moved into the calving stalls, and the waterer in the main corral had to be thawed out because either the wind had found a way to freeze the inlet pipe or the heat tape had quit working. At 8 a.m. when Maisie woke up, she realized Roman had not made it in yet for his breakfast, so she did what she always did; she got up to go and check on him.

She forced herself out of her warm bed; six weeks of the calving regime having taken their toll. She walked over to her dresser and pulled out a drawer. Damn! Wouldn't you know it? She was out of clean underwear, just as Sabine had been before her. Worse still, she had not run the washing machine the previous day, so everything was still in "the stink pile" as she called it. Oh did Sabine ever feel better that this sort of thing happened to others, though most would never admit to it. Oh well, decided Maisie, she would go without underwear for now, run up and check on her husband, he would not know anyway, and then she would come back down to the house and run a load of personal laundry in the washing machine. Slipping on the pair of jeans closest to hand and a heavy sweatshirt, she headed for the door, her ample bosoms reveling in unexpected freedom. Roman had just finished up bedding another stall, ready for an expectant mother.

"Ah, there you are, honey," he said, happy to see her. "I need another bottle of Biomycin and another of NuFlor. We're plumb out of both and we need to dose 56's calf because it's not feeling so hot. So would you do me a favour and nip into town right away and pick some up at the vet's? We really don't want to be caught without it."

"Sure", Maisie said, always quick to oblige. "I'll grab a coffee and head on out. Have I got time to pick up a few groceries? We've got almost nothing to eat."

"Of course, just as long as you hurry!" How many times has that particular phrase invited disaster?

Maisie was quick. The vet clinic was not busy and she was in and out within three minutes. On to the grocery store she went, the big, new Sobeys that she so enjoyed: "Slobbeys", her husband called it. Trying her best not to dawdle, she latched on to two cartons of milk and was halfway down the cereal aisle looking for Roman's favourite. Her eyes were taking in an older man and his wife obviously in to do the weekly shopping, with the man's face announcing to all that he was essentially a prisoner of war. But suddenly there he was looking directly at her with the most quizzical of expressions and nodding at the same time. She looked away, her mind scrambling. Was he someone she was supposed to know? Had he recognized her, and as so often happened, had she forgotten who he was? She glanced back again and only then felt the unrestricted movement beneath her sweatshirt. She was about to give him a drop-dead glare when once again he gestured downwards with his head. There, on show for all who cared to see, was a massive clump of pubic fuzz. Her heart all but stopped, she said. All the colour drained from her face as she tugged frantically at a zipper that was bound and determined it would never close again. She was about ready to pass out with embarrassment when the man's wife looked her way.

"Are you all right, dear?" she said, seeing a fellow creature apparently in some distress.

"Just feeling a little fuzzy," Maisie heard herself say, at which not only did the husband almost collapse in hysterics, he backed into the pyramid of cans that were in a splendid soup display, sending dozens of cans of soup tumbling into the aisle.

"Albert!" screamed the man's dragon. "Now look what you have done! I can't take the old fool anywhere," this last comment directed at Maisie who had inexplicably dumped her shopping basket on the floor and bolted, prompting everyone around to think that she was the guilty party.

What Sabine found so healthy about this story was that Maisie was unafraid to tell it. Beyond this, so many farm women were able to laugh so easily at themselves, maybe in part because they saw themselves too often in some reflection or other, dressed like wandering scarecrows or frumpish aliens. Practical farm clothing, coveralls and such, could hardly be called stylish at the best of times. These ladies were not afraid to share their most outrageous experiences with others, and once the telling of such tales began, there was no end to them, especially of the ones involving shenanigans with the husband. Not that Sabine was liberated enough to tell her "La Senza" tale to anyone, not yet.

"Did you tell your husband when you got home?" Paula Dewhurst, one of the other women in on the conversation, had to ask.

"Well, he would probably have heard about it sooner or later, so yes, I told him. Besides, he had to know why I had come home without any groceries. He couldn't stop laughing for a whole week. And he's taken to walking around saying things like, 'My wife is one of them fuzzy-wuzzies down on the farm.' But let me tell you, his turn will come. I'll tell you something else, too. I now have an emergency drawer of underwear."

So do I, Sabine was thinking, so do I.

Paula, being Paula, had to add her ten cents worth. "You know what, sometimes I get to thinking we should force our menfolk to wear some of the underthings they think we should wear. Take my old man, for instance. He seems to think that all I need to wear underneath is a skimpy bit of string and lace, preferably in neon purple. So there I am, putting on my heavy duty work bra—you girls know the sort, one from which there can be no escape—and he has the nerve to say, 'Oh, so we're off with the heavy armour to take on the Taliban today, are we?' I mean, can you imagine what would happen if these two hummers got loose chasing a cow? In three seconds I'd be on my back like an upturned tortoise." Paula, it has to be said, was also well built.

Sabine could not help but laugh. After all, she had worked too often beside her dear friend Sybil, Siggy's Sybil, whose hippy attire, airy as it was, put enough flimsy lace and string on display to keep the men around mesmerized for hours. Not that she did it deliberately, not Sybil;

that was just the distracted way she was. What Sabine found refreshing about such characters was the attitude that said, "Take me as you find me".

Stella would have said they were "too earthy, too bucolic" for her, as though this implied some sort of rustic coarseness that put them beyond her pale as far as intimacy was concerned. Sabine was getting to know them in a far different way; they were simply unafraid to be who they were. They would never need regular makeovers or "life coaches", no personal trainers to define who they thought they ought to be. They did not need tubs of oil-of-this or lotion-of-that to keep their supposed unsightly wrinkles at bay. In any crisis, udder balm would do just fine. These were country ladies whose husbands knew enough to tread softly and to bring home the odd bouquet of roses or bottle of Chablis. Like Hugo Hartford who was married to the fiery Marta.

Once again, the story took place during the calving season. After three weeks of being confined to barracks, so to speak, not only did Marta agree that Hugo should take a night out to play hockey with the boys, his team aptly named "Rocky Men O' Paws", she actually insisted that he do so, provided he was back by eleven o' clock that night, because it was calving season nonetheless. Because the calving season was a given, she did not make any stipulation about the sort of condition in which he should return; he knew enough and was responsible enough not to come home incapacitated. Besides, she had booked a girls' night out for the following Friday. Furthermore, she knew she needed time to herself, even if that time was shared, consumed, by expectant bovine companions and their young. Having Hugo around all of the time, she explained, was like having a pesky mosquito trapped in one's ear. He needed time, she needed time; so off he went to his hockey, and her body released an involuntary sigh of relief.

"Old farts' hockey" would not be complete without a jug or two of suds after the exertion, so Hugo permitted himself the usual "one for the road". And another, then another: to the point where the road had to be someone else's concern. They were celebrating the birth of a teammate's twin girls; at least that was the official explanation, even if after two hours Hugo could not remember which teammate it was. Inevitably he had to make the decision to abandon his truck in town and catch a ride home in a taxi at two in the morning. "I'm a little on the late side," he had to confess to his partners in crime, still partying. From there on, his company was not particularly welcome to anyone. His attempts at song on the way home caused the taxi driver to threaten to deposit him on the side of the road. And as he foresaw, there was no ecstatic welcome when he got home, not with his admitted shortcomings and his wobbly condition, and worst of all, with his blatant and callous disregard of a wife slaving away at home taking care of their mutual economic interests. But there was more to it, more that he could not have known; not that his addled brain would connect the dots in its present state, anyway.

For Marta, the whole night had been not a quiet evening but a nightmare. She had been unable to call her devoted husband on his cell phone because she had found it on the kitchen table, right where he had left it. Probably by design, she thought sourly. She had gone out to the barn at 8 p.m. Everything looked good. The cow that had calved at five had cleaned off her baby; both were now lying side by side, snug and content in the straw bedding. Okay, so Dumbo, the calf with the huge ears and no evident brain, would have to be shown how to access the groceries once again, but he would have to go hungry until she had done her outside check. At least there were still three empty stalls still available in the barn. Armed with one of those flashlights boasting zillions in candlepower, she made her way first into the holding pens and then into the field, at once realizing this could be a long night. An older cow had just dropped her calf, but no panic: she was up and doing her thing. There was certainly no need to bring her into the barn yet, seeing that she was in good fresh bedding. Oh, oh, there in the far corner was a brindle heifer eyeing her with intense suspicion and, it seemed, keeping her rear end out of Marta's line of sight, forcing Marta to walk the full length of the field to check her out. Sure enough, she was in the throes of calving, but there was only a single foot showing. Where was the other one? Quietly and without fuss, talking softly to her all the way, Marta got the animal into the maternity stall in the barn. Before rushing off to the house for a glove and a bottle of mineral oil for lubrication, she gave the heifer some chop to settle her down.

As she left the house, she glanced at the clock. Hmm, 10.30 p.m., Hugo should be home any time soon. She returned to the heifer. The birthing had progressed no further, as she expected. She coaxed the heifer into the head-gate and restrained her. Putting the glove onto her right hand and arm, and oiling it liberally, she inserted her hand into the animal's vulva. Yes, as she had surmised, one of the baby's legs was folded back so that no matter how hard the mother was to push, the calf was stuck. Marta began to manipulate the baby, gratified to feel a strong reaction as she did so. The heifer immediately began contracting ever more strongly, crushing Marta's arm so hard she cried out in pain, cursing Hugo at the same time. Where the hell was he? Where had the idiot got to? Oh well, she would have to do it on her own. After one particularly strong contraction, Marta was able to push the calf back in, and struggling desperately to reach the uncooperative foot, finally she was able to grab onto it and pull it out alongside the other one just in time. She withdrew her hand. After five mighty contractions from the mother, the baby was spat out, literally. Marta was exultant, so proud of her heifer, of the calf, of herself. But there was nobody around with whom she could share the moment. Where the heck was her man anyway? Had he gone and got himself into an accident?

"Typical man," said Maisie gratuitously.

"Typical man," echoed Marta continuing the story.

Having moved the heifer and baby in the barn out of the maternity pen and into one of the spare pens, Marta went back outside to finish up the check she had begun at 8 p.m. Murphy of Murphy's Law fame will tell you that trouble always comes in threes.

"Keep a close eye on 72," Hugo had blurted out just as he left, as if anticipating problems and feeling guilty that he would probably not be around to help. "She's either going to give birth to a monster, or she's going to have twins."

Well, 72 had not been neglected so much as omitted by Marta, and there she was, flat out in the bedding in the corral. A calf was on its way out, had been on the way out for some time if its swollen tongue and nose were anything to go by. The head behind the tongue and the nose was seemingly wedged *in situ*.

"I swear it! These husbands of ours wish these things on us sometimes," Paula commented.

Marta did the obvious; she went back to the house for the calving chains, sat herself down behind the exhausted cow, attached the chains to the calf's forelegs with the double loop so favoured by the vets, and began to pull. It was akin to trying to pull a brick through a keyhole, not helped by an old mama exhausted by her exertions. But at last something went in Marta's favor; the cow, suddenly deciding that she resented the human intrusion into her back end, struggled unsteadily to her feet. Too tired to fight, she was easily cajoled into the maternity pen in the barn.

"So now it's 11:30, and still no Hugo," said Marta. "So I phone up the vet on-call and tell him the situation."

"'Bring her down to the clinic', he says, half asleep. It was the new guy; Greg I think his name is."

"'No, you don't understand', I tell him. 'My husband Hugo has the truck, and he's still at work'. I lied. I had to. I couldn't tell him my husband was probably carousing in the Rocky Hotel. 'I have no way of getting her to town'."

"'Have you not got a neighbor who can help you?' he says. I know what he was thinking. He'd have to come out to the farm and do a C-section on some old crock tied up to a tree."

"That's what he'd have to do for a lot of folks around here," commented Maisie.

"So I tell him flat out, no, I don't have a neighbor and would he please get his sorry ass into his truck and get out here without wasting any more time."

"'You realize it costs more to…' he's saying, when I yell 'I don't give a monkey's tutu what it costs. Get that carcass of yours out here now!'"

"'Okay, okay,' this Greg says. 'Give me directions and I'll be on my way. But you'll also be paying mileage. You know that, don't you?' he says."

"'Will you stop yakkin' on about your mileage, and get your sorry ass out here like I told you', I said. Well that guy may have been a smart cookie to make it through veterinary college, but he sure had a hard time following a set of directions in the dark. I think he took the scenic route via Abraham Lake. He finally gets to our place at 12:30, and still no sign of that bugger Hugo."

Marta met the vet at the gate. Young and good-looking, she hastened to add, her hostility for his tardiness deflated as he expressed his apologies. She led him to the barn. To Marta's mind, he took laboriously long to put on his coveralls and gloves and lay out his paraphernalia. But then again, she found herself gratified because this man was obviously very methodical and meticulous about business. Finally he got around to checking the cow.

"I think there's a chance we can get it out of her if you help me," he said.

"Don't think so, if you will pardon my saying so," said the slurred voice at the entrance door of the barn. "You're gonna have to go the whole nine yards and cut him out." There he was; Marta's husband and soul-mate, grinning stupidly at them in all his inebriated glory, propped up against the doorframe to stop himself from falling down.

"You know, Sabine, that vet heard words I never knew I knew, words that a respected member of the community should not have heard. Like, I just let rip and told my old man exactly what I thought of him, and you know what? He just told me to lighten up a little or my rad might boil over."

"'And how the bleep did you get home?'" I'm screaming at him. "'Did you drive home in that state? You did, didn't you?' Oh I was so mad, and so relieved to see him, both at the same time, I wasn't making any more sense than he was."

"As a matter of fact," he said, "I didn't drive home. I left the truck in town and came home with a detonated driver."

"You mean 'designated', I corrected him."

"Yeah, detonated," he says.

"I told him he was bloody well detonated, coming home in such a sorry state as that. I mean, can you imagine what the new vet was thinking?"

Completely unfazed, Hugo continued to advise the poor vet that he would have to do a full C-section; this, after the vet had quietly insisted that he and Marta could get the calf out with or without Hugo's help.

"I would help you guys, but I am indisposable right now," said Hugo grinning.

"You mean 'indisposed'," said the vet softly.

"Yeah, completely indisputable," said Hugo.

"You mean plain bleeping useless and despicable," Marta told him.

Committing to any delicate undertaking with a critical audience, not just watching but critiquing every move, is hard enough at the best of times. However, when that audience should be playing a primary role but is not even in sufficient control of his own limbs to offer any meaningful physical assistance, the whole business takes on the connotations of an issue. Especially when despite everything Marta and the vet tried, that calf stayed put, resolutely stuck.

"See, you gotta C-it, C-it, C-it, see, you gotta C-it, C-it, C-it, and so say all of us. And so say all of us. See, you gotta C-it…" Hugo was singing without reserve.

"Tell him if he doesn't shut the hell up, we're gonna sedate him," the vet muttered through clenched teeth. Marta did what only Marta could have done. She strode over to her mate, grabbed his legs and upended him into the pile of well-used, odiferous bedding ready for removal and piled near the door. The resultant hoots of laughter only indicated how deep into the sauce Hugo had been. Thankfully, the ensuing commentary was not much more than an unintelligible mumble, seeing as Hugo was largely horizontal and talking into the straw. He was apparently still concerned how "indisputable" he was.

"The man, your man, is unfortunately right. We're going to have to do a C-section," said the vet. He and Marta both heard the "I told you so" from the flopped-out figure of humanity beside the door before it keeled over in well-deserved slumber, one arm stretched obliviously into the remains of fresh cow dropping.

"You know what? When that calf came out," Marta continued telling her story, "We both realized, me and the vet, there was no other way we would have got him out. So how did that inebriated fool of a husband of mine know that?"

"Was the calf still alive?" Sabine always concerned herself about the living first.

"Yeah. A bit the worse for wear, mind you, and with great big fat lips and swollen nose and tongue. But as soon as we had fixed Mama-cow up, she was right there with him doing her thing. Calf was up and sucking away when I came by in the morning. Of course, we gave it colostrum before we quit for the night."

"What about your husband?"

"Ah, there's where the story ended so perfectly. We left him there to sleep it off. I heard him stumble back into the house at six in the morning, just as I was setting off to go do a check. There he was, cow poop in his hair and all over his face. So I tell him, 'see what happens when you neglect your darling wife? You get yourself deep in shit.' I left him to go have a shower."

All this postulated yet another recognition for Sabine: Physically weaker, maybe, but not weaker overall, and decidedly not subservient, the farmwomen she had gotten to know gave as good as they got. Whatever chauvinism their husbands might display, it was all show and tell; men could not be overtly chauvinistic and get away with it, not if they wanted their wives to be a viable part of the team. So too, the notion of sexism and so-called women's liberation were non-issues.

One of the other interesting things that Sabine mused upon, after five years on the farm, was that misfortune sought out male and female without discrimination, and this fact alone discouraged any sort of superiority complex on the part of one or the other. So it was that the day after Sabine had contrived to wrap the disk that she was towing around one of the trees bordering the driveway because she was fiddling with the air conditioning knob and not watching where she was going, Aubrey got his comment of "What are you? Stupid?" shoved right down his craw, not by her but by fate. He was barreling down the gravel road, on his way back to the yard with the tractor and the empty fertilizer spreader to meet up with the tender truck scheduled to deliver another load to him from the depot. He turned in the driveway to see his wife standing there, phone in hand. He stopped and got out.

"Phone for me?" he asked brightly.

"Nah. It was the fertilizer depot. The tender truck is going to be a bit late. Where did you leave the spreader?"

"Uh?" Aubrey turned. No spreader! His heart missed several beats, his mind raced. Speech is always retarded in crises like this. "If…see… where…what if? Oh no! Oh hell, please no!" He leaped back into the tractor, reversed at high speed down the driveway and out onto the road. There it was, skewed sideways in the ditch, teetering at such an angle that one good push would have flipped it on its side.

"Oh Sheesh kebabs," came Aubrey's laundered language. "Oh bloody Sheesh kebabs in a charcoal brassiere, so what the hell do I do now?"

The urgency of the situation was not lost on him; the man in the tender truck would be arriving any minute, even if he were late. It would not do to have him see the company spreader hanging around in the ditch. Okay, like it had done before in the field way back when, the pin had popped out when he hit a bump, but he, Aubrey the conscientious operator, had not bothered to attach the safety chains to the drawbar. He had not needed to because in the field he would not be going fast enough for the pin to pop out. Except he had not been in the field; he had been on the road to get to the field, a road designated by government as a "secondary highway", no less. Imagine the consternation: here was a retired policeman, a custodian of law, order and safety, and he had not done what the law had required him to do—secure an implement in tow—because he did not think for a minute that the pin could pop out. But pop out it had, and now the company spreader was making an exhibition of itself in the ditch, with the company man about to crest the hill and see such folly with his own two beady eyes. The story would reverberate outwards from there like an echo bouncing off the walls of the grandest of canyons.

He climbed out of the tractor "to study the situation", a phrase he always used to downplay crisis to Sabine. A chain. What he needed was a chain. He could hook it up to the spreader's hitch and gently turn the machine and tow it back onto the road. Trouble was, where in the blazes was the chain?

"You need this?" Sabine's voice took him by surprise. She had walked out onto the road dragging their twenty-foot logging chain behind her. Ah, but the lady was brilliant, no two ways about it!

"Well yes. How did you know? And thank you. Where was it?"

"Well, if it was where you last left it, it would have been wrapped around that dead tree you were trying to pull out of the bush last fall, and nobody would have remembered where it was. So I went out and brought it back and hung it in the shop, where obviously you never noticed it." None of this was said in triumph or with a view to criticizing; it was just a statement of plain and undeniable fact, but it sure put the shine on his wife's brilliance.

"Bless you," he said nonetheless. "Now I'll set up the tractor the way I want it. Then you can drive, and I'll signal from the ground. How's that?"

"Fine by me," said Sabine confident with her own competence, in and of itself a recognition that had she not known what she was doing, she would have said so. With signals that had been refined between them by years of much trial and plenty of error, the spreader was back on the road in minutes, hitched back up to the tractor.

"We make a hell of a team," beamed Sabine.

"We make a heck of a team," Aubrey corrected her. They both laughed knowingly, conspiratorially; both thinking that what the company man had not seen, his heart would not care to grieve.

It was soon after this incident that the final realization hit Sabine, the recognition that so many farm women were actually defined by their farm and the whole farming world. This was a world of shifting realities: of cycles and seasons, of living and, yes, dying; of accommodating and adapting oneself to an existence that called its own shots. This was not a world where it was either worthy or useful to go tilting at windmills; it was not a world where to be a strident feminist burning your bra or a red revolutionary advocating better working conditions made any sense. Maybe this was why so many farmwomen felt so comfortable within their own bodies and within their own skins. They did not care, nor did they have any need to project an image aping some glam movie celebrity; it was so obviously inappropriate, and it was false. As if to underline that sentiment, their handbags were liable to contain a multi-tool, a jack knife, a couple of fencing staples, maybe a roll of insulation tape, perhaps a bolt or two. Even more than that, the average farm wife never seemed to confuse instant knowledge with the hard-earned wisdom garnered from a life lived experientially. The average farm wife lived life, experienced it, and savoured it where she could. This was the notion that prompted Sabine to put pen to paper and to try and encapsulate the thought.

THE FARM WIFE

She is in her own right the first line of defense,
The second line of offense, depends who's the enemy.
She is by common sense the keeper of the keys
To armoury, bank and heart, unequivocally trusted
To stand by her man as much as she knows
He will do the same, an equal, complementary,
Unless he comes home drunk, disorderly and disheveled,
Or with some unanticipated new toy, truck, bike, boat, hot tub, babe.
Disheveled? He's always disheveled. No matter, he can look like hell
As so many do to citified eyes, just call it the 'bucolic look'.
She'll still be there beside him, the power behind the throne,
The boot behind the drone, never afraid to call a spade
A spade and a fool a fool, and yet so full of motherhood;
She has to be, surrogate to calves, kids, lambs and chicks,
Her arms are ever wide with welcome,
And so Madam, it is with a sense of honor
We award you your Ph.D.,
A Ph.D. in life.

Chapter Fourteen
FOR BETTER OR FOR WORSE

"So, young fellah, where are all you farmer types gonna spend your Saturdays now, tell me that?" Aubrey had joined the monthly get-together of his RCMP pals at the local Tim Horton's.

"What are you talking about?" Aubrey responded, reaching for a donut.

"Don't tell me you haven't heard," said Bud. "Your precious auction mart is gone. Sold up! The big box boys are coming in. Your favourite place on this earth will soon become a spanking new shopping center." The news hit Aubrey like a brick thrown full-force into his stomach.

"I don't believe you," he managed. "You boys are having me on. They couldn't do that. They wouldn't get away with it. That auction mart is much too important to us, to the whole rural community."

"Ah, but sad to say my good friend, this rural community that you talk about is not so important to the movers and shakers of the town. You know that. Everybody knows that, surely?"

The analogy of farming becoming an out-of-control roller-coaster reasserted itself in Aubrey's mind. But now the twists and turns of the run were beginning to defy the laws of reality, to buck all the norms of agri-business. The sudden plunges seemed to invite you headlong into yet another disaster, another one you could not possibly survive; but survive you did, if only just! But taking away the auction mart was like chipping away at the bricks and mortar of the farmer's livelihood. Damn it all, it was like obliterating a piece of the farmer's identity.

"And what does Clayton Cole have to say about all of this?" Aubrey asked.

"Not the right question," said Bud.

"What do you mean, not the right question? Tell me what the right question is, then."

"The right question is what can Clayton Cole say about it? You know how hard the Coles fought to get any recognition for the role the auction mart plays in the community. Nobody outside of agriculture gives a fiddler's fart. Hell, they wouldn't even agree to put in a proper access road for your man Clayton. Now you watch just how quick they put in an access road so us town folk can rush in and buy up our bargain lawn furniture from Taiwan and our stonewashed jeans from some sweatshop in India. But don't you go worrying about Mr. Cole. He saw the writing on the wall a long time ago. Shrewd businessman that he is, he knows what he's doing."

Nonetheless, like most of the neighbours, the Hanlons were devastated.

"There goes the greatest recycling business of all time," commented Sabine, her mind's eye parading all of the bargains and treasures she had harvested at the mart over the years. "Yet another nail in the rural coffin," she felt compelled to add, not quite ready to voice the same unsettling questions nagging at her brain. If Clayton Cole could see the writing on the wall, why was it that they, the Hanlons, could not see it? Where would they sell their calves now? What should they be doing?

During these times of stress and downturn, stories began to take wing, taking off on flights all of their own. Economic bad times tend to bring out both the best and the worst in people. Especially their stories.

There was the story of J-D, the same Jim Delamere that Pete and Aubrey assisted in his time of need. His neighbours, also a young family, lamented to him that they were looking to sell off part of the herd they had so painstakingly built up because they were short of hay. J-D said nothing but delivered thirty large round bales into their yard the next day. When the neighbours arrived home and found the bales, the husband phoned several people before it dawned on him where the bales had in all likelihood come from. He phoned Jim.

"Look, I got more than I need, and you need more than you've got," Jim said, "so I can help you out."

"But, but we can't afford to pay you," said the neighbour desperately. "That's why we need to sell off some cows. How much do you want for the bales?"

"Nothing! Maybe you can help us out when we have a tight year. There are fifty or so more here, if you need them."

"But, but you can't just go round giving your bales away," said the grateful neighbor not quite believing his luck. "I mean, you guys have to live too."

"Look," J-D apparently said, "we have come to understand how far we're all in this together. I learned that the hard way. I know you'd help me if I got in a fix so don't sweat it. If it really bothers you, replace the bales next year. End of conversation."

But then again, things did not always happen that way. Pete actually caught a man stealing his hay, not just a single bale but a full trailer load of ten bales. Pete had been stacking his bales in his bale yard during the day and had left the tractor there in order to finish the job the following morning. That evening after dark, he slipped over to a neighbour's to return a compression tester he had borrowed. On the way home, he could have sworn he had spotted movement in his bale yard, so he went to investigate. He came upon a heavy-duty pickup and trailer with a tractor, his tractor, loading up bales in the pale moonlight. The tractor stopped and a man climbed down.

"This is where I'm supposed to be pickin' up them bales for Charlie Thompson, right?" he said hastily, a little too hastily.

"Right," said Pete, playing along in the hope that he could figure out whom the man might be. He recognized the voice but could not quite place it, probably because the fellow was deliberately slurring his words. The man's insistence on pulling down his tuque and pulling up the collar of his coat made it difficult to see the face. "But why the hell are you loading bales at this time of night?"

"Well, you know how it is. I work all day in the oil patch, so this is the only time I can get here," said the voice.

"But why not use the lights? I mean, how can you see what you're doing?"

"Ach, for the life of me I couldn't find the light switch," said the man almost whining. "Besides, there's just enough light to get by."

"I see. So that's what you're up to these days, eh Stiffy? Stealing bales out of farmers' yards and peddling them off to the highest bidder, right?" Pete's mind had finally connected with the voice. The man was "Stiffy" Westlon who lived on a tumbled-down acreage ten miles further west; "a rat-bagger's paradise" is how Quincy Klug would have described it, which was good coming from Quincy. Pete knew the place. It was so ramshackle it barely merited the title of someone's fixed address he said.

"Wha', what d'ya mean?" Stiffy's voice rose a couple of octaves. "I'm pickin' these here bales up for ol' Charlie, Charlie Thompson. He tol' me he'd bought 'em from you. Now if he's bull-shittin' me, why I'll unload 'em right now and be on my way."

"Slow down Stiffy, slow down. This Charlie Thompson, who is he? Where does he live?"

"Sheesh, you gotta know Charlie Thompson. Everybody knows old Charlie, don't they? Lives out east of here a ways."

"Oh that's right, too. His place goes by the name of Imaginary Acres, right?"

"Yeah right," said Stiffy, visibly relieved that he might be off the hook. "That's the place, out east of here."

"Uh huh. Look Stiffy, here's what we'll do. You unhitch your trailer right here, right now, and you go home. You get your friend Charlie to phone me tomorrow and we'll straighten this whole thing out. You come back after work tomorrow night and pick up the bales and the trailer."

Stiffy hesitated for a split second. "Sounds good enough to me," he blurted, trying to remain as casual as he could. Pete watched him unhook the trailer and drive away. As soon as Stiffy was good and gone, Pete went back to the house and picked up Jeannie.

"Come on, dear, we're gonna catch ourselves a skunk." He told her the story. Together they went to where their machinery was stored and removed a harrow off the field set. They took it up to the bale yard and laid it upside down across the gateway to the bale yard, covering it over with grass and dirt; nobody would ever see it in the dark.

"My bet is that he'll be back before midnight," said Pete.

He was. Better yet, because it was not too cold a night, Pete was in a nice warm truck concealed behind the bales waiting to see how everything turned out. He knew it was going to be dramatic because Stiffy, maybe because he was so intent on getting in and out of there in nine seconds flat, was driving like a madman. There was a series of popping sounds as all four of his wheels traversed the teeth of the harrow, and the vehicle came to an untimely stop. Stiffy climbed out, bent over the front wheel to see what had happened, and went ballistic. He cavorted around his truck like a demented ape, ranting and raving and shouting abuse at the sliver of a moon. Pete watched, in some awe it should be said, as Stiffy climbed back into his truck, roared back over the harrow and blasted off down the road driving on his rims. He had learned an expensive lesson: enough for Pete to tell him that he would not press charges when he came back for the trailer the next day, minus the bales, of course, and boasting four new tires on his truck.

There were stories of those who could not or would not buy themselves and their family any Christmas gifts that year. There were tales of this company shutting down that person's credit, of banks threatening foreclosure, of accidents and yes, one suicide caused by trying to carry on without the wherewithal to do so. Then, when the "calf run" came on in the fall, a time when so many farmers marketed their calf crops through the auction marts, stories abounded of buyers—usually characterized as seedy mafia types—discounting animals for a slightly frozen ear or tail, or too woolly a hair coat, or even because of the tiniest stub of a horn where the dehorning paste had missed in the spring. With all the talk getting so outrageous, it was a wonder that calves were not being discounted because of the poor body condition of their owners, Aubrey was thinking. That is, until he and Sabine went through the wringer themselves.

"Get rid of 'em as soon as you can," was Pete's counsel. "The price is set to take a real tumble."

Easier said than done, now that their local mart was defunct. Where should they ship their calves—to the mart in Red Deer or the one in Rimbey, to Olds or to Innisfail? What format should they choose, load-lot, pre-sort, or the good old "these here calves are from the Hanlon spread in Rocky Mountain House," which is what they had always done. Just as they were about to settle on a particular option, another horror story would pop up and cloud their vision, and so they dithered another day or two. Then there were all of the added costs. The sales commission on each animal was now higher than they had ever paid; plus there were the deductions for this and that, brand inspections, Hartford Insurance and Alberta Cattle Commission, and the like. Then there was the expense of trucking, something that they had never had to itemize as a major item before. It was not as if they could ship their 85 or so calves in their own stock trailer. Ironically, it was the trucker who ended up making the decision for them; he was available Thursday afternoon, and the presort calf sale for Olds was on Friday morning.

"Let's go for it," said Sabine innocently.

"Go for it," Aubrey told Stewart the trucker after Stewart had explained the idea behind the presort procedure.

"See, your calves get mixed in with the calves brought in by all of the other folks. They sort 'em all out according to weight and size and colour and breed, something along those lines. The boys in Olds are good at their job, so don't worry on that score. Anything that does not fit into any group is sold separately. You know, frozen ears, wobbly on the legs, that kind of thing. So if your calves are all over the shop in weight and size…"

"They are," said Aubrey and Sabine in unison.

"Then you should do better this way because buyers here are looking for uniform groups. Better yet, they're not allowed to pull any out, unless of course there is something clearly wrong with one."

With Pete and Jeannie on hand to help sort, things went well and Stewart was on his way, well on schedule, with the first of two loads. The "Bovine Chorale" began in earnest immediately after he left. Sabine hated it, hated this one time of year more than any other. Even though she had never had children of her own, her motherhood instincts still kicked in. Was she not, after all, a kind of surrogate mother to all of her cows and their babies? She felt their loss as her own, empathized with their incomprehension as those same humans who had cared for them all spring and summer now took their babies away. They bawled for the rest of the day and most of the night, with Sabine sharing their angst. What really hurt, however, were the bovine looks of, were they contempt, dismissal or betrayal that they reserved for their treacherous human caregivers the next day. They knew by then who had instigated the kidnapping of their little ones. Oh, they knew, no matter how hard Sabine tried to salve her conscience by talking to them and telling them that their responsibilities were now to the babies they were carrying in their bellies. Both Aubrey and Sabine were happily in the habit of talking to "their girls", although on this occasion Aubrey did not have much to say.

Attending an auction in hopes of bagging a bargain is one thing. Attending an auction where your stock is on offer and the prices of your particular commodity are trending downwards into the basement is akin to being forced to attend your own trial on trumped-up charges with no provision to defend yourself. Aubrey was stoic. Sabine feigned light-heartedness, that is until the full significance of the presort format hit home. Not that their entry into the packed sale hall was not traumatic; it was, and the sale had not yet commenced. In a way, it was easy to forget that this was a place of business and not entertainment. The hall was packed with folks like themselves; those not buying or selling were spectators with a vested interest. What were the prices doing? Should they hold onto their own calf crop or consign it next week before the prices dropped even further? What was the loonie doing against the greenback? What were the buyers doing, the heavy-hitters working for the big packers and the feedlots? They were all there, falsely affable or poker-faced depending on the required image for the day. Seated before the specially placed phones and catered to by waitresses slipping in from the café with a burger or a coffee, the buyers were the ones who would be footing the Hanlon paycheck for the year. Sabine would have served the coffee laced with a dram or two of vodka, would even have had the waitresses display a bit of cleavage if it would have helped her hopeless cause.

The auctioneers strode in, all purpose and business; their clerks trailed behind ready to face the world. All groomed in western style, they were very professional, very focused; they had to be, for there were over three thousand calves to auction off this day. The beginning of the sale was announced. The first bunch was ushered in. Fifteen black steers, all uniform in size and shape, the electronic readout showing a combined weight of 8100 lbs for an average of 540 lbs each. They were beautiful, outstanding, their coats all shiny, but the bids languished at a paltry 80 cents a pound. The auctioneer persisted, dragging the price up to 88 cents before bringing down his gavel. Sabine was sick to the stomach. This was awful. This was ten cents lower than they had hoped for. She looked at her hands, then at her feet, and stayed staring at the floor until the next group was brought in. This time there were a dozen red steers, just as good as the first group. They fared no better. But by the seventh or the eighth groups, the price had climbed grudgingly up a solid five cents and that was where it stayed.

The atmosphere of despair and resignation was almost tangible. People who made their living this way looked constantly down at their boots or escaped, momentarily, to the café for another slug of strong coffee. The buyers were scoring, and they knew it. One notably obnoxious John Wayne throwback strutted about in the front, until a burly cowman sitting in the corner cautioned him, "You'd best be sitting yourself down, young fellah, before I get to putting you down." Many in the hall heard the exchange; some applauded it. The man sat down in a hurry. Nobody needed a know-all so brazenly poaching in their troubled waters.

"When can we expect to see our calves come in?" Sabine leaned over and quizzed Aubrey half an hour later.

"When? What do you mean when? They're all mixed in. Some of ours have come through already."

"What do you mean, 'mixed in'? I've not seen any of ours."

"Presort, remember?" said Aubrey patiently, realizing how uptight his wife was feeling. "Ours are mixed in with other people's calves. Size, colour, weight: Remember what Stewart said?"

"How…how can we figure out how well we're doing then?" Sabine raised the obvious question.

"There's no way of knowing until we pick up the cheque. That's the point. You take the chance when you mix them up. We're doing as well as anybody else who brought cattle in, if that's any consolation."

It was not; not any consolation, that is. The Hanlons hunkered down, not so much attending the sale as enduring it, with Sabine only spotting three of their calves as they flowed through. The cheque, their take-home pay for the year, meant that they were paying themselves somewhere around eighteen cents an hour for all the work of the past year, according to Aubrey. Yet surprisingly, he was not bitter. "We're all of us in the same boat," said Aubrey philosophically.

Sabine did not find herself quite so philosophical. She put pen to paper in her own unique way and came up with her own view of what happened at the auction.

AS IF THEY KNOW!!

I watched myself go down today, I watched myself go down.
And the talkers … They just kept on talking,
Not even looking
As we ranchers surveyed our own demise,
Presided over our own economic funerals.
Economic? More, much more than economic!
And the talkers … They kept on talking
Not even sensing
As we wilted in a shroud of despair,
As we saw our year's work slide under the hammer,
Hammered under, token dollars and token cents.
"It's a serious situation," they pronounced gravely,
As if they even knew. As if!
Damn that man with his gavel.
Damn that cowboyed buyer with his smirk,
His cowboy hat unsoiled by cowboy sweat.
Damn that ringman, poking machoed hell,
That's my girl you're poking, my baby,
To him not life, just a commodity, a piece of meat.
And they keep on … Keep on talking
As if I, as if we may have recourse
They talk…
As if they can weigh our sadness.
I look around at once proud faces
Now unsmiling, burned and cowed,
Masking pain and slipping, again and again
To study booted feet.
Maybe, maybe it's time to go,
Time to move on.
The talkers, they'll keep on talking
As if they know!

"We both chose to do it, for better or for worse," added Sabine.

"So we did, oh yes, so we did!" Aubrey sighed into his lukewarm coffee.

It was the closing of the auction in Rocky Mountain House that prompted the Hanlons, and Aubrey in particular, to tune into what was happening more broadly in their industry in contrast to what was happening in Alberta's resource industry. As much as the fortunes of the one were spiraling downwards, so the fortunes of the other were climbing to dizzying heights. Experienced agricultural professionals, mechanics, partsmen and others, were being seduced in droves by the lure of oilfield wages. Agricultural dealers could not compete, so they had to get by with part-timers and retirees, with apprentices and those with no experience whatsoever. Taking a tractor to the local dealer for repair was increasingly a hit-and-miss affair; usually with a much higher than necessary bill at the end because of the time taken on the job, compounded by the level of inexperience and the number of novices learning their way through. Young men whose eyes once were focused on farming abandoned that road for the good things life in the oilpatch would bring. Farming was becoming the domain of the old and the increasingly infirm. Those farmers who tried for a while to work off-farm only to invest their loot on-farm soon saw the futility of pouring their money down an unrewarding sink-hole. More and more of them put their land and their cows on the block, and chased after the toys instead: boats and bikes and monster trucks with all the chrome. The shortage of labour grew so that even the local stores had to pay $12 an hour starting wage for the most menial of jobs, with the more aggressive offering a sign-on bonus to get ahead of the others. In the meantime, those left on the land watched their own income spiraling downwards, undermined by rising costs and stumbling returns. For the Hanlons, less so, but for many others bitterness tinged their voices as they became marginalized players in the boom that was leaving them behind, the returns for their time leaving them earning far below minimum wage.

Aubrey was determined not to become resentful. After all, he had to remind himself constantly, they were the ones who opted to go into farming. But when the first ever landman to set foot on their property arrived in their yard one evening, Aubrey near boiled over. The moment the man introduced himself and said what his business was, Pete's disparaging joke immediately came to mind.

"How do you know when a landman isn't lying?" went the joke.

"When his mouth stops moving," went the answer.

It was unfortunate that Aubrey was unloading a trailer of square bales

208 *For Better Or For Worse*

and stacking them in the cramped confines of a dusty old granary. He was sweating, itching from the hay dust, and downright grumpy because he had to get the bales under cover before the forecasted rain mixed with snow blighted the landscape. It was also unfortunate that the man was both loud and smelled of alcohol, having spent the previous hour or two in one of Rocky's many watering holes. Aubrey could care less about the man's story, could never have known that the man's wife had left him that very morning for a six-figure driller. His opening remarks were offensively short.

"We need access to your land," he said.

"We? Who the hell is we?" snapped Aubrey.

"Oh, we are Majestic Geophysical. We would like permission to seismic your land."

"Is that right? What if I don't want you people on my land? What then? What if I don't want an oil or gas well, or even a bloody diamond mine?"

"Frankly, my friend, unless you own the mineral rights under your land, and I can tell you that you don't, you don't have a choice."

"What do you mean, I don't have a choice? I own the land, don't I?"

The man sighed as if he was dealing with an eight-year old with a learning disorder. "You own the surface rights but not what is underneath. We are working for a company that has paid good money to see what might be under your land."

"And so, where the hell do I fit in then?" Aubrey was unashamedly belligerent.

"Where? Nowhere, really. We pay you a standard access fee to your land. We do our job. We pay you for any damage we do, and we leave your land pretty much as it is. If an oil company figures out from the data we provide that there is something worth going after, then they will approach you themselves."

"And tell me I have no rights, just like you just did, huh? What if I don't want them to move in?"

"Then they go to court and you will be ordered to cease and desist. You cannot stop them."

"You know what? I think you would do better to come back in the morning when my wife is around. Then we can sort all this nonsense out over a cup of coffee, which by the way is something you could do with."

The man realized he had overstayed his welcome and overplayed his hand. "Sure thing," he said. "I'd help you with those bales but I have a bad back."

"No worries. See you in the morning."

The next day, the man was a totally different person. He had slept off the whisky, had slept off the departure of his flighty wife, was glad of it in fact, and this left him purposeful and pleasant to deal with. And so the Hanlon land was explored over.

The next dealings the Hanlons had with the oilfield folks involved the laying down of a pipeline across their land to connect two wells, one north and one south of the quarter section they had purchased from Stanley Himilton. The landman this time was an ex-farmer who was easy to get along with. Aubrey and Sabine heard him out and both realized at once that the windfall would bail them out from their financial squeeze at the time. Fifteen thousand dollars would be a boon after the pathetically low calf cheque. They were all scheduled to meet up with the contractor two days hence.

Every walk of life has them, the sort whose knowledge of life is much too vast to be constrained by the limits of a brain. The chosen contractor had not even made it out of his truck before Sabine felt offended. It was a massive machine. All new and shiny with its several antennae proclaiming great importance and its acres of chrome and myriads of lights screaming style, it was a bottomless money pit. When the man finally did make it out of the cab, his dismissive glance of her was all too obvious, and intended so; this was a man for whom a woman was no more than a hood ornament. He moved forward and tried to intimidate Aubrey's hand. Sabine merited no more than that first cursory look.

"So I take it these folks know what I want," he boomed at the landman.

"They sure do," said the landman quietly, as if already trying to minimize the damage.

"Good deal. Good deal. Actually, I need to put one more designated work space over there," he pointed. "That'll be okay with you, I'm sure," he bulldozed Aubrey.

"You'll be paid extra," said the landman, again trying his best to keep the contractor's role to a minimum.

"Pay, pay; that's all we ever do for these farmer types. We pay and pay," the mouth seemed driven to comment.

"*Excuuuse me my good man,*" Sabine's reaction took him by surprise. "Have you any idea what us farmers are getting for our calves right now? We deserve to be paid. It's our land."

"Waal, what have we got here," the man spun around as if stung by a bee. "A little lady with spirit. A spitting little wolverine, and so pretty with it."

Before Aubrey and the landman could respond, Sabine had given voice to what they were all thinking, and in the very same words. "Sir," she said, "why don't you just fuck off and leave us to deal with this gentleman." Aubrey could not believe it; his wife had used the dread f-word, full frontal! What was more, it had the desired effect. The man paused as if to say something, thought better of it, jumped back into his truck and took off in a cloud of angry dust.

"Good riddance to bad rubbish," commented the landman. "Trouble is, he's very good at what he does. One of the best."

Strange that it should be so, but Sabine felt violated as soon as the pipeline construction crew moved onto the land. They were meticulous about how they went about the project, but still there was a massive scar left behind in the fields. Yes, they put all of the topsoil back and then reseeded to hide their footprint. But what could not be hidden was the fact that Aubrey and Sabine made more in one single year from the seven acres allocated for the project than they would have done had they farmed the same acres for four years in a row with a bumper crop every year. That fact alone was unpalatable enough without the sense of shame that Sabine felt in offering up their land to such violation in the first place. Once again, Sabine resorted to paper…

THE OILMEN COMETH…

If they had come upon my land
And they had not paid me,
That would have been violation.
If they had come upon my land
And told me to get thee gone,
That would have been usurpation.
But they came upon my land and they paid me, oh so well.
And so I became their whore, I laughed along with them,
Passed the time of day, cavorting with their largesse.
I watched them attack my ground scraping away its goodness
So they could bury their secrets of who gets the benefit,
Of how long it takes before age and corrosion,
Yes, corrosion eats away their labour,
Their pipes suppurating unseen below,
Contaminating not their land
But mine after they are long gone,
Leaving me only with their money
Like a sexually transmitted disease.

Chapter Fifteen
TIME AND A HALF

*N*umbers.

Many a wise farmer could explain to you the thing about numbers is that they can tell you what you really *do not* want to hear as much as what you *do* want to hear. With the greatest of versatility, they can spit out an epic tall tale just as quickly as a chintzy short story. Believe in them too implicitly and you can find yourself believing someone you would not ordinarily trust; someone in a suit with an agenda that is not yours. This is when you can be easily convinced that you have already effectively passed away because the figures supposedly tell you so.

The Hanlons, like so many others, were forced into the realization that in today's world, farming in Canada was predicated primarily on numbers and not on lifestyle. To survive as a farmer, you simply could not ignore the industrialization of agriculture and its quantification. You might lament it but you sure could not change it. The days were gone when you could perceive your animals, for example, as their own intrinsic versions of the gift of life; in the modern world, they were first and foremost a commodity to be traded back and forth like any other, like coffee or cocoa or diamonds. To you, herd health might mean protecting the well-being and, yes, the happiness of your critters, but that was the narrow view, quaint and romantic. Herd health was more about protecting your investment and maximizing your returns. The banker and the accountant, of course they would tell you that, especially when your paycheque held so much benefit for them. Crass commercialism had gone most of the way in de-romanticizing "animal husbandry" and the nurturing of the soil. The era of every animal, and every machine for that matter, having its own leisurely story had been sacrificed to the frantic struggle for economic survival. If the numbers did not line up favorably enough in the banker's firmament, you could be quickly dispossessed. Passion for the land, for its innate sanctity, had been cheapened by the "clinicalism" of numbers, and to Aubrey and Sabine it did not feel good.

Of course, like anyone who prided themselves on being progressive, they attended a variety of field days, checking out the new way of doing things, but invariably they got the sense that the gurus of the latest methodology or technology were all too often like fundamentalist preachers trolling for converts to their particular brand of the gospel. No question, there were evident benefits to holistic farming and no-till seeding, to methane digesters and Environmental Farm Plans, but both Aubrey and Sabine kept thinking that this was on the same level as renovating the superstructure when the ship was holed below the waterline. When it came right down to it, when so many in the agri-sector could only keep the farm alive by going to work off-farm, there had to be something wrong structurally. Would it make sense to people if their banker, for instance, had to work an extra day a week in the pizza parlour just to keep the swivel chair in his office? Would they be accepting of their doctor having to double up as a bartender one night a week just to make ends meet? Yet, for some reason it was now considered *de rigeur* that the folks who produced the food should have to do something extra. It was considered perfectly normal that the folks who cared for the nation's most precious resources, the soil and the water, should have to go and get a job in another field and extend their work week to 80 or more hours Why was this? Was it necessary because of a cheap food policy adopted by successive governments, devised to harvest the urban consumer's vote at the expense of the producer on the land? Was it because of unwillingness on the part of all levels of government to readdress what agriculture should be doing for the country? Or was it simply because of the obvious disconnect between the predominantly urban types strutting the corridors of power and wielding their bogus authority over an increasingly disenfranchised agricultural community? All of the above, Aubrey found himself thinking.

Again, what was the point of all the incredibly high-tech equipment agricultural companies were pushing so hard if Joe Farmer needed half a lifetime to pay for it? So what if the combine could go from field to bowl with all a person needing to do was to add milk to the cereal? So what if it had every monitor you could think of, plus a built-in shower and sauna for those hot days? These were machines that the average farmer could only drool over at the trade fair.

Ah, the trade fair. It was always a great day out when the Hanlons hit Agri-Trade, in Red Deer, with Pete and Jeannie to "go and see all that we cannot afford," said Pete. There were dozens of gleaming machines and booths patrolled by shoals of sales people, every one of them as slick and as polished as the products they were doing their best to hustle. These people held a special fascination for Aubrey, while the others, Pete, Jeannie and Sabine, simply ignored them. The younger ones, the faster swimmers perhaps, could sum up the state of one's money belt or bank account in seconds, their beady eyes suddenly clouding over when PFS (Poor Farmers Syndrome) telegraphed itself. Aubrey never knew, before going to the fair, that Poor Farmers Syndrome was so evident for all to see. There were two or three other types in the salespersons' sea. The "grouper", too rotund and too experienced to waste energy where it was clearly not needed, was content to sit by his lair waiting to swallow up any moneyed innocent that strayed too close. Then of course there were the sharks, always the sharks, many bearing scars from previous encounters. These were the most dangerous, luring the unwary into that "exceptional deal". And, alas, all of a sudden you found you had landed yourself a brand-new four-wheel drive loader tractor with self-leveling bucket and ninety-six equal payments over the next eight and a half years. All this, without the busty maiden sitting in the cab, which was the bait that first caught your eye and lured you in. Finally, there were the seasoned campaigners, the killer whales, the ones who only did business when they were hungry. When they weren't hungry, they were the most enjoyable because they would do tricks instead, only too pleased to pass the time of day explaining all the newest gadgets because you showed a genuine curiosity even if you had no money—no worthy *numbers* that is to say.

Aubrey knew he was becoming more and more negative. Indeed, he felt it was becoming something of a disease, and one that he had to keep from infecting his wife; for the farm had been, and still was, a huge part of their adventure together. Farming these days was a tough row to hoe, but when there was a panting creditor or a whining banker at the end of the line with hand outstretched, it became a double struggle—even if the banker was a Peter Walshe awaiting an installment on the mortgage. In fact, that was almost worse because Peter was always so understanding, always so ready to work with you and not against you. So Aubrey's final response, invariably to himself was, "We'll go another year, I guess." Through all of his self-doubt and his wavering self-confidence, Sabine was the rock, the one who strode ever onwards, looking neither to the left nor to the right. Or so he liked to think. But even Sabine was showing signs of ag-fatigue.

A holiday, or so it is often said, provides the time to recharge the batteries. A holiday for those who allow themselves to become entrapped by the farm is more than simply charging batteries, however. It allows farmer folks to more fully recover a balanced perspective. For people under siege, and most farmers were people under siege, it allows a little escape. The problem was that Aubrey and Sabine were too far down-in-the-mouth to even consider a holiday. Yes, they could afford it financially. But as it so often is with farmers, they were reluctant to spend money on themselves when they still had a fertilizer bill to pay, still had an outstanding invoice from last month's fuel delivery. There would undoubtedly be an upcoming repair bill, too, if the year was anywhere near normal. It was Pete who broke the logjam, Pete and Jeannie.

"We've come for payment," he said as they sat down for a visit in the Hanlon home one afternoon.

"Payment? Did you say payment?" Sabine had to jump in, her face trying vainly not to show her worry. "Do we owe you guys money too?"

"No, not money," Pete said gently. "You owe us time, and because you can't even remember, the bill has gone up to time and a half. Then there's the fact that you're so late in paying, which means that you people are up to double time on this particular bill."

"What the hell are you smoking?" Even Aubrey's voice betrayed serious discomfort.

"Ah, so it's the pair of you now that's got Debtors' Alzheimer's," Pete's eyes were twinkling. "Do you remember way, way back when we had that mother of all parties…?"

"How could we forget?" sighed Sabine.

"And you remember how you, dear Sabine, were worried about us doing so much for you, moving your cows and all that, and you were concerned how you would get to paying us back?"

"And you said you wanted to borrow the boat," said Aubrey. "Take it. She's all yours."

"Whoa, boy! Whoa! Hold your horses there, big fellah!" Jeannie was determined to put her two cents in. "That was only a part of the deal, remember?"

"Huh?" said Aubrey.

"What do you mean only part of the deal?" asked Sabine, still very unsure about how far they may have over-extended themselves without even knowing it. "Do we owe you money too?"

"We also get the whole crew," said Pete. "For free. Not that the crew is that competent by all accounts, but then you have to take your chances if your crew is manning a vessel with a chancy name like 'Loosey Goosey', right?"

Sabine looked across at Jeannie who winked. That was when she burst out in delight. "You guys are something else!" she shouted. "But before you complete the press-ganging of your crew, we had better make some bookings. Besides, the captain here will have to dig out his sextant and his anchor and his commodore's hat. You had also better understand that the crew needs to find quarters since they're both too superstitious to sleep on any rig named 'Loosey Goosey.'" Sabine's laugh lines were back.

"All taken care of," Jeannie announced smugly.

"What do you mean, all taken care of?" Aubrey intervened. "So where and when are we going?"

"You tell them," Jeannie nodded over at her husband.

"Well, on June 21, next, we shall all assemble on parade at the Hanlon farm gate; you with your boat in tow, us as passengers in your cruiser of the highways, your diesel pickup. We shall embark at 0:500 hours for the port of Penticton, where we shall lay up and rest our landlocked limbs for forty-eight hours. All passengers and crew will disembark and set off on a one-day wine tour to stock up on that most essential of victuals for the voyage, namely Okanagan grape juice of distinguished vintage. Upon our being sufficiently loaded, manner of speaking of course, we shall set sail for French Creek Cottages just outside of Parksville, on Vancouver Island, where we are designated to meet up with the landlubbers Delamere. Once there, we shall repose for a balmy ten days before re-embarking for the voyage home. Any questions?" Pete was really enjoying the act.

"Yes. Are the accommodations booked, and if so, whom do we pay and how much?" It was back again to the issue of numbers for Sabine.

"All taken care of," said Jeannie tersely. "We're sharing a cottage for four on the beachfront."

"What do you mean, all taken care of?" Aubrey took over the questioning. "You have to let us pay our way…right honey?" he appealed to Sabine for support.

"Right," said Sabine. "We can't have you paying for our holiday. We might be poor, but we ain't quite broke yet."

"Who said anything about a holiday?" Pete again. "You guys are not on holiday. You're the ship's crew, remember? The presence of you, your truck, and your boat are payment for services rendered by us to you in hauling critters from one Quincy Klug's place to yours."

"You can't be serious; you can't do this." Sabine was exasperated. "We have to pay something."

"Ach, take us out to dinner," said Jeannie. "It's a deal then?"

"No, hold it!" bellowed Aubrey. "We cannot go for free. We have to pay *something*. We can't just take your charity."

Pete spoke very quietly, but the message hit home just the same. "Look, there is something uncivilized, uncouth about a couple of really good friends who are not able to accept a gift graciously. Now Jeannie and I happen to know that neither of you is either uncivilized or uncouth. We value you both in our lives. If we didn't, we would not be doing this.

Besides, you're the ones providing the boat and all the transport. So please, no more of this protesting, okay?"

"Okay," said Sabine with the warmest of smiles.

"Okay," Aubrey grunted into his coffee.

It was almost as if the trip had been designed with Aubrey and Sabine in mind. The stopover in Penticton was merely the first step in the unwinding process; it certainly deflected both of their minds away from the farm. The fortuitous meeting up with a farm couple from Iron Springs was a further catalyst for mental cleansing. Elvis and Sylvania Hexstead were beef and grain farmers with the same old tired concerns as everybody else, but with a whole different attitude. "You gotta live first and farm second," declared Elvis. "For my old daddy, music always came first; that's why he named me Elvis. And my wife's dad, why, he goes and names his daughter after a light bulb. I guess he was making good and sure I'd see the light." Clearly both of them took life as it came. "Life is something to be enjoyed," said Elvis, "but too many folks have to make up their mind to do just that. Say, we're taking ourselves out on a wine tour, too. Why don't you join us? We have one of them fancy vans that seats six. Sylve will do the driving, won't you honey? She doesn't exactly go overboard when she's wine-tasting, do you hon? So, all of us folks can be doing the serious testing while she's doing the driving. What d'ya say?"

"Good enough for me," said Sylvania.

"Perfect for us," said Jeannie who had fretted that she would have to be the designated driver.

The tour was a blast. They sampled pinot noir and pinot blanc, cabernet sauvignon, merlot and shiraz, blanc des blancs, and Chablis. And the more they tasted, the more Elvis sang off-key, imperfectly assisted by Aubrey and Pete, and later on by Sabine. She maintained decorum until almost the end when she could no longer resist entering the fray the moment the boys launched into a very wobbly version of Paul Anka's "Diana".

"Oh Aubrey," she shrieked more than squeaked, "I'm but a fool, don't ever squeeze me, don't ever be so cruel…"

They also made a substantial contribution to the local economy. Elvis was more the "single-focus" type. When he came across a wine that he particularly liked, he bought a case; his achievements for the day amounted to an astonishing eight cases, "to drink off poor calf prices", he said.

"He normally buys about four cases," commented Sylvania, "but then he's never been in such bad company."

As for the others, they bought a bottle here and a bottle there, and pretty soon they had the equivalent of two cases of their own. The problem was, the more wine they tasted, the more pleasing to the palate all of it became. It was a day to remember, a day so far removed from cows and all that manure that a good deal of mental space was created.

The holiday on Vancouver Island turned out just as such holidays are intended: relaxing, fun-filled, relieving. Jim and Sonya Delamere were already there, ensconced in their own beachfront cottage alongside the one Pete and Jeannie would share with the Hanlons. Jim Delamere was a totally different man; his foray into dirty dancing with death had made him immensely stronger and more self-assured. Once his finances had been brought back on track thanks to a favorable reassessment of that notorious overpayment, he had never looked back. The Delamere farm had become one of the most progressive in the area, not so much flourishing as holding its own. What small farm could possibly flourish in such twisted times?

Cold Okanagan white, or slightly chilled red, together with the salmon and the prawns, the clams and the shrimp and the mussels tended to over the BBQ on a succession of gorgeous summer evenings by the sea would have sufficed. The forays onto the beach with two little farm girls exploring the mysteries of the ocean were a bonus; so much so that their parents could happily abscond into time for themselves, knowing their little ones were in such good hands. Indeed, for Aubrey and Sabine who had never had children of their own, being involved with the Delamere twins offered an insight into a world they had never seen since their own childhoods: a world full of innocence and wonder, so beautifully captured by a treasured interchange on the beach.

"You know what, Uncle Orby," said five-year old Molly Delamere with the most serious of faces. "God must have a great big hole in one of his moneybags."

"Oh and why do you think so?" responded a puzzled Aubrey.

"Oh because look at all the sand dollars we keep finding. God makes them, you know." Molly was still deadly serious.

"And how do you know that, little missy?" asked Sabine.

"It's a well-known fact," said Francis, coming to her sister's defense by mimicking a worn-out TV commercial.

As if the unhurried leisure was not enough in itself, the outings in the boat were downright magical. It did not matter that the fishing was poor, or that they lost the only salmon to strike the line. What mattered were the ambiance and the chatter of the two little girls as they counted the "diamonds" in the boat's wake, or as they searched for the mermaids that Francis assured her mother came out at night. "I even seen one," Francis said.

"Me too," said Pete, eyeing his wife with a grin.

It was their last day on the coast that set the scene for one of those pivotal conversations that can occur unexpectedly among good friends. The three men, Jim, Aubrey and Pete, had gone out on the boat for one final attempt to catch that elusive salmon. Be darned if they did not go and hook two at the same time, one on each line. The ensuing scene could only have been described by an onlooker as "slapstick comedy in omnivision". It began when Pete's fish decided that being on the starboard side of the boat was not conducive to escape so it made a violent run to port. Aubrey at the controls attempted to make a minor correction in course. "Minor" was more like major and served only to entice Jim's fish on the port side to head strongly for starboard. When it comes to farmers who think they are fishermen, inexperience only seems to compound their landlubberly ways. Both men arose out of their seats to do what their fish had done, switch sides so that their lines did not become crossed. As a quick, clean maneuver, it was spectacularly unsuccessful; they collided heavily amidships, both falling heavily to the deck. Pete's rod was jerked from his hands and was making a fast getaway over the side, aided and abetted by one very vigorous salmon. Somehow Jim spotted it, twisted over like a contortionist, and grabbed onto it before finishing up in a sitting position. The trouble was that the rods were identical. Pete was up on his feet in a flash. He seized one of the rods Jim was holding, the one that Jim had actually started out with, and began reeling in frantically. The fish was gone. No, wait a sec, there was a brief tug, then slack and more slack. The fish was gone now for sure, had to be. Only in Pete's mind. Maybe it had stopped to have a bit of a snooze, perhaps it was looking in the mirror to check out its new nose ring. Whatever the case, it suddenly went back on the offensive. That was when Pete discovered two things: the power of a Coho on the run, and the unfortunate fact that his line was hopelessly tangled up with his ex-rod, by way of the cover on the auxiliary outboard motor, before disappearing off into the sea. Miraculously, the fish was somehow still on the other line too, so both fishermen ended up not only fighting fish, but also working with and against each other, all at the same time.

Aubrey would have earned the MVP award for the day had he remained dedicated to keeping the boat's prow stolidly into the wind, but the Most Valuable Player category vapourized with the appearance of Pete's fish at the side of the boat. Aubrey switched off the motor; deserting his post, he reached for the net and galloped over to retrieve Pete's trophy, landing it onto the deck for Pete to pick up in wild exultation. Only then did he realize that a "Loosey Goosey" left to her own devices was a girl with a mind of her own. Wind and current had turned her head and she positively flew right back the way she had come. Inevitably this provided a welcome slackening of the line for Jim's fish. Once again the farce of fish but no fish, lost fish, gotten-away fish, was played out with Aubrey and Pete being rudely reminded that Pete's line was still in some bizarre sort of tango with Jim's. The fish in the water now ran Jim's line taut, and kept on heading for Japan or somewhere. That pulled Pete's fish out of his hands, propelling it over the side and back into the swim. Aubrey made the wisest choice he could have in the circumstances; he went back to his post and restarted the boat's motor to nose back into the wind. The boys would have to do it on their own without his help. To his utter amazement, they succeeded, and within six or so minutes, both fish were at the stern. Pete netted first one and then the other, the second rendered half invisible by a mare's nest of nylon line wrapped haphazardly around its body. That was when they began to laugh, exultant and uncontrolled laughter, the best ever stress reliever known to man. Aubrey switched off the engine and allowed the boat to drift for a good ten minutes as they told and retold the story to one another in the manner of small boys who have just discovered Merlin's secret. Then they headed home as the triumphant hunters they saw themselves, their incompetence as fishermen layered over with fine words.

The critical conversation came that night just as the sun was setting. The fresh salmon, barbecued by the ladies of course seeing as the three Nimrods had more than earned their keep, was stunningly good. The best white of the Okanagan had loosened tongues and mellowed perspectives when Sabine commented wistfully that she wished they could all afford to do "this sort of thing every year".

"Ah but you can," offered Jeannie.

"Not with our calf prices always going down and our input costs always going up we can't," said Aubrey backing up his wife, and suddenly realizing at the same time that if she was this turned off by farming, maybe they needed to bring the whole issue out into the open.

"Yeah, that's the worst of it," said Jim. "We just don't have enough fingers to put in the dike."

"Hold on now, fellahs, hold on! Don't let this evening turn into a drowning of sorrows and a trashing of what we all do." Pete was more animated than they had ever seen him. "Don't forget how good farming has been to us. Don't forget farming defines who we are, and I for one would not want any one of us sitting around this table to be anyone other than who they are. Our animals, our land and the way we interact with them, the seasons, the weather, they all have become a part of our psyche. Sure we have maybe more than our fair share of bad experiences, but don't ever forget that we have some real good ones, too. So where's the problem? The problem is that we unconsciously allow one single dimension, the dimension of numbers, to stake too big a claim. Sure we have to pay attention to numbers, all of us, but we have to see them as no more than what they are and then we have to get ourselves beyond them. We can't let this one dimension define our whole existence. Yes, we're in tough times, every one of us, but let's quit crying the blues for a change. Remember, farming is what brought us all together here, and what a wonderful experience it has been."

"Beyond anything we could have imagined," said Sonya.

"And I vote for the same again next year. Let's all book before we leave." Sabine surprised both herself and Aubrey.

"So look how a really great experience has changed our outlook so much," Pete was determined to finish.

"You can say that again," Jim agreed. "It's just too easy to narrow down the whole world to one single issue until it blocks out everything else. I know; I've already traveled down that road."

"Gopher vision," said Aubrey. "We can never see the whole horizon at any one time."

"We were never meant to," said Pete. "So we have to concern ourselves with the good things in life, just like our friend Elvis did. The farming experience, as we all know, can be both good and bad. But experience by itself is not something we can choose. Experience is not really a choice because it's going to happen to you regardless. So as I say, experience is not a choice but our attitude is. We can change it if and when we want. Attitude lets you make sense of experience, even control it to a point."

"Ah, but however positive your attitude might be, you still can't control all of the numbers. If calf prices are down, they're down and that's all there is to it." Sabine wanted so badly to air her own worries that it never dawned on her, nor Aubrey, that Pete's speech was aimed specifically at them.

"That's true," said Pete. "Very true. But don't forget that numbers exclude more than they include, and they can always be rearranged. They exclude all of those things on which we cannot put a price. They can reduce everything we do to a single dimension, but because we have allowed them to become so important in the way we do things, we can easily let ourselves be controlled by them. There are always creative things we can do, always, to make changes. It all comes down to will. Too many folks try to carry on with the farm when they would be far better off to get out. They prolong their own agony, and keep on prolonging it. Farming is not an easy life, I don't care what people say. It's perfectly legitimate to stand up and say, 'I've had enough; I don't need to do this any more!' This is not an admission of failure. It's a recognition of a broader reality, and one in which numbers should only play a limited part."

"Okay, so what do we do?" asked Sabine. "The numbers tell me that we've pretty well run out of options. In fact, I would have to say they have forced us into a bit of a corner. So how the heck can you be creative when you don't want to lose either the farm or the animals?"

"You?" said Pete homing in on what he wanted to say. "You make some bigger decisions. Decide first if you want to hang in or bail out. If you want to hang in, think about subdividing that rental place of yours and selling it. Sure it has brought in a bit of income, but it has given you plenty of grief as well. With the oil boom going on, there's a whole lot of money going around and you deserve some of it, no?"

"When would you ever counsel a person to quit?" It was Jim who asked the question Sabine so wanted to ask but did not dare for fear of exposing her hand.

"When a person does not want to do it any more, or when he or she can't do it any more. They will know in their own soul if they want to quit. It's as simple as that."

No doubt about it, Aubrey and Sabine had to do a little soul-searching, and soon.

Author Biography

Colin and Felicity Manuel were both born and raised on farms in Kenya, East Africa. In 1975, they made the move to Canada where Colin joined the teaching profession and Felicity worked in a bank. The couple's yearning for the land led them to the Rocky Mountain House area in Alberta, where they purchased *Shambani*, Swahili for "Home Farm" and from there all manner of fun things unfolded. In essence then, these writings are a salute to our neighbours because it is those same neighbours who have so enriched our lives. If quality of life resides in the company you keep, then boy were we ever blessed!

The 3 books in the trilogy by Colin Manuel…

"Footloose in the Front Forty!"
"Fancy Free in the Back Thirty!"
"Down to the Last Quarter!"

And then there's "Lucky…
a Bovine Look at Genius Humanitas"…
the life of an Alberta cow.

Illustrator Biography

In addition to illustrating numerous books, Ben's art is extensively published by Leanin' Tree. He has won many awards over the years, including the 2011 Moonbeam Award for children's books, 15 medals from Cowboy Cartoonists International, and a very large spot on his mother's fridge. A family man with a wife and two daughters, he lives high on top of Bizwanger's Hill in west central Alberta, where he can happily watch the world go by, grabbing what he can from life and living it to the fullest. When he's not making pictures, you can find him making music as he travels regularly throughout western Canada and the US to slather audiences with his twisted western wit. To add a further dimension to Ben's art, visit his website at www.bencrane.com.